PRAISE FOR ROBERT BAILEY

Rich Blood

"*Rich Blood* is a deliciously clever legal thriller that keeps you turning pages fast and furious. Robert Bailey's latest is wildly entertaining."
Patricia Cornwell, #1 *New York Times* bestselling author

The Wrong Side

"Bailey expertly ratchets up the suspense as the plot builds to a surprise punch ending. Readers will impatiently await the next in the series."
—*Publishers Weekly* (starred review)

"Social tensions redoubled by race intensify a workmanlike mystery."
—*Kirkus Reviews*

Previous Praise

"*The Professor* is that rare combination of thrills, chills, and heart. Gripping from the first page to the last."
—Winston Groom, author of *Forrest Gump*

"Robert Bailey is a thriller writer to reckon with. His debut novel has a tight and twisty plot, vivid characters, and a pleasantly down-home sensibility that will remind some readers of adventures in Grisham-land. Luckily, Robert Bailey is an original, and his skill as a writer makes the Alabama setting all his own. *The Professor* marks the beginning of a very promising career."
—Mark Childress, author of *Geo*

"Taut, page turning, and smart, *The Professor* is a legal thriller that will keep readers up late as the twists and turns keep coming. Set in Alabama, it also includes that state's greatest icon, one Coach Bear Bryant. In fact, the Bear gets things going with the energy of an Alabama kickoff to Auburn. Robert Bailey knows his state, and he knows his law. He also knows how to write characters that are real, sympathetic, and surprising. If he keeps writing novels this good, he's got quite a literary career before him."

—Homer Hickam, author of *Rocket Boys / October Sky*, a *New York Times* #1 bestseller

"Bailey's solid second McMurtrie and Drake legal thriller (after 2014's *The Professor*) . . . provides enough twists and surprises to keep readers turning the pages."

—*Publishers Weekly*

"A gripping legal suspense thriller of the first order, *Between Black and White* clearly displays author Robert Bailey's impressive talents as a novelist. An absorbing and riveting read from beginning to end."

—Midwest Book Review

"Take a murder, a damaged woman, and a desperate daughter, and you have the recipe for *The Last Trial*, a complex and fast-paced legal thriller. Highly recommended."

—D. P. Lyle, award-winning author

"*The Final Reckoning* is explosive and displays every element of a classic thriller: fast pacing, strong narrative, fear, misery, and transcendence. Bailey proves once more that he is a fine writer with an instinct for powerful white-knuckle narrative."

—*Southern Literary Review*

"A stunning discovery, a triple twist, and dramatic courtroom scenes all make for a riveting, satisfying read in what might well be Bailey's best book to date . . . *Legacy of Lies* is a grand story with a morality-tale vibe, gripping and thrilling throughout. It showcases Bailey once more as a writer who knows how to keep the suspense high, the pacing fast, the narrative strong, the characters compellingly complex, and his plot full of white-knuckle tension and twists."

—*Southern Literary Review*

"Inspiring . . . Sharp in its dialogue, real with its relationships, and fascinating in details of the game, *The Golfer's Carol* is that rarest of books—one you will read and keep for yourself while purchasing multiple copies for friends."

—Andy Andrews, *New York Times* bestselling
author of *The Noticer* and *The Traveler's Gift*

RICH
BLOOD

ALSO BY ROBERT BAILEY

BOCEPHUS HAYNES SERIES

The Wrong Side

Legacy of Lies

MCMURTRIE AND DRAKE LEGAL THRILLERS

The Final Reckoning

The Last Trial

Between Black and White

The Professor

OTHER BOOKS

The Golfer's Carol

RICH BLOOD

ROBERT BAILEY

THOMAS & MERCER

Published by Thomas & Mercer, Seattle

www.apub.com

Amazon, the Amazon logo, and Thomas & Mercer are trademarks of Amazon.com, Inc., or its affiliates.

ISBN-13: 9781542037273
ISBN-10: 1542037271

Cover design by Shasti O'Leary Soudant
Cover image: © Judy Kennamer / Arcangel

Printed in the United States of America

For Joe and Foncie Bullard

PART ONE

1

Waylon Pike had never killed anyone before.

He'd done other things. Terrible, awful things. Some of which he'd served time for doing. Some he hadn't.

But in his forty-two miserable years on this earth, he'd never taken a life.

He'd thought it would be harder. That there would be cold feet, nerves, something.

But Waylon didn't feel a damn thing.

As he waited for the car that would take him on his way to do the deed, Waylon cast his rod back in the water and gawked at the fireworks lighting up Lake Guntersville. He wondered how many of these pyrotechnic devices had been purchased at one of the outlets in and around his home in South Pittsburg, Tennessee. Waylon had worked a job in high school at the supercenter off the interstate and learned quite a bit about roman candles, smoke bombs, missiles, rockets, crossettes, ground spinners, and every other kind of firework you could think of. He'd always had an affinity for explosives. Both the ones that provided visual entertainment . . .

. . . and the devices that did a little more than decorate the sky.

His first brush with the law had been for lighting a roman candle in a friend's truck and shooting the projectile out the window at an oncoming car. He'd gotten youthful offender status, and the misdemeanor didn't even show up on his record. Waylon should have been relieved to escape punishment, but, if anything, his initial foray into crime only made him want to go further. When he was nineteen, he'd torched a restaurant at the behest of the owner for the insurance proceeds. The fire was investigated, but he was never charged or suspected of arson. The owner gave him 10 percent of the payout, and Waylon was on his way to a career of being a "fixer" for people.

And a life of trouble. He had a rap sheet that included convictions for theft, arson, and possession of cocaine, and he'd served two different stints in prison, the last of which had wrapped up a year ago.

Waylon wondered as he reeled his line back in and recast if he'd ever had a chance in life. If the stars were just aligned for him to be a criminal.

When he'd met Jana Waters, he'd felt that his luck had changed. She was a rich, bored housewife who seemed to be tortured by her life of affluence. They'd met at a bar and gotten drunk, and then he'd enjoyed her talents inside her vehicle in the parking lot of the bar. Waylon smiled at the memory. Since that initial romp, Jana had hired him to do an endless array of handyman tasks at the family mansion on Buck Island. She'd also referred him to some of her rich friends, and so he'd made a handsome wage these last nine months. Waylon had been a terrible student, but he was great with his hands. Whether he was hired for engine repair, house fixer-upper projects, or boat maintenance, he was a "good man to have around," as Jana had told him and her friends. He had to admit that he enjoyed going legit. Doing honest work and getting paid for it. Of course, he was screwing another man's wife, but all was fair in love and war, right? Adultery was a sin, not a crime. And he was going to hell anyway. Might as well go happy.

Waylon had known it couldn't last. Before long, he figured he'd be dragged back into his old life. Something or someone would pull him to crossing over again. It was as inevitable as Auburn rolling Toomer's Corner after a big win or an Alabama loss.

He hadn't figured that Jana Waters would be the instrument behind his return to his seedier past, but life was full of surprises, wasn't it? He glanced at his watch and then back at the lake. The night was dark now, but there would be more fireworks. It was the Fourth of July after all. He reeled the line back in and grabbed his tackle box. Then he crossed the highway and climbed into his truck. Just a fisherman finishing up for the day.

He still had a few minutes before the pickup would happen, but he remained calm. Cool. Almost numb.

In approximately sixty minutes, he would kill a man.

Waylon Pike watched the fireworks show. And waited.

2

Jana Waters gazed into her almost empty glass of vodka. She bit her lip and then drank the rest before sliding it across the bar and standing.

"Leaving us so soon, Ms. Waters?" the bartender asked with a tease in his voice.

On a normal night, Jana might blow the handsome young lad a kiss. What was his name? Keith? Kenny? She couldn't remember. But tonight, her heart wasn't in it.

"Will you be here tomorrow?" he asked.

Jana blinked, managing to find her patented fake smile. "If you're lucky."

"Yes, ma'am," he said, his face blushing.

Jana turned and walked toward the exit. Fire by the Lake was a restaurant that sat right on Lake Guntersville off Highway 69. It had been one of her favorite haunts for years, even before the ownership changed. She felt eyes on her as she strode toward the door. That was nothing new. Jana Waters always left a wake coming and going.

She walked to her car, keeping her shoulders back and eyes forward. The wind off the lake was warm and sticky. When she reached her Mercedes SUV, she gazed out at the blacktop, glaring at the huge billboard that hugged the edge of the road.

INJURED AT WORK? GET RICH.

Below the tasteless slogan was her brother's smiling face and the message to call an equally crude telephone number—1-800 GET RICH—for legal services. She hadn't seen Jason in three years, but he was never very far from her thoughts because she passed at least five of these monstrosities every time she drove anywhere. Guntersville to Boaz on Highway 431. I-65 all the way to the beach. Hell, even Lusk Road past Signal Point to Alder Springs.

It didn't matter. Jason's billboards were everywhere, and in each of the highway posters he flashed his bleach-whitened teeth and dirty-blond stubble, which some woman—probably his trashy ex-wife or his bitchy law partner—must've told him looked cool. Jana thought he looked ridiculous, and she'd told him as much the last time they'd spoken. She'd told him a lot of things then, and he'd fired some choice words back. Seeing him now, smiling down at her as if he were enjoying the crisis she was in, made her want to vomit. She stuck her middle finger at the advertisement and slid into the driver's seat. Before starting the car, she sucked in a deep breath and felt her heart rate speed up.

She glanced at the clock on the dash. 8:55 p.m. The meeting was supposed to happen at 9:00. As she backed up her vehicle and turned for the exit, she glanced out the window at the dark water and full moon. A cascade of roman candles lit up the sky followed by the machine-gun sound of God knew how many other kinds of fireworks.

It was the Fourth of July. She should be sitting on the screened porch of her home on Buck Island, watching the show with her husband and daughters. Maybe walking down to the dock for a better look. Grilling dogs and burgers. Listening to Darius Rucker or Kenny Chesney or some other lake-appropriate artist. Maybe the girls could've had friends over. Or perhaps a boyfriend?

Jana felt her eyes welling up, and she ground her teeth, refusing to wipe away the tears. She glared at the billboard of her brother again.

She would not be weak. That had never been her style, and it wouldn't be now.

She pulled the Mercedes onto Highway 69 and accelerated east toward town. As the strip mall drew near, she clicked the right-turn blinker and pulled into the lot. She parked under an unlit streetlamp.

Ten seconds later, the passenger-side door opened, and a man climbed inside. He smelled of mint chewing gum with the slightest tinge of body odor. Jana fought the urge to gag.

"Ready?" he asked.

Jana tried to speak, but the words wouldn't come. She glanced at him, nodded, and edged out of the space.

Seconds later, she was back on the road.

As she passed the causeway, fireworks illuminating the lake, Jana thought of her girls. And Braxton. Her husband.

What in the hell am I doing?

3

The club felt good in the surgeon's hand.

The grip was sticky, and though he wasn't wearing his customary FootJoy StaSof glove, he still had firm control over the eight iron. He looked down at his feet, which were adorned with blue-and-black Tevas, and then the scuffed Titleist golf ball. He waggled the clubhead and set it behind the ball on the green nylon mat. Then he began his swing, turning his shoulders behind the ball and cocking his wrists. At the top, he shifted his weight from his right leg onto his left and fired the clubhead at the ball. There was a satisfying thwack at impact, and the ball lifted into the air and out over Lake Guntersville. Because of the full moon and the fireworks being shot in every direction, he could see that the ball curved gently from right to left, traveling perhaps 130 yards before disappearing into the dark water.

Dr. Braxton Waters breathed in the humid air and took a few seconds to admire his handiwork. He was hitting balls off the dock just like in his favorite Darius Rucker song, "Beers and Sunshine," which he'd listened to a few minutes earlier. Now playing on his Alexa: "Wagon Wheel," another goody by the pop star turned country artist. Normally, these tunes would have lifted his spirits, even if he was in a bad mood. Launching balls into the water usually helped relieve stress as well, and the shot he'd taken was as close to perfect as could be.

Alas, nothing seemed to be working tonight. He set the club down and grabbed his empty pint glass, then stuck it under the keg tap and began yet another pour.

Braxton took a long pull from the glass and then snatched the bottle of tequila and poured another shot. Chasing Patrón with pale ale. *The rich man's guide to getting wasted,* he thought, chuckling bitterly and kicking back the shot. Then he raised the pint glass and took a long sip of beer. No lime. No salt. No problem.

Braxton burped and grasped the golf club, stumbling back to the mat as Darius sang about dying free in Raleigh.

"Dying free," Braxton bellowed out over the lake, knowing his words would be drowned out by the wind and sound of firecrackers. He placed another ball on the green carpet and gazed out at the muddy water. Then he turned back to his empty house, lit only by the overhead chandelier in the den. There was a time when the Fourth of July had meant that the lawn between the boathouse and mansion would be filled with people of all ages mingling, drinking, and dancing. Four years ago, he'd hired a live band, and a lot of the neighbors had come over along with some of the girls' friends. That was while things with Jana were still cordial.

Braxton sighed and lined up to the golf ball. He jerked the club back and brought it down onto the mat. The ball squirted dead right. A cold shank. The worst shot in golf.

"Figures," he said. He rolled another ball over and hit another "lateral shot," as he preferred to call it, hating even to whisper the word *shank.* Braxton closed his eyes and felt unsteady on his feet. He thought of his oldest, Niecy, a rising sophomore at Birmingham-Southern College. He'd almost begged her to come home. "Your sister could really use some time with you," he'd pleaded. He dropped the club and pulled out his phone to look at her text, which had been nice but firm.

I'm sorry, Dad, but I can't be around Mom right now. Every time I come home, she sucks me into her drama and it becomes a huge fight. I'm going to Destin with some friends. I asked Nola to come with us, but she said no.

Braxton flung his phone into a lawn chair and picked up the golf club, waggling it several times in frustration. *Nola* . . . his youngest daughter was sixteen. About to be a junior in high school, assuming she passed her summer classes. She'd been hit the hardest by his and Jana's estrangement. Due to her poor grades, they'd had to pull her out of Randolph, the private college prep school in Huntsville, and she was barely getting by at Guntersville High. Once a bright-eyed, curious, happy-go-lucky child, she'd become a moody and edgy teenager who'd withdrawn into herself, barely speaking to him or her mother.

Jana said it was Braxton's fault. That he hadn't spent enough time with her. That he'd spoiled Niecy with attention and glossed over his youngest.

For a while, he'd believed her spiel. He was an orthopedic surgeon. One of the best in north Alabama and, by far, the most proficient in Marshall County. He had a ridiculous schedule of operations and worked sixty to seventy hours a week almost every month of the year. He'd tried to cut back when Nola switched schools, but dropping hours meant fewer surgeries and less money. Braxton was well off, but the mortgage on their house was steep, and Jana's spending habits and drug use kept him in constant danger of being in financial peril. He was forty-nine years old, in the prime of his medical career. He needed to be working.

Braxton rolled another ball over. He took a three-quarter swing and this time hit the ball flush. He breathed a sigh of relief. Even when he was drunk and at the end of his wits with his crazy wife, the last thing he wanted to add to his plate was a case of the shanks.

He giggled at the absurdity of the thought and then plopped down in the lawn chair, surveying his texts. The only message from Jana today had come in around 6:00 p.m.

Out tonight.

Braxton scrolled down, pausing briefly at a message from Colleen, the CRNA who'd been with him for over a decade. For the past few years, since Jana's craziness had escalated, they'd engaged in an on-again, off-again affair that was currently off.

Happy fourth! I wish things could have been different . . .

Braxton gave his head a jerk. He wasn't sure how he felt about that. Truth was, he hadn't been the perfect husband. He'd made mistakes, but his indiscretions were nothing like his wife's. They hadn't put his family in danger.

He clicked over to his phone call summary and looked at a set of unfamiliar digits with a Boaz location. Braxton had screened the number at least five times before answering yesterday afternoon. He'd figured it was another extended-warranty reminder and had readied himself to hang up, but instead the voice that had come over the line had sent a shiver up his arm.

"Dr. Waters, this is Tyson Cade. I'm sure you know who I am. Your wife owes me $50,000. She hasn't paid, though she's done other things to grant herself more time." There'd been a pause, and Braxton had forced himself not to respond. "I've run out of patience, Dr. Waters. I want my money, or there will be consequences."

"How soon?" he'd managed.

But the line had gone dead, and Tyson Cade hadn't called back. Braxton had broached the subject with Jana last night, but she'd bolted before he'd gotten any of the details. "I've got it under control," was all she'd said.

Braxton cringed, thinking about the sheer lunacy of his wife's response. Nothing was "under control" in Jana's life. She'd been a spiraling typhoon for years, which was why Braxton would be filing for divorce. He'd hired an attorney, told Jana, and let the girls know. All that was left was filing the paperwork, which he planned to do as soon as he figured out how to handle Mr. Cade.

He'd tried to call the dealer back today, but the cell number had already been disconnected. It had probably been a burner phone purchased at Walmart. Braxton figured that the methamphetamine king of Sand Mountain had a basket full of such devices.

"Tyson Cade," he whispered. "What have you done, Jana?"

He'd thought her shenanigans would only hurt him financially. In fact, for a while, he'd embraced the concept of separate lives, having his own side fun, but Jana's drug use and volatile behavior had finally forced him into pursuing divorce.

Dealing with Tyson Cade, though, was a new low, even for Jana. She'd put Braxton and their daughters in peril. He stumbled back to his beer, then took another sip and poured himself an additional shot of Patrón. He toasted the sky and chased the tequila with another long pull from his pint.

Braxton figured that, if Cade really wanted his money, the drug lord would call back. He'd been waiting all day. Nothing.

He'll call back, Braxton knew. There was no way in hell Jana could come up with that kind of cash by herself, and Cade wasn't going to kill the golden goose. Braxton had already called his banker. He could put together the funds, but it was going to hurt.

He stumbled back toward the mat but decided against hitting any more balls. Darius was now singing "For the First Time," and Braxton collapsed into the lawn chair. He gazed up at the moon and wondered, as the song went, when was the last time he'd done something for the first time.

Yesterday, he thought. *Yesterday I spoke with a meth dealer.*

He reached for the pint glass on the ground and knocked it over. Too tired and drunk to get up for a refill, he gaped up at the sky. "Fuck it," he said out loud.

"Fuck it all."

4

The plan had been to kill the doctor inside the house.

Waylon would walk around the side of the home and use the key he'd been given to enter the laundry room before sneaking downstairs to the man cave, where he would find the surgeon either shooting pool, fiddling around on his computer, or watching TV. If possible, he'd come up behind him and kill him without being noticed. If Dr. Waters did see him, Waylon would feign having to come by and pick up a tool he'd left in the workshop attached to the man cave. He'd go inside, come out with a hammer or a screwdriver, and then try to catch the doctor unaware and shoot him in the head.

Was it a good plan? Waylon was by no means a criminal mastermind, and he knew that Braxton Waters lifted weights and was in good shape. There could be a scuffle, which might leave a trail that he'd been in the house.

Waylon had begun to doubt the wisdom of his scheme as he approached the mansion. Then he heard music coming from the dock.

He grinned as he ambled down the grassy slope toward the water. He couldn't believe his luck. Braxton Waters was lying down on a lawn chair. Waylon edged to within ten feet of the doctor and saw that Waters's eyes were closed. Then he noticed the quarter-full tequila bottle and the knocked-over pint glass.

A ripple of relief ran through his body. There'd be no confrontation. Waylon studied the lake. He could see the boathouse of the neighboring home, but the lights were off, and it was at least four hundred yards away. In the other direction, he saw fireworks still being shot over the lake. *Perfect,* he thought.

He tiptoed forward and took out his 9 mm pistol and held it in his gloved hands.

Waylon Pike glanced to his left and right and then back up at the house. He saw nothing suspicious, no movement. He peered out at the lake. No boats were in the area.

When the next round of fireworks began going off in the distance, he pointed the gun at the head of Dr. Braxton Waters.

And then he pulled the trigger.

———

After cleaning up the mess, Waylon walked around the side of the house.

His ride was waiting.

He slid into the passenger seat and closed the door.

"Well?" his benefactor asked.

"Done," Waylon said.

5

Jana Waters woke up on the floor with her daughter screaming.

"Mom! Wake up, Mom!"

Jana tried to look at her daughter, but her eyes had crusted over with gunk. "Wh-wha-what is it, baby?" She managed to pull herself up to a sitting position, her daughter standing over her. Then she took a deep breath and exhaled as the sun from the floor-length window warmed her face.

"Mom, why are you on the floor? And where's Dad?"

Jana turned her head away from the heat coming off the glass. "Nola, can you get me a wet rag?"

She heard a frustrated sigh followed by footsteps marching across the hardwood floor. Seconds later a damp piece of cloth was pressed into her hand. Jana wiped her eyes and placed the cloth on her forehead. She opened her eyes, and, though the corners of her lids still felt gritty, she could see her daughter standing above her with arms crossed.

"What's going on, Mom?"

"When'd you get home?"

"Five minutes ago."

"What time is—?"

"Noon. I told you and Dad that I'd be home from Harley's at twelve. You still haven't answered my question. What's going on? And why're you passed out on the floor? God, Mom. And where's Dad? His car's in the garage."

Jana winced. She put her hand on the cold floor and pressed herself up to her knees. As she moved, a wave of nausea rolled through her body. "Honey, I'll answer your questions as best I can, but can you get me some water?"

This time Nola didn't move.

Jana climbed to her feet and put her hand on the couch to steady herself. She blinked out the window toward the lake as her head began to pound. She squinted at her daughter, who'd wrinkled her face up in disgust.

"Fine, I'll get it myself," Jana said. She shuffled toward the kitchen, noticing that her feet were bare and that she was still in the sundress she'd worn last night. She grabbed a glass from the cabinet, put it under the automatic ice maker, and cringed at the sound of the ice clunking against the sides of the cup. Then she filled it with water from the sink and took a long, slow sip, spilling some of the liquid down the front of her dress. Behind her, she heard her daughter calling for her father as she walked downstairs toward the man cave. Jana drank two more glasses of water and then splashed some on her face. *Better,* she thought, as she saw Nola running back up the steps.

"Mom, he's not here." Her daughter's voice now sounded worried instead of mad.

"He's probably fishing with Burns," Jana muttered. "Or maybe they took the Jet Skis out."

"I'm going to go check the boathouse."

"No," Jana said, feeling a tickle of fear run down her arms as she began to get her bearings. *No,* she thought, going over the events of the previous night in her jumbled mind.

"What do you mean, no?"

"I mean, let me do it. Why don't you be a dear and fix me a bagel? Or some cereal?"

"Are you joking?"

Jana began to walk toward the stairs with Nola on her heels. "Is that so much to ask? To make your mom a little breakfast?"

Nola didn't respond as they reached the foot of the stairs and opened the door to the outside. As they walked across the grass, Jana put her hand over her eyes to shield her face from the harsh, glaring sunlight. She heard a horn coming from the lake.

"There's Burns," Nola said. She was walking side by side with Jana, and they both waved at a man passing by in a small bass boat. "No one's with him," Nola added.

Jana heard music coming from the dock and recognized the voice of Darius Rucker, Braxton's favorite singer. As they walked down the wooden pier, she saw the golf mat, the bucket of balls, and the knocked-over pint glass. *No,* she thought again.

"Dad!" Nola shouted, and Jana winced as her head pounded and heartbeat raced. Nola took off in front of Jana and walked into the boat-house. As Jana reached the structure, Nola came out. "All three Jet Skis and both boats are still in there." She frowned. "Why's the music still on?"

Jana edged her way to the green mat. She turned and saw the golf club and, next to it, the kegerator. On the wooden floor, a bottle of tequila, almost empty.

"Mom?" Nola's voice came from behind her.

When Jana turned, her daughter's hands were shaking as she pointed down at the dock. "What's that?"

Jana approached, and when she saw the red substance below her, she dropped to her knees. She knew exactly what it was. What it had to be.

"Is that blood?"

Jana gazed up at her daughter. Nola Waters had reddish-blonde hair like her father and Jana's own sky-blue eyes. Her light skin was even paler than usual in the glow of the early-afternoon sun.

"Mom?" Nola pressed, taking a step backward. "Is it?"

"Baby, I don't know—"

Nola's gasp interrupted whatever Jana was planning to say. The sixteen-year-old pointed toward the water, her arm wobbling.

Jana wheeled and saw a cap in the water about ten feet away. It was navy blue and had *GL* inscribed on the front in red and, underneath, in smaller text, *Gunter's Landing*. Braxton wore this hat when he was playing golf.

No . . .

Jana felt her breath catch as she managed to get up and walk toward her daughter. Nola was shivering. Jana tried to put her arm around her, but the girl shook it off.

"Honey, give me your cell," Jana said, trying to keep her voice calm.

Nola managed to take out her phone from her shorts pocket, and Jana clasped both hands around the device. Her hands quaked. "Nola, look at me, honey."

The sixteen-year-old crossed her arms and glared at Jana. The girl's bottom lip trembled. "Do you think Dad is . . . ?" She pointed at the cap and covered her mouth as tears flooded her eyes.

"No," Jana said, forcing calm into her tone as adrenaline coursed through her veins. She looked to the blood on the dock floor and the cap in the water and pressed three digits on the phone. Seconds later, Jana heard the dispatcher pick up.

"911. What's your emergency?"

"My name is Jana Waters, and I live on Buck Island." She cited the street address and sucked in a breath. Nola stared out at Lake Guntersville. "My husband is missing," Jana managed. "It looks like he was down on our boat dock last night or this morning, but . . . we can't find him."

6

A rescue team and four sheriff's deputies arrived in less than ten minutes.

The officers asked Jana and Nola to wait inside, but mother and daughter wouldn't abide. Instead, they watched from the backyard. Nola sat in the grass and rocked back and forth against her knees, while Jana paced back and forth across the lawn.

Jana felt jittery and took a Xanax. She offered Nola one, but the teenager refused, glaring at her mother once again until Jana broke eye contact.

The sedative did nothing to calm Jana's nerves. As the search continued, she had to cross her arms to keep her limbs from shaking. She forced herself to mention other possibilities to Nola. Perhaps Braxton had nicked himself trying to cut some rope in the boathouse or attempting to change the pony keg in the kegerator. He'd gone for a swim and his cap fell in the water. Or he was on a boat ride with another friend that he hadn't bothered to tell Jana about. She and Braxton barely communicated anymore, so that wouldn't be a stretch.

But Nola said nothing. There was no hope in her eyes, and Jana knew why. Her father's cell phone was on the dock. His car was in the garage. All their boats and Jet Skis were in the boathouse. Jana had called Burns and all Braxton's other friends, and none of them had seen him or been with him last night or this morning. She'd reached out to Marshall Medical Center North and South, but no one had heard from Dr. Waters since yesterday morning.

He's dead.

Jana knew it. She'd known it since seeing the blood and hat, same as Nola.

After an hour and a half of dragging the lake bottom, one of the rescue divers emerged from the water and yelled something to the officers on the dock that Jana couldn't make out. There was a discussion with the members of the emergency team in the small police boat, and then two of the officers leaned over the stern toward the diver in the water, who'd been joined by two other divers holding something in their hands.

"Oh no," Jana whispered, looking at her daughter, who'd risen to her feet. Seconds later, a body was pulled from the water and placed in the boat.

Jana opened her mouth to scream, but the sound of her voice was drowned out by the bloodcurdling cry of her daughter, who'd started to run toward the dock.

7

Lynette Pike lived in a double-wide trailer on the outskirts of South Pittsburg, Tennessee. She'd lived alone for most of the past thirty-two miserable years since Irv had been killed when his log truck rolled over. Her only son, Waylon, came home from time to time, usually in between prison stays, and Lynette barely blinked when he arrived on the morning of July 5 with a tote bag in his hand and grin on his face.

She made him breakfast and wondered what he'd done this time. Waylon was always running from some kind of trouble. They barely spoke while he ate, and, despite her misgivings, Lynette was glad her boy still came home. She and Irv hadn't been June and Ward Cleaver, but at least Waylon hadn't left and never come back like so many of her friends' children. When her son was in trouble, he came to see his momma, and that made Lynette happy.

And happiness, she knew damn well, was fleeting.

After he finished, he kissed her cheek and went back to his room, which she still kept clean for him, never knowing when he might drop in.

"How long you staying?" she asked.

Waylon had almost shut the door but kept it half-cracked. He shrugged. "Don't know. Maybe couple of weeks. Maybe a few days."

"You in trouble?"

He smiled. "Love you, Momma."

She returned the smile despite herself. "Love you too," she said as the door closed behind him.

———

Waylon clicked the lock and placed the tote bag on the tiny twin bed. He took a deep breath, unzipped the container, and poured out the contents.

He giggled as stacks of hundred-dollar bills fell onto the navy comforter. Ten hundred-dollar bills per roll, and there were fifteen rolls. *"Fifteen thousand dollars,"* he whispered. Exactly what he was told he'd get.

"I did it," he said, speaking louder now as he recalled the events of the prior night when he'd shot Dr. Braxton Waters three times in the head. He'd checked the doctor's pulse and confirmed he was dead. Then he'd kicked the poor sap's body over the side of the dock and watched as it disappeared into the muddy water. He'd hesitated when he saw the blood on the floor by the lawn chair. Nothing he could do about that. He'd cursed under his breath when he saw that Waters's cap had fallen over the edge and was floating in the water. He'd tried to retrieve it, but the hat had already drifted a couple feet off the dock, and Waylon didn't want to risk jumping into the water.

"Fuck it," he'd whispered then.

He lay down on his bed of money and imagined Jana Waters's naked body. Her firm ass and perky breasts. She'd been a high-energy bitch and the best lay he'd ever had in his life.

And she's made me a rich man, he thought, wrapping his hands around a wad of cash and throwing it up in the air like he was tossing a football. Waylon giggled, thinking how damn easy it had all been. "Thank you, Jana," he said out loud, chucking another wad of bills up into the air and closing his eyes as the money landed softly on his face.

8

The holding cell stank of stale urine and body odor. Other than a cot, the only thing held within the four gray cinder block walls was a porcelain toilet.

Jana sat on the floor with her back pressed against the hard wall. She tightly gripped her knees, but that no longer helped control her convulsions. Her arms shook and her teeth chattered. Sweat streamed down her face, back, and ribs. She needed a Xanax. Craved one. But she hadn't been given any of her prescribed medications since she was brought in.

How long had she been here? Four hours? Eight? In her mind, she replayed the moments on the dock right after her dead husband's body was pulled from the lake.

Nola running down the pier with Jana trying to catch up. Her daughter covering her eyes and wailing at the sight of Braxton's corpse, which was covered in mud and milfoil. Jana trying to hug Nola and being pushed away. Officers descending on mother and daughter and urging them to let the crime scene technicians do their jobs.

Then Nola in Jana's face. Yelling. Hitting Jana's shoulders with her fists. *"This is your fault. You did this. Where were you last night? Why were you on the floor when I got home? Why weren't you with Dad? You did it, didn't you? You killed him!"*

Jana had put her hands over her face to block the blows, but Nola's anger had only intensified. Finally, her daughter pushed her so hard that Jana lost her footing and fell backward onto the ground. Jana looked up at Nola, holding her arms toward the child. *"Nola, how could you think . . ."* She'd trailed off, her voice quivering.

"I know this is your fault," Nola had said as an officer had gotten between the pair. *"It has to be."*

Jana gazed at the gray cinder block and bit her lip to try and maintain control of her teeth. *She'll pay for that,* she thought. *Treating me like a criminal after all I've done for her. Braxton barely spent any time with her anyway. Where was he during all the dance practices and soccer trips and gymnastics classes? Where was her beloved father when she went through puberty early? Or when Jay Little broke her skanky heart last summer? She needs to check herself.*

Jana let out a ragged breath. A wave of nausea was coming on, and she swallowed hard. *I . . . need . . . a Xanax.*

The only thing that seemed to keep her mind off the withdrawal was the anger permeating every pore of her being.

"This isn't my fault," she whispered, remembering her daughter's words. *If Nola had kept her mouth shut, I'd be taking visitors at the house. Friends and colleagues, paying their respects and dropping off food. That's what should be happening . . .*

Instead, she was here. In this stink hole going through the first stage of benzodiazepine withdrawal.

Why won't they give me my damn Xanax?

Jana closed her eyes. By now, they must have found the drugs. Before being taken to the jail, she'd been told by one of the deputies that the sheriff's office had obtained a warrant to search the house and all the vehicles for any evidence linked to Braxton's death. Jana had a stash of pot in the trunk of her Mercedes. Worse, she'd hidden the coke she'd bought from one of Tyson Cade's dealers in a drawer in her bedroom closet, and there was also a baggie in the glove compartment of her SUV. She couldn't remember if she'd used it all last night or not. Whether she was deemed a suspect or not in her husband's death, Jana figured there was a good chance she'd be charged with possession of an illegal substance.

But she knew that the sheriff's department was fishing for something bigger than a drug charge. Jana had already been interrogated twice since she'd been brought to the jail, and the questions had focused solely on her whereabouts last night and her estranged relationship with her dead husband. Jana understood that the spouse was always a suspect in these types of cases—she watched enough Investigation Discovery to understand that. But Jana also knew that this situation was different. "Where there's smoke, there's fire," the saying goes, and she'd created a good bit of smoke in the last couple of years.

Her use of pot, alcohol, and benzos had probably contributed to her problems, but that alone wouldn't have been enough. And she had a prescription for Xanax, didn't she? Yes, she sometimes exceeded four milligrams a day and her oldest daughter would fill scripts for herself and give them to Jana, but so what? She'd suffered from anxiety since she was a teenager, and the benzos took the edge off. As did the alcohol. And the pot. Everyone she knew did some combination of the same thing.

No big deal, nothing to see here.

Jana's recent taste for cocaine was a different story. Her association with Tyson Cade had put her and her family in peril. She'd gotten behind on her payments, which had led to . . . *consequences.* Why in God's name had she taken up with Cade? Now she was hooked on coke, too, and she knew she was withdrawing from that as well. If only they would give her a Xanax, she could keep it together.

Jana continued to convulse in the cell. Withholding her meds was all part of the plan. They were trying to make her uncomfortable, hoping she would say something to hang herself. Jana tried to focus on what the deputies must be discussing. What had she told them?

She rubbed her hands over her face and, with a burst of energy, scrambled toward the door of the cell.

"I need a Xanax!" she screeched. "Y'all trying to kill me? Can't you see I'm having withdrawals?" She beat on the door several times and rolled over on her back, gazing up at the ceiling, which was also gray cinder block.

And then her thoughts gradually turned over to Waylon Pike. He'd been obsessed with Jana and literally had nothing to lose. Easy to manipulate. Valuable.

What did I do? she thought as her arms and legs continued to shake.

The door clanged open, and a pair of guards stepped inside along with a woman in scrubs who identified herself as the jail nurse. Jana turned away and squeezed her eyes shut, seeing Waylon's dull eyes in her mind.

What did I do?

———

After being examined by the nurse, Jana was finally given a Xanax. One of the officers asked if she wanted to make a phone call. She said yes and was led down a narrow corridor to a room with a desk and phone.

"Five minutes," the guard said.

Jana felt better as the calming medicine worked its magic. She gripped the telephone and placed the receiver in front of her mouth, which was a chore since her hands were shackled together.

Who could she call? Her daughters? Both would be reeling from their father's death. She couldn't put this on them.

Who then? Jana couldn't think of a single friend who'd be willing to lend her assistance.

If only her father were still alive. He'd know what to do. How many times had her dad bailed her out of jams? But he'd died three years ago, and her mother a year before that.

Jana needed a lawyer, but there were none in Guntersville she trusted.

Finally, closing her eyes and grinding her teeth together, she realized there was only one option. She couldn't remember his cell phone number, but that didn't matter. Everyone in the state of Alabama knew how to reach her brother.

Setting her jaw, Jana dialed the digits she'd seen on a thousand billboards.

1-800 GET RICH.

PART TWO

9

"Jason James Rich."

The voice was a deep baritone. Distinguished, firm, but with the slightest twinge of condescension. It belonged to Winthrop Brooks, the chairperson of the Alabama State Bar Disciplinary Commission. Brooks wore a charcoal suit and a maroon tie, complementing the reading glasses that hung low on his nose. He was bald except for a couple of gray patches on the sides of his head. To Jason, he looked every bit the no-bullshit commercial litigator that he was.

Brooks sat in a burgundy leather chair in the middle of an elevated platform. A microphone had been placed in front of him, but it wasn't turned on.

Jason stood and squinted up at the chairman. He'd had one case against Brooks that had settled for just north of a million dollars. That didn't create a conflict of interest, but Jason doubted that it garnered him any favor with the man, whose client probably hadn't been pleased at having to shell out seven figures. He glanced at the other three members of the commission. Seated to Brooks's left: Mary Crosby, a forty-five-year-old real estate attorney from Dothan, and Gary Debro, a fifty-two-year-old insurance defense lawyer from Decatur. To the right: Josephine Scales, a young prosecutor for the Fayette County District Attorney's office.

"Yes, sir," Jason said. His voice felt dry, and he knew it sounded hoarse. He'd dressed in a navy suit with a light-blue tie. During his drive from the Perdido Addiction Center to Montgomery, he'd passed three billboards where he was wearing the exact same thing.

IN AN ACCIDENT? GET RICH.

INJURED IN A FALL? GET RICH.

HURT ON THE JOB? GET RICH.

Each advertisement had Jason's goofy, smiling face. Normally, Jason might have chuckled at being in the same suit as in the ad; today, he felt nothing but a dull sense of numbness. Rehab had done that to him. At first, during the detoxification period, he'd been keenly aware of everything happening. Now, with only a week left of his mandatory three-month stay, he could barely feel anything at all. Almost as if he was a spectator to his shit show of a life.

Even today, "on the outside," as a criminal might say, life seemed odd and disjointed. Though he'd been given his phone for the trip, he hadn't even turned it on. In truth, he hadn't wanted to use it. His partner was keeping him updated on his cases during her regular visits, and sadly, he could think of no one else he needed or wanted to call.

"Mr. Rich, we've reviewed the findings of the general counsel's investigation and his recommendation," Brooks continued, his tone stern. "However, before we make our decision whether to approve his proposal, we wanted to hear from you in person."

Jason glanced to his left, where the only other person in the boardroom sat. Anthony "Tony" Dixon was the general counsel for the Alabama State Bar. Like Jason, Tony was thirty-six years old, and they'd been in the same law school class at Cumberland. They hadn't been friends, nor had they run in the same social circles. However, Jason had always felt that Tony was a solid person and smart lawyer. He'd been fortunate that Tony was heading up the investigation.

"Mr. Rich, you understand that this is the second time that you've been investigated due to a disciplinary complaint."

Jason managed a smirk.

"Something wrong, Mr. Rich?" said the chairman.

"That first complaint was dropped, and I wasn't punished in any way."

"You got into a fistfight with Nate Shuttle on the courthouse steps in Walker County," Mary Crosby chimed in. She raised her eyebrows, but her voice carried no irritation. Perhaps amusement? Curiosity?

"Yes, ma'am," Jason said. "I believe Mr. Dixon's investigation concluded that I wasn't the aggressor in the altercation, and, if I'm not mistaken, Mr. Shuttle had to pay a fine. Isn't that right, Tony?"

The general counsel nodded. "That is correct. There was no discipline cited, but you were given a warning for . . . inciting the confrontation."

"And remind us how you did that?" Ms. Crosby asked.

"I called him a fucking prick," Jason said, sneering up at Winthrop Brooks. "Pardon my language."

"You also broke his nose," Brooks said.

"After he pushed me and took a swing," Jason said. "You should read Tony's report."

Brooks's face turned red. "I have. And I've also read the one we're here about today. Everyone involved in the deposition of your client, Ms. Eileen Frost, back in February—opposing counsel, his associate, the court reporter, and Ms. Frost herself—reported that you were under the influence of alcohol and acting impaired during the proceeding so that the deposition had to be stopped due to your erratic behavior. You were reported to the bar and agreed to an emergency suspension of your license pending a ninety-day stint in a rehabilitation facility. That about cover it?"

Jason swallowed, tasting bile in his mouth. Any bravado he'd felt after bringing up his avoidance of punishment for the fight with Nate was gone. He hung his head. "Yes," he said. "I would add that my partner recently settled Ms. Frost's case for $950,000, and she was ecstatic. It was a good result."

"Yes," Brooks said. "We know. We've spoken to Ms. Frost. In fact, we've spoken to almost every current and former client of your law firm. While none of them were displeased with your representation, several, including Ms. Frost, admitted to smelling alcohol on your person and having questions as to your sobriety during consultations." He took off his glasses and scrutinized Jason with a cold gaze. "Mr. Rich, you understand that this behavior is improper, unprofessional, and unethical."

"Yes, sir," Jason said.

Brooks put his glasses back on and gave his head a jerk. "Mr. Rich, I have to say that I don't understand you." He took out a piece of paper and slid his spectacles up his nose. "We've meticulously combed through your background as a student and lawyer, and it's impeccable. Golf scholarship to Davidson College in North Carolina, where you graduated with honors. Law review at Cumberland School of Law along with being on the trial advocacy team that won a regional championship. Two years as an associate at Jones & Butler and then nine years as a solo practitioner. You made *Super Lawyers* magazine in the 'rising star' category. And you and your firm have been a leader in handling pro bono cases for the indigent." He paused. "And yet you seem to be on a mission to get yourself disbarred. The fistfight with Mr. Shuttle was the only other formal complaint besides this one that's ever been lodged against you, but the general counsel's investigation has revealed a laundry list of bizarre incidents over the past couple of years." Brooks cut his eyes to his associates on the platform.

"One court reporter"—Mary Crosby began—"who happens to be the daughter of a federal judge, said you streaked the Quad in Tuscaloosa after taking a doctor's deposition."

Veronica Smithers, Jason thought, not saying anything.

"You gave both of your clients a Gatorade bath after a mediation," Gary Debro added, his tone incredulous. *"In the opposing counsel's conference room."* He paused. "With a full cooler of ice."

Jason again kept his mouth shut, forcing a frown.

"You got into a mud wrestling match at the Rock the South concert in Cullman last summer with a female patron and were escorted by the police off the premises, along with the woman, and charged with disturbing the peace," Josephine Scales said.

Jason winced.

"Mr. Rich, you have anything to say?" Mr. Brooks asked.

"I . . . uh . . ." He swallowed again and took in a breath. "The Gatorade bath has become a firm tradition after successful results, and I paid for all the cleaning charges. We, uh, probably should limit those celebrations to our office."

"You think?" Debro asked.

"Yes," Jason said. "And as far as the whole Quad thing, I was kind of dating Judge Smithers's daughter at the time." He shrugged. "With Rock the South, we were in a weather delay, and there were at least a hundred people there playing in the mud. The criminal charge—which was a misdemeanor—was dropped. And I wouldn't describe what the woman and I were doing as . . . *wrestling.*"

"What would you have called it?" Scales asked.

Jason shifted his eyes to her. "Making out? Hooking up?"

Scales's face turned crimson, and she looked down at the table.

"Those are only a few of the more volatile incidents, Mr. Rich, not to mention the fact that you've cluttered up the entire state with your tacky billboards," Brooks said, his tone now one of exasperation.

Jason ground his teeth together. He shot Tony a glance, who shook his head as if to say, *Don't do it. He wants you to lose your temper.* Jason took a deep breath and glared at Brooks. He resisted the urge to remind the commission that his billboards had been approved by the board.

Brooks looked down his nose at Jason for a full five seconds before continuing in a softer, compassionless voice. "I knew your father."

Jason licked his lips and forced himself to breathe. White-hot rage surged through his body and mind.

The chairman frowned and rubbed his chin as if he were in deep thought. "Lucas Rich was a fine lawyer and an even finer man. The epitome of *class* . . . and *professionalism.*" He hesitated. "I was sorry to hear of his passing."

Jason crossed his arms to keep them from shaking. "Thank you," he managed, then took another deep breath and cut to the chase. "Mr. Chairman . . ." He looked to the others. "Members of the commission . . . I regret my behavior very much, and I'm ready to comply with the recommendations of the general counsel."

"OK," Brooks said. He snatched another document and brought it to his face. "Let's go over Mr. Dixon's proposal, shall we? Your license to practice law will be reinstated when you meet the following conditions. First, your completion of a ninety-day inpatient rehabilitation stay. Correct?"

"Yes, sir," Jason said.

"Of which you have already completed eighty-three days. Right?"

"Yes. I was granted an eight-hour furlough for this hearing, and I'll be drug tested on my return this afternoon."

"Good," Brooks said, squinting up from the page at Jason. "Let's hope you pass that test," he said, oozing sarcasm. He returned his eyes to the proposal. "Second, you'll receive a public reprimand by the commissioners of the Alabama State Bar at one of their next meetings."

"Yes, sir."

"You will pay a $2,500 fine."

"Yes."

"And the last provision requires that, after you finish your rehabilitation, you'll cooperate with the recommendations of the Alabama Lawyer Assistance Program."

"That's correct."

Brooks leaned back in his chair and rapped his knuckles against the table. "The commission will now discuss the proposal, and Mr. Dixon will notify you of our decision within the hour." He scowled at Jason as if he were a roach he'd just stepped on. "You can wait outside."

———

Forty-five minutes later, Tony took a seat next to Jason in the hallway. Tony let out a long sigh that conveyed his fatigue.

"They didn't go for it, did they?" Jason asked.

"No . . . actually . . . they did," Tony said. "The vote was three to one. I'm sure you can bet who voted against you."

"Brooks."

"I can neither confirm nor deny."

Jason gazed up at the ceiling and took in a deep breath. "Thanks, man."

"No need for thanks. It's a fair deal. But Jason . . ." Tony stood. "This is it. If you get hauled back in here, you're done. The commission was adamant that your reprimand will include a zero-tolerance policy for any future findings of inappropriate or unethical conduct."

As the general counsel began to walk away, Jason called after him. He thought about standing, but his legs felt rubbery and weak. "The bar won't get any more trouble from me, Tony." He cringed at the desperation he heard in his own voice. "That's a promise."

Tony turned and put his hands on his hips. "I hope you keep that pledge." The general counsel inspected Jason with flat eyes. "This is your last chance."

10

The mood in the conference room was grim. The officers' faces were tight. Though the air-conditioning was going full blast, to Sergeant Hatty Daniels, the space felt hot and stuffy. Tension gripped the space like a boa constrictor. Like the other lawmen and women, Hatty focused on the head of the table and waited.

At last, Sheriff Griffith cleared his throat. "Y'all know the deal. Based on Clem's autopsy report, the cause of Dr. Braxton Waters's death was three gunshot wounds to the head from a nine-millimeter pistol. He was obviously then pushed or rolled into the lake. Time of death has been approximated at between nine p.m. on July 4 and one a.m. on July 5. Isn't that correct, Clem?"

"Yes, sir," said Dr. Clem Carton, the county coroner.

"People, it's July 7. Dr. Waters has been cold for sixty hours, and we still don't have any leads other than his wife."

"Who has a rock-solid alibi for almost the entire four-hour window." Hatty's voice was stern as she inspected the sheriff from her spot at the other end of the table. She had dark-brown skin, short hair, and a no-nonsense disposition. She was the best investigator in the department, and that's why she'd been assigned the gig. "Jana Waters was seen on a video surveillance camera entering the Hampton Inn on Highway 431 at nine forty-five p.m., and the same camera shows her leaving at three a.m. on July 5. There were cameras at all exits, and she never left the hotel. Her Mercedes remained parked in the same spot for over five hours." Hatty paused and leaned her elbows on the table. "Though possible, it is unlikely that Ms. Waters killed her husband unless she hired someone to do it, and so far we have no evidence of that."

"She was having an affair with Tyson Cade," Sheriff Griffith fired back.

"So you say, Griff, but we have nothing proving that." Hatty gave him a weary smile, and he grunted. She had a solid relationship with the sheriff and was the only person in the room who would dare call him "Griff" under the circumstances. But she wanted to get her point across. "All we have is circumstantial evidence linking Ms. Waters to Tyson Cade. Calls to strange numbers."

"Cade was at the Hampton too."

"I know, and I suspect he was there to see Ms. Waters, but we don't have a room attached to either one of them, and the cameras coming out of the elevators never give us a clear view."

"What about the drugs?"

Hatty nodded. "We've got her dead to rights on coke and marijuana possession, and we've charged her accordingly. That gives us the right to hold her, but, unless some facts surface to show that she'd hired someone to kill her husband, we don't have enough to charge her for the murder."

The sheriff again grunted. "Do we have a single other suspect?"

"Our best angle is probably the handyman, Pike, but—"

"We'll get to him in a minute, but first let's cover all the other alternatives. Did the doctor have a mistress?"

Hatty let her hands fall to the table palms down. "Several of the staff at the hospital said that Waters was having an affair with his CRNA, Colleen Maples. We've spoken to her, and she denied anything but a professional relationship. She also said she was at the Rock House on the Fourth with a group of three other women for dinner, and her story is corroborated by all of them. A waiter at the restaurant also remembers seeing her there, and her credit card receipt shows she cashed out at eight fifty-eight p.m. Maples lives in a small house near

Camp Cha-La-Kee, and two of her friends joined her for some drinks and to watch the fireworks on the lake. Everyone left around one a.m."

"So nothing but smoke on the affair, and she has an alibi."

"Yep," Hatty said.

"Damnit," Griffith said, wincing. "What about enemies? Did Waters have any business associates that he'd wronged? Patients that he'd mistreated? Any damn thing?"

"Not that I've found. Of course, there was the malpractice case that tried last year . . ." Hatty trailed off, and there were several nods around the room.

Dr. Waters had been sued for medical negligence by the family of Trey Cowan, who'd been the star quarterback of Guntersville High School five years ago. A genuine blue chip prospect with offers to play from every top college program in the country. He'd committed to Auburn, but Nick Saban and Alabama were still after him, and many thought he'd flip his senior year.

In the last game of his senior season against Scottsboro, Trey had broken the tibia in his right leg. Though serious, the fracture was a common injury, and players typically recovered within six months. But Trey hadn't recovered. He'd developed an infection after surgery, and, though the wound eventually healed and his leg was saved, he could never play football again and walked with a pronounced limp. Trey's mother, Trudy, a longtime waitress at Top O' the River, had filed a lawsuit on her son's behalf against Waters. After three years of discovery, depositions, and two failed mediations, the case went to trial. Eight days later, the jury came back with a verdict in favor of the doctor.

"Have we spoken with Trudy? Doesn't she live in Alder Springs?" the sheriff asked.

"Yes and yes," Hatty responded. "Deputy Mitchell"—she cut her eyes at an officer to her right—"drove out there yesterday evening. Isn't that right, George?"

"Yes, ma'am," Mitchell said. "I spoke with Trudy after she got off work. She spent the Fourth at her neighbors', the Albrights, who had a party. Trudy was there until well past midnight and walked the quarter mile home. There were about ten folks at the party. All have confirmed her attendance."

"So she has an alibi." Hatty stated the obvious.

"What about Trey?" Griffith asked.

Hatty crossed her arms and glanced at Mitchell to continue.

"He went to the party at the Brick downtown. Was there until around nine. Told the bartender he was going to watch the fireworks on the lake from the Sunset Trail."

"Did he?"

George shrugged. "When I spoke with him, he said he went alone."

"How did he get to the trail?" the sheriff asked.

"He said he walked."

"You don't believe him?"

"That's a good three-quarters of a mile at least," Mitchell said, scratching his chin. "Long stroll for a man with a limp."

"What does Trey do now?" the sheriff asked.

"Works for the city, doing odd jobs," Mitchell said. "Umpiring Little League. Chains crew for football games. Doing sanitation work at different municipal facilities."

"He had a full ride to Bama, didn't he?"

"He had a full ride everywhere," an officer leaning against the wall said, his voice low. "Until Doc Waters botched his surgery."

"Speak up, Kelly," the sheriff said. "How do you know Trey?"

Deputy Kelly Flowers stepped forward. He was an athletic man in his midtwenties with thick forearms. "I was a senior wide receiver when Trey was a sophomore. He was great even then. Already getting offers. I caught ten touchdown passes that year."

"I remember now," the sheriff said. "Advanced to the quarterfinals, didn't we?"

"Yeah."

"You still keep up with him?"

"Not much," Kelly said. "It's sad, you know. Trey was a god around here for three years. And now he's cleaning bathrooms and getting yelled at for bad calls in Little League games."

Silence in the room. Griffith finally spoke. "Bring him in, all right, Kelly? We need to at least talk to him, and it'll be easier coming from you."

"Sheriff, he can barely get around. There's no way he could've killed Dr. Waters."

"He managed to make it to the Sunset Trail . . . or so he says. He also has a clear motive and no alibi. Bring him in."

"Yes, sir," Kelly said.

"What about Walter Cowan?" Griffith asked, moving his eyes around the room.

"Trudy said she hasn't heard from Walt since the divorce became final," Mitchell said. "She thinks he's working construction down on the Florida Panhandle somewhere, but, in her words, she 'doesn't know and doesn't care.'"

The sheriff gazed up at the ceiling. "OK . . . let's talk about the handyman now." He leaned his elbows on the table and formed a tent with his hands. "Have we located him yet?"

"Waylon Pike," Hatty said, a touch of annoyance in her voice. This was the one avenue of investigation that she and the department had whiffed thus far. "He did a good bit of work for the Waterses as well as several other families on Buck Island, including the Burnses, Campbells, and McCarys. Jackson Burns said he saw Pike at the Waters home on the morning of July 2 and that Pike had swung by and built a set of steps with a railing in the Burnses' guesthouse that afternoon. He hasn't seen or heard from him since then."

"Do we have any information on Pike? Address? Cell phone number?"

"Both," Hatty answered. "He was living in an apartment back behind Gunter Avenue, but he wasn't there when we tried to see him. We got a search warrant, but his apartment was clean. We called his cell, went straight to voice mail."

"Did we track it?"

Hatty nodded. "The last time it registered to a cell tower was on July 3, and he was at the Brick downtown. We checked with the bartender there, and she recognized his picture. Said Pike liked to watch the Braves game from the bar and drink a couple of draft beers during happy hour."

"So he has no alibi, he's apparently left town, and he's turned his phone off." For the first time, Sheriff Griffith's tone contained a trace of hope. "Suspicious, I'd say."

"No doubt," Hatty agreed.

"Any thought as to where he might be? Did Burns say anything?"

"Burns told us that he thought Pike said he was from somewhere in Florida or Georgia, so we've sent an APB to all counties in both states." Everyone in Guntersville called Jackson Burns, the owner of Burns Nissan Mazda, by his last name.

"Not much to go on," the sheriff lamented.

Hatty held out her hands. "We've got nothing else."

The room was silent for several seconds. Finally, Griffith stood. "I've got a press conference in the morning. Unless we get a break between now and then, I'll say the investigation is ongoing, and we're pursuing several leads. We don't have forever, people. Every day that goes forward without a suspect charged with this murder is a day that makes it harder for Shay Lankford to get a conviction, and you can bet your ass that she's riding mine twenty-four seven. We need to make a damn arrest."

"We do, Sheriff," Hatty said, also standing and trying to make eye contact with as many of the officers as possible. "But first things first."

Griffith rubbed the back of his neck and gazed at her. "We have to find Waylon Pike."

11

Waylon couldn't help himself. He'd been back home a week, and he was restless. He was also tired of his mother. The way she frowned and pursed her lips every time he described his work in Guntersville was a dead giveaway that she knew he was in trouble. Slinking home after getting in a fix had been Waylon's pattern his whole life, and Lynette Pike was no fool.

I've got to get out of here . . .

His instructions had been clear. Lay low. Stay the hell out of Marshall County. Don't bring any attention to himself.

He'd planned to take some of his blood money and go to the beach. Drink beer on the sand for a couple of weeks. But, if he were honest with himself, that was a pipe dream. Waylon Pike didn't have the first clue about how to have fun on the coast, and sitting in a lawn chair all day in the hot sun sounded boring. Maybe the mountains then, he'd thought. Hike the Appalachian Trail? Get a cabin in Gatlinburg? Or what about the lake? He'd worked on a lot of boathouses around Lake Guntersville. He could rent a place over by the Nickajack Dam near Chattanooga. Or how about Lake Burton over in Georgia? Wasn't that where they filmed *Deliverance*? He loved that movie. Hell, screw this local mess. Why not see the country? He had enough cash to easily get him to California. Or Colorado. He could maybe become a ranch hand or something on a spread like the one in *Yellowstone*. Maybe get branded like those bunkhouse boys. Cool, right?

Wrong.

All his ideas sounded lame or like they required too much work.

Truth was that the only vocation Waylon Pike enjoyed was crime, the only thing in life that he'd ever been good at.

And he'd just killed a man. His first murder. He'd hit the top of the criminal food chain, and it had been easy as damn pie. A week had passed, and the Marshall County Sheriff's Department hadn't come calling. From what he'd read on the internet, they didn't have a clue.

He wanted to celebrate. To get drunk and blow off steam.

And he wanted to be with a woman. Yes, by God, he missed some of the female companionship he'd enjoyed in Guntersville, and all the adrenaline and success of his latest venture had made him horny as hell. Being cooped up in his mother's shack for a week had only heightened his desires. He'd thought about paying for a whore. He knew where to look for that kind of fun and wasn't above it.

But Waylon was a man of means now. *Well heeled,* as he'd heard his mother describe rich folks. With the kind of cash he could sling around, he ought to be able to pick up a woman. Maybe not Jana Waters quality, but something.

So on July 11, seven days after killing Dr. Braxton Waters, Waylon drove across the Alabama state line and stopped at Fat Boys Bar & Grill in Bridgeport. When he saw the Harley-Davidson motorcycles parked out front, Waylon smiled, breathing in the scent of exhaust and, from inside the building, grilled burgers.

He took a seat at the bar and ordered a cold PBR, cheeseburger, and fries. Waylon took a long sip from the chilly mug and exhaled.

He had $1,000 cash in his pocket. He was about to get drunk, and judging by the three or four good-looking women he'd already seen in the place, he'd have every opportunity to get thoroughly laid. After drinking another long gulp from the beer, he held up his glass to the mirror behind the bar and winked at himself.

———

Tara Samples was a slightly husky woman with a gap in her bottom teeth that you couldn't see unless she smiled big, which she hardly ever did. She loved draft beer, cheap bourbon, and Alabama football. She'd let ROTC put her through four years at Jacksonville State University and, in return, had served one tour of duty in Afghanistan. Tara had been home in Bridgeport for a decade since turning in her uniform. She owned and operated her father's hardware store, attended church every Sunday, donated money to North Jackson High School, her alma mater, and was a fine tax-paying citizen.

However, every so often, when her PTSD would rear up, Tara had to have, as John Anderson liked to sing, a straight tequila night.

The evening of July 11 happened to be one of those occasions, and Fat Boys was her preferred destination. After three shots, she noticed another one placed next to her that she hadn't ordered.

"Buy you a drink, ma'am?"

Tara turned and peered into the dull eyes of a man she didn't recognize. Then she pulled back and sized the stranger up. She saw the veins sticking out of his arms, the stubble on his face, and the calluses on his hands. Tara had never married, but she enjoyed a good romp, especially to close out a night of liquor shots.

And the rougher the better. In the army, she'd fucked in closets, gotten diddled while driving an open jeep across the desert, and on one particular batshit night in Ghazni, had a three-way with two superior officers. She squinted at the man, took the shot glass, and kicked it back before slamming it down on the table.

"Another?" he asked.

He'll do, Tara thought, nodding and placing her hand on the back of his stool.

———

Six hours later, Waylon lay on his back and looked up at the stars. He was hammered, on the verge of exhaustion. Next to him, Tara ran her fingers down his stomach to his groin. "You got anything left?" she asked.

Waylon guffawed. "Ma'am, no ma'am. Sergeant, you have wiped me out."

They'd had three more shots at the bar, and then they'd retired to her place, and she'd broken out the handle of Jose Cuervo. She lived in a one-story rancher on two acres of land. After downing half the bottle, most of a saltshaker, and a full lime, she'd taken the sheet off her bed and laid it down on the grass in the backyard.

Though not much of a looker, Tara was an incredible lay, and Waylon figured his sack was bone dry after the marathon she'd just put him through. When the sex was over, Tara had started talking about her time in the army. Her kills.

She'd taken three lives that she knew of in Afghanistan. Waylon had been interested in the details. Two had been machine gun kills. Enemy soldiers who'd crossed her path and would've shot her if she hadn't been quicker. She'd used an M27, a gun that Waylon had read a lot about. He asked her if she still had it, but she ignored the question.

The one that bothered her was her third kill. The last one. She'd come up behind a man in close quarters. Too tight for a gun, so she'd had to use her knife. She'd slit his throat, heard his groan. Felt the air seep out of his lungs and smelled his breath as he dropped to the ground. "I still hear that motherfucker's groan in my dreams, and I wake up and my bedroom smells of his stale stench."

She explained that she preferred sleeping outside and pointed to the bed swing she'd hung on the porch. "Great for sleeping, not so much for fucking."

Waylon had listened to this stranger's tales of murder and been awestruck. Envious even. Why hadn't he ever joined the army? His skill set would have been perfect.

He reached for the tequila bottle as Tara lay beside him. He took a long pull and felt a bit dizzy. He wanted to tell this woman about his kill. He had to tell someone. What would be the harm? This bitch was piss drunk. He could always deny everything if she somehow remembered what he'd told her.

Waylon took another sip. He glanced at Tara, who'd closed her eyes. They were both naked, their bodies glistening with sweat, the air reeking of tequila. He closed his eyes and opened his mouth.

"I killed a man," Waylon Pike said.

12

Hatty Daniels didn't hesitate when the tip came in. It was a little less than an hour to Jasper, Tennessee, and she arrived in forty minutes, her siren blaring the entire way. Deputy George Mitchell rode shotgun but barely said a word during the ride.

Both knew what was at stake. The Waters murder was a week old, and the Marshall County Sheriff's Office was being inundated with news coverage, most of it bad. There had even been calls for Sheriff Griffith's firing.

Homicide was rare in Guntersville. The crime rate itself was higher than the national average, but that was due to theft, burglary, and other property offenses. Violent acts were typically limited to assault and robbery charges.

A murder on Buck Island was unheard of.

Griff was feeling the heat, and he'd had another full-force meeting the previous evening that was even more dire than the first. They were seemingly out of options. There was still no direct evidence against Jana Waters, no additional suspect had emerged, and Waylon Pike had seemingly disappeared.

The call from the Marion County Sheriff's Department had come at 4:30 p.m. A woman named Tara Samples had told the Bridgeport, Alabama, police chief about her encounter with a South Pittsburg man who claimed he'd shot and killed a doctor who was hitting golf balls on his boat dock. Samples, a retired veteran who owned a local business, had heard a news report about the murder of Dr. Braxton

Waters and had come in and given a statement. She'd taken a selfie with the man and gave his photo to the police as well. The Bridgeport PD had contacted the authorities in South Pittsburg, and one of the deputies, a longtime resident, recognized the man as Michael Pike. Michael *Waylon* Pike.

Pike had been found at his mother's house and taken to the Marion County Jail in Jasper, where he was being held for a number of outstanding warrants and questioning in the murder of Braxton Waters.

Though the Samples woman was admittedly drunk at the time Pike told her about killing the doctor, she had a reputation for being a no-nonsense woman who wouldn't have reported a crime if she didn't really think something was wrong. "Tara is the opposite of a drama hound," Hatty's source in the Bridgeport PD said. The photograph that Samples had taken had been sent to Hatty, who'd verified with Jackson Burns that the man in the picture was indeed the Waylon Pike who'd been working for him and several others on Buck Island, including the Waterses.

Once they arrived at the jail, a brief conversation was had with the sheriff. Instead of overwhelming Pike with officers, a low-key approach was agreed upon. Hatty and George would go in, and everyone else would view a live video feed. They were then led down a narrow hallway to the interrogation room. Inside the tight space, Waylon Pike sat in an aluminum chair with his head resting on a wooden table. He didn't look up as they entered.

"Mr. Pike, you have a couple visitors from Guntersville," a Marion County guard announced and then closed the door.

Hatty cut her eyes at George, who cleared his throat and sat down in one of the aluminum chairs. She continued to stand.

"Mr. Pike, we came down here to arrest you for the murder of Dr. Braxton Waters."

Pike kept his head on the table, but Hatty saw his neck twitch and eyes blink open. He said nothing.

"If that's how you want it to go, then we'll just take you with us and be on our merry way," Hatty added.

Pike sat up straight and folded his arms across his chest. His brown hair was disheveled, as if he'd been dragged out of bed, and his face was covered in several days' worth of stubble. He looked at George first and then Hatty. "Dr. Waters?" he asked.

"Don't play dumb with us," George said. "Several of the Waterses' neighbors remember you working on their house, and a Bridgeport woman has given a statement that you confessed to killing him." That was a bit of an exaggeration. Tara Samples had said that Pike confessed to killing a doctor on the physician's boat dock. He hadn't mentioned Waters by name. "You remember Ms. Tara Samples," George continued. "You met her at Fat Boys Bar & Grill last night and spent the rest of the evening with her."

"She was drunk," Pike said. "So was I. I didn't say a damn thing to her."

"She begs to differ. She's a retired veteran with impeccable credibility."

"Like I said, she was hammered."

Hatty took a step forward and sat down next to George. "The Marion County Sheriff's Office searched your mother's home." She looked up at the ceiling before lowering her gaze to the suspect. "They found the money."

Pike bit his lip but otherwise managed to keep a poker face. *Impressive,* Hatty thought as she continued. "What's a guy like you doing carrying around $14,000 in cash in a duffel bag?"

"Pretty risky to keep it in the house, don't you think?" George chimed in. "At least bury it in the backyard or something. But, on the flip side, where does a guy like you hide that much money? I mean, it was under the floor. If your mother hadn't told the officers where you keep stuff, they probably wouldn't have found it."

Pike's mask of calm was teetering. He stared down at the table, his forehead and cheeks reddening.

"You have two outstanding warrants from other states for speeding and petty theft," Hatty chimed in. "You're still on probation for the arson conviction for which you served three years in the Limestone Correctional Facility, and those out-of-state arrests are a violation of your probation and your parole. You're going to jail, Waylon. Probably back to prison regardless of whether you're convicted of Dr. Waters's murder." She leaned her elbows on the table. "But we're going to convict you. We have a statement that you said you did it."

"That's hearsay," Pike said, meeting her eyes and darting his gaze to Mitchell. A tell. He was beginning to panic.

"Actually, Waylon, it's not," Hatty said. She'd heard Shay Lankford argue this exception in court enough to commit it to memory. "A statement made by a defendant to another person is considered a party opponent admission. It is by definition *not* hearsay. Tara Samples's statement comes in." She flung her hands up in the air. "Of course, what Marshall County jury is going to believe a retired veteran?"

"She was drunk."

"You keep on saying that, but she remembers what you said very well. You were talking about 'kills.' She told you about her escapades in the army, and you had to say something, too, didn't you?"

Pike glared at Hatty but said nothing. "What about the money?" she continued. "You didn't get that from fixing someone's boathouse. And why'd you leave Guntersville right after Dr. Waters's murder?" She looked at George. "What do you think, Deputy?"

"I think it's obvious someone paid Mr. Pike here a handsome fee to kill Dr. Waters."

Pike glanced down at the table, keeping his arms crossed tight to his chest. An extremely defensive position. *Almost got him.* "Waylon," Hatty said, lowering her voice, "tell us who hired you to kill Dr. Waters. It's your only way out. If you don't, you're going to ride the needle.

Brutally executing a human being and then kicking his body over the side of his boat dock? There's no way a Marshall County jury won't return the death penalty." Hatty leaned back in her chair, letting her words hang in the air.

"What's it going to be, Pike?" George asked.

———

Waylon Pike kept his gaze fixed on the table, not moving. His mind raced with possibilities . . . doubt . . . frustration. How could he have been so stupid? Leaving the money at his mother's house. Telling Tara Samples about his kill. He blinked but didn't look up from the table. *Let's not make it worse,* he told himself.

This wasn't the first time he'd been questioned by police officers. *They want to deal,* he knew. But if he started trying to negotiate, there was no going back. They'd know he did it.

Were they bluffing? He finally lifted his head and looked at the Black woman and her hard-ass partner. Both were staring at him with confident, calm expressions. If they were the least bit nervous about what he might do or say, they weren't showing it. They'd told him they were going to arrest him. Were the money and Tara's statement enough? He should get a lawyer, but, if they'd confiscated his cash, he couldn't afford one. It had been a week since Braxton Waters's murder, and he knew they had to be feeling pressure to do something. If he didn't talk, would they charge him?

His gut said yes.

Waylon cleared his throat and looked past the two officers to the closed door. He'd been in fixes before, but nothing like this. How could his own mother have sold him down the river? The money should have been safe.

"All right, George," the Black officer said. "Charge him."

"Wait," Waylon said, hearing the panic in his voice and gritting his teeth. He lowered his eyes to her. "What's the deal? I ain't talking unless I have a deal."

"That's not the way this works," she fired back. "We don't negotiate until we know what you know. Only the district attorney can make an offer."

"I want immunity," Waylon said. "Complete immunity or I say nothing."

The woman glanced at her partner and then back at Waylon. "No chance. You murdered Dr. Waters. You're going to be put to death unless you talk. If any deal's struck, it's going to be on your sentence. I suspect that our prosecutor will be willing to negotiate, but immunity would be an outrage."

"It's really simple, Pike," the male officer said. "If you don't give us some information right now, we're going to charge you and take you in. If you want any chance at a negotiated plea, you need to start talking."

Waylon averted his eyes, thinking about his benefactor.

"Who paid you the 14K?" the woman asked.

Waylon gazed at her. "It was fifteen."

"Who?" she persisted.

Waylon Pike sighed. "The doctor's wife," he finally said.

13

Jana Waters lay on her back on the hard cot. She'd been in the holding cell for over a week now, and she felt better. Exhausted but improved. She still craved a Xanax, but the jail physician had put her on a tapering dose of the benzodiazepine, and she was now getting .5 milligrams a day. That was a lot less than she typically took, but it was something. She was able to think now, and she'd been thinking hard. Her brother needed to call her back. She knew lawyers in Marshall County—good ones—but she figured that none of them would want to touch her case. Braxton had been a popular figure in town. In some way, shape, or form, he'd treated many of the lawyers or someone in their families. There would be conflicts of interest and, even if there wasn't a true conflict, what attorney in his right mind would want to get involved?

Barry Martino came to mind. He was a criminal defense attorney whose son Deak was the same age as Nola. Jana remembered him talking about one of his criminal cases at a Guntersville High basketball game last year. If Jason continued to ignore her, she'd call Barry.

When the cell door slid open, Jana cocked her head toward the opening, expecting a corrections officer with a food tray. Instead, Sheriff Richard Griffith, who Jana had met at several fundraisers, strode inside, flanked by two officers. Jana rose to her feet.

The last person to enter the cell sent a wave of gooseflesh up Jana's arms.

Shay Lankford wore a crimson suit. She was a tall woman with an athletic figure who Jana used to see all the time at the Downtown Gym, where they both used the same personal trainer. She'd been elected district attorney three years ago in a close election, becoming the first female head prosecutor in Marshall County history.

Jana and Braxton hadn't voted for her. Jana had found Shay to be aloof and unfriendly. The woman barely spoke to her at the gym or anywhere else but was able to turn on the charm when she spoke to a group or a jury. She was always dressed to the nines. Even at the gym, her clothes, hair, and face were perfect.

"Ms. Waters," Shay said, stepping forward as the three law enforcement officials gave way.

"Shay," Jana said, glaring at the other woman, not breaking eye contact.

"We have Waylon Pike in custody," Shay said. "And he's told us everything."

Jana kept her gaze fixed on the prosecutor. "Did he kill my husband?"

Shay's lips curved into a tight smile, and Jana felt a ripple of agitation.

"He did exactly what you paid him to do," the district attorney said.

Jana's heartbeat raced. "Wh-wh-what?" she managed.

Now Shay grinned full out, showing her pristine white teeth, her eyes glowing with intensity. "You're really something, aren't you? I understand that you haven't cooperated with questioning from Officers Daniels and Mitchell."

"Not until I speak with an attorney."

"You've had a week to get a lawyer. What's the holdup? The court will appoint you one. All you have to do is fill out the paperwork."

Jana scowled. "I'm Jana fucking Waters. I'm *not* going to take a court-appointed lawyer. My brother just happens to be one of the best attorneys in the state, and I'm not going to do anything until I speak with him."

Shay cocked her head. "You mean . . . the billboard guy?" She glanced at the sheriff and the other two officers, and they all shared a look of amusement.

"He practices in Birmingham," Jana said.

Shay rolled her eyes. "Jana, we know what you did. We've talked with your bank. We know how much money you took out the day before your husband's murder, and we know that we found the same amount on Mr. Pike. He's confessed to the crime and given a sworn statement that you paid him to do it."

Jana's hands began to quiver. "He's lying."

"Are you going to tell us what happened?" Shay fired back.

Jana shook her head. "Not until Jason gets here."

Shay shifted her eyes to Sergeant Daniels. Then the prosecutor took a step backward, and Hatty Daniels took her place.

"Jana Rich Waters," Hatty said, her voice strong, "you are hereby charged with capital murder in unlawfully and intentionally causing the death of your husband, Dr. Braxton Waters."

Jana's legs shook, and she sat down on the hard cot. She peered past the woman and the other people in the cell to a spot on the gray cinder block wall. As Hatty continued to speak, Jana became numb, not realizing that tears had begun to slide down her cheeks.

"You have the right to remain silent . . ."

PART THREE

14

The Flora-Bama Lounge and Package Store was one of the most iconic watering holes on the Gulf Coast. Football legends like Kenny "the Snake" Stabler had been known to tie one on at the beachside saloon, and the bar's annual mullet toss was one of the biggest events on the Florida Panhandle. In his breakthrough novel, *The Firm*, John Grisham even had Mitch McDeere make a stop at the legendary establishment while being chased down the Redneck Riviera by the Mafia.

Less than a half hour after being discharged from the Perdido Addiction Center, or the PAC, as the residents and staff called it, Jason Rich sat at a table near one of the outdoor stages of the famous bar. From his spot, he could look past the singer and see the emerald waters of the Gulf of Mexico. Jason could almost taste the salt air coming off the breeze.

In every direction, he saw people drinking. Three college girls wearing bikini tops and blue jean cutoffs split a pitcher of margaritas to his right. Behind him, a couple of middle-aged men drank Miller Lite longnecks. And below the stage was a group of fortysomething women all drinking different-colored concoctions with straws in their plastic cups. Cosmopolitans, martinis, kamikazes, tequila shots . . .

Jason turned toward the front of the restaurant. High above the building and about a hundred yards south of the Flora-Bama was a billboard with his smiling mug gazing back at him.

INJURED AT WORK? GET RICH.

On the lower edge of the giant highway poster was a tiny script of legalese that could barely be read from a car but which every attorney advertisement had to include: "No representation is made that our quality of legal services is greater than the quality of legal services performed by other lawyers."

What bullshit, Jason thought. That was exactly what was being represented. Or at least that was the intent. The hypocrisy of the statement was galling, but all lawyers that wanted to make money had to include it. Whether it was an obnoxious billboard, a television commercial, or a social media post, every plaintiff's firm that wanted to make a buck advertised why their services were indeed better and then put the magic "we aren't really saying that" qualifier at the bottom.

A waitress stopped in front of his table. She wore a white tank top with the name of the restaurant embroidered in pink in the middle. She also sported white denim shorts and a blue cap with *War Eagle* written in orange on the front. "Get you a drink?" she asked.

Jason was struck by so many powerful urges at once. Outside of group therapy sessions and the disciplinary hearing a week ago in Montgomery, he'd spent the past ninety days in almost total isolation. Romantic entanglements with other residents were forbidden at the PAC, but that hadn't stopped several couples from hooking up.

But Jason had avoided all of it. He'd come to treatment to get away from the world, and any additional relationships would have complicated matters. But now, at the by God Flora-Bama, everything he'd sought to avoid was right in front of his face in all its glory.

Alcohol.

Drugs.

Women.

Sex.

Jason gazed up at the beautiful waitress, who blinked back at him in confusion. "Sir? Get you something? How about a beer?"

"Corona," Jason finally managed. "With a lime."

She sashayed away, and Jason shook his head. *What am I doing? Why am I here? Do I really want to quit this soon?* He envisioned the patronizing face of Winthrop Brooks, the chairman of the state bar's disciplinary commission. Wouldn't this little scene make that prick happy?

"I knew your father," Brooks had said. *"The epitome of class . . . and professionalism."*

The comments were meant to be a dig. Lucas Rich was a well-respected member of the Alabama State Bar until his death, everything his tacky son wasn't.

Jason glanced again at the billboard in the distance.

The waitress placed the cold bottle of beer on his table. "Do you want a menu?"

"No," Jason said. "Thank you. Just the beer for now." He lowered his eyes and didn't watch as she walked away. He studied the Corona, a beer he only drank by the ocean. Kind of like as a kid, he ate Cookie Crisp cereal at the beach because it was the sole time his mom would let him have something besides raisin bran or Total. Corona with a lime. The taste of the tropics. Like the commercials with the couple sitting under the umbrella, each person holding one of the Mexican beers with the scene framed by blue water.

Jason moved his gaze to the only other object on the table. His iPhone. For years, he'd kept the damn thing in his pocket and checked it every couple of minutes. Even while at the urinal, he'd pull out the phone to look at Twitter while he did his business. Though his time in rehab had been awful, the absolute best part was being away from his phone. The constant interruptions. The clutter. The texts, emails, tweets, Insta posts . . . He rarely used the device to make phone calls and doubted anyone else did either.

Since checking out of the PAC, he hadn't turned his phone on. He knew he was only postponing the inevitable, but something was holding him back. Hell, he'd ordered a beer before turning on the phone. He was going to break his sobriety before he checked his messages. What sense did that make?

Jason looked at the full bottle and then back at the phone several times. He turned and glanced again at his massive billboard. There were at least ten more in both directions along the Emerald Coast Parkway. With a cap covering his head, the bill tucked down over his eyes, he doubted anyone in the bar would recognize him. He'd gotten a few strange looks early on at the PAC, and two patients had asked him about taking on their respective divorces (which he'd politely declined), but that was as close as anyone had come to acknowledging him as a lawyer. Another silver lining to rehab.

He scanned the stage. The singer was now crooning Jimmy Buffett's "Changes in Latitudes, Changes in Attitudes," and Jason glanced at the open bottle with lime. He touched the cold glass and abruptly removed his hand as if he'd held it over a burning stove. When was the last time he'd been here?

There had been a lawyer convention a couple years ago at the Perdido Beach Resort, which was across the bridge at Perdido Pass. After the last speaker, Jason and a few colleagues had spent the next eight hours at the Flora-Bama. If he remembered correctly—and that was debatable—a few of them had ended up skinny-dipping in the gulf.

A good story, but was it a good night? He'd woken up at 3:00 a.m. in a condo with a woman he barely knew, his head raging with a hangover. Jason again peeked at the Corona. If he took a sip, he knew he'd be headed for a similar night, a disaster for his career.

Quit being a pansy and check your damn phone.

Jason snickered at the self-talk. Was that his own voice? Or perhaps Izzy had crept into his subconscious. As the thought of his law partner came to him, his mouth formed a true smile, and for a brief moment, he felt better. And also guilty. He'd left her holding the fort for three months, and he was going to dive right back into the bottle? What kind of douchebag was he?

A most remarkable douchebag . . . That, no doubt, was Izzy's voice.

Looking from the bottle to the phone, he finally grabbed the device and clicked the power button with his thumb.

He had over a thousand emails, several hundred texts, and at least fifty voice mails. He ordered some fried crab claws and a water and skimmed through as many of the messages as he could stomach while he ate. Izzy had eventually responded to the work-related emails. The rest appeared to be some variation of spam. Most of the texts were repetitions of the emails. As for the voice mails, Jason didn't bother. He couldn't recognize any of the numbers, and he figured they were all car warranty scams or some other mess.

After devouring the crab claws, he pushed the empty plate to the edge of the table and took a long sip of water. Then he glanced at the full beer bottle. He again touched the glass.

"Something wrong with the beer?" the waitress asked as she picked up the remains of his lunch.

"No, just not thirsty."

"Let me know if you want to try something else. We've got several craft brews on tap, including the Fairhope 51, which is a smooth pale ale. That's my favorite." She winked at him and walked away.

Jason looked at the phone and thought about calling Izzy. His last few texts were from this morning, and they'd all been from her.

Just checking to see if you're back amongst the living.

Call me when you're out.

Starting to get worried. Today was discharge day, right?

As he glanced at the screen, a new text popped up, also from Izzy. This one made Jason flinch.

Have you heard from Jana yet?

Then seconds later, another from Izzy.

Don't you dare say yes until you've talked with me.

And a third.

That is the last thing in the world you need.

And a fourth.

You owe her nothing.

Now Jason's heartbeat was racing. What the hell? Maybe he should look at his voice mails. But before he could check them, the phone started to ring.

The sound was almost foreign to him, as he hadn't heard the jingle in ninety days. He cocked his head and considered the screen. It was a 256 area code, and below the digits that he didn't recognize was a location. Guntersville, Alabama.

Jason let the phone ring without answering. Then he checked his voice messages and saw that he had five from the same Guntersville number.

Jana . . .

"Shit," he said and reached for the beer bottle. He held the glass to his forehead and closed his eyes. *Just a tiny sip. One little taste . . .*

Jason took out his wallet and placed a twenty and a ten on the table. Still clutching the bottle, he brought it to his nose and breathed in the scent of beer, lime, and salt. He again closed his eyes. *One fucking sip . . .*

The phone began to ring again. He didn't have to look at it to know that it was the same number, but he gazed at the screen anyway, confirming his suspicion on the second ring. *Jana . . .*

He'd spent so much time in rehab trying to get a handle on his dysfunctional family. Now here he was, at the most famous bar on the panhandle, being tempted by a beer and his crazy sister. He'd been out less than an hour.

Three rings.

Jason gazed past the stage to the gulf, clutching the bottle in a death grip but not taking a drink.

Four rings.

Five.

Six.

Jason set the drink down and answered the phone.

"This is Jason Rich," he said, hearing the quiver in his voice as he walked away from the table and the still undrunk bottle of Corona. As his feet touched the sand and his eyes fixated on the ocean, he heard the voice that haunted his dreams.

"J. J., it's me. Where've you been?" Jana's voice sounded breathy and desperate.

Jason said nothing, cringing at her use of the pet name J. J., which she'd done since they were kids. While his investigator, Harry Davenport, sometimes referred to Jason as J. R., which he rather liked, he couldn't stand J. J. He wasn't sure if it was the nickname itself or the fact that his sister used it that made him hate J. J., but hate it he did. Memories flooded his mind, and he envisioned the lone photograph that he'd brought to the PAC, which was now tucked away in his suitcase. The one from Space Camp when they were kids. Jana with her thousand-megawatt smile and Jason with his bowl cut and braces, perpetually inadequate in his older sister's presence. A mere accoutrement to her life.

"What is it, Jana?"

"I-I-I need your help."

15

"Jason, have you ever heard of 'gaslighting'?"

Three weeks into his therapy, after he'd been through detox and enough sessions for his counselor to get a feel for him, Jason's therapist brought up this phenomenon.

"No," he said.

"It's a situation where a person manipulates another person by psychological means into questioning his or her sanity." Michal studied Jason from across the small circular table that separated them. "Sound like anyone you know?"

Jason squinted back at her. He'd begun to get used to being sober, and the last week or so of therapy had focused on his family relationships, particularly with his father and sister. "What are you talking about?"

"Do you remember the story you told me yesterday?"

Jason shrugged but said nothing. Talking about Jana always made him uncomfortable, even in the quiet space of Michal's office.

"You caught her having sex in high school. Her boyfriend was dropping her off. Your parents were asleep. You had walked to a friend's house and were on your way back. You go past the vehicle and see her naked in the cab. She's in his lap thrusting back and—"

"Stop," he interrupted.

"I'm only retelling what you told me."

"I know. I just . . ."

"You said that she saw you watching her."

Jason looked away, not wanting to meet his counselor's gaze. He nodded.

"And what did she do when she came inside the house?"

Jason tried to marshal his courage as he spoke. "She acted like nothing had happened. Fixed herself a bowl of cereal and asked me if Mom and Dad were still up."

"Did you say anything to her?"

"I asked how she could do that with her boyfriend in our driveway, and she acted like I was crazy. She said she'd been dropped off by her friend Susan. Then she told me I needed to quit it with all of my teenage fantasies. Called me a Peeping Tom. She said that if I told Mom and Dad what I thought I saw, she'd tell them about how I watched her in the shower and that she'd caught me masturbating to a *Playboy* magazine."

"And how did that make you feel?"

"Crazy," Jason admitted. "And scared."

"Scared of what?"

"That she might tell my parents what I'd done."

"What *you* had done?"

"Yes."

Jason hadn't liked being cross-examined. And even in the comfortable and confidential confines of the PAC, Jason's heart rate sped up every time Jana's name was mentioned. Sharing with Michal about his sister's behavior was liberating. But it was also terrifying. Jason wondered what Jana would say if she found out what he'd told his therapist.

"You're crazy, Jason. You're a drunk. A druggie. A weak-ass loser who can't handle his life." That's what she had told him when he had suggested that she might want to seek treatment for her drinking problem over three years ago. Or that she and Braxton should go to marital counseling. She insisted that he was the one with the problem. Not her. Him. He was the one whose marriage was in shambles, who needed to drink to get through the day.

"Take care of the log in your own eye, baby brother."

She'd said it then, and it was no doubt what she would have told him if she could have been a fly on the wall during his therapy. The perpetual devil on his shoulder.

And now she needs my help . . .

———

The sound of a honking horn pulled Jason from his reverie, and he looked in the rearview mirror. A man in a pickup truck was giving him the middle finger. Jason was in the left lane and had slowed his speed to sixty-three, seven miles under the speed limit. There was an eighteen-wheeler in the right lane, and the person driving the vehicle behind Jason couldn't get around.

He gave the man a thumbs-up, and the pissed-off gentleman laid on his horn again. Jason pressed his foot to the accelerator and moved his vehicle over into the right lane. As a parting shot, the pickup driver flipped him the bird again as he drove by. Jason waved. He saw a green sign indicating that Montgomery was ten miles away, and he needed to make a quick stop in the state capital.

———

The headquarters of the Alabama State Bar were located on Dexter Avenue in downtown Montgomery. In his first few years as an attorney, Jason had served on the executive committee of the Young Lawyers Section, which was a fun gig where he got to meet a lot of other attorneys and became friendly with the leadership of the bar.

But that chumminess had ended when he'd started his billboard campaign. There had, of course, been complaints at the use of his last name to insinuate that choosing him as an attorney would lead to big money.

IN A CAR ACCIDENT? GET RICH.

Jason's point, however, was that he was simply suggesting that prospective clients contact him if they had a particular legal problem, and there was no prohibition in the rules of ethics against that. Besides, underneath the jingle—which always contained a question followed by the "GET RICH" answer—was the following verbiage, which brought home Jason's point: "Call 1-800 GET RICH and let attorney Jason Rich and the Rich Law Firm help you." And, of course, he also had the magic "no representation" language at the bottom of each billboard. The bar had reluctantly agreed that the billboards were within the rules but recommended that he change his jingle in light of the controversy.

Jason hadn't budged. He had too much invested in his billboards and wasn't about to change them unless the bar made him. This refusal had brought about resentment, which no doubt hurt his cause when complaints began to roll in regarding his erratic behavior. He'd narrowly avoided punishment for his fistfight with Nate Shuttle, but the chickens had come home to roost when he was accused of being impaired during the deposition of Eileen Frost.

After checking in at the front desk, Jason was brought into a large conference room. Photographs of prior presidents of the Alabama State Bar adorned the wall, but Jason paid them no mind. He just wanted to get this embarrassment over with, but, alas, a wait was in store.

After thirty full minutes, a woman and a man finally entered the room. The man Jason had met numerous times before. Edward Raleigh had been the executive director of the bar for almost Jason's entire career as an attorney. Ted was an all-business administrator and a hell of a fundraiser. During Ted's tenure, the annual meeting of the bar, which had alternated between the Grand Hotel in Point Clear and the Sandestin resort in Destin, Florida, had almost doubled in attendance and sponsorships. The director was not one for small talk and got straight to the point.

"I'd apologize for the delay, but you called a few hours ago, and Ashley and I had to move some meetings around."

"No problem," Jason managed. He glanced at the woman, who'd taken a seat next to Ted. She had red hair and a smattering of freckles on her face. He would have guessed her to be in her mid- to late thirties. She smiled at him, and her eyes were kind. Jason returned the gesture.

"I'm Ashley Sullivan. We haven't met, but I pass by about five of your billboards on my way to work every morning."

"Like seeing an old friend, huh?" Jason asked, surprising himself at how easy the old retort had come back to him. How many times had he heard that same comment from opposing counsel, court reporters, and even judges over the years?

She laughed, and even tight old Ted Raleigh managed a grin.

Jason gave a half-hearted chuckle. "Where's Tony?" he asked, hoping that his old classmate would be present.

"He's giving a CLE on ethics in Huntsville," Ted said. "I'm sure he would've wanted to be here, but, like I said, you didn't give any of us much notice."

"No, I guess I didn't," Jason said. He took the piece of paper he'd brought with him and slid it down the table. "Well, there it is. Ninety days. I'm a new man. Clean and sober. Ready to tackle the world."

Ashley retrieved the certificate, eyeballed it, and peered at Jason. "The Perdido Addiction Center was a good choice."

"Changed my life," Jason lied.

"Did it?" she asked.

Before Jason could respond, Ted grabbed the certificate and stood up. "Jason, I'm going to leave things with Ashley. I'll make a copy of this for our files, and you can pick it up at the front desk when you leave. We have already received your payment of the fine." He paused, and Jason saw a gleam of pleasure in the executive's eyes. "Your public reprimand will be at the bar's next meeting on August 24 at nine a.m."

"Good," Jason said. "And that'll be it, right? The bar will unhook the leash."

"Not exactly. I'll let Ashley fill you in on the rest."

———

Once Ted closed the door, an uncomfortable silence engulfed the room. When Ashley had done nothing to break the quiet, Jason finally couldn't stand it. "All right, what now? Do we hold hands and sing 'Kumbaya'?"

"I'm waiting for you to answer my question," Ashley said. When Jason raised his eyebrows, she leaned her elbows on the table and squinted at him. "Did ninety days at the PAC really change your life?"

Jason cocked his head at her use of the acronym. "You seem awful familiar with—"

"Five years ago," she interrupted, "I was there one hundred twenty days. One more month than you. Since then, I've been in the Lawyer Assistance Program. Last year, Ted made me the president."

"Did you get a cool trophy too?"

"Every day is a challenge when you're an addict," she said, ignoring his dig. "Treatment isn't a quick fix. Do you understand?"

He had heard Michal say the same thing on numerous occasions. "Yes."

"Good. Now, what's your plan for ongoing treatment?"

Jason thought back to the discharge instructions he'd been given by Michal. She would continue to provide telephone consultations until he could find a suitable local therapist. It was also recommended that he join a weekly AA group.

Jason cleared his throat and conveyed all this information to Ashley, who frowned.

"Same as me," she said. "The PAC is great—don't get me wrong. I wouldn't be where I am without what they did for me. But rehab, regardless of the place, is only the beginning. Eventually, you come down from the mountaintop. You forget about the benefits of sobriety and want a drink. Have you thought about having one yet?"

"I drove straight to the Flora-Bama after discharge and stared at a Corona for thirty minutes." He paused, surprised at how easy it was to confess the truth. "I didn't drink it."

"Good," she said. "But when will the next temptation come, Jason?" she asked, her voice lower. "Before your first deposition? Court date? Mediation?"

Jason looked down at the table.

"The Lawyer Assistance Program provides a road map for continued sobriety."

Jason glanced up at her.

"Sounds like complete bullshit, doesn't it?" she asked, smirking. Jason couldn't help but laugh.

"Yes."

"That's because it is. There's no road map. No secret sauce. Every day is going to be challenging."

For a moment, there was another lull in the conversation, and Jason felt his face growing hot. He covered it with his hands. *I can't do this,* he thought. *There's no way...*

Seconds later, he heard Ashley's voice. She'd moved down the table and was now sitting directly across from him. "Jason, can I ask you another question?"

He lowered his hands and wiped his eyes, which had become moist. "Yes."

"Why didn't you drink that Corona?"

Jason snorted as he thought of the phone call he'd received.

"My sister," he said.

Ashley gave him a warm smile. "That's good. Your family can support you during this time."

Jason wanted to laugh like a maniac. Instead he closed his eyes, thinking of Jana and knowing that helping him was the last thing on her mind.

16

Izzy Montaigne was pacing back and forth in her office and speaking into a Dictaphone when Jason barged through the door.

"Honey, I'm home," he said, holding out his arms.

She stopped and let the hand holding the recording device fall to her side. "Why haven't you answered any of my phone calls or texts today?"

"Nice to see you too," Jason said, plopping down on the love seat in front of his partner's desk. It was 5:30 p.m., and the firm's staff, which consisted of two secretaries and three paralegals, had left for the day. Only Izzy remained, but Jason had known she'd be here. She'd rarely left work before seven o'clock since he'd hired her out of law school eight years ago.

Izzy sat on the edge of her desk and folded her arms. "Did you take the case?"

Jason put on a fake smile. "Hey, rehab was great. Thanks for asking. I'm actually feeling well."

"Did you take the fricking case?" Izzy snapped.

"Not exactly," Jason said. "I'm going to meet with her."

"You're taking the fricking case." Izzy threw down her recorder and began to pace again. "If it's not bad enough she sabotaged your marriage, sent you into a tailspin that led to rehab, now she's going to screw up your career too. A clean trifecta from the Wicked Witch of the South."

"West," Jason corrected.

"We're in the South, dipshit."

"I love the way you talk to your boss," Jason said. "I should fire you for such gross misconduct."

"Please do, Jason. I get a six-figure job offer every day from some of the biggest firms in the state. Jones & Butler. Faulk & Stephens. Jackson & Meyers. You name it."

"But you're hopelessly devoted to me."

A tiny, tight grin formed on Izzy's mouth. "I'm not taking a pay cut, and the fact of the matter is that I make too much money working here to leave for other pastures unless the grass on the other side is green as goose crap."

"You have a way with words, you know that? We have got to get you in the courtroom."

"Is that why you took the case? To get me some trial experience? Or was that your own reason for telling that witch yes? How many trials have you handled since becoming a lawyer?"

Jason formed a goose egg with his index finger and thumb.

"And so you're thinking the best way to break that streak is with a capital murder case representing your crazy-as-hell sister in a county where, if you don't have local counsel, you're screwed harder than a virgin on prom night?"

Jason squinted, trying to understand the analogy. "Wait, what?"

"You know what I mean."

Jason rubbed his hands down his pant legs. "I do."

"Then why in God's name are you going to Guntersville?"

Jason took out his cell phone, brought up the text he wanted, and pushed the phone into Izzy's hand. "Read it."

Izzy gazed down at the screen and read the message out loud. "Uncle Jason, this is Nola. I tried to call but you didn't answer. You probably didn't recognize my number. Please help us. I don't know why you've been gone for so long. I know you and Mom had an argument after Grandpa's funeral, but she really needs you now. Please come home.

Dad is dead and Mom's in jail and we don't know what to do. Niecy said I shouldn't call you. That you've quit on us, but I don't believe that. Please, Uncle Jason. Please come." Izzy looked up from the phone and gave it back to Jason. She shook her head. "So Jana is now using her daughter to try to guilt you into taking her case."

Jason had received his niece's text on the way from Montgomery to Birmingham, and if he were honest, he didn't know what to make of it. Izzy very well could be right, but he wasn't about to admit that to her. At least not yet. "You don't know that. Nola could have sent that on her own without any encouragement from Jana."

"Maybe . . . but I doubt it. Even if she did, you can't save Nola from her mother."

"I have to go," Jason said.

Izzy froze for a moment. "OK," she said. "But you don't have to take her case. You just got out of rehab, Jason. You need to be—"

"What? I need to be what? Resting? Meditating? Taking it slow?" Jason snorted. "Iz, I left the PAC and went straight to the Flora-Bama. I ordered a beer and was about to drink it when Jana called from jail."

Izzy blinked and rose from the desk, walking a full circle, until she took a seat next to Jason on the couch. "Every time I visited, you said things were going fine."

"I thought they were," he said, leaning his head back and staring up at the ceiling. "But by the time I was discharged, all I wanted to do was forget about what happened. Alcohol has always been my solution to dealing with problems. Rehab helped, but it didn't solve anything. It just reopened all the wounds."

After several seconds of silence, Izzy touched his shoulder. "The PAC was only the beginning, Jason. You know that, right? It was never going to be a complete fix."

He recalled what Ashley Sullivan had said at the bar office. "Everyone's a therapist, right? What, did you google how to help a person coming out of rehab?"

She thumped him on the knee with her index finger. "Nope. Just plain common sense."

If anyone had ever been blessed with her fair share of walking-around smarts, it was Isabel Montaigne. She'd struggled with dyslexia as a child and barely gotten into Birmingham School of Law. After working her ass off to make her grades, there'd been no job offers coming out of school, and thus she'd interned with Jason's fledgling firm without pay before he could afford to offer her an associate's job.

She was the first person he'd hired, and it was the best decision he'd ever made as a lawyer. Izzy worked like a dog, daylight and dark, and, within months, she began to run the office. She handled buying firm computers, software, furniture, and legal supplies. She haggled with legal malpractice insurance carriers and obtained the best deals. She became the firm's shrewdest screener of new cases and was a natural at evaluating the ones that offered the best chance for a quick, lucrative settlement. When the firm had made enough money to add staff, she interviewed and hired the folks they needed. She did it all, allowing Jason the freedom to work cases as fast as possible up to the settlement stage.

Finally, and most importantly, it had been Izzy who'd recommended the billboard campaign. "It's a different world, Jason, but, as Coach Bryant liked to say, 'The same things win that always won, and we just have a different bunch of excuses if we lose.'" Izzy was a die-hard Alabama football fan, and the first thing she did after making enough money was to buy season tickets. She quoted Coach Paul "Bear" Bryant like she was reciting scripture, and in the state of Alabama, that wasn't too far off.

After echoing the Bear, she'd elaborated: "If people see your smiling mug with a nice jingle to the side of it as they're driving home or to their place of business or the grocery store or wherever they're going every single day, you'll be the first person they think of when they need a lawyer. Sounds too simple, but the ones doing it are winning. I've had

Harry performing reconnaissance of the plaintiff's firms, and it's not the blue bloods making all the money. Sure, the old guard gets theirs, but the ones that are breaking in all have billboards." She had cackled. "People are lazy, Jason Rich." She liked calling him by both names when she was rolling. "We can capitalize on that."

And so it began. First, they had two or three on I-65 from Birmingham to Montgomery. Then they added some on I-20/59 to Tuscaloosa. Once their first seven-figure settlement had rolled in, they'd doubled down and placed billboards everywhere. Mobile. Dothan. Orange Beach. Fort Payne. Gadsden. Auburn. Troy. He'd been present for the unveiling of the first one in Guntersville, knowing his father, venerable old Lucas Rich, would have to drive home from work every day and see his son's smiling face. After saturating Alabama, they went into Florida, Georgia, Tennessee, and Mississippi. Jason and Izzy became licensed in each state, and the firm continued to expand its reach. There'd been talk of adding partners, especially when Jason went to the PAC, but neither of them wanted that. "Me and you, Jason Rich," Izzy would always say. "Me, you, and . . . Harry."

"Earth to Jason." Izzy waved her hands in front of his face and playfully punched his shoulder.

Jason gazed down at the floor, depression beginning to sink in. He enjoyed thinking about the success of his firm and his partnership with Izzy. But, despite it all, his life had spun out of control. "Sorry. Got a lot on my mind. Jana and her kids are in real trouble, and I may be the only one who can help them."

She leaned close to him and spoke in a low tone. "Why do you want to help *her*? After all that Jana has done to you. After how she acted after your dad died? And the way she treated Lakin? Why?"

Jason winced at the sound of his ex-wife's name.

"Why can't you let her go?" Izzy pressed.

Jason leaned his elbows forward on his knees and placed his face in his hands. "I don't know," he finally said. "But something inside me says that I'm never going to be able to do that unless . . ." He looked up at her. " . . . Unless I go home."

Izzy stood and paced to the window, which overlooked downtown Birmingham. The sun was setting on the Magic City, and a few blocks over, the Barons were about to start a series with the Montgomery Biscuits. Jason stood and took a place next to her, admiring the city. "Remember when we didn't have any windows?" he asked.

"That first office off 280 was such a dump," Izzy said, her voice monotone.

"We've come a long way."

"And you're going to risk everything by taking on a capital murder trial. What if you lose? What if you embarrass yourself? We could be finished."

"One case won't make or break us."

She turned and looked at him. "That's bullshit and you know it. In this racket, you're only as good as your last case." She paused. "The word is already out, you know. A few reporters discovered that Jana is your sister, and two of them called this afternoon, wanting to know if the rumors were true. That Jason Rich of the Rich Law Firm was going to take on one of the most high-profile murder cases in the last twenty years."

"What'd you say?"

"No comment. But it's not going to end. You're going to put yourself and our firm in the spotlight over there. You've never tried a case to verdict. If you lose and you lose badly, as you damn well probably will since the witch is probably guilty, then everything everyone says about us will be proved true. We're frauds. We aren't real lawyers. We're ambulance chasers. Snake oil salesmen. You'll give each of our competitors an advantage, and we'll become a laughingstock overnight."

Jason gritted his teeth, knowing that she was right but not appreciating the insight. "You're welcome to leave at any time. Just as you were when I was sent to rehab."

She punched his arm and, this time, there was nothing playful about the gesture.

"Ouch."

"Don't patronize me. I'm not going to walk out on you. Without you, I'd have nothing. I owe you my whole career. I would never have broken in as a lawyer if you hadn't given me a chance."

"Those other firms were all stupid."

Her voice began to shake. "No, you were the stupid one. You gave me a chance without any reason to do so."

"Hiring you was the easiest and smartest decision of my life."

She wiped her eyes before the tears could fall. "If you represent Jana, that's going to be the worst."

"You don't know that."

"My gut tells me you're stepping onto a land mine."

Jason leaned his forehead against the warm glass. He gaped at the traffic on the highway. "I'm going to drive to Guntersville and check things out. I have to do that anyway." He hesitated. "They're my family, Izzy. They're the only family I've got, and they need me right now."

"You've also got me and Harry," she said. "We need you too."

"I know."

"When are you leaving?"

"Tonight. Gonna go check on things at the apartment, then head out."

"Everything's fine there. I had it cleaned for you yesterday, and Harry and I have been looking in on things a couple times a week."

"Thank you," he said, turning toward her. "I mean it. Thank you."

"My pleasure," she said. "I'm really glad you're back, even if you're going to risk everything we've built."

Jason started to protest, but Izzy's smirk stopped him. "Sorry, I couldn't help myself. Come on." She bolted past him toward the door.

"Where are we going?"

"If you're heading to Guntersville to possibly take on the trial of the century, I'm not letting you take that clunky SUV you drove to Perdido. No way, no how. Not on my watch."

Jason beamed as they reached the elevator. "You got my car fixed?"

After they stepped inside and she pressed the button for the first floor, she inspected him with brown eyes that radiated intensity. "If you're hell bent and determined to do this, you're not going as some limp-dicked shadow of your former self." She poked him hard in the chest. "You're going home as Jason motherfucking Rich."

17

The car was a midnight-black Porsche 911 convertible. The license plate advertised the brand.

GETRICH.

Jason had been in a fender bender the week before he went to rehab, so he'd taken his other vehicle—a ten-year-old Ford Explorer that he kept for investigation trips where he needed more space. He had always enjoyed fast cars, and this was the third vehicle made by the German auto manufacturer that he'd owned. He looked at his partner.

"Go," she said. "I'll have Harry take the SUV to your place and park it."

"Thank you, Izzy."

"You're welcome."

"I'm sorry to have to put you in this spot. It's not fair, especially after having been gone so long."

"You never have to apologize to me, Jason Rich. Never. Ever." She opened the door for him, and he climbed behind the wheel. She shut the door, and he felt the keys being pressed into his hand. When he took them, she closed her hand around his. "I think you're an idiot for even considering this case, but if you do take it, Harry and I have got your back."

"I know."

She released his hand, and he started the car, feeling his energy levels increase with the sound and feel of the engine. He peered up at her.

"Don't forget who you are," she said.

He put the car in gear and pressed his foot on the accelerator. The Porsche sprang forward like a pent-up cheetah. He clicked the button that made the top roll back and grinned as a hot breeze flooded his nostrils. As he passed by the Barons' stadium, he clicked on the radio and hooked up his phone to the Bluetooth. Then he turned the volume up.

The first song on his playlist seemed appropriate for where he was going.

"Highway to Hell," by AC/DC.

Feeling a combination of exhilaration and fear, he howled up at the sky and pressed the accelerator to the floor.

18

By the time Jason reached his apartment, the euphoria that had gripped him pulling out of his office was gone. The Porsche was only a car, and he was still a thirty-six-year-old divorced alcoholic who would now be practicing law under a zero-tolerance policy and whose sister was batshit crazy, in jail for possibly murdering her husband.

"Be sure to take it slow as you ease back into practice," Michal had advised in one of their last sessions.

If he took on Jana's defense, he'd be handling the biggest case of his life. Not exactly following the discharge instructions.

He parked and walked inside. A few moments later, the elevator reached the top and opened into his penthouse condominium. It was an appropriate residence for a wealthy, single attorney. Mountain Brook was the ritziest neighborhood in Birmingham, and his place overlooked the main drag of the village, only a couple of miles from the city's oldest country club. He enjoyed the game of golf, but being a plaintiff's attorney didn't allow for many rounds. His brother-in-law, Dr. Braxton Waters, had been a scratch player. As he began to pack his things in a duffel bag—his suitcase was still in the SUV, and it was probably premature to think of staying more than a couple of nights—and picked a dark suit from his closet, he tried to remember the last time he'd seen Braxton. Christmas four years ago? The lake the summer before? Jason couldn't be sure. There'd been a time when he was close with Jana's husband and her two daughters, but that was long ago.

Now Braxton was dead. And what of the girls? Niecy was in college. Had she come home to be with Nola? Where were they staying? Braxton's parents were deceased, but his mother had a sister who lived in Guntersville. Jason felt guilty for not checking in or returning Nola's text, but he had to visit Jana before he did anything else.

He zipped up his bag and took a last look around the place. He'd bought the apartment a few weeks after his divorce had been made final and now he wondered if he'd ever spent a single night in the place when he wasn't drunk or high. The apartment had two bedrooms, but only one was ever used.

The other room contained the boxes that he'd brought with him from the house he and Lakin had shared. Jason leaned against the doorframe and gawked at the cardboard containers, losing himself in painful memories.

They'd been married five years and lived in a two-story brick home in Vestavia. But three and a half years ago, the final decree of their divorce was signed on January 29, 2015. Exactly thirty days later, on the morning of February 28, Jason's father had suffered a heart attack in the shower. Lucas Rich had been able to crawl to his phone and call an ambulance, but he'd passed before arriving at the hospital.

Nothing had been the same since.

"Jason, let's talk about what happened with Lakin." Michal had pushed him in their sessions to explore the hard questions concerning his marriage. *"Were there any issues or problems that kept coming up?"*

Lakin had wanted kids. Jason couldn't, or maybe the proper word was *wouldn't*, commit to having a family. *"Why couldn't you, Jason?"* His therapist asked probing, thoughtful questions about whether the couple's marital issues were connected in some way to Jason's family history.

He didn't have all the answers. All he knew was, at the end of the day and as Jimmy Buffett liked to croon, it was his own damn fault. Had he loved Lakin? Yes, he had. She was a court reporter when they first met. He'd been taking a host of stressful depositions in Nashville, and Lakin was the stenographer. She was good at her job. Witty, funny, and smart. He enjoyed talking with her during breaks in testimony. When the last deposition concluded, he asked her to have a drink on Broadway, which led to dinner, and which resulted in an unforgettable nightcap in his apartment that didn't end till the following morning.

Since opening his law practice, Jason had dated many women, but none who were as much fun as Lakin. They laughed. They partied. They enjoyed each other's company. And they eloped nine months after the tryst in Nashville.

Had Jason's family approved of Lakin? Hell no, they hadn't. Lakin was from Talladega, Alabama. Her father had spent a lifetime in stock car racing, working the pit crews for Bobby Allison and the Alabama Gang. Her mother was a waitress at Huddle House. The only money Lakin had was in her purse. Lucas Rich had wanted his only son to marry a woman with a dowry, who came from "good stock." He frowned on Lakin, telling his son that he could have done better. Ironic, really, since Jason had never managed to please his father, but somehow, suddenly, he was too good for his bride?

Meanwhile, Jana ignored her new sister-in-law, deeming her "trashy." On their rare visits to Guntersville, Jana barely acknowledged Lakin.

And Jason's mother would not challenge her husband or Jana. Joyce Rich was polite. She sent a wedding gift. But she never embraced Lakin as her daughter-in-law.

Lakin probably could have handled being rejected by Jason's family, but Jason couldn't. Nor could he get on board with his wife's desire to have a family of their own. As the years went by, he worked more and drank too much. He wouldn't commit to having kids and, eventually, was unfaithful. If he were honest, he knew he had given Lakin no choice but to divorce him. He'd damn near begged her to do it with his actions.

And when his father had died thirty days after the divorce became final, he'd felt something inside himself snap. He'd become a ship without a rudder, slowly self-destructing until he drank three Bloody Marys before the deposition of Eileen Frost.

And now here he was. Staring at the boxes that held the ruins of his former life. Regardless of whether he took Jana's case, what was he going to do with the rest of his life? If he was honest with himself, there was nothing for him in Birmingham anymore except his law firm, which had run fine and dandy without him around. Hell, maybe he was holding Izzy back.

You're the brand. He could hear his persistent partner's voice in his head. *Maybe so,* Jason thought, as he locked the door to the apartment. *But that's about all I am anymore.*

He rode down the elevator gazing at the tile floor, trying to quiet his thoughts. When he stepped back out into the muggy night, he saw a familiar face leaning against the side of the Porsche.

Harold Michael Davenport wore a black T-shirt and faded jeans. A cigarette dangled from his mouth, which he dropped and stomped out as Jason approached. "Don't tell Izzy, aight?" he asked, glancing down at the flattened nicotine stick.

"Hear no evil, see no evil," Jason said, holding his fist out, which Harry nudged with his own.

"Heading out already?"

"No time like the present." Jason scratched his neck and gazed back at his condo. "Besides, that place gives me the heebie-jeebies. I think I'm gonna sell it."

"And go where?" Harry asked. His voice was gravelly, scarred from years of smoking. At five feet nine inches tall, he was a couple inches shorter than Jason, but his arms were taut with lean muscle, and his hands were as rough as sandpaper.

"I don't know."

Harry took a pack of Marlboros out of his back pocket. He lit another one and blew a cloud of smoke into the air. "Want one?"

"No thanks."

"I thought everyone that went to rehab ended up addicted to cigarettes."

"Not this cowboy."

"You got that right."

Jason cocked his head. "What?"

"You're a cowboy, all right. Never tried a damn jury trial in your life, fresh out of rehab, and going to Marshall County to take on a capital murder case." He exhaled a ring of smoke. "That would make damn Roy Rogers proud."

"Yippee-ki-yay," Jason said. He threw his duffel into the convertible and shook his head. "You and Izzy sure do jump to some conclusions. I haven't said I was taking the case yet. All I'm going to do is talk with my sister."

"Right," Harry said.

"If you came here to harass me, I'll be on my way," Jason said, walking around the front of the car and opening the driver's side door.

"I came to drop off the Explorer, and I wanted a word with you."

"Well, you've had several words, and I have a long trip ahead of me. Is there anything else? I'm fine by the way. Rehab was great. Feeling awesome. In case you were wondering."

"Bullshit. You look like you could fall off the wagon any second. Hell, it's fifty-fifty whether you make it to Guntersville without having a drink. There're a lot of convenience and liquor stores between here and the Marshall County line."

"What do you want, Harry? You're starting to piss me off."

"I want you to go back upstairs. Tell your crazy sister to fuck off and take this thing slow."

"What thing?"

"The rest of your life, amigo. I'm your friend, remember? Good ole Harry. I've saved your ass more than a few times, and I've been wiping it for the last couple of years while you've wallowed around feeling sorry for yourself." He took a step closer, poking his finger hard into Jason's chest. "Going to Guntersville is too much, too fast, too soon. You're gonna get hurt, brother."

Despite his irritation, Jason smiled. He'd met Harry at Sammy's exotic dance club in Birmingham. Jason had been interviewing one of the dancers, an eyewitness to a car wreck involving Jason's client, when a few of the patrons had taken exception to his monopolizing the young woman's time. Harry Davenport was the bouncer at Sammy's and ceased the impending fight before Jason got roughed up. As they walked out of the place, Harry had given Jason his card, saying he did private investigating as his main business and was a cooler on the side. Jason had hired him on the spot, and he'd become the firm's strongest asset outside of Izzy. He knew Harry, like Izzy, was just watching out for him.

"Look, Harry, I'm a lawyer. My sister has been charged with capital murder. Her daughters have lost their father. They need me. And besides, Guntersville is my home."

"You haven't been around in a few years. They'll manage." Harry's face tightened. His jaw was set, his eyes grave. "And don't give me any of this homecoming crap. I thought you hated your childhood."

"Doesn't mean I can't and shouldn't try." Jason cocked his head at the investigator. "What's the deal, Harry? I mean, I know you and Izzy don't want me to take this case, but aren't you being a little over the top? I mean, I have to at least go to the funeral."

"Why? Have either of them been there for you when you needed help? Did either of them write to you in rehab? Or call you after you split with Lakin?"

"She's still my sister, and her daughters are my nieces. I have to go." Jason slapped his hands together. "I can't run from my problems, and there's never going to be a perfect time to break back into practicing or to visit my sister."

"It's a shitstorm up there," Harry said, his voice lower.

"What do you mean?" Jason sensed they were finally getting to the point.

"I mean, when Izzy said she thought Jana was going to contact you, I did some preliminary investigation."

"And?"

"And it's bad. There's a handyman who's confessed that Jana hired him to kill Dr. Waters. There're rumors that she was in deep with the meth trade. Ever hear of a place called Sand Mountain?"

Jason squinted. "I grew up in Marshall County, remember? Course I have."

"Then you know that there are places on Sand Mountain that are off the grid, which makes it a great place to make and sell methamphetamine." Harry let out another puff of cigarette smoke. "And to get rid of people who get in the way. You know the name Tyson Cade?"

Jason shook his head.

"You will if you take Jana's case. He's the meth czar of Sand Mountain. My contacts in Marshall County say that all illicit drug sales go through Cade." He narrowed his gaze. "They also say that Jana was screwing him."

"Great."

"The rumor swirling around Guntersville is that she owed Cade a lot of money and was . . . *working* it off until she could pay him back. Dr. Waters had a huge life insurance policy. He was about to divorce her. You can deduce the rest."

Jason rubbed the back of his neck. "Thanks for the sneak preview."

"Cade is *not* someone to mess with, Jason. I understand that you feel you have to go and see for yourself, but please, let someone else represent Jana. Fine, go to the funeral. Help the kids out as much as you can. Then refer Jana to a criminal defense attorney. Someone who knows what the hell they're doing." He patted Jason's shoulder.

Jason climbed inside the car and turned the key. As the Porsche roared to life, he gazed up at his investigator.

"You know I'm right," Harry said.

Jason peered over the steering wheel. When he spoke, it was more to himself than his friend. "Have you ever wondered who you really are? I mean, beyond what you do for a living, who you marry, who your friends are, how you spend your time . . . but literally, who in the hell you are. That simple, little question." He looked at him. "Like me. Beyond the billboards, the addictions, my crazy family, my broken marriage, my successes and failures and bullshit, who am I?"

"We all wonder that, amigo," Harry said, his voice subdued. "And some of us never figure it out."

Jason put the car in gear. "Maybe not. But I think that's what this is for me."

As he began to pull out of the parking lot, he heard Harry's voice behind him.

"Hey, J. R."

He hit the brakes and looked over his shoulder at his investigator, who was silhouetted by the streetlamp above the sidewalk.

"Don't get yourself killed."

PART FOUR

19

When the man walked into the Alder Springs Grocery, he could tell the store clerk was watching him. He bought a Sun Drop, an oatmeal cream pie, and a pack of sugarless chewing gum. When he placed the goods on the counter, he winked at the clerk, whose face had turned almost as red as her hair.

"What's up, Doob?"

Marcia "Dooby" Darnell rang him up and met his eye. "Tyson," she said, as if saying the name pained her. "That'll be six dollars and eighty cents."

He handed her a ten-dollar bill and held up a hand when she started to collect his change. "Keep it."

She slid the plastic bag to him, and he took it without breaking eye contact with her. "Heard anything about the good doctor's murder?"

She winced. "Only that his wife's been arrested and she looks guilty as hell."

"How's that?"

"That Pike fella confessed and said he was paid by Ms. Waters to kill her husband."

"Everyone's heard that," Tyson said. "You know anything else?"

She averted her eyes as another customer entered the store. "Hey, Marvin."

An old man grunted at her as he made his way back to the cold drinks cooler. She peered back at Tyson. "I heard that her brother may represent her. The guy on the billboards."

"Jason Rich," Tyson said. "I've also heard that. Know anything about him?"

She shook her head. "Nah, the Riches lived out on Mill Creek. The daddy was a lawyer in Guntersville. They didn't get up this way much, and Jason went to private schools. I don't think he's been back in town since high school."

"Anything else?"

"Nothing good."

"Spit it out."

"I heard Jana was screwing you to pay off her drug habit."

Tyson cocked his head. "Now where would you hear such a tacky rumor?"

Dooby Darnell grinned, showing off a set of perfect white teeth, a nice contrast with her auburn hair. "My first husband always said I was tacky trashy, and he meant it as a compliment."

"I think you're beautiful." Tyson took a hundred-dollar bill out of his wallet and placed it in her hand. "If you hear anything else about Dr. Waters's murder or his wife's case, you let me know."

"You're going to get me fired," she said with a slight tease in her voice, folding the bill and putting it in her pocket.

"I hope I do. Then you can come work full-time for me." He winked again and turned for the door.

———

Once outside, Tyson Cade breathed in the humid air and opened his soft drink. He took a long sip and winced as the tangy citrusy taste hit his tongue, sending sugar and caffeine flooding through his blood vessels. He looked back at the store and belched, remembering all the times he'd walked here during middle and high school, scrounging up enough money for the snack that he'd just bought.

Now he flung hundred-dollar bills around for information, but back then, he was lucky to get out of there with change. He'd come a long way since growing up the bastard son of Ruthie Cade a half mile away in the veritable heart of Sand Mountain. He wished he could feel pride in his accomplishments, but that was a rare notion for Tyson.

There was too much stress in his world to fool with pride. If he ever became satisfied, if he ever congratulated himself for a second, he'd get caught. Or worse . . .

. . . he'd end up dead.

As he recognized the sedan in the distance, Tyson opened the oatmeal cream sandwich and took a large bite. Three bites later, he'd downed the whole thing, and he wadded up the plastic and threw it in the trash can by one of the gasoline pumps. The black unmarked police car rolled to a stop next to him, and he climbed inside, still chewing the delicious Little Debbie goodness.

"We've got a problem," the driver said.

With his mouth full, Tyson gestured with his hand for the man to fill him in.

"There's a hole in Pike's confession. He says Jana gave him the money in person the night of the Fourth, but you and I both know that's impossible."

Tyson swallowed. "We know no such thing. And besides, so what? Pike admitted to killing Waters. Said he was paid to do it, and Jana took out that exact amount of money a day before, right?" Tyson chuckled. "And how do we know that Jana didn't give him the money?"

"Tyson, come on."

"A woman as conniving and smart as Jana Rich can do a lotta things you might think were impossible. Trust me on that one."

"Tyson, you had guys watching her. And you met her at the Hampton Inn. The odds that she was able—"

"Fuck the odds. Pike says she paid him, and it sounds like the only hole is some circumstantial bullshit." He slapped the man on the shoulder. "Come on, Kelly. Don't be a pansy. Surely your prosecutor can get a conviction off what she has."

"She can, but a good attorney might be able to make some hay." He glanced at Tyson and then back at the road. "And enough hay could cause us some problems."

Tyson took a long sip of Sun Drop. "Well, first she has to hire a lawyer. And once she does, her counsel will . . . have to be properly informed of what's at stake."

Deputy Kelly Flowers sighed and rubbed the back of his neck as the car hurtled down Hustleville Road. "Tyson, you've got to tell me the deal, man. Did you hire Pike to kill Dr. Waters? Am I an accessory to murder?"

Without any conscious thought, Tyson grabbed the gearshift on the vehicle and dropped it into neutral. The car whined, and Kelly pulled over on the side of the road. "What the—" Kelly started, but stopped when Tyson shoved the barrel of his Glock into his throat.

"You need to calm down, Kelly, and think through this thing. Even if I did hire Pike, would it be wise to tell you? Is there any percentage in you knowing my shit?" He pressed the gun harder into the officer's throat. "The answer to both of those questions is no. Now, I pay you a handsome amount of money to keep me abreast of the goings-on of the Marshall County Sheriff's Office, and I make sure that you have the freshest product at the cheapest price, don't I?"

"Y-y-yes," Kelly managed. "Tyson, put the gun—"

Tyson forearmed the deputy up under the nose, and Kelly yelped in pain as blood gushed out of his nostrils. "You're in no position to give me orders, Deputy. If I wanted to kill you right now, I could do it, and there's nothing anyone would say or do. Five people on either side of this road could witness it, and they'd all say that they didn't see anything. And it wouldn't make a tinker's damn that you're an officer. You know why? Because this is Sand Mountain, bitch." He forearmed Kelly again, and the officer's eyes rolled back in his head.

Tyson eased the gun off the lawman's neck and leaned back in his seat. "Drive."

———

Five minutes later, Deputy Flowers pulled into a used auto parts place on Highway 75. "Thanks for the ride," Tyson said, stepping out of the car and drinking the last of his Sun Drop. He motioned for Kelly to roll down the window. Holding the empty bottle in his right hand, Tyson leaned his elbows on the seal and squinted at the officer.

"Let me know when she lawyers up," Tyson said.

"Yes, sir," Kelly said.

"Is there anything else? Any other news?"

"I . . . I spoke with Trey Cowan."

Tyson smirked. "What the hell for?"

"Trey has a motive because of the malpractice lawsuit. And he doesn't have an alibi." He paused. "The sheriff wanted us to check all our boxes."

"So . . . what was the golden boy doing on the Fourth of July?"

"Watching fireworks from the Sunset Trail . . . by himself."

"My, how the mighty have fallen. That kid is going to rue the day he chose not to work for me. But what the hell? You can't fix stupid." Tyson flung the empty bottle of soda into the footwell of the cop car and grinned at the officer. "Speaking of which . . . what happened back there was a warning, Kelly. You'll only get one. Stay in your lane. Do as I say. And everything will be fine. In a few short months, Jana Rich will be convicted of murdering her husband, and you'll stand to gain a sizable raise."

Kelly wiped blood from his nose and nodded. "Yes, sir."

"That's my boy," Tyson said, winking at him just as he'd winked at Dooby Darnell at the grocery mart. Then he turned and walked toward the entrance to the store. As he did, he put three sticks of gum in his mouth and tossed the wrappers on the ground, drawing a dirty look from one of the salesmen that evaporated when the man recognized Tyson. After shooting him the middle finger, Tyson laughed.

Littering might be illegal in Marshall County, but, as Tyson had told Kelly Flowers . . .

. . . *this is Sand Mountain, bitch.*

20

Jason had never loved Lake Guntersville. Weird, since he was born and raised there, but he just never took to it. Jana, of course, was the opposite. She'd gotten up on her skis the first attempt, had tubed, wakeboarded, and boat surfed like a champion. She could line a fishing pole after a cursory explanation from their father and was driving the boat at ten years old. She'd been the proverbial duck in water, while Jason had been, as his father joked, like a monkey fucking a football.

Confidence is a strange thing. When you are good at something, you want to do it more and more, and confidence breeds repetition and practice, which produces excellence. Jason had never felt confident on the water. Everything took him longer to do, and his sister was always three steps ahead. When he was thirteen years old, they'd boated over to Goat Island, a popular spot with a cliff that kids and adults liked to jump off. The highest precipice was fifty feet up in the air. Naturally, Jana climbed to the top and jumped from it without a moment's hesitation. When Jason managed to jump from the smallest cliff—still a good twenty feet high—his feat felt like a failure. A whimper in the face of Jana's scream.

The memories had flooded Jason's brain during his drive home, and, as Harry had warned, he did pass a few convenience and liquor stores that seemed to be calling his name. Fortunately, he'd pressed on without stopping, though the Porsche had topped out at 110 miles per hour several times, and he was lucky he didn't get a ticket.

Now, sipping hot complimentary coffee from a Styrofoam cup that he'd gotten in the Hampton Inn lobby, Jason gazed out at Lake Guntersville, thinking of his jump from the Goat Island cliff those many moons ago and his insufferable sister, who he'd be seeing again in a little less than an hour. He'd gotten the hotel room for a couple of nights with the option of extending his stay if needed. In all honesty, Jason didn't have a clue how long he'd be here. He'd thought about going out to the family homestead, and he knew he would eventually, but first he needed to get his bearings.

And see Jana . . .

Jason sighed and glanced behind him and up the hill to the hotel and then to his right, where there was now a waterfront Wintzell's Oyster House. As he'd driven through downtown Guntersville at eleven o'clock last night, he hadn't noticed many changes. Now, in the daylight, he could see a few subtle signs of what some people would call "progress." Jason figured that most lawyers who were from out of town would stay at this very Hampton Inn during a trial week. It was a mile from the courthouse and a stone's throw to Wintzell's, which would be a good place to unwind after a long day in court.

Just the thought of it made him crave a shrimp po'boy and a beer, and he shook off the images. Standing on a wooden dock that jutted out from the hotel parking lot, Jason could see boats on both sides of the Highway 431 overpass.

And in the north and south directions, he could see billboards with his smiling face on them.

IN A WRECK? GET RICH.

Jason cringed, feeling the butterflies in his stomach. He hadn't seen Jana in three years. His visit to her in the jail might cause a commotion, given the press coverage the case had generated. Izzy had sent an email that morning, saying that the messages from reporters were beginning to pile up. They needed to answer them soon.

Soon, Jason thought, finishing his coffee and trying to calm his beating heart. He hadn't worked as a lawyer in over ninety days, and it felt weird being in a suit again. He had actually lost some weight in rehab, so his trousers felt baggy and his coat a little big.

The heat wasn't helping. Jason guessed the temperature was in the midnineties with an index well above a hundred. Sweat beads were beginning to form on his forehead.

While he hadn't taken to the lake as a kid, Jason had gradually learned his way around. If a person took a boat under the overpass and drove it about a quarter mile past Wyeth Drive and Signal Point, they'd eventually hit the Veterans Memorial Bridge. Hang a right and look to the left, and the boatsman would see Buck Island, where the rich and powerful of Marshall County lived.

And where Braxton Waters was murdered on the Fourth of July.

Jason took a last sip of coffee and flung the empty cup in a trash can. Then he climbed into his Porsche. He'd already packed his briefcase, which looked professional but contained only a couple of blank yellow notebooks. He'd hoped that a cup of coffee and the smell and feel of the lake would relax him, but he'd had no such luck. If anything, he was more on edge.

Jason fired up the sports car. He wished he could say it was good to be home.

21

The Marshall County Sheriff's Office was housed in a redbrick building on Blount Avenue. After trying and failing to find a parking spot in the lot, Jason parked on a side road and put a dollar in the meter. He then walked the block and a half to the entrance. By the time he trudged through the door, his sweat had started trickling down the small of his back.

He wiped his forehead with the back of his hand and walked to the front desk. His heart sped up as he locked eyes with the desk clerk. In his eleven years as an attorney, Jason had never been to visit a client in jail. All his cases had been civil personal injury matters. Nothing criminal.

The clerk was a middle-aged woman with short dark hair and glasses. "You an attorney?" Her voice sounded tired and scratchy.

Jason cleared his throat. "Yes." It was the truth after all.

"Who're you here to see?"

"Jana Rich Waters."

She blinked. "What's your name?"

"Jason Rich."

"You related to her?"

"I'm her brother."

She blinked again and cocked her head. "Jason Rich. As in 'Call 1-800 GET RICH'?"

He put his finger to his mouth. "Don't tell anyone, OK?"

"You look different in person than on your billboards."

Jason didn't know what to say to that, so he kept his mouth shut.

"I pass three of 'em coming to work. You got Highway 431 covered up."

"Yes, ma'am." He smiled, but she didn't.

"So, are you her attorney, or are you just here for a visit?" the woman asked.

Jason answered on instinct. He didn't want to have to come back if visiting hours were later in the day. "This is an attorney consultation."

"All right then," she said, looking to her right and pushing a couple of buttons on an electronic box on the wall. Seconds later, a buzzer sounded, and a metal door to Jason's left slid open. The clerk led him down a long hallway and into a tiny room containing only a folding table and two aluminum chairs. "An officer will bring the detainee down in a few minutes."

"Thank you," Jason said, his mouth dry, his heart now racing.

"You all right?" the woman asked. "You're sweating pretty bad."

"I'm fine," he managed, running his hand over his damp forehead again. "Just not used . . ." He stopped himself. "Fine," he repeated.

She shrugged and shut the door behind her.

Jason tried to take a deep breath but found that it was impossible. All he could manage was several short, choppy gasps. Was he about to hyperventilate?

He reached for the table and tried to steady himself. Then he slowly sat down, opened his briefcase, and took out a blank yellow pad and two pens. He set them on the table and placed the case on the linoleum floor.

A cacophony of sounds erupted outside in the hallway. People talking. Someone laughing. Murmurs. A cough. The same buzzer sound he'd heard when he was let in. The jingle of chains. Footsteps.

Jason grabbed his pen and wrote the date and his name on the top of the pad, just like he was in high school about to take a test. He snorted at the ridiculous notion and, for a split second, almost relaxed.

Three hard knuckle raps ended that sensation in an instant. His stomach clenched as the door swung open. A thick-armed officer stepped inside. Behind the man, Jason heard whimpering.

"Mr. Rich?" the deputy asked.

"Yes, sir," Jason said, standing as the officer veered to the side. Behind him, a female guard escorted a woman in an orange jumpsuit with shackles on her hands and feet into the room. The woman was crying and looking down at the floor. The cuffs on her hands were removed, but her feet remained chained together.

"Deputy Anderson," the male cop said, pointing at the female officer, "will be standing outside the door. Just knock a few times when you're done."

"OK," Jason said. Then the officers exited the room, and the door slammed shut.

For at least five seconds, the only sounds in the room were their breathing. Finally, Jason reached out and touched her hand.

"Jana?"

She had crossed her arms tight to her chest and was shivering.

"Jana, look at me," Jason said, finding his voice.

She straightened and pushed her blonde hair out of her face. Her crystal-blue eyes, the whites red from crying, pierced his own. She looked both sad and angry. "Where've you been?"

"I got here as soon—"

"I've been calling for days. I left three messages. I called that bitch partner of yours, and she was no help at all. You need to fire her."

"Great to see you too, sis," he said, turning and taking a seat at the table. "Please, sit down."

Jana huffed but did as he asked. "What the hell, J. J.? Why did it take you so long—"

"I've been in rehab," Jason interrupted, figuring he'd get right to it. "Ninety days at the Perdido Addiction Center. I didn't have access to my phone until yesterday afternoon."

She gazed at him and wiped her tear-streaked eyes. "Well, I didn't know that. Are you . . . better?"

"To be honest, I have no idea," Jason said. "I was about to have a drink within an hour of discharge, and then I listened to your message."

A tiny smile played on her lips. "So I saved your ass again."

Jason pondered whether his sister had ever saved his ass but decided not to argue.

"Well . . ." She slammed her palms down on the table and set her jaw. "Now I need you to save mine."

22

Almost an hour later, Jason stared at his notebook, which was now full of writing. His sister continued to talk, but he was only half listening. She'd pretty much said the same thing over and over again in ten-minute intervals.

She didn't kill Braxton.

Yes, she took out $15,000 from her and Braxton's joint account the day before his murder, but that was because she was afraid that Braxton was going to cut her off. He'd been threatening to do so for months, and she couldn't risk not having any money.

She barely knew Waylon Pike. He'd done some work at their house. He'd worked for several families on Buck Island, in fact. Quiet, unassuming guy. She thought he might have a learning disability and had no idea why he'd make up such horrible lies about her. She didn't give Pike any money other than a few hundred bucks here and there for making repairs to their boathouse and home. As far as she knew, the $15,000 was in an envelope in a shoebox in the back of her car.

Where was her car? She didn't know. Probably impounded by the sheriff's office. "If the money's not there, I want you to file a lawsuit against the county. I want it filed by the end of the day. I want to sue Waylon Pike too."

It was a rant, Jason knew. He'd met several people, men and women, during his group sessions at the PAC who would go on and on about all their misfortunes, continually saying the same thing over and over again until the therapist mercifully cut them off and tried to redirect them to the main issue: their alcohol and drug problem.

Jason attempted to do the same thing here. "Jana, I understand that you have a lot to get off your chest, but I need you to answer some basic questions."

"OK," she said, crossing her arms over her chest. "Shoot."

"Where were you the night of the Fourth of July?"

"I was at Fire by the Lake. I wanted a nice spot to view the fireworks and have a couple of drinks."

"Who were you with?"

"By myself. I spoke with the bartender. His name's Keith, I think. Maybe Kenny. He's nice, and I've seen him there numerous times."

"What were you doing drinking alone?"

"I didn't want to be at home. Braxton's been cheating on me for years. He's screwing his nurse anesthetist, Colleen. He's turned the girls against me, brainwashed them into thinking I'm crazy. All I wanted was to have a few drinks."

"When did you leave?"

"About nine."

"Then?"

"Are you going to take my case?"

"I don't know. Why does that matter?"

"Is this conversation privileged?"

"Yes. It's a consult. I'm your attorney for the limited purpose of this meeting. Everything you tell me is protected by the attorney-client privilege." He paused. "What happened next?"

"I drove to a strip mall about a quarter mile down Highway 69. I parked and a man got inside."

"Waylon Pike?"

"No."

"Who was it?"

"I don't know."

"What do you mean you don't know."

"Exactly what I said. I don't know."

Jason frowned. "What happened then?"

"I gave this man some money, and he gave me a ziplock bag with a gram of cocaine inside."

"Jesus Christ, Jana."

"Fuck you, J. J. You're the addict, remember. So I did some coke because my family was falling apart and my husband was boning another woman. What's your excuse?"

"How much did the gram cost?" he asked through clenched teeth.

"I don't remember."

Jason just stared at her.

"I don't."

He knew she was lying but decided not to push it. "Then what happened?"

"He got out of the car, and I drove to the Hampton Inn."

Jason added that to his timeline on the notepad. "Why?"

Jana cleared her throat. "My husband was having an affair. I was lonely and angry."

"You do any of the coke?"

"Two lines in the parking lot of the hotel. Another once I got inside my room."

Jason made more notes. "Who'd you meet?"

"Does it matter?"

"Well, it could provide you a complete defense to the crime if whomever you met backs up your story."

"No, it won't," Jana said. "They're saying I paid Pike to kill Braxton. It doesn't matter where I was. I could have stayed at Fire by the Lake. I could have been at the Hampton Inn. I could have been on fucking Mars."

"Good point. But humor me. Who'd you meet at the hotel?"

She peered down at the table. "Tyson Cade."

Jason felt a trickle of fear run through him as he remembered what Harry had told him. "The meth czar of Sand Mountain," he announced. "Good grief, Jana. Why in the world would you get mixed up with a guy like that?"

She scowled at him. "When was the last time we spoke, Jason? Dad's funeral? You abandoned me when I needed you most. When my world was falling down all around me. When my husband started conspiring to ruin everything I'd established in this town. I started doing coke to take the edge off and give me more energy for all of the bullshit I'm involved in. DAR. PTA. Hospital boards. Blah. Blah. Bullshit. Bullshit. And, yes, I was having sex with my supplier because I owed him money. There. Happy?"

"I thought Cade was a meth dealer."

"Tyson does it all."

"You always were attracted to talent. So is that what you did? You drove to the Hampton Inn and fucked Tyson Cade all night. Were there any other takers? Did any of his sergeants take a turn?"

He saw the slap coming and made no move to block it.

His face stung, and he stood and put his hands up. "All right, I'm sorry," he said. "I went too far and I'm sorry. But if you hit me again, I'm out of here."

"I'm not a whore, Jason. But I wasn't going to be lonely on the Fourth of July. I wasn't going to let that bastard defeat me, you understand?"

"What I understand . . . ," Jason said, wiping his still hurting cheek, "is that you have one hell of a motive for murder. You were worried about a possible divorce. You were cheating on Braxton with a drug dealer. You believed your husband was cheating on you. You also thought he was about to cut off the financial gravy train, which you were using to buy cocaine and which you needed to pay off your dealer. That about cover it?"

She crossed her arms again and looked up at the ceiling.

"Jana?"

"Yes, that's all true."

"And this Pike fellow has confessed to the police that you paid him $15,000 to kill Braxton?"

"Yes," Jana said, still staring upward. "He's lying."

"But you actually took fifteen grand out of your bank account just before the murder? So is that supposed to be some kind of crazy coincidence?" Jason did nothing to contain the exasperation in his voice.

"Either that or someone's trying to frame me," Jana hissed. "That's the only explanation."

"And I haven't even gotten to the life insurance policy that I'm sure Braxton had. Had he changed the beneficiaries to Nola and Niecy yet, or were you still set to receive millions upon his death?"

Jana glanced at him and then looked back at the table. "I don't know."

Jason rolled his eyes. "Jana, how in the hell is any lawyer supposed to defend you?"

"I didn't ask any lawyer. I'm asking you. My brother."

"Is that supposed to be a compliment? Communication is a two-way street, Jana, and you haven't spoken to me since Dad died either. You were a complete zero when I went through my divorce. If anything, you seemed happy about it."

"Don't blame me that you married a trashy redneck slut. You can take the girl out of Talladega . . . or should I say *Dega*, like the NASCAR blowhards do . . . but you can't take the Dega out of the girl."

"So says the girl who was messing around with a meth dealer the night her husband was murdered." Jason got up and put his notepad in his briefcase. He couldn't get to the door fast enough. "Good luck, Jana."

"Are you going to represent me?"

"No," he said. "I suggest you call one of the criminal defense lawyers in town."

"I've called all of them. No one'll take my case."

"The public defender then?" Jason said, knocking on the door three times.

"Marshall County doesn't have one."

"Then ask the court to appoint you one."

"J. J., please—"

"Don't J. J. me," he said, wheeling toward her. "You ask for help, but then you do everything you can do to make me feel like I'm going crazy. The truth is that I believe you probably killed Braxton. And, if you didn't kill him, I bet he's dead because of you."

She glared at him. "Go then. I don't need you. I don't need any damn body. I'll represent myself."

"That would be a mistake."

"Calling you was a mistake," Jana hissed. "Expecting the only family I have left to offer any support was a mistake. Get out of my sight, Jason. There's a bar right down the street. The Brick. They have great happy hour specials."

Jason started to fire something back, but the buzzing sound of the door opening interrupted him. The female guard stepped inside. "All done?"

"Yes," Jason said, scowling at his sister. "We're done here."

23

Jason walked with his head down as he exited the consultation room. He wanted to get out of the building as fast as possible, but as he was led down the hall, he realized that a swift departure wasn't going to happen. There was a barrel-chested man in uniform who appeared to be waiting on him at the end of the hall. Next to him was a tall, thin woman with dark-brown hair wearing a maroon suit.

"Mr. Rich, I'm Sheriff Richard Griffith." He cocked his head at the woman. "And this is the district attorney, Ms. Shay Lankford."

Jason held out his right hand and shook both of theirs. He managed a smile, as did the sheriff, but the prosecutor remained stone faced.

"Mr. Rich, are you going to be representing your sister?" Shay asked.

Direct and straight to the point. Jason felt wobbly on his feet. "Honestly, ma'am, I don't know what I'm going to do. I just met with her in my capacity as a lawyer. As I'm sure you know, criminal law isn't my cup of tea."

His words did bring a slight grin to Shay's face. "Yes, I was aware of that. Ms. Rich has been adamant that you were going to be her lawyer, but I have to say I'll be surprised if you take this on."

Jason felt a tickle of irritation. He wanted to get out of this place. "Why? Because I'm her brother? Or because I'm a personal injury lawyer?"

"Both. But mainly because you don't do criminal work, and you haven't tried many cases."

"Trust me, sir," the sheriff said, his voice gruff but not unfriendly. "You don't want any part of this."

"Hearing that a lot," Jason said. "But I'll make up my own mind." He turned to Shay. "Any chance I can get a copy of that confession from Waylon Pike?"

She didn't hesitate. "There's no discovery in a criminal case in Alabama until after the indictment is handed down by the grand jury. However, if you enter an appearance, I'm happy to give you a copy of Pike's statement."

"Great," Jason said, slapping his hands together. "Well, Sheriff, Ms. Lankford, I just got into town, and I need to see my nieces."

"They're at the house on Buck Island," Griffith said. "Their aunt's with them."

Jason wrinkled up his face. "Isn't that where—"

"The boathouse has been roped off with yellow tape," the sheriff added. "And our crime scene technicians have already done a thorough search of the home."

"OK," Jason said. "Well, thank you for letting me know."

"Neither of the girls have come to see their mother since the arrest," Shay said. "In fact, she's had no visitors."

"Well," Jason said, "thanks for updating me. I'm going to go now." He stepped toward the sheriff, who moved out of his way.

"Mr. Rich?" Shay called after him.

"Yes," he said, looking over his shoulder at her.

"I know this is a difficult time for you, but I'm going to give you some unsolicited advice."

"OK," Jason said.

"See your nieces. Be with your family. But don't try to be a hero. Jana is guilty, and I bet, deep down, you probably know that. Let the court appoint her an attorney and go back to taking million-dollar settlements. Given what you've been through this year, I doubt a murder trial is the best way to break back in."

A surge of anger ran through Jason's body. How in the hell could she know that he'd been in rehab? His thoughts must have registered on his face because Shay took a step forward and spoke in a low tone that only he could hear. "I make it a point to research my opponents. I know you've been to treatment. I know you had a bar complaint. I know you and your sister have been estranged for years." She took a step closer and spoke directly in his ear. "I also know that she's batshit crazy with a strong motive to murder her husband and a dump truck of evidence against her. Let this one go, Jason."

He took a step back from her. So it was "Jason" now. He had to admit that the prosecutor was intimidating, both in look and manner. His legs again felt wobbly. "I'll think about it."

"One more thing," Shay said, her voice louder as she resumed her position next to Sheriff Griffith. "There're some reporters outside. I'm sure word has gotten out that you're here. Like I said, our detainee has had no visitors and no attorney, and you're a recognizable figure because of your billboards. There's a back exit that will allow you a faster retreat. I'll walk you myself."

"Save you some time and a lot of hassle," the sheriff added.

Jason began to understand the seeds that Shay Lankford had been planting. "And it would save you guys the publicity," Jason said, feeling a renewed strength in his voice. "If Jana has to have an appointed lawyer, it's not nearly as interesting. It looks like she's guilty before the case even starts. But if I take the case . . ."

The prosecutor and sheriff said nothing.

"I'm going out the front," Jason proclaimed.

24

Jason made a beeline toward the sidewalk that would take him to his car, telling each of ten or twelve reporters "No comment" in response to their questions. If he decided to take the case, then perhaps some grandstanding would be in order. But not now. The only publicity these guys were going to get was confirmation that he was in town and had seen his sister.

And if that made Shay Lankford and Sheriff Griffith nervous or anxious in any way, then Jason was glad. He could see the look of superiority in the prosecutor's face, along with the same condescending tone he'd heard from so many other lawyers during his eleven years of practice.

"You aren't a real lawyer."

"How many cases have you tried?"

"You run a racket, not a law practice."

While Shay wasn't ugly about it, the thoughts were written all over her expressions and tone of voice. Jason had dealt with smugness before. In the personal injury world, it simply didn't matter. Jason and Izzy signed up cases. Most of their matters involved people who'd been injured badly in a car accident, trucking collision, or premises accident. The law was simple, the burden of proof easy. And the insurance companies on the other side always wanted to settle regardless of whether you were a billboard lawyer or in a blue blood firm.

About the only areas of law in Alabama where an attorney could get courtroom experience trying cases was criminal law, either as a prosecutor or a defense attorney, or in the specialized area of civil law called medical malpractice. Because physicians were reported to the National Practitioner Data Bank and their state medical board if they settled a case, medical malpractice cases often went to trial.

Jason had avoided med mal cases like the plague, not because he was scared of the courtroom but because of the massive expense involved for a roll of the dice in front of a jury. In his career, he'd focused on the sure thing and worked his ass off marketing his ability to bring that sure thing to his clients. He knew how to investigate a case and had become adept at taking and defending depositions.

But, in eleven years, he'd only seen the inside of a courtroom for status conferences and motion hearings, and he'd begun to let Izzy handle those.

Jason walked briskly to his car, working up another sweat as the midday heat ratcheted up. He didn't hear footsteps behind him, so he figured the horde of press had given up. As he opened his door, he felt a hand on his arm. He glanced over his shoulder and saw a small woman wearing wire-framed glasses.

"I said no—"

"This isn't an interview request," the woman said. "You don't remember me, do you?"

Jason blinked his eyes and focused on the petite woman with light-brown skin. "Kisha?" he asked. "Kisha . . . Humphrey?"

She smiled at him. "It's Roe now. Kisha Roe. Married name."

"It's great to see you!" Jason said. They'd been the only two kids from Guntersville in their class at Randolph, a small private school in nearby Huntsville. In elementary and middle school, their parents had carpooled together. Kisha had always been near the top of the class.

"So you're a reporter now?"

"I prefer *journalist*," she said with a tease in her voice. "I write for al.com and the *Advertiser-Gleam*. But my dream is to be a forensic investigative reporter for *Dateline* or I/D." She raised her eyebrows.

"And my sister's case would be the perfect vehicle for that. You slumming for an exclusive?"

She reached out and punched his shoulder lightly. "No, silly. I was saying hi to an old friend. I also wanted to say that I'm sorry. I'm not sure if you were close with your brother-in-law, but I can't imagine how your family is handling all this.

"Of course . . . ," Kisha continued, "the murder of Dr. Braxton Waters is the most high-profile homicide in north Alabama in years. Probably the biggest since the Jack Wilson murder in Huntsville in the early nineties."

Jason shrugged, not knowing the reference.

"The ophthalmologist who was killed in a murder-for-hire scheme. His wife was arrested and convicted of murder, but her twin sister, who many believe to be part of the plot, was found not guilty in a separate trial. Paula Zahn, who is my absolute hero, did a great piece about it on I/D. You should watch, especially if you take Jana's case."

Jason didn't have the foggiest clue what she was talking about but found himself enjoying the conversation. Kisha had always been like a cool breeze. Easy to be around, smart, observant, and curious about life with a whimsical streak. It didn't surprise Jason that she'd gone into journalism.

"What is the scuttlebutt about Braxton's murder?"

Kisha cocked her head and raised her eyebrows. "Ah, you want something from me?"

"Just some local gossip from an old friend. Too much to ask?"

"If you take the case, will you keep me in the loop?"

Jason extended his hand. "You scratch my back, I'll scratch yours. How about that?"

She squeezed his hand. "It's great to see you. How about dinner tonight? I'll introduce you to my better half."

"Great."

"The Rock House. Eight o'clock. We'll save a spot at the bar for you. Sound good?"

"Perfect," Jason said.

"Perfect," she echoed, and then Kisha was off down the sidewalk.

———

Seconds later, Jason was turning onto Blount Avenue. He sucked in a breath as the Porsche began to climb the Veterans Memorial Bridge with picturesque views of Lake Guntersville on either side of him. Off to his right, he saw the piece of shore known as Buck Island and the first of an impressive lineup of mansions that all fronted the water.

Jason put his right-turn blinker on as he saw the GUNTER'S LANDING sign and then Buck Island Drive.

He took in a deep breath and exhaled, trying and failing to relax. He knew this next part might be as hard as or harder than what he'd been through at the jail.

Family . . .

25

Tyson Cade glanced at the number calling in on his phone. He was on Highway 75 headed toward Fort Payne. He had several stops to make. A meeting with a supplier. Another with a buyer. Dealing drugs wasn't a nine-to-five job. It was a twenty-four hour, seven-days-a-week, 365-days-a-year gig. If you didn't have the energy, you had no business playing the game. If you weren't smart, you'd end up in jail. If you were dumb, you'd end up dead.

Tyson was only twenty-nine years old, but he felt like he'd lived two lifetimes. The one before he started dealing, when he graduated near the top of his class at Guntersville High and played baseball for a year at Snead State. And the one after, when he'd risen in the ranks by outworking everyone and becoming Johnny "King" Hanson's right-hand man. When King finally got caught and sent to prison, the "kingdom" went to Tyson. To oversee it, he had to stay on top of everything. His supply. His demand. His meth cooks.

And his buyers of high-end product like opiates and cocaine. These folks, like Jana Waters, were sometimes the hardest to deal with, but they brought in the biggest profit. A rich doctor's wife shouldn't have been a money problem, but damned if Braxton Waters hadn't chosen to play hardball. He was going to divorce Jana, and he was using her coke habit as leverage.

He'd underestimated Tyson, as had Jana. A fatal mistake, quite literally for Dr. Waters.

Tyson grabbed his cell and focused on the digits. How many burner phones out there had he dispensed to his crew? He'd lost count. This looked like one of the numbers, but he wasn't sure.

Screw it.

"Yeah."

"Jana Rich had a visitor today." Deputy Kelly Flowers's voice came through on the receiver. His voice was high. Keyed up.

"1-800 GET RICH?"

"Yep."

"He take the case?" Tyson asked, seeing a green sign indicating fifteen miles to Fort Payne.

"He said he was going to think about it."

Tyson tapped his fingers on the steering wheel. "Maybe we should help him come to a decision."

"You think that's wise? The sheriff and Shay tried to get him to go out the back door to avoid publicity, and the sonofabitch marched out the front like he was the mayor."

Tyson chewed on a nail and spat what he'd bitten off into the footwell. "Well, we're gonna do more than make a suggestion."

"Who?"

"You let me take care of that." Tyson ended the call and set the phone in the passenger seat.

Up in the distance, he saw a billboard advertising Miller Lite and then, just past it, a familiar face sporting a dark suit and a big smile.

Tyson almost laughed at the coincidence, but he didn't. Instead, he sneered at the man on the billboard and tipped his hand to his head, deciding that he would handle Jason Rich himself.

"Be seeing you soon, Counselor."

26

Jason pulled into the circle driveway and parked behind a silver Toyota 4-Runner. There were a couple other cars in the wide parking area, including a red Jeep Wrangler and Ford pickup. Jason walked toward the front door and rang the doorbell. He had to admit that he was almost as nervous to see his nieces as he'd been to see their mother. Three years was a long time in a kid's life. An eternity.

The door swung open, and a woman stood in the opening. She was almost as tall as he was with her father's strawberry-blond hair and mother's blue eyes.

"Uncle Jason?" she asked, creasing her eyebrows.

"Nola?" Jason figured it had to be Nola because Niecy had darker hair.

She brought her hands to her mouth. "Oh my God. It's . . ." Tears came to her eyes, and Jason stepped over the threshold and put his hands on her arms.

"I'm so sorry about your dad."

She leaned into him for an awkward hug. "Thanks. It's . . ." She didn't finish. Instead, she looked down at the marble floor and stepped out of the way so that he could enter the grand foyer. It was a little past noon, and Jason could see Lake Guntersville in all its glory straight ahead through the full-length glass window. Buck Island was situated right on the main channel, so the view was breathtaking. To his left, there was a windy staircase with framed photographs of the two girls adorning the wall as the steps ascended to the second floor. Past the stairs was an archway into a huge kitchen that opened into a family room with more spectacular views of the lake from each of the windows. Nola walked toward the kitchen, and Jason followed, taking in the mansion and wondering how anyone could be unhappy living in such a palace.

It was the cliché of all clichés, but Jason knew it was true: money can't buy happiness. But, as he looked out the window at the sunshine and saw the sailing vessels moving up and down the waterway, Jason couldn't help but think of the Chris Janson song "Buy Me a Boat," which he enjoyed blaring in his Porsche.

As he entered the family room, his other niece was gazing at her phone. She wore cutoff jeans and a white tank top, and her brown hair was covered by a black-and-gold Birmingham-Southern baseball cap. When she looked up, she didn't stand. "What're you doing here?"

Jason straightened and glanced at Nola, who was peering at the floor again.

"Well?" Denise Catherine Waters had been called "Niecy" since she was born, a nickname bestowed on her by her father.

"I just wanted to see how y'all were doing."

She snorted. "Well, let's see here. Our dad's dead. He was murdered about a hundred feet from where we're sitting."

Jason glanced out the window at the boathouse and saw the yellow tape blocking the path to the dock.

"And, as luck would have it, he was apparently killed by our precious mother, who's been in jail for the last week."

"You don't know that," Jason said. "She's innocent until proven guilty." The words sounded so lame coming out of his mouth that he almost gagged.

"Oh, whatever, Uncle Jason. Oh, that's right. You're a lawyer. You know all about this stuff. You have a bunch of billboards. We should definitely listen to you."

Jason was flabbergasted by Niecy's tone and rough words. He'd never shared a cross word with Jana's eldest daughter.

"All I was trying to say is that she hasn't been convicted."

"Waylon Pike confessed to killing Dad, and Pike said that Mom paid him to do it. Why would he lie about that?" Niecy spat the words.

"To get a deal," Jason said. "He's caught with his pants down, and he's giving them a bigger fish." He immediately regretted how crass he must sound to his nieces as he tried to explain the case. "Putting an ex-con like him in jail is nothing, but nabbing the doctor's wife? A much bigger get for the district attorney."

Niecy's face softened, but not by much. "You don't know that."

"No, I don't," Jason said. "But you asked why Pike would lie, and I gave you a reason."

"Why did it take you over a week to get here?" Niecy challenged. "Dad was killed on July 4. It's July 13. Where've you been?"

"I sent you a text," Nola said, her voice tentative. "A few days ago."

Jason felt like he was a foot tall as he turned to Nola, his face becoming flushed. "I'm so very, very sorry. I, uhm, I was in rehab until yesterday without any access to my phone. When I got out, I had several messages from your mother." He froze, trying to cope with the guilt and shame that bloomed in his chest. "I came as soon as I could." He looked at Nola. "I'm sorry I didn't respond to your text. I . . . I should have. I just needed to see your mom first."

Niecy's lips had started to tremble. "How about the last three years? When everything around here was going to pot, why'd you disappear? Right after Paw Paw died, you might as well have died too."

Jason again looked at Nola, who gazed at him with a curious stare.

"I didn't . . . handle your grandpa's death very well. I'd just gotten a divorce, and I wasn't ready to lose him too."

"But you and Paw Paw weren't close," Nola said. "Mom has told us that."

Jason lowered his eyes to the floor. "That's true. We weren't. But . . ." Jason trailed off. This was a question he'd gotten a lot at the PAC, and he still didn't have a great answer. "Look, I've made a lot of mistakes since Dad died. My life went off the rails, and I ended up in rehab. I stayed away from y'all, because your mother . . . has always made me kinda crazy. She says things . . . does things . . . that make me feel like I'm less of a person. She's done that since I was a kid, and . . . after the divorce and Dad's death . . . I just couldn't take it anymore. I couldn't be around her, which meant I couldn't be around you guys. I'm sorry."

"You were the only normal family we had," Nola said, her voice practically monotone compared to Niecy's. "We always looked forward to seeing you, because you actually stood up to Mom's BS."

Jason didn't know what he was more surprised by, being referred to as "normal" or the difference in Nola's and Niecy's demeanors.

"I was a junior in high school the last time you were here," Niecy said, her tone still intense. "I was looking at colleges, and you said you'd love to show me Davidson, where you went. We even talked about meeting up for spring break in the Carolinas and looking at a bunch of other schools. Remember that? Wake Forest. UNC. Duke. Maybe even the College of Charleston. A road trip with my uncle Jason . . ." Her lips began to quiver again. "You remember?"

Jason did. He closed his eyes, thinking back to Christmas three and a half years ago. He'd been excited about Niecy's college choices, and they'd mapped out a trip, clearing it with Jana and Braxton.

"Why didn't you call me?" Jason asked, but he knew what she was going to say before the words came out of her mouth.

"*I did call.* I left you messages on your cell and office phones. Emails. Facebook messages. And you know what I got in response? Nothing. Zilch. Zero. Squat."

"I'm sorry, honey. I—"

"Don't call me that. Don't call me anything. Don't even look at me." She brushed past him without looking. "Nola, I'm going out. If you want to come with me, let's go now. I'm not going to hang out with this loser any more than I have to."

"Niecy, wait," Jason said. "Please. Stop. I went to see your mom in the jail."

Niecy stopped on a dime and turned toward him. She placed her hands on her hips. "And?"

"And she wants me to represent her."

Her laugh was high, sounding off. Almost hysterical. Jason wondered when was the last time Niecy had gotten any sleep. He noticed that her eyes were red rimmed, probably from fatigue and crying. "You? The billboard PI lawyer? Isn't a criminal case out of your league?"

Jason raised his eyebrows.

"Oh, I'm on the prelaw track at Southern. I'm going to be an attorney too, Uncle Jason. But not a snake oil salesman and ambulance chaser like you. I'm going to be a corporate lawyer. A *real* attorney like Paw Paw."

"Good for you," Jason said, growing tired of her act. "Is that 'snake oil salesman' a line your mom used? Or perhaps you heard your grandpa call me that."

She didn't answer.

"There's no telling what you've heard about me." He looked back at Nola. "Well, you can bet that ninety-nine percent of whatever your mother has told you is a lie."

"So you're not an ambulance chaser?" Niecy challenged.

"I'm an attorney who represents clients who're injured in accidents. I've obtained almost $30 million in settlement money for my clients."

"Put it on a billboard," Niecy said.

"I did," Jason said. "It's on the one on Highway 431 that you pass every day when you go into town. Any *other* suggestions?"

At this, Niecy cracked the faintest of smiles. "If you've stayed away from us all these years because your life was in shambles and you can't handle Mom, if Mom is such a *liar*, then why would you even think about taking her case?"

Jason opened his mouth to respond, but nothing came out. Why indeed.

"My *suggestion* would be that you give that some more thought. Come on, Nola."

Niecy stormed out of the room, and Jason heard the front door slam shut. He felt a hand on his shoulder. "I'm sorry, Uncle Jason," Nola said. She started to go, but Jason called after her.

"Nola, wait. Is anyone staying here with y'all?"

She stopped and rolled her eyes. "Technically, Aunt Cathy is."

"What do you mean, 'technically'?"

"She's eighty-seven years old and can't get around that good. She's been here two or three times in the last week but only stayed the night once, and she said she can't do that anymore because she almost fell." Nola shrugged. "Aunt Cathy's nice, but it's not like she was close to our family. She's just literally the closest living relative. That is . . . besides you."

"So y'all have been alone this whole time?"

"Burns comes by every day. Brings us takeout. Lets us hang at his house and watch movies. We spent the first couple of nights after Dad's death over at his place in one of the guest rooms. He's been really great."

"I'm glad," Jason said, feeling relieved that they at least had someone to watch over them and guilty that he'd been out of contact until today.

Several loud honks from a car horn pierced the air, and Nola cringed. "I need to go. Regardless of what Niecy said . . . I'm really glad you're here."

Jason peered at the teenager, the hurt radiating from her eyes as his own guilt intensified. He wanted to say, "Me too," but he knew it would sound like a lie.

Because it's a lie, he thought.

Nola walked away before he could respond.

27

Jason spent a few minutes pacing around the main level of the now-empty house. Since his arrival in Guntersville, he hadn't had much time to think, but he did now, and he was consumed by one all-powerful thought.

I need a drink.

Jason walked down the stairs to the basement and Braxton's man cave, where he'd spent several Christmases and Thanksgivings drinking cocktails, beer, and wine from his brother-in-law's stocked bar. As he reached the foot of the stairs, he glanced at the bar and saw that it was just as he remembered. He walked over to the glass cabinet and contemplated the bottles of bourbon, vodka, and gin that adorned each shelf. His mouth felt dry, and his heart rate picked up speed. He couldn't get Niecy's words out of his mind.

He had abandoned his family. Jason glanced from the liquor bottles to the refrigerator and opened it. There were several beers inside.

"Go ahead. Grab you one. I don't think Braxton will mind anymore."

Jason turned at the sound of the deep voice and saw a large man standing at the foot of the stairs.

"Hope you don't mind, but I'm going to give us some more light." The man flicked a couple of buttons on the wall, and the room became bright. Jason noticed a massive television that hung on the far wall, where his brother-in-law had enjoyed watching Alabama football games. There was an old-fashioned movie theater popcorn maker to the side as well as the portraits that many Alabama football fans had in their lairs. *The Goal Line Stand* against Penn State in 1979. *The Kick* by Van Tiffin in '85 to beat Auburn. Pictures of Coach Bryant and Coach Saban.

"Jackson Burns," the man said. He wore a golf shirt, baggy shorts, and flip-flops and shuffled toward Jason with his hands stuffed deep in his pockets. "We've met before, but it's been a while. Call me Burns. In this town, I'm not sure if anyone knows my first name anymore."

"I remember," Jason said, shaking the man's meaty hand. Burns was about six feet tall, which was the same height as Jason, but he must've weighed a hundred pounds more, probably topping out close to 275 pounds. "You used to take us out on your boat in the summer when my wife and I came for the weekend."

Burns snapped his fingers. "That's right. Lakin, right? Sorry to hear about the divorce."

The comment stung, and he was a bit surprised that Burns knew about the breakup of his marriage. But he knew he shouldn't be. Burns and Braxton had been good friends for years. Next-door neighbors. The subject was bound to have come up.

"Been through that myself," Burns said, grabbing a beer from the fridge. He popped the top and took a long swallow. "Shan left me over Christmas. Guess she'd finally had enough of being a car dealer's wife." He snorted. "You know how it is. Crazy hours, never home, always on the lot chasing the next sale." He took another gulp of beer. "She and my two sons live in Huntsville now. I get to see the boys every other weekend and on Tuesdays, but Tuesdays during the school year hardly ever work out."

"I'm sorry," Jason said. "You have kids?"

Jason shook his head.

"At least it was clean, then. No baggage. And I don't mean to say my boys are baggage. The damn baggage is Shandra. She's always going to be Jack and Charles's mother. I won't ever be rid of her, and I'll probably be cutting a fat alimony check to her the rest of my life, not to mention child support for the next fifteen years. Be glad you don't have to deal with that hassle."

Jason didn't know what to say, so he kept his mouth shut. Burns finished off the beer and grabbed another from the fridge. "Go on. Take one. Don't make me drink alone." Jason hesitated but then took a can.

Burns walked to the door leading out to the porch and opened it, stepping out into the hot sun. "Where'd the girls go? I was going to take them to lunch over at Top O' the River."

"I don't think they were expecting me to show up. Niecy got pretty upset."

Burns chuckled. "She's a fireball, that one. Got her daddy's brains and momma's temper." He popped the top on his can and took another long sip. Jason tried his best not to focus on the drink in Burns's hand. "I suspect your niece was a little pissed that you haven't been around in a while."

"You suspect right."

"You and Jana grew up in Marshall County, didn't you?"

Jason nodded. "Little cove called Mill Creek."

"That's right. I remember Jana showing us the old homestead. Good fishing up that way. I'll still go over there and try to find some bass or catfish in and around those boathouses."

Jason remembered all the mornings he would wake up and see a small bass boat circling his family's boathouse. "Yep," he said, smiling.

"How long's it been since you were out to Mill Creek?"

"Forever and a day. With Mom and Dad both gone . . ." He trailed off.

"I actually knew your dad. Lucas Rich. Had a law office on Gunter Avenue forever. When he retired, they turned the old building into a barbecue joint." Burns gave his head a jerk. "Sad. That why you became a lawyer? Because of your old man?"

Jason frowned. "I guess that was part of the reason."

Burns sipped his beer. "No shame in that. I followed my old man into the car business. So I have to ask, Why didn't you take over the family practice?"

"That's . . . kind of a long story," Jason said, not wanting to get into it, staring at the beer can still in his hand.

Burns looked out at the lake. "Guessed it must've worked out for you. Based on your billboards, I'd say you're making a killing."

Jason continued to examine the beer, running his finger over the opening. "We're doing OK."

For a few seconds, neither man spoke, and Burns drank his beer. "Do y'all still own the place out at Mill Creek?"

"As far as I know," Jason said, scratching the back of his neck and looking again at the beer can, wanting so badly to open it. "Jana would have needed to get my approval to sell." He shook his head. "I'm not sure what's happened to the house. I think Jana was going to try to rent it out."

Burns took another long sip of beer and began to amble down toward the dock.

"Are you sure it's OK—?" But Jason cut himself off when it was obvious the other man wasn't going to stop.

"If it's like everything else in Jana's life, I suspect your Mill Creek house is a disaster."

"Tell me," Jason said, peering at the approaching boathouse and then back to Burns.

"She and Braxton were having problems, I know that. Jana had gotten into drugs, and she owed quite a bit of money to credit card companies . . . and her drug supplier."

"Tyson Cade," Jason said, and Burns looked at him.

"You know Cade?"

"By reputation only."

"Well, his rep is well earned. He's the last person you want to get messed up with, but you know your sister. She'd find trouble in a house full of nuns."

Burns stopped at the edge of the water. "Why are you back in town, Jason?"

"I would have thought it was obvious," Jason said, feeling defensive. "My brother-in-law's been murdered. My sister's in jail. I wanted to check on my nieces and see Jana."

Burns took another sip of beer. "You sure waited long enough."

Jason gazed at the untouched beer. "I was unavoidably detained," he said.

"Right," Burns said.

"I was in rehab for three months without access to my phone. I found out about the murder and Jana's arrest yesterday, and I came as soon as I could."

"Rehab, huh?" Burns asked, looking at the can of beer. "For alcohol? Drugs?" He hesitated. "Sex? Gambling?"

"Alcohol," Jason said.

Burns made a "give me" gesture with his free hand. "Here, you don't need that, then." Jason handed the beer over, then watched as Burns downed the rest of his can and crushed it. "Rumor on the street is that you came to town to be Jana's lawyer. That true?"

Jason scanned past the boathouse to the dark water. "I came back primarily to see my family. But yes, I'm considering taking the case." He glanced at Burns. "Did the police ever talk with you?"

"Oh, yeah. Several times. At first, I think Nola thought Braxton might be with me. We played a lot of golf together and would go on Jet Ski rides and fishing excursions all the time."

"Had you seen him on the Fourth?"

Burns popped open the beer that Jason had given him and took a long drink. "Nah. We had a huge sale at the dealership. I was there until ten p.m. With the kids and Shandra gone, I didn't want to be home.

When we closed the lot, I went down to the Brick and had a couple rounds with some of my salespeople. I got home after midnight but was up early the next morning to go fishing. I was on my dock when I heard all the police sirens." He tipped the can back. "It was crazy."

"I bet," Jason said.

"Listen," Burns said, finishing off the can and crushing it just as he'd done with the last one. "If you're seriously considering representing Jana . . . which I think would be crazy as hell . . . then there are some things you need to know."

"What things?"

"You hungry?"

Jason wasn't, but he decided to be agreeable. "Starved."

"Good. Come on." He started back toward the house.

Jason followed. He couldn't resist pushing the man a little. "What things?" he repeated.

Burns opened the door and looked at Jason. His eyes, while red, were sharp. "Waylon Pike," he said.

28

They went to the restaurant in Burns's twenty-four-foot MasterCraft runabout, which Jason had ridden in before during happier times. The boat was still in excellent shape, and despite his hesitancy at riding in anything motorized with Burns given the man's heavy alcohol consumption, Jason had to admit that he enjoyed the trip down memory lane. Burns never stopped talking and took on the role of tour guide, pointing out the different landmarks along the way. These included the mansions on Signal Point Drive, which, according to Burns, were "nice but not quite up to Buck Island"; the Wayne Farms Chicken and Feed Plant, which was on the corner of Highway 227 and Signal Point and gave off a strong aroma that reached their boat as they passed by; the Paul Stockton Causeway on the right and Wyeth Drive on the left. And, then finally, Top O' the River sitting perched on a hill on Val Monte Drive.

As they approached the docking station, Jason glanced off in the distance and saw the Hampton Inn, thinking of his sister's tryst there on the night of the Fourth of July with Tyson Cade. Guntersville was a small town, but the lake made it seem bigger, more mysterious.

Fifteen minutes after docking, they were seated in the upstairs dining room of the restaurant, which smelled like pine trees and fried catfish. It wasn't unlike the feeling of stepping into the Grand Hotel in Point Clear, Alabama. The vibe was comfortable, and Jason had to admit that he was surprised to feel his stomach rumbling, his hunger piqued. When a waiter brought them a tin plate covered with corn bread, slaw, and onions, Jason and Burns dug in.

With his mouth full, Burns took a long swallow of Miller Lite and pointed at the plate. "This is the best part. The catfish is good, but this right here sets the tone, you know? Kind of like ordering the sausages and cheeses at the Rendezvous in Memphis before they bring out the dry ribs."

Jason had to agree. The food was delicious, and he washed it down with a sip of cold sweet tea. "Burns, you said you know some things about Waylon Pike."

Burns's face was now puffier than when they'd first met, and his eyes had grown redder. Definitely on his way to being three sheets. "I know a lot about him," he said.

"Tell me."

"Well, I know he met Jana at Fire by the Lake, which is a little dive off Highway 69. Good fried shrimp, decent bar. Anyway, they must've had a couple drinks together, and Pike told Jana he was a handyman and voilà. Next thing you know he's doing some fixer-upper projects for them."

"Was Pike's relationship with Jana anything more than professional?"

Burns rubbed the stubble on his cheek. "Son, I don't want to speak ill of your sister."

"Speak ill. It's fine. I want to know everything I can about Pike." He paused. "Did they have an affair?"

He chuckled. "I'm not sure I'd call it that. A bartender I know at Fire by the Lake. I think his name is Keith, but it may be Kenny, said that he saw Pike and Jana fogging up the window of Jana's Mercedes after closing time."

Jason thought it was odd that Burns also had a hard time remembering whether the barkeep's name was Keith or Kenny. *Isn't that exactly what Jana said?*

"Next thing you know, Pike's working on the Waterses' boathouse," Burns said, holding out his hands. "Turns out that Pike did good work, and Jana spread the word about how 'handy' he was to have around to the other folks on the island, including yours truly."

"Did Pike do any work for you?"

"Yes. Put a new roof on my boathouse. Built some shelves for my office and bar. And once my divorce was final and the boys were out of the house, he did some yard work for me."

"Sounds like you were around him a lot. He seem like a killer to you?"

Burns's mouth curved into a drunken smile. "Whoever *seems* like a killer? I mean, to me, Waylon was a good ole boy. Showed up on time. Did his job. Kept his mouth shut. Wasn't a bit of trouble. He worked for several of my other neighbors, and he was fine for them too. No problems. No complaints. Now . . . did he enjoy tying one on when he was through working? I suspect he did—in fact, I joined him a couple of times myself at the Brick—but there's nothing wrong with that. Hell, I'm tying one on right now."

Jason thought about that. Burns was getting pretty loose. "If you don't mind me asking, do you drink like this every day?"

He considered his glass. "No, but since Shandra left me, I probably drink more. As a car salesman, I'm on all day long. Seven in the morning to ten at night. You gotta do something to unwind, you know what I mean?"

Jason did. It was one of the reasons he'd ended up in the PAC. But Burns's comment brought up an interesting question. "Why aren't you working today?" he asked.

"I've taken a good bit of time off since Braxton's murder. Had to answer a lot of questions from the sheriff's office since I was next-door neighbors and knew Pike pretty well. And Braxton and I were best friends." He looked out the window. "We'd been best friends for thirty years."

"I'm sorry," Jason said.

"It's just, you know, Braxton and Jana and their girls. I mean, they weren't perfect, but they were kinda like my family once Shan took off. I ate dinner over there a lot. Saw somebody in that family almost every day."

"Did you see Jana much in the last six months?"

He stared at the table. "No. She was gone a lot." He glanced up at Jason. "I know she and Braxton were having problems."

"How?"

"Braxton told me."

"What did he tell you?"

"That he was worried about her drug use."

"Did he ever say he was thinking about filing for divorce?"

"Yeah," Burns said. "The last time he mentioned that was the Sunday before he was killed. We played eighteen holes over at Goose Pond. Took my boat. When we finished up, we had an early dinner at the Docks." He took a slow sip of beer, then eyed the bottle as he began to peel the label off. "That was probably the last time I saw him."

"What did he say?"

"That he'd been to see a lawyer and she'd drafted up a complaint for divorce."

Jason felt his stomach tighten. "Who was the lawyer?"

"Candace Gordon. A local. Her office is on Blount Avenue."

"Did he say he was going to file?"

Burns chewed on a toothpick. "Yep. He said that he'd already told Jana the night before and that she'd stormed out of the house. He also said Jana was in a lot of financial trouble, and he wasn't sure how he was going to get her out of it. That he was going to be moving money out of their joint accounts after the Fourth so that she couldn't bankrupt him."

"Jana said that Braxton was cheating on her. Any truth to that?"

Burns looked behind their table and then around the restaurant. It wasn't a stealth move, especially given his increasing drunkenness. "You didn't hear this from me."

"OK."

"He had a thing for a nurse or something over at the hospital. Colleen Maples. I think he'd been tapping that for a while."

Now it was Jason who looked around the restaurant, as Burns had gotten a bit loud. "How long is a while?" Jason said, keeping his voice low in the hopes that Burns would do the same.

"Years." No such luck.

"Did he tell you about her?"

"Oh, yeah. There wasn't much Braxton kept from me."

"What did he see in this Colleen?"

Burns took his hands and placed them over his chest. "Big ol—"

"All right," Jason interrupted before he could say anything more. People were beginning to stare." I get the picture.

"And Jana? Did she cheat on Braxton with anyone other than Waylon Pike?"

Burns waited as the waitress delivered their entrées. Both men had ordered the catfish special. Once she was gone, he leaned his hefty forearms on the table. When he spoke, Jason had to blink back the scent of alcohol on his breath. "I don't think Jana cheated on Braxton until she found out about Colleen. And, outside of maybe a one-night stand with Waylon, I'm not aware of any other affairs." Burns stared down at his plate of food and then cut into his catfish. "I'm no shrink, but I think Jana had a really hard time with your Dad's death. She worshipped that man. Then when Braxton stepped out on her, she started drinking and doing more drugs, and things got out of control. Don't get me wrong, now. Her and Braxton's marriage was volatile. Jana was a drama queen, always stirring something up. But there was nothing dangerous until these last couple of years."

Jason peered down at his plate, thinking his sister's behavior wasn't all that different from his own. What if he hadn't been reported to the bar and been forced to go to rehab? Would he be in a jail cell by now? The thoughts depressed him, but they also made him see Jana in a different light. "Anything else you can tell me?"

Burns chewed his food. "Yeah, but you're not going to like it."

Jason waited.

"The night before Braxton was killed, I was out on my boat. I'd gone fishing over by where you're from actually, near Mill Creek. Anyway, I saw Jana sitting out on her dock drinking something. Sounded like she was drunk and maybe on something too. Slurring her words pretty bad."

Jason wondered what condition Burns had been in, given how much he'd had to drink today. "What happened?"

"I asked her how she was doing, and she said, 'Just fine for someone who's about to lose everything.'

"I asked her what she meant, and she got mad. She said I knew damn well what she meant. That Braxton was going to divorce her. That he was going to move all their money into an account that she couldn't access. That he was cheating on her and was now going to leave her penniless too. I didn't know what to say, so I just told her I was sorry. Then she said something you ain't gonna like."

"What?"

"That there was no way in hell she was going to let him cut her off and leave her with nothing. And that she'd taken $15,000 out of one of their accounts that afternoon."

"Good lord," Jason said. "Why would she tell you that? You're Braxton's best friend."

"I don't know. I kind of think she wanted him to know. Besides, I was friends with Jana too. Like I said, the Waterses were kind of my family."

"Did you tell Braxton about the money she'd taken?"

"No," he said. "I probably should've, but I felt sorry for her." He took a bite of his food and pointed his fork at Jason. "I haven't even told you the worst thing she said."

Jason braced himself. "OK."

"She said she'd kill the bastard before she'd let him ruin her life."

Jason examined his plate. After all the corn bread and slaw, he wasn't hungry anymore. *Another damn confession,* he thought. "Well, I suspect the sheriff's investigators were pretty interested in that conversation." Jason wasn't a criminal lawyer, but he knew that what Burns had just told him was a party opponent admission. It was, by definition, not hearsay and could be used against Jana at the trial.

"They were. Of course, I never believed that she'd actually do it."

"Pike apparently signed a statement saying that Jana paid him fifteen grand to kill Braxton," Jason said.

"I've heard that too."

"Do you believe it?"

Burns leaned back in his chair. "Well, that matches the money she took out. And as for Pike, he seemed like a good ole boy, but you know your sister, Jason. She can cast a spell on people. She's about ruined her two girls. Neither one of them wants to visit their mother in the jail because they're scared of what she might say. Jana plays with their emotions, and they know she'll make them feel guilty. She's written them both nasty letters asking them why they haven't come to visit. Nola's been hit especially hard because she told the sheriff's investigator that she thought Jana did it. Jana basically told her in the letter that it was Nola's fault that she was in there."

"Good grief," Jason said, rubbing the back of his neck with his hand. That sounded just like his sister.

"You want some friendly advice?" Burns asked, his voice slurring slightly.

"Let me guess. Don't take the case."

He made the gun symbol with the index finger and thumb of his right hand. "Pow," he said.

"Thanks," Jason said.

"She's guilty, Jason," Burns said, taking a large bite of catfish. "She's guilty as sin, and there ain't nothing you, Clarence Darrow, or Perry Mason can do about it."

Jason took his glass of tea and held it up in a mock toast. "Innocent until proven guilty?" he asked.

Burns shook his head and spoke with his mouth full. "Guilty."

29

Jason drove the boat back to Buck Island. Jackson Burns the tour guide was gone, and the large man was now lying on his back, drifting in and out of sleep. Though he hadn't driven a watercraft in years, Jason found that he rather enjoyed the task, and, as the cliché goes, it was a bit like riding a bike. By the time he reached the Veterans Memorial Bridge and saw Buck Island in the distance, he was smiling.

Given what Burns had told him over lunch, he really didn't have any reason to be happy, but he felt better nonetheless. Again, perhaps it was the air hitting him in the face. Or maybe hearing how Jana had spiraled out of control after their father's death made him feel better about his own demise.

"Thanks for driving," Burns said, patting Jason on the back. The car dealer's voice was hoarse and thick with drink and fatigue.

"No worries," Jason said.

"Here, let me get this last part. The boat slip can be kinda tricky."

They switched places, and Burns guided the boat into the slip with Jason hopping out and cranking the lift until the boat was out of the water. Once Burns was safely on the dock, Jason peered west and saw the Waterses' boathouse a quarter mile in the distance. "Burns, when did you say you got home the night of the Fourth?"

The other man sighed and leaned against the side of a chair. "It was actually the fifth by then. Past midnight, probably closer to one a.m."

"Did you come down here?"

Burns chuckled. "Hell no. I passed out in my bed."

"Could you hear anything coming from the direction of Jana's property?"

"Nah. All I heard was the occasional firecracker."

They trudged up to Burns's house, which was every bit as impressive as the Waterses' home. When they reached the porch, Jason turned back toward the water and saw a nest of clouds moving in from the south.

"Rain on the way," Burns said. "Maybe it'll cool things off."

Jason nodded, but if he knew Alabama in July, he figured that any rain would only make things stickier and muggier. Regardless, the current breeze coming off the lake felt good.

"You want me to give you a lift back to your car?" Burns asked.

"No, that's OK," Jason said. Jason wasn't about to get in a vehicle with the drunk salesman. "The walk will do me some good."

Jason followed Burns through the house, and they said their goodbyes in the foyer.

"If you need anything, let me know," Burns said. "And give the girls a little time. Their world's been turned upside down. They'll eventually warm up to you." He squinted at Jason. "That is, if you stick around. Are you?"

"Am I what?"

"Gonna stay."

"I don't know. Still feeling things out. Is there going to be a funeral for Braxton?"

Burns shook his head. "Niecy says they aren't going to do any kind of service or memorial until after their mother's trial. She doesn't want to deal with the publicity, and I don't blame her. What those girls need more than anything is some stability." He rubbed his bloodshot eyes. "And time."

"Makes sense," Jason said.

They shook hands, and Burns held on to Jason's. "Remember what I said. I think it's great that you've come back to reconnect with Niecy and Nola. God knows they need some family. But don't let Jana sucker you into taking her case. She did it, Jason."

"You really think so?" Jason asked.

"There's not a doubt in my mind." He let go of Jason's hand. "And I bet, if you really think about it, there's not one in yours either."

———

Jason decided to walk down Buck Island Drive instead of trying to navigate the trees and landscaping between the two backyards. It was only a few hundred yards between the two houses, but Jason's legs felt heavy as he neared the Waterses' estate. The boat trip and the lunch with Jackson Burns had been exhilarating and stressful, and he was beginning to come off the high of being on the windswept lake. It was 3:30 p.m., and he still had a lot to do.

And much to think about.

As he approached the driveway, he heard the sound of a car coming from behind him. He turned and saw a black Mustang that was slowing down. As the passenger window rolled down, Jason saw a man behind the wheel.

"Jason Rich?" the stranger asked. He was in his late twenties, if Jason had to guess, with a close-cropped haircut. He wore a navy T-shirt, and Jason could see the veins snaking over his muscles as his hands gripped the wheel.

"Who wants to know?" Jason asked.

"You don't know me?"

Jason shook his head. "Should I?"

The man looked back at the road. "You will."

"What—?"

"Soon," the man said, and the car lurched forward. The vehicle turned around in the Waterses' driveway and then raced back toward Jason.

He stopped in his tracks, unsure of whether he was going to have to dive out of the way, but the man just waved as he headed back toward the highway.

What the hell? Jason wondered as he tried to calm his breathing. His adrenaline had spiked, and his senses were on high alert. For all the glamour of the houses that lined the waterfront, Buck Island Drive wasn't the most impressive of streets. In fact, there was barely enough room for two vehicles. He started to walk again, picking up his pace. As he entered the driveway, he only saw his Porsche and was relieved.

Though he wanted another chance to talk with his nieces, his interaction with the Mustang driver had spooked him. Had the man been following him? And if so, why?

Marshall County was a weird place, Jason knew. His father used to say that 95 percent of the area were good, law-abiding folks. But that other 5 percent could best be described as "outlaw."

Jason took in a deep breath as a steady rain began to fall. He hopped into his Porsche and fired it up, exhaling slowly in the small confines of the vehicle. He'd been back home less than twenty-four hours, and the overriding vibe had been fear and dread with a side of guilt.

Who was that guy? he thought as he pulled back onto the blacktop.

30

Tyson Cade watched his rearview mirror as he skirted Buck Island Drive and turned onto Highway 431. The Mustang, like all his vehicles, was a loaner. Tyson never drove the same car more than a few times without switching it up. He was a man of many looks. Sometimes he shaved. Sometimes he didn't. His hair vacillated from high and tight to long and loose, depending on the season. And his cars and boats vacillated from big to small, luxurious to old and rickety. About the only common denominator was speed.

Tyson liked to move fast. He thought he'd scared the lawyer, but he didn't want to do anything but plant a seed. The real party would come later.

Though he thought there was a chance that Jason Rich would come to the correct conclusion on his own, it wouldn't hurt to impress upon him the significance of his decision.

Tyson grabbed his cell and punched a button.

"Yeah?"

"I've got a tracker on Rich's car."

There was a momentary pause. "Good." A couple of seconds of silence and then Kelly Flowers added, "When?"

"Tonight," Tyson said.

"Do we need reinforcements?"

Tyson visualized Jason Rich's soft, pampered face. "No, but let's have some muscle available just in case. Comprende?"

"Sí."

Tyson clicked the phone dead. *Soon,* he thought, echoing what he'd told the billboard lawyer. *Very soon . . .*

31

By 8:00 p.m., all Jason wanted to do was go to sleep, but alas, the night was young. He still needed to meet Kisha at the Rock House. If there was a chance in hell that his sister might be innocent of hiring Waylon Pike to kill her husband, he needed additional information. All his conversations with Burns and Jana had revealed were a whole lot of reasons to think she was guilty.

As he drove down Blount Avenue and hung a left on Loveless, he saw a smattering of cars parked along the street adjacent to Gunter Avenue ahead. Though it took several minutes, Jason finally found a parking spot and ambled up the sidewalk toward the quaint restaurant, which had several couples and families eating outside on the patio on wrought iron chairs and tables. He stepped inside and saw Kisha waiting on him. She waved and he headed toward her, taking in the Rock House. He'd eaten here a couple times before with Jana and Braxton. The food was excellent, and the vibe was simultaneously rustic and modern. There were two dining rooms separated by a wall and then a narrow hallway that contained the cozy four-seater bar. Jason took a seat next to his former classmate at the bar and saw that another woman was seated next to Kisha.

"This is my wife, Teresa Roe," she said. Jason nodded at the other woman, who was taller than his old friend, with long, straight black hair.

"Nice to meet you," Jason said, trying not to be surprised by the revelation that his old friend was gay.

Seeming to sense his thoughts, Kisha smiled big. "I came out a couple years after college. We met at the mullet toss down at the Flora-Bama. You ever been to that?"

Jason nodded, not really thinking about the famous festival held every April at the beachside saloon but instead dwelling on the untouched Corona bottle that he'd left sitting at the table after taking Jana's call. He found himself wondering what happened to it. Did the waitress with the Auburn cap throw it away? Put it back in the fridge to be enjoyed by another patron? He took in a deep breath, realizing that his visit to the Flora-Bama was just over thirty hours ago.

"Earth to Jason." Kisha interrupted his reverie.

"The mullet toss," he managed. "How romantic."

They all laughed, and Kisha described her meetup with Teresa at the bar of the Flora-Bama. They'd both been there with friends and ended up avoiding the iconic tossing of the fish and taking a long walk on the beach, "where one thing led to another." They were married six months later.

"I'm happy for y'all," Jason said. When the waiter, a nice woman named Susan, asked for their drink orders, Kisha ordered a cosmopolitan, Teresa a martini, and Jason a club soda with lime.

"Not partaking of the spirits tonight?" Kisha asked with a tease in her voice.

"No," Jason said. He thought about mentioning rehab but changed his mind. Kisha was a reporter after all, and it wasn't the best of ideas to be a complete open book to the press.

"So have you decided whether you're going to take Jana's case?" Kisha asked, the tease in her tone gone.

"Not yet. I was kinda hoping that my old high school friend might fill me in on what she knows." Jason chortled. "Go Raiders," he said, mimicking the cheer for Randolph High.

Kisha shared a brief glance with Teresa and then peered at Jason. "Well, I know that the sheriff's office has arrested Waylon Pike, a handyman who did odd jobs for your sister and some others on Buck Island. And I know Pike confessed that Jana paid him to kill Dr. Waters."

"I've heard that as well," Jason said. "Was there some sort of announcement?"

"Press conference couple days ago. Right after Jana was arrested."

Great, he thought. *The whole county knows.*

"I've also heard that Jana took out a lot of money either the day before or two days before the murder," Kisha continued.

"How much?" Jason obviously knew the answer but was curious if the amount had become public.

"Fifteen thousand dollars," Teresa added, leaning forward to make eye contact with Jason. "I'm a bartender at the Brick downtown, and that's the scuttlebutt around the bar."

Great, Jason thought again. He twisted in his chair so that he could face them. "Have either of you heard anything that might suggest that my sister didn't do it?"

Kisha winced and glanced at Teresa, who shook her head. "I'm sorry," Kisha said.

"What about other enemies? Did Braxton have anyone gunning for him that you're aware of?"

Kisha opened her mouth to say something, but stopped and rubbed her chin.

"What?" Jason asked.

"Well, I was about to say that Dr. Waters was probably the most beloved physician in town, which is true. He was. But . . ." She trailed off and took a drink.

"You thinking about that malpractice case?" Teresa chimed in.

"What malpractice case?" Jason asked.

Kisha scrunched her face. "Don't tell me you don't know. You're a lawyer. I would have thought Braxton or Jana would have said something to you about it."

"I hadn't talked to either of them in years. Can you fill me in?"

"Well . . . ," Kisha began, leaning closer to him. "Trey Cowan, quarterback of the football team, broke his leg in the last game of his senior season. Had offers from everyone. Ranked a five-star prospect by Rivals and 247Sports. Anyway, Dr. Waters did his surgery, and something happened after the procedure. A complication. Trey wasn't able to play ball again, and his family sued Dr. Waters. The case took two weeks to try, and the jury came back with a defense verdict."

Jason wasn't surprised. "Has there ever been a medical malpractice plaintiff's verdict in Marshall County?" he asked.

"No," Kisha said, her eyes wide. "And that was one of the big talking points heading into the trial—whether the Cowan case was going to break that streak." She took a sip of her cosmo. "It didn't."

"Those cases are hard to win," Jason said. "Especially in small counties that revere their doctors."

"You really didn't know?" Kisha asked.

"No," Jason said.

"Well, Trey went from being a town celebrity to an afterthought. He walks with a limp and works for the city. His family . . . is kind of rough."

"What do you mean?"

"I mean Sand Mountain."

"Ah," Jason said.

"The mom, Trudy, lives out on Hustleville Road right in the heart of meth country."

"You mean Sand Mountain SlimFast?" Jason asked, remembering the colloquial expression for the illegal Marshall County export.

"Damn right."

"Is Cowan connected to Tyson Cade?"

Kisha cut her eyes at Teresa, who squinted back at Jason and spoke in a cautious tone. "I really don't know. I hear a lot of things at the Brick, and I can't imagine there not being some connections, but if there are, it's not something that either one of them publicly acknowledges."

She hesitated and took a small sip from her drink. "The thing is, Jason, that a lot of folks think Dr. Waters screwed up. There're rumors that he was hooking up with his CRNA and they were having an argument during and after Trey's operation."

"What?" Jason asked.

"True," Teresa said. "I mean that there were rumors of a spat between them, not that there actually was."

"And the complication?"

Teresa nudged Kisha's elbow, who seemed to be champing at the bit to take this part. "He got an infection, which is a known complication," the reporter began. "But the plaintiff's lawyer argued that if Dr. Waters had done proper follow-up and timely ordered antibiotics, the infection would've resolved without issue."

"Who was the plaintiff's lawyer?"

"Local guy named Sean Calloway. He was in over his head. First med mal case."

"And the defense attorney?"

"Knox Rogers. You heard that name before?"

Jason had. Rogers had a reputation for being one of the most skilled civil trial lawyers in the state and made his reputation trying medical malpractice cases. "He's good," Jason said.

"They won on a causation defense," Kisha continued. "In other words, even if Dr. Waters was guilty of negligence, his failure to follow up didn't cause any harm. The die was cast after the surgery. And Sean hadn't gotten any causation experts."

Jason sipped his club soda. "So the Cowan family had reason to be pissed off at Braxton. They're from Sand Mountain. And they might be hooked up with Tyson Cade."

"I'd say it's possible but unlikely." Teresa's voice was firm, matter of fact.

"Why?"

"Because Trey's a good guy. I see him down at the Brick quite a bit, and he's a sweetheart. Not the sharpest tack in the box but not a bad actor."

"Losing your dream in life might make someone do crazy things."

Kisha gave a swift nod. "Might."

"So Trey Cowan is a possible avenue of investigation," Jason said. "Do you know where I might find him?"

"He goes to the Brick for happy hour a lot during the week," Teresa said. "I see him almost every time I'm there."

"He also umpires baseball games out at Ogletree Park, but the season's almost over," Kisha said. "The Brick's probably your best bet."

"Thank you."

For the next thirty minutes, they made small talk, and Susan took their orders. Jason requested a french dip, which turned out to be outstanding. Kisha asked him if he was going to visit his family home, and Jason avoided the question, saying he wasn't sure. He had so much to do.

As they were paying the tab, Jason thanked the couple and insisted that the meal was on him. As they walked outside, Jason took in the cooler air and was thankful for a reprieve from the heat. He hugged both women and then caught Kisha's hand.

"Can you think of anyone besides the Cowan family who might've had a bone to pick with Braxton?"

"Maybe the CRNA? Her name's Colleen Maples, and the gossip is that she and Dr. Waters had recently broken off their relationship."

Jason glanced down at the sidewalk and then back up at his old friend. "Any other avenues worth pursuing?"

"Only one, but I'd think hard and fast before I went down it."

"Tyson Cade," Jason said.

Kisha squeezed his hand. "Be careful."

32

Tyson Cade watched the tracking app on his phone, which showed Jason Rich's Porsche as a red dot approaching Blount Avenue. If he were coming back to the hotel, he would have needed to head south on Gunter, but it looked like the lawyer was moving north.

Interesting, Tyson thought. Was he going back to see his nieces again? If so, there was no choice but to wait. Tyson wasn't a patient man, but he gave it five more minutes. Rich's car appeared to stop for a few minutes, and Tyson figured that the attorney was getting gas at a convenience store. Then the red dot continued along Highway 431. When it passed Buck Island Drive without turning, Tyson rose from his seat and paced until he noticed the dot turning onto Highway 79.

Then he snapped his fingers and punched a button on his cell. "Change of plan."

"But we've got everything set up here," an anxious voice answered.

"I don't care," Tyson said. "I think I know where this bastard's going."

"It'll be easier to get the drop on him when he comes back here." The voice on the line continued to sound agitated.

Tyson watched his screen as the dot slowly moved down Highway 79, otherwise known as Scottsboro Highway. "I'm not sure if he's coming back."

33

Jason turned left onto Mill Creek Road and let out a deep breath that he hadn't realized he'd been holding. He passed by the first few houses, wondering if any of the neighbors were the same from when he was a kid. As he reached the two-story home made of wood and rock, he felt a lump in his throat. He parked in the concrete driveway, cut the ignition, and eased out of his vehicle. Then he fumbled through his keys until he found a rusty gold one that he hadn't used in three and a half years.

Jason trotted up the steps that led to a stoop and then the front door, almost able to hear the thudding of his heart. He stuck the key in the hole and twisted, half expecting it not to work.

"I'll be damned," Jason said as the door gave and he pressed across the threshold. A pungent, musty odor almost made him gag. The heating and air had been turned off, and the house was hot. Instinctively, he reached for the light switch by the door, but it didn't work. Obviously. Jana must have turned off the electricity and water soon after their father died.

The door opened into a den with a fireplace and then a large kitchen with a double island. To the right of the den was his parents' bedroom. He glanced inside, remembering how he'd slept between them on stormy nights when he was young. Jason was now sweating profusely, partly from the heat, partly from the feelings the place brought back. He stepped into the bathroom and gazed at the shower where his father's heart had stopped working. He wondered sometimes about his dad's final moments. Where had he left his phone? How far had he crawled to get it? As he struggled for breath, what had the old man been thinking about?

Knowing his father, Jason suspected that Lucas had been focused solely on survival. But what about after he dialed 911? In the minutes before the ambulance arrived? *Did he think about me? Did he have any regrets?*

Jason felt his eyes growing moist and shook off the depressing thoughts. He left the bedroom and walked downstairs to the basement. He opened the door and stepped out onto a covered patio. The half-moon above shone its light onto the middle of the cove, and Jason gazed out at the dark water.

Why had he come here? What was it he wanted to see? Or feel?

Jason trudged around the side of the house with his head down. He reached inside the Porsche and took out the six-pack of Yuengling beer he'd bought at a convenience store. He'd been fighting it all day long, but he was tired of resisting. The day had been difficult. Jana had basically kicked him out of the consultation room, and all he'd learned about his brother-in-law's murder was that it sure as hell seemed like she was guilty. Just like his work partners and everyone else said. He was tired and strung out and wanted a damn beer. Might as well fall off the wagon at the old homestead.

"Mind if I have one of those?" The voice came from the front of the house, and Jason jumped, almost dropping the carton. He took a step toward the sound and saw a man sitting on the front steps. He had short hair and wore a navy T-shirt.

"I saw you earlier today. Out on Buck Island Drive."

"Yes, you did," the man said, continuing to sit. "Tyson Cade. Pleased to meet you."

Jason's heart fluttered. "What do you want?"

"A beer." He held up his hands, and Jason pitched him a bottle. Tyson caught it and twisted the top off before throwing it out into the grass and taking a long sip. "You're not going to make me drink alone, are you?"

"I've lost the urge," Jason said. "What can I do for you?"

Tyson stood and approached Jason. "The answer to a question."

Jason wrinkled his face. "What?"

"Are you going to take your sister's case?"

A surge of adrenaline flowed through Jason's body. Or maybe it was cortisol. He doubted he could outrun Tyson Cade. The other man was younger and, judging from the veins that protruded from his arms, much stronger.

Tyson reached into the front of his pants and took out a pistol. "Are you?" he asked.

"What's the correct answer here?" Jason asked.

"No," Tyson said. "The correct answer is no."

"Why do you care so much? She's guilty, right?"

Tyson grinned. "Right."

"Then why do you care?"

"Let's just say that if Ms. Waters ever testifies, she knows some things that could hurt my operation."

"Like the cocaine you sold her." Jason knew he was violating attorney-client privilege, but he didn't care. He had a gun pointed at him by a drug dealer.

"You're a sharp cookie." Tyson took a step closer.

"I would think you'd want to be paid for the coke she bought from you."

"Oh, I will, but first things first," Tyson said. "If Jana takes the stand and implicates me, or worse, if she cuts some kind of a deal to bring me down . . ." He stopped. "Well, I can't have that. You understand, don't you?"

"It would be your word against hers, right? I'm sorry, but I can't imagine my sister's word being all that trustworthy."

Tyson rubbed his chin. "I like a man who gets to the point, but your sister is far smarter than to get mixed up with a man like me and not take precautions."

Jason squinted at him. "Does she have something else on you?"

"I don't know. Does she?"

Jason gazed at the man, at the gun he was holding, resisting the urge to put his hands up. "I still don't get it. Why am I a threat? Why are you here waving a gun at me?" He paused. "Could it be that my sister is innocent? That you paid Waylon Pike to kill Braxton, and now you want to make sure she gets convicted?"

"Try again, Counselor. Pike has already confessed that Jana paid him to kill the good doctor."

"He could've just been doing what you told him to do."

"Mr. Rich, it is my wish that Jana have an appointed attorney. One who will negotiate a deal that doesn't involve me."

"You mean someone who's in your pocket. Or too lazy or scared to want to mess with you."

"Like I said, you're a sharp cookie."

"Well, I haven't made my mind up."

"Fair enough." Tyson held the gun steady. "But I'd like to come to an arrangement with you before I leave. If you do take the case, I'd like your word that Jana isn't going to implicate me in any drug deals."

"What if I refuse?"

Tyson cocked the gun. "Those two nieces of yours sure are pretty. It would be a shame if me or one of my deputies had some unsolicited fun with them, wouldn't it? And, worse, it would be tragic if something bad happened to those young ladies."

Jason's breath caught in his throat, picturing Nola and Niecy as he'd seen them yesterday. Niecy's spunk and anger. Nola's earnestness. Both so vibrant. Expressive. Smart. And beautiful. *And this sonofabitch just threatened them.* His head felt light and his stomach queasy. He resisted the urge to grab his knees. He glared at the drug dealer, who had his pistol pointed at Jason's head. "What are you saying?" he managed to get out.

"I'm saying I'd hate for them to end up dead in the lake like their father." Tyson moved closer and pressed the gun into Jason's chest. "Do you understand?"

A chill enveloped Jason as he gazed into Tyson Cade's eyes. The younger man wasn't bluffing, and Jason again envisioned his nieces. This time, their expressions were blank, their bodies cold and unmoving, as they sank to the bottom of Lake Guntersville.

"I need your promise on that, Counselor," Tyson continued, "or you may end up dead in that cove tonight." He waved his gun toward the boathouse.

Jason tried to think, choosing his words as carefully as he could. "If I can figure out what it is she has on you, will you back off?"

"I'm not negotiating here," Tyson said.

"I'm not sure she can win if she doesn't testify," Jason said.

"Then she'll lose. Not my problem." Again, he dug the pistol into Jason's chest. "Waiting for that promise, Counselor."

Jason let out a ragged breath. "I promise."

"Good," Tyson said, finishing the rest of his beer in one gulp and then tossing it in the front yard. "I'm really glad we had this conversation, aren't you?"

Jason didn't answer as he watched Tyson Cade walk down the driveway toward a black truck that had been pulled to the side of the road. The drug dealer looked at Jason over his shoulder and waved, as if he were saying goodbye to an old friend, before hopping in the vehicle.

Seconds later, he was gone.

Jason stood stock still in the driveway for a long time, gaping in the direction of the truck that had whisked his new nemesis away. Despite the July heat, he was freezing, and his fingers and hands were twitching. He couldn't get the images of Nola and Niecy out of his mind.

He walked back into the house and locked the door. He set the carton of beer on the kitchen counter and gazed out at the water. He wanted a beer. He wanted to drink all five of these Yuenglings. He wanted that badly. Craved it. Needed it. His throat felt dry, and his hand reached for the bottle and then pulled back as if he were putting his fingertips over a fire. He stepped away from the alcohol and trudged down the stairs. He lay on the couch in the den where he'd played video games as a child. He stared up at the ceiling.

What have you gotten yourself and your family into, Jana?

Jason closed his eyes. He had another thought before exhaustion overcame him.

What in the hell am I going to do?

34

Jason awoke to the sun shining bright rays through the window behind the couch.

He shaded his eyes from the glare. He pulled himself to a sitting position, his body stiff and sore. The boat ride yesterday had been rough in patches, and his lower back and neck were suffering the effects.

He walked to the window and looked out at the cove. What he saw was what he remembered seeing every day of his childhood. Fishing boats in the middle of the lake and around several of the boathouses.

But the boats weren't what held his eye. He also saw someone paddling a kayak. The craft pulled up to the adjacent boathouse, and a thin woman with a deep suntan hopped out and pulled the kayak onto the dock.

"I don't believe it," Jason said to himself. He opened the door and walked swiftly toward the woman. Once he reached the dock, he began to jog. She was just coming out the side door of the boathouse when he caught up to her. He sucked in a deep breath of the humid air and smiled.

"Jason James Rich," she said, squinting at him with one eye open and the other closed. She wore a gray tank top and athletic shorts, which showed off the wiry muscles in her arms and legs. Sweat glistened on her forehead and neck, and her brown hair was tied up in a ponytail. "You look like shit."

"Thanks," he said. "Savannah Chase Wittschen." His grin widened. "You look fantastic."

She poked his chest. "You call me Savannah again, I'll push you in this lake."

"Chase. I . . ." He couldn't think of the words. "I . . . can't believe you're here."

"Why? This is my home." She gestured at the single-story brick house next to the Riches' home. "Papa and Mimi both passed on, and I've always loved it here. Unlike you, Mr. Famous Billboard Lawyer." She hooked a thumb toward the shore. "Saw your ride. Porsche 911 convertible. Nice."

"Thank you."

For a moment, they studied each other. Then Chase pressed past him and spoke without looking at him. "About to make some coffee and breakfast if you're hungry."

Jason watched her. Chase Wittschen had been his only friend at Mill Creek. She went through the Guntersville public school system while Jason had been a Randolph private school lifer. But in the summers, especially during elementary and middle school, they'd been inseparable. When Jana and her friends would go jet skiing or wakeboarding or swimming, Jason would find Chase, and they'd take kayak rides or hike in and around the cove. Back then, Chase always wore overalls, and her curly hair was cut short like a boy's. She'd taught him how to fish, chew tobacco, and steer a kayak and paddleboard, though none of it had taken very well. Chase had loved the water and all its mysteries, while Jason had simply craved the attention she gave him.

But their relationship had changed once they were in high school. They still hung out, but teenage hormones eventually got in the way.

He hadn't thought of Chase in years. They'd lost touch after high school, and last Jason had heard, she'd moved out west and was working at one of the national parks.

He took in a long, low breath. As he followed her up the dock, he found that he was smiling, just as he'd done when he was driving Jackson Burns's boat yesterday and felt the wind caressing his face.

The good vibes dissipated the minute Jason entered the kitchen. On the counter, he saw a rifle, three pistols, and two other long-barreled guns.

"Getting ready for war?" Jason asked, feeling uneasy as he took a seat at a wooden table.

Chase was making eggs in a skillet on the stove. "Shouldn't you be?" she asked, peering at him over her shoulder. "If you're going to be having late-night confrontations with Tyson Cade."

Jason's stomach tightened, and he raised his brow. "You saw that?"

She continued to toss the egg yolk in the pan with a fork, talking as she worked. "I had that bastard between the crosshairs of my AR-15. It was all I could do not to pull the trigger. Would've done this whole county a lot of good."

"How do you know him?"

"I've been back a couple of years. I keep my eyes and ears open. Coffee?"

"Please," Jason said, watching as his old friend poured him a cup from an old-school drip maker and placed the mug in front of him.

"Thank you," he said, wincing as he took a sip of the scalding-hot liquid. "And thanks for having my back last night."

She turned and put a paper plate of eggs and two pieces of wheat toast on his plate. "It's not the Cracker Barrel, but it'll do."

"It looks wonderful," Jason said. Chase placed some Smucker's grape jelly and a couple of forks on the table, and they both dug in. The food hit the spot, and for a few minutes, Jason forgot about Tyson Cade's threats, his sister's murder case, and the decision he had to make soon.

"Thank you," he said after devouring the breakfast.

"Welcome," she said. She took a sip from her mug. "I'm sorry about your brother-in-law."

"Heard about that?" Jason asked.

She rolled her eyes. "I'd have to be an ostrich not to have heard about it. I assume you're in town to save your sister's ass?"

He gazed out at the water. "I don't know what I'm doing. I mean . . . I did see Jana at the jail yesterday, and she asked me to help her, but that's not the only reason I came home."

She crossed her arms. "Why then?"

He looked at her. "Honest? I just got out of ninety days in rehab. Alcohol addiction. I almost fell off the wagon within an hour of being discharged, and then Jana called me and told her sob story. I didn't know what else to do. I was hoping coming here would help me figure it out."

She whistled between her teeth. "That's a lot."

He chuckled. "Thanks."

"It is," she said. "I'm not being cute. It is a lot to deal with at one time. Has coming here helped?"

Jason took a sip of coffee and covered his face with his hands. "I almost got drunk last night. Probably would have if a meth dealer hadn't threatened to rape and kill my nieces and finish me off too."

"So . . . sounds like the answer to my question is no."

"Correct."

"Have you reached out to AA? Tried to get in a group?"

He rolled his eyes. "No."

"Well, do you want to get better?" She snapped the question, her voice harsh. Chase had never been one to mince words.

"Why'd you cover me last night?"

"Because I didn't want you to get hurt."

Jason held his coffee mug with both hands and inspected the steam coming off it. "Why? The last time we were together . . . I hurt you."

"That was a million moons ago, Jason. We were young and foolish. I don't hold that against you."

"We should've at least talked about it. I'm . . . sorry."

"Yeah, we should've. And I'm sorry too. You were a jerk . . . I was naive . . . we were seventeen." She grabbed the empty plates, before throwing them in the trash and beginning to clean the skillet in the sink. "What's your business with Tyson Cade?" she asked. "Why would he be waving a gun in your face and making threats?"

"Guess."

She continued to scrub the pan. "Jana."

"Bingo."

"Let me guess again. She was buying from him . . . and probably sleeping with him too. Close?"

"And you're on to Final Jeopardy."

"So . . . what? That doesn't explain why he'd be threatening you and your nieces."

"He's worried she'll testify that she bought drugs from him and that she has evidence, a tape maybe, that the police could use to bring charges. That she'll cut a deal to avoid the death penalty or a life sentence by giving them the county's drug lord."

Chase put the pan on a paper towel to dry. "Those sound like valid worries to me. That is, if I were a drug lord. What does he want?"

"For me to not take the case . . . or, if I do, to promise him that he won't be implicated by her."

"And if you don't do either, he said he'd kill you and your nieces?"

"Yes."

"Jesus. You should probably report that to the sheriff's office."

"What good would it do? Seems like that would escalate the situation and put Nola and Niecy at greater risk." He took a last sip of coffee. "I don't think Tyson Cade plays by the same rules we do."

"So what are you going to do?"

"I don't know," he said. "Based on what Cade said, it seems like one wrong move by Jana's attorney could cause irreparable harm to her daughters." He stood up and stretched his sore back. "They're the only family I have."

"Sounds like you really don't have much choice then."

He blinked and looked at her. He was expecting to hear the same advice he'd gotten from Izzy, Harry, Jackson Burns, and Kisha Roe. To run like the wind from this whole situation. "You think I should take the case?"

"If you want to protect your family, that seems like the only option."

Jason peered out at the lake, remembering something he'd noticed last night. "Our house doesn't seem near dusty enough. Do you know if someone's been keeping it up?"

"I was always pretty good at picking a lock," Chase said, a slight tease in her voice.

"Why?" Jason said, turning toward her.

She walked toward him and placed her cup on the table. "I guess . . . with the way it was left . . . all the furniture still there . . . I thought someone might be coming back one day. And I've got a lot of free time on my hands."

"Why's that?"

Her face went blank. "It's a long story, and you probably ought to be going. I can't imagine how many folks have already called 1-800 GET RICH by now. And . . . it appears that you might be venturing into some criminal law, eh?"

"Eh," Jason echoed. He grabbed the door handle leading to the outside deck. "Thank you."

He started out the door, but Chase's voice stopped him. "Wait."

She walked forward and pressed a pistol into his hand.

He looked at the weapon and back at Chase.

"I'm not going to be able to watch your back every second."

"I don't have a gun permit."

"The next time he threatens to kill you, he's probably not going to ask for one." She smirked and cocked her head.

"Good point," he said, sticking the gun in his pocket. "Where'd you get the arsenal in there?"

"Like I said, long story."

She turned, and Jason reached for her arm, squeezing it gently. "Thanks again," he said.

"You gonna be around?" she asked.

Standing there, in his crumpled suit with a loaner gun stuck in his front pocket, badly needing a shave and a shower, Jason felt self-conscious and a bit ridiculous as his heart rate picked up speed. "I think so," he said.

35

An hour and a half later, Jason walked through the doors of the Marshall County Sheriff's Office. He went to the reception desk and saw the same woman he'd seen the day prior.

"Well, well, well. Back again so soon, Mr. Rich?"

"I'm here to see my sister." He paused but didn't break eye contact. "My client."

"OK," she said, looking hard at him. "I'll let them know. Have a seat, and someone will be right out."

Jason took a seat and crossed his legs, trying to look relaxed. He'd driven straight from Mill Creek to the hotel. He'd showered, shaved, and put on a fresh shirt and tie. He was wearing the same suit, but he'd only brought one, and a quick ironing job had smoothed out the wrinkles. On the way to the Hampton Inn, he'd called Izzy. When she'd answered, he'd forgone any pleasantries. He'd made up his mind.

"I want you to draft me up a notice of appearance as counsel for Jana."

"Are you out of your—"

"I also want you to look at discovery in criminal cases in Alabama and see what we can get."

"I haven't handled a single criminal matter in my life, and neither have you."

"Well, with this one and one more, we'll have handled two. I don't have time to argue with you, Izzy. I have to do this to protect my family."

"Jason, talk to me. What's happened?"

"Call Professor Adams over at Cumberland. We've given a lot of money to the school. Tell her we'd like her to consult with us, and we'll pay her a handsome fee to be a guiding post." He'd paused to catch his breath and could tell his partner was furiously scribbling notes. Pamela Adams was the dean of criminal law at Cumberland and the best teacher Jason ever had. She'd probably agree to consult for free given the high-profile nature of the case, but he knew you got what you paid for.

"Anything else?" Izzy asked. The protest in her voice was gone.

"Yeah. Send Harry. ASAP."

He'd clicked End without further discussion. That was how he rolled when he worked. No wasted effort. No squandered time. It felt exhilarating and oddly comforting to be back in the arena, even if defending a murder case was uncharted territory.

Jason watched the double doors to the side of the reception area swing open. District Attorney Shay Lankford walked toward him with something between a smirk and a scowl.

"I saw your notice of appearance."

Jason smiled. Once engaged, there was no one faster on the draw than Izzy Montaigne. She'd filed the notice within an hour of their call. "Yes. I've decided to represent Jana."

"Does your client know?" Shay asked.

"Why would you ask that?"

Shay shrugged. "Let's just say the guards that bring Jana her meals have reported that she seems to say a lot of ugly things about you."

"She's my sister. We fight like hell, but we're family." The words sounded odd coming out of his mouth.

Shay stepped closer. "I hope you aren't planning to turn this case into some kind of circus."

Jason frowned. "What are you suggesting?"

She crossed her arms. "Oh, come on, Captain Billboard. You're a walking publicity stunt. Just don't expect Judge Carlton or Judge Barber to put up with any kind of shenanigans."

Jason felt a trickle of anxiety run through him. He didn't recognize the names of either of the two circuit court judges. Undeterred, he forced a grin. "I'm going to be myself."

Before Shay could respond, an officer approached them. "The detainee is in the consultation room."

The prosecutor gestured for Jason to follow the deputy.

He started to walk toward the double doors but then looked over his shoulder at Shay and added, "You said if I entered an appearance, you'd give me a copy of Waylon Pike's confession. I'd like it before I leave today."

Shay pursed her lips. "Certainly."

"Good," Jason said. "Looking forward to working with you."

36

Once they were alone in the room, Jana spoke through clenched teeth. "Well, you've got a lot of nerve. Coming back here after making such an ass of yourself yesterday. I'm not in much of a forgiving mood."

"Shut up," Jason said.

Jana recoiled. "What . . . what did you say to me?"

"I said shut up," Jason said. "I'm in no mood for your lunacy, Jana. Tyson Cade almost killed me last night. He held me at gunpoint and said that if you testified in this case and implicated him in any way in any kind of drug deal, that he would kill me, and that he would rape and kill Niecy and Nola."

Jana's eyes went wide, and she shook her head back and forth, as if she didn't want to believe it. "He's bluffing."

"He thinks you have something on him. Do you?"

She averted her eyes, looking up at the ceiling.

"Do you?" Jason pressed.

"Maybe."

"What in the hell does that mean? If I'm going to represent you, we can't keep secrets from each other."

"Whoa, now. Who's saying that you're doing any such thing. I don't want that anymore."

"Too late," Jason said. "I'm not going to let you endanger your children and my nieces. I've already entered my appearance as your attorney. I'm taking the case, and you need to start talking."

She crossed her arms. "That's not legal. You can't represent me without my consent."

"We're in Marshall County, Jana. It's the Wild, Wild West, and I'm not in the mood for your bullshit. You need a lawyer, and there aren't any other takers. I'm all you've got, and I'd say that makes you pretty damn lucky."

"Oh, really. Why's that?"

"Because every member of that jury will have driven by four of my billboards coming and going to trial. I'm a household name, and what I lack in experience in criminal law, I make up for in recognition." He rubbed his hands together. "Your case needs smoke, bluster, and bullshit, and I've made a career out of all three."

She looked at him, and tears suddenly appeared in her eyes. She grabbed his hand. "Thank you, J. J."

Was it true affection? Or an act? With Jana, he could never tell.

"You're welcome," Jason said. "Now, I need you to tell me something."

"Anything," she said, squeezing his hand.

"You took out $15,000 from the bank the day before Braxton was killed. What did you do with it? I'm not buying your story that you left it in your car."

Jana peered down at the table. "I gave it to one of Tyson's deputies. The money was a down payment on what I owed him."

Jason took in a deep breath and exhaled. "How much did you owe?"

"Fifty grand."

"Jesus," Jason said, running a hand through his hair. "How do you know that the man was with Cade?"

"I just did. With Tyson, I'd get calls from strange numbers. I'd be told where to be. And then I'd go. On the night of the Fourth, I went to a strip mall, and I gave the money to one of his men. Then I drove to the Hampton Inn, where I met Tyson. What I did with him was also . . . a payment."

"Oh, Jana," Jason muttered.

"Don't you dare judge me. You have no idea what I've been through these past three years. My husband abandoned our marriage. My kids were brainwashed. So I got into drugs."

"The bottom line is that there's no way you can defend yourself on the stand without implicating Tyson Cade?"

She held out her palms, exasperated.

Jason stood and began to pace the room. "Then you can't take the stand."

"The hell I can't. I've got to tell the jury I didn't do it. That I didn't pay Waylon Pike to kill Braxton. Don't I have to say that?"

Yes, Jason thought. "I'm not sure I'd recommend you taking the stand even without this Cade business," he said, not looking at her.

"Why?"

"Because I don't think a jury in this county will believe you." He looked at her. "I'm not sure I believe you."

"Fuck you."

"No, thanks," Jason said. "Look, I'm going to bring some paperwork by so that we can turn the power and water on out at the house at Mill Creek."

"Why? You can stay at my house at Buck Island."

"No. I'm staying at Mill Creek, and that's final. I'm going to ask the girls to stay with me. I'm assuming that's OK with you."

She hesitated.

"Jana, we both know that Tyson Cade wasn't bluffing. He doesn't look like the kind of dog that just barks. Nola and Niecy will be safer at Mill Creek with me."

She hung her head but finally nodded. "Please take care of them, Jason." She sniffled. "I don't know what I'd do if . . ." She trailed off.

"I will." Jason leaned in and kissed her cheek. "I promise." He walked to the door and knocked three times. "I'll be in—"

"J. J., I gave that money to Tyson Cade. What if he gave it to Pike to kill Braxton? I mean, that's probably what happened, don't you think? He set me up to take the fall." Her voice was high. Desperate.

"Why would he do that?" Jason asked.

When a guard opened the door, Jason said, "False alarm. A few more minutes, OK?"

The officer rolled his eyes, and the door slammed shut.

Jason approached his sister and leaned his hands on the table. "Cade wouldn't want to hamstring his money sources. With Braxton dead and you in here, where's he going to get the rest of the money you owe him? Doesn't make sense." He stared at Jana, who'd closed her eyes.

"There's no way we can win, is there?" she asked.

"I don't know," Jason said, taking a seat. He didn't want to give her any false hope. "But the state has to prove their case beyond a reasonable doubt, which is a much higher standard than the personal injury cases I typically handle. That's one thing we have in our favor."

She snorted and looked at him. "Presumed innocent, right? We both know that a jury in this county is going to presume I'm guilty."

It was the most honest thing he'd heard his sister say in a long time, and Jason was taken aback.

"You know I'm right," she added.

"Yes," he said.

"So what do we do?"

"We go after Waylon Pike with both barrels. He's cut a deal to save his ass. I'm getting a copy of his statement, and I'll sic my investigator on him. If the jury doesn't believe Pike, then the state's case turns to shit."

A tiny smile came to Jana's face. "Thought you said you didn't do criminal work."

"I don't, but I remember a little from law school, and I'm a fast learner. To win, we'll have to discredit Pike, but that's not all."

"What else?"

Jason raised off the seat and paced back to the door. Again, he knocked three times.

"J. J.?"

"We have to give the jury something else to believe. A plausible alternative to you paying Pike."

"How are you going to do that without involving Tyson Cade?"

Jason took in a deep breath and exhaled as the guard opened the door. "I have no idea."

PART FIVE

37

"ALL RISE!" The bailiff bellowed the two words that started any legal proceeding, and Jason shot off his chair and buttoned his coat. Next to him, Jana also stood. Behind them, the courtroom was full to capacity. Though Jason had tried to keep his eyes in front of him when he'd made his entrance, based on the glances he'd allowed himself, most of the spectators were media types.

After a three-second pause, Judge Ambrose Powell Conrad stepped through a side door and strode to the bench. In Marshall County, the two circuit court judges were Virgil Carlton and Terry Barber. When both had recused themselves due to having been treated as patients by Dr. Waters, an out-of-county judge had had to be appointed to handle the case.

Powell Conrad was once a lifetime prosecutor, starting off as an assistant district attorney for Tuscaloosa County and eventually rising to the top post. Two years ago, he'd been elected a circuit court judge. Conrad was a bit of a celebrity in the state of Alabama, as he was heavily involved in the apprehension of noted killer James Robert Wheeler in Hazel Green, Alabama, in 2013. Judge Conrad had lost sight in his left eye during his quest to bring in Wheeler and thus wore a black patch. Because of that, a lot of local Tuscaloosa attorneys referred to him as "the pirate."

Because Conrad had made his career as a prosecutor, he had a reputation for being a hard-ass. Though Jason had a few cases pending in Tuscaloosa, none had been assigned to the former district attorney.

"All right then," the judge said, grunting and pushing the microphone away from him. "Please be seated."

Jason and Jana took their seats while Judge Conrad turned to his bailiff. "Travis, what's the deal with the mike?"

"Sorry, Your Honor. Judge Barber was in here doing pleas this morning. He likes to use it to be heard."

"Well, if I use it, I'm gonna burst everyone's eardrum in here." He turned to the gallery. "I'm loud . . . if y'all haven't figured that out yet."

Nervous laughter filled the courtroom, and Jason forced a grin.

Judge Conrad leaned over the bench. "State of Alabama versus Jana Rich Waters," he said, and his voice resonated off the walls. "Is the state ready to proceed with the arraignment?"

"Yes, Your Honor." Shay Lankford rose and spoke with an air of complete calm.

"And the defendant?"

"Yes, Your Honor," Jason said, standing and trying to keep his legs from wobbling.

"OK, let's get on with it. Ms. Waters, will you please stand."

Jana did as instructed.

"Ms. Waters, to the charge of capital murder, how do you plead?"

She cleared her throat. "Not guilty."

"All right. Will the attorneys approach?"

Jason walked around the table and strode toward the bench.

"How long do y'all need? It is the middle of August now. Can we get it tried early next year? Maybe the first week of February?"

"That's fine with the state," Shay said. "But we'd prefer an earlier setting."

"Judge, we'd also like the case to be tried sooner," Jason said. "Ms. Waters is being held without bond, and her youngest daughter is a high school junior who needs her mother. We'd ask for the quickest setting we can get."

"You sure that's wise, Counselor?" Judge Conrad asked, raising his eyebrows.

"It's what my client wants," Jason said. "She's entitled to a speedy trial."

Judge Conrad scrutinized him with a wry grin. It was the way you looked at someone you knew was doing something foolish.

Insane, more like it, Jason thought, forcing his own smile.

Then, after giving his head a jerk, Conrad licked his index finger and shuffled through a stapled sheet of papers. "Looks like I've got room the week of October 22. That's two months out." He paused and squinted at Jason. "Speedy enough?"

"Yes, Your Honor."

"Madame Prosecutor?"

"That's fine, Judge."

"All right then. Please take your seats."

Once they did, Judge Conrad stood and peered out over the gallery. "The trial of this case will be held on October 22, 2018." He banged his gavel on the bench. "Court adjourned."

———

After saying his goodbyes to his sister, Jason strode down the staircase to the first floor. When he exited the courthouse, at least six microphones were pointed in his direction. He looked for Kisha, found her, and winked. She elbowed her way to the front and spoke over the crowd. "Do you have any comment on the arraignment of your sister?" They'd planned this moment earlier in the day. Kisha was to refer to Jana as his sister. Always. Jason would be owning his family connection to this case, not running from it.

"Jana is not guilty," Jason said, glancing at the different cameras. "My sister has been wrongfully charged with this crime. The state's entire case rests on the word of a convicted felon. A jealous handyman who they arrested more than a week after the murder of my beloved brother-in-law. It's obvious that Mr. Pike's story is a lie. Made up to save his own skin. My sister, Jana Waters, has been a respected member of this community her whole life, and I'm confident that a jury will see this for what it is in two months. A hatchet job." Jason glared at several of the cameras. "This case is an outrage, and, before I'm done, the people who've put my sister through such misery will pay for how they've wronged my family."

"Mr. Rich—"

"That's all for now." Jason walked toward his Porsche with cameras flashing in every direction. Once inside, he backed out onto Gunter Avenue and spun his wheels as he accelerated away from the courthouse.

His phone rang before he'd gone fifteen feet.

"Yeah," Jason said.

"Are you out of your mind?" Izzy asked. "You're gonna be held in contempt for commenting on evidence."

"You think?" Jason asked. "There was no gag order."

"There will be now. Your comments about Pike go over the line."

"Good. To have any chance of winning, we're going to have to shake things up."

"Jason, are you sure you know what you're doing? You don't have the cleanest record with the bar, and your public reprimand is in a few days."

"I know what I'm doing," Jason said, trying to keep his tone confident. "You know how we roll, Iz. We make our adversaries uncomfortable; we keep them on their toes. That's what drives settlements, almost as much as exposure. When the other side hates to have to deal with you, that's an advantage."

"I know, but this isn't a car wreck. You really think these tactics are going to work in a murder case?"

"I don't know, but we can't sit here and do nothing, or we'll take a beating. My sister's character has been assassinated in the press ever since she was arrested. It's time to take a swing at the state, and everything I said was spot on. To win, we have to discredit Pike. I needed to plant that seed."

He heard a few chortles on the other end of the line.

"What?" Jason asked.

"Well, you certainly planted it. How fast do you think you'll get a reaction?"

"Soon, I'd imagine," he said.

"Yeah," Izzy agreed. "Very soon."

38

Soon turned out to be thirty minutes.

Judge Conrad, who had yet to leave Guntersville, ordered an emergency hearing. When Jason returned to the courtroom, the sandy-haired, heavyset barrister was scowling, his face as crimson as Alabama's football helmets. At the prosecution table, Shay Lankford glanced at Jason and rolled her eyes, her arms crossed tight.

"I should hold you in contempt," Judge Conrad said.

Jason held his eye. "Forgive me, Your Honor, but I don't understand the problem."

"Commenting on evidence to the press? A huge no-no, Mr. Rich. Potential jurors will likely have heard your comments, making it harder to impanel a jury. Do you understand?"

"Yes, sir, but what about the press conferences the sheriff held denouncing my client?" Jason asked. "Potential jurors probably heard his remarks too." He hesitated and chose his words carefully. "There was no gag order in place, and I was exercising my right to freedom of speech. Said another way, Judge, the state started it."

Judge Conrad grunted. "I'm imposing a gag order from this point forward. No comments to the press from either side. Anyone violating this order will be held in contempt. Is that clear, Mr. Rich?"

"Yes, sir."

"Shay?"

"Yes, Your Honor." Her face was flushed, and she kept her arms crossed. Jason could tell that he'd rattled her. *Good,* he thought. He hadn't taken this case to make friends.

"Mr. Rich, the only reason you're not in a jail cell right now is because your actions, while deserving of punishment, did *not* violate an order of this court. If you so much as breathe heavy around a reporter or a member of the press, you'll find yourself locked up for a week. You hear me?"

"Yes, Your Honor."

"All right then," Judge Conrad said, glowering at Jason. "Get out of my sight."

———

Shay caught up to Jason outside the doors to the courtroom. "That clown act might scare an insurance adjuster, but all it does is make me more determined to see Jana spend the rest of her life in prison. You understand?"

"Nothing I told the press was untrue," he replied. "Waylon Pike is a con man, Ms. Lankford, and you know it. Your case is weak." He started to turn away, but her voice rang out behind him.

"If Jana didn't pay Pike, then who did?"

He continued to walk, but Shay wasn't done.

"If you don't have an answer for that, Mr. Rich, then your client is going down."

39

They huddled at Café 336 at the Bakers on Main shopping center a couple of blocks from the courthouse. Jason ate a chicken salad sandwich and chips and washed it down with tea while Harry gave him a breakdown of his investigation.

"The Cowan kid is mostly doing grounds crew work right now for the city, mowing grass for the city parks and doing other odd jobs. Goes to the Brick almost every night for happy hour. That bartender, Teresa, is usually working there."

"Have you spoken to him?"

"A couple of times. Small talk about the Braves game on the TV. He's not overly talkative."

"Does he have a girlfriend? Love interest? Anything?"

Harry shook his head. "None of that. He drinks a little too much, but he lives in an apartment close to the Brick, so he always walks home."

"From what you've seen, is there a chance in hell he could have come up with $15,000?"

"Not on what he's doing for the city. But his apartment is nicer than what you'd think a minimum wage city employee could afford, so there must be a nest of some sort. I've heard rumblings that his father may have taken out one of those loss-of-value insurance policies. If that can be confirmed, then it's possible that he could have had 15K stashed somewhere."

"We need to confirm that," Jason said. "Any word on where the dad is?"

"Working construction in the panhandle."

"Find him, Harry. What about the mom?"

"Lives off of Hustleville Road. Works at Top O' the River as a waitress. I've tried to speak with her a couple times, but she's blown me off each time." He gulped down some tea. "Wasn't rude. Just said she didn't want to talk."

"Same question. Any chance she could have fifteen grand in cash lying around?"

"None," Harry said.

"What about the CRNA, Maples?"

"Finally was able to speak with her yesterday."

"And?"

"Verifies everything that's in the investigator's report produced by the state. Admitted that she had an affair with Dr. Waters but said it ended months ago. Admitted that she'd initially denied the affair when questioned by the police but owned up to it after being shown text messages between the doctor and herself. Last saw him on July 3. They had a surgery together that morning. She sent him a text the night of the Fourth, which is in Investigator Daniels's report."

"Happy fourth! I wish things could have been different . . ." Jason spoke the words straight from memory. "And her whereabouts on the Fourth?"

"Ate with friends at the Rock House and watched the fireworks from her cabin on the lake."

"Which is where?"

"On the main channel off Highway 69."

"Pretty close to Fire by the Lake?"

Harry squinted. "A mile maybe. If that."

Jason wiped his mouth with a napkin. He looked around the café, which was pretty full at 1:30 in the afternoon. He saw a couple of people glance his way, but most folks were just enjoying their late lunch. "Let's talk about your interview with the bartender at Fire by the Lake again."

Harry crossed his legs and gave his head a jerk. "His name's Keith, not Kenny. About twenty-seven years old. Said that Jana was a frequent flier. Came in at least once a week for a cocktail or draft beer. Sometimes alone. Sometimes not."

"And, when she wasn't alone . . . ?" Jason flinched, waiting for it.

Harry grimaced. "She was there with Waylon Pike."

"Damnit," Jason said, thumping the table with his index finger. "Anyone else?"

"No," Harry said.

Jason finished the rest of his tea in one gulp. "Back to Maples. She's a CRNA who lives on the water. She clearly had the funds to pay fifteen thousand in cash."

"Clearly. But what's her motive? By her own account, she'd ended the affair."

"But she was still pining after him as late as two hours before he was killed. Maybe her text was a way of saying goodbye."

"You're reaching, J. R."

"I know," Jason admitted. "Still, a jilted lover is someone with motive. But Cowan is the better play. Stronger motive. And wasn't Pike known to frequent the Brick as well?"

"According to our friend Teresa, the answer is yes," Harry said. "They were at the bar on several occasions at the same time, and she thinks she saw them talking at least once, maybe twice."

"*Thinks* being the operative word."

"It's better than nothing," Harry said. "We can't prove what they were talking about, but the fact that they were seen together in close proximity to the time of the murder shows that Cowan had the opportunity to hire Pike to kill Dr. Waters."

"Which leaves us lacking only confirmation of means," Jason said. During his conversations with Professor Adams, she'd stressed that a criminal defendant needed the means, opportunity, and motive to commit the act. It was the rule of MOM, as she called it. "To prove the crime of murder, those three elements must always be shown," she'd added. "If you're going for an alternative killer, you need to show that this other person had all three."

"I'm headed to Panama City in the morning," Harry said. "I'll track down Mr. Cowan and get our confirmation, one way or the other. What about Braxton's lawyer in the med mal suit?"

"I finally got a meeting set up. Took forever because the guy's always in trial."

"When?"

"This afternoon. Meeting him in Huntsville at a brewpub there that he likes."

"You're an alcoholic. You sure that's a good idea?"

Jason ground his teeth together. "Trying to be agreeable. I need something from this guy."

"What?"

"Anything? An angle. Something I'm missing. Knox Rogers was around Braxton, Jana, and the Cowan family for two and a half years. If Cowan is our alternative killer, who better to fill me in on his possible motive than Braxton's attorney in the malpractice case."

"I hear you, but I wouldn't get my hopes up."

"Thanks. What about Braxton's office staff?"

"I've spoken to his receptionist and medical assistant, and neither had anything we could use. Still trying to track down his nurse, but she's in surgery almost every day."

"What's her name again?" Jason asked.

"Beverly Thacker." Harry started to stand but then sat back down. "You know it's not too late to get out of this, J. R. You could withdraw. The court could appoint Jana another lawyer. You could still look after your nieces, just like you're doing now. You don't need this, man. We don't need it."

Jason rose to his feet. "I've told you, Harry, I don't have a choice. One wrong move by Jana's defense lawyer, and Nola and Niecy get hurt, you understand?"

Harry also stood and grabbed his arm. "Have you considered how you're going to feel if *you* make that wrong move? You already waived a preliminary hearing. Was that wise?"

"It's what Jana wanted. Besides, all the state would've had to do is introduce Pike's confession to show probable cause and have the case bound over to the grand jury. I didn't want to waste any time. I knew she'd be indicted, and I wanted to get us to the arraignment as fast as possible so that we could have a quicker trial date."

"Why?"

"Because whatever happens here, good, bad, or ugly, I'd rather it happen fast for my family's sake."

"You're walking through a minefield—you know that, don't you?"

"Yes," Jason said. "Again . . . better to walk fast."

Harry leaned forward and whispered into Jason's ear. "The private security detail we've hired is the best around. They removed the tracking device that Cade put on your car, and the guards are watching you and your nieces like a hawk." He peered down at the table. "But Cade's people are watching too."

"I know," Jason said. "And I appreciate all you've done, Harry."

"It may not be enough. Cade is smart. His people are good. What I'm saying, amigo, is that I can't guarantee your family's safety."

"I understand," Jason said. "Have you learned anything more about Cade's connection to Pike or Cowan?"

"Nothing."

Jason turned to go, but Harry held on to his arm. "What if I do find a connection to Cade? How are we going to be able to use it, given the threats he's made?"

Jason wiggled out of his grasp. "We'll cross that bridge when we come to it."

40

Tyson Cade put two packages of Twinkies on the counter along with a twenty-ounce Sun Drop.

"What's the good word, Doob?"

It was 2:30 p.m. at the Alder Springs Grocery. A slow time for a stop in, though things would pick up soon when school let out. Dooby Darnell pushed her bangs out of her eyes and seemed to flinch a little. "Nothing, Tyson. That'll be five dollars and thirty-seven cents."

Tyson dangled a one-hundred-dollar bill in front of her. "Heard anything about the Jana Rich murder case?"

She ran both hands through her fluffy auburn locks. "Trial in October," she said. "That and her lawyer . . . her brother . . . has moved back to town and is watching over her girls." She glanced around the store. "I've also heard rumors that he's set up some kind of fortress over there at Mill Creek. A lot of security."

"Anything else?" Tyson snapped. "That's old news."

"I'm sorry," she said.

"What about Trey? He been in here recently?"

"Earlier today," Dooby said. "Picked up a few things to take to his mom's."

"And how is Trudy?" Tyson asked.

"Fine, I think."

Tyson put the hundred back in his wallet and gave her six bucks. "Keep it."

Then he started for the door.

"There was an investigator in here last week. Left his card. Was asking a whole lot of questions about Trey and Trudy." She hesitated. "And you."

"Did you keep the card?"

She reached under the counter, then held it up for him to see.

Tyson walked over and snatched the card out of her hand. "Harry Davenport," he said. Then he winked at her. "You done good, Dooby girl." He reached into his wallet and took out the hundred again. He placed it in her hand. "I've given you my emergency number, haven't I?"

"Yes."

"If this guy"—he flicked the card—"swings by again, I want you to call me on that line. Got it?"

"Yes," she said.

"Good," Tyson said. "Bye now."

———

Out in the parking lot, he ate one of the Twinkies in one bite and downed half the soft drink. Then let out a long burp. He was on edge, having barely slept in the last few days. Business was booming all over Sand Mountain, and it was hard to keep up with the demand. He'd heard about Jana Waters's arraignment earlier today as well as Jason Rich's efforts to make his house safe out at Mill Creek. According to one of his guys who'd recently scoped the place, Rich had hired at least four security guards. One was at the house at all times. One shadowed Nola on her way to and from school, and one watched the back side of the house and the water. Another watched the college girl, Niecy, at Birmingham-Southern.

Tyson figured that the best way to ambush the lawyer, if that was needed, would be by boat, but the bridge at Mill Creek was small, and a large craft wouldn't fit underneath. He could send a crew on Jet Skis, but that would be too loud. A fishing boat was probably the best option, but Tyson knew he wouldn't go that route either. There was too much security, not to mention the rednecks who resided on either side of the Rich home. Chase Wittschen was ex-military, and the Tonidandel brothers, who lived across the street, weren't to be messed with either. If Tyson tried to hit the house, it would be World War III, and he wasn't sure if he could win.

Any way he sliced it, if he was going to remind the billboard attorney of his obligations, he'd have to do it away from his home. *Which is better anyway,* he thought as the unmarked police car rolled to a stop beside him. He climbed inside.

"Talk," he said as soon as his butt touched the seat.

Deputy Kelly Flowers pressed the accelerator and cleared his throat, not looking at Tyson. "Rich seems focused on Trey Cowan. He's got an investigator. I believe his name is—"

"Harry Davenport," Tyson said, holding up the card Dooby had given him. "What's his story?"

"Was a bouncer at Sammy's in Birmingham for a couple years."

"Nice place," Tyson said.

"Before that, he was in the army Ranger program."

"Great," Tyson said, taking a gulp of Sun Drop and belching. "Any chance Trey could be involved in Dr. Waters's murder?"

Kelly glanced at him. "Not that the sheriff's office is aware of." He seemed to be weighing whether to say anything more, no doubt remembering how their last ride had ended.

Tyson grinned at him. "Relax, Kelly. I'm not in the mood to teach any lessons today. And I don't have the time. But to respond to what you're no doubt thinking, I'm not aware of any involvement on Trey's part."

"I've heard he might have done a job for you a month or so before the murder."

"Who told you that?"

Kelly again glanced at Tyson. "His mother. Last time I was at Top O' the River. I'd eaten with some of the other officers. She asked whether I knew anything about Trey working for you."

"What did you tell her?"

"The truth. That I hadn't heard any such thing. Then she said Trey took a trip for three days in June and didn't tell anyone where he was going. He left his car here and must have driven something else. She was worried that he might have made a delivery for you."

Tyson frowned. "Even if she was worried, why would she tell you? Aren't you supposed to be an officer of the law?"

"Me and the Cowan family go way back. I'd never arrest Trey unless I was forced to. Trudy knows that."

"Does she also know that you work for me?"

"Of course not," Kelly said. "Nobody knows that."

For a moment, there was silence, and then Kelly asked the question hanging in the air. "Tyson, did Trey make a run for you?"

"No," Tyson answered.

"Then where'd he go?"

"Beats the hell out of me. Doesn't his father live in Florida?"

"Yeah, but according to Trudy, Trey won't have anything to do with him."

"Maybe not," Tyson said. "But money is a strange motivator."

"What does that mean?"

"Maybe the golden boy wanted some dough? Maybe he borrowed fifteen grand from his old man so he could pay Waylon Pike to kill Waters?" Tyson chuckled. "Wouldn't that be some shit?"

"You don't really believe that, do you?" Kelly asked.

Tyson's grin faded away. "Do you really think I'd tell you what I believe, Kelly?" Tyson waited a beat and changed the subject. "What's Rich up to? What's the scuttlebutt in the office?"

"He shook everyone up with his press conference today, which immediately led to a gag order from Judge Conrad."

"Do the sheriff and the district attorney still feel confident in a conviction?"

"Yes, but they're concerned about Pike."

"Why?"

"He's a convicted felon, just like Rich said on television today. They're concerned about his credibility."

"Don't they have more?"

"Of course. They have motive out the ying-yang with Dr. Waters's affair and his threat to file for divorce. Plus, no one had more contact with Pike than Jana Waters. *And* she's one of the richest women in town, and she did take out $15,000 cash from the bank the day before the murder."

"Sounds rock solid to me. Jason Rich is going to have to be a magician to get his sister out of that."

"He's not going to roll over. That seems pretty clear."

"Maybe not," Tyson said. "And as long as he keeps his word about not implicating me, I don't care what he does. Hell, I almost hope he wins."

"You're not serious?" Kelly asked.

Tyson thumped the deputy on the side of the head with his index finger like he might be a five-year-old kid acting up. "You're not going to make me beat your ass, are you, Kelly?"

"No, sir," Kelly said.

"Good."

"Now, is there anything else you can tell me about what's going on with Jana's lawyer?"

Kelly rubbed the side of his head. "He's receiving a public reprimand by the Alabama State Bar in a few days at their monthly meeting in Montgomery."

"Really?" Tyson asked. "Montgomery, huh?"

"Yes. Rich had to go to rehab for ninety days for being drunk during a deposition. The reprimand deals with that. Apparently, he has to stand before all the bar commissioners while they publicly shame him." Kelly whistled through his teeth. "Sounds awful."

"It does," Tyson said.

And it also sounds like an opportunity, he thought.

41

Jason found Knox Rogers sitting by himself on a wooden bench on the outside patio of Yellowhammer Brewing. The attorney had salt-and-pepper hair and sported large circular glasses, faded jeans, and a white button-down with the sleeves rolled up. He had what looked like a case file laid out on the table and was marking medical records with a yellow highlighter. As Jason approached, the man leaned back and held his glasses out from him.

"Well, God-a-mighty," Knox said. "You look just like your billboard."

Jason sat on the other side of the bench and extended his hand. "Jason Rich."

"Knox Rogers," he said, taking a long sip from his glass. "Really. I think that's the same suit and tie that's on the one on the parkway." He winked. "I passed it on the way here."

"My wardrobe is pretty limited right now," Jason said. "Thanks for making time for me."

"I'd say get a beer, but I suspect you probably shouldn't be doing that."

Jason tensed. "You know . . . about my problem."

"I've got a lot of lawyer friends in Birmingham," Knox said.

"Why'd you insist on meeting here then?"

"Because I come here every Tuesday or Wednesday afternoon, depending on my trial schedule, for a couple of india pale ales and some good old vitamin D while I think through whatever case is on my mind. There's never anyone here in the middle of the day, and I didn't want anyone in my office to know that we were meeting. I doubt anyone here cares."

Jason glanced around and saw a couple of bearded guys drinking beer inside and a woman with purple streaks in her hair nursing a cold pint and working on a laptop at one of the inside tables. No one else was outside.

"I doubt anyone does," Jason agreed.

"So what can I do for you?" Knox asked. "I assume that you're interested in what I can tell you about the medical malpractice action that the Cowan family brought against Dr. Waters." He took a sip of beer, his eyes never leaving Jason's. "I also assume that you're looking at either Trey Cowan or perhaps his mother, Trudy, as an alternative suspect. Someone else to shine the spotlight on so the jury might be confused enough by the prosecution's evidence to find reasonable doubt." He set his glass down. "Sound close?"

Jason gave him a sheepish smile. "You get right to the heart of it, don't you?"

"I don't suffer fools, and my time is valuable." His tone was matter of fact and bordering on arrogant. Jason had heard that Knox Rogers was able to get juries to eat out of his hand, but that he could be intimidating to other attorneys. *Especially those that don't know what they're doing,* Jason thought.

"I understand," he said. "And you're correct. I want to know what you can tell me about the med mal case. The Cowan family and especially Trey would seem to have a lot of reason to be mad at Dr. Waters. Is that a fair assessment?"

"Yes," Knox said, enveloping his pint glass with both hands and peering at the ale. "They were very angry, especially his mother. I remember it was difficult to get through her deposition. She kept yelling at Dr. Waters from across the table. Saying that he ruined her son's life." He looked up from the pint. "I'll get you a copy of the transcript."

Jason was shocked. "Thank you."

"You should also look at the trial transcript. I think we have a copy of it somewhere. After the jury returned a defense verdict, the Cowan family appealed, so we had to put the whole record before the appellate court, including the transcript. As I recollect, Trudy Cowan made similar comments during the trial. Her testimony was genuine. Very effective."

"What about Trey?"

He shook his head. "He was pitiful. Numb to everything, it seemed. I can't remember him saying anything other than he trusted that Dr. Waters would fix him, and he didn't."

"And the father?"

"A drunk. Smelled of alcohol on the day of his deposition. You'd know something about that, wouldn't you?"

Jason ground his teeth and tried to keep his temper in check. So far Knox Rogers had been of great help. He could endure a few wisecracks.

"I'm sorry, I couldn't resist." Knox took a sip of beer. "I like a cold one or a nip of whiskey as much as anyone else, but I have no respect for someone who would do that while representing a client's interests, especially during something as important as a deposition."

"My client wasn't compromised," Jason said, keeping his tone low. "Only my law license."

"So you say."

Jason crossed his arms and stared at the other man. "What can you tell me about the case? Why were the Cowans suing?"

"It was a surgical repair of a broken tibia. A routine operation in most cases, but infection is a possibility. With Trey Cowan, the hardware became infected."

"I've heard that Dr. Waters failed to follow up in a timely way."

"That was one of the allegations. He didn't come back to see Trey that afternoon or the next morning. He assigned it to a physician's assistant, and the PA forgot."

"Isn't that malpractice?"

"No," Knox said. "The patient was being followed by nurses as well as anesthesia. And the PA did see him the following morning, and antibiotics were ordered."

"Were they ordered soon enough?"

"That was the heart of the case. The plaintiff argued that there was an eight-hour delay without treatment, which was a breach of the applicable standard of care and which caused irreversible damage to Trey's leg."

"And the defense?"

"One . . ." He held up his index finger. " . . . that there was no substantive delay and any gap in time between treatment was within the standard of care. And two . . ." He held up a second finger. " . . . that even if there was a true eight-hour delay, the damage would have occurred regardless." He took a sip from his glass. "I'm fairly confident that it was the causation theory that sealed the deal for us. Only an infectious disease doctor could testify on whether earlier antibiotic treatment would have made a difference. We had such an expert, and the plaintiff didn't."

"Who was the plaintiff's lawyer?"

"Sean Calloway. He was a friend of the family and a local." Knox winked. "But he'd never handled a medical malpractice case, and it showed."

Jason gazed down at the picnic table, thinking of his own case and lack of experience handling criminal trials. Would he make a similar mistake in representing Jana?

"The family was too beholden to locals. They never should've let Braxton do that surgery. He was a good doctor, but they should've taken Trey to Birmingham. That's just my opinion."

"And they should've gotten a medical malpractice lawyer."

"Yes, they should've. Sean argued the hell out of that case. He did a good job and made us sweat out the jury's verdict. But, even if we would've lost the trial, I think we'd have gotten the verdict reversed due to his failure to have an infectious disease doc."

"Why did the Cowans appeal?"

"Desperation. When their motion for new trial was denied, it was the last avenue they had. They took it, but it was no use. That trial transcript was as clean as a whistle."

Jason gazed at the other attorney's half-drunk beer, taking it all in and thinking of something else. "Did you hear anything about Dr. Waters having an affair with a CRNA at the hospital? A woman named Colleen Maples?"

Knox grinned. "Yes, I did. And I was scared to death that his relationship with the nurse anesthetist was going to steamroll our case."

"Why?"

"Because they were heard arguing during the procedure. And when it was over, a nurse witnessed Braxton follow Maples down a hallway. She said the CRNA was crying."

"Jesus. Did any of that come into evidence?"

"No," Knox said. "Because the lawsuit centered around improper follow-up after the surgery and not anything that occurred during the surgery, we argued that any evidence of their personal relationship or an argument between them would be overly prejudicial."

"But did the argument have anything to do with *why* Braxton failed to follow up? Could he have been distracted?"

Knox grabbed his pint glass again with both hands and turned it back and forth in his hands. "Braxton denied that allegation."

"And Maples?"

"She said she couldn't remember what happened after the surgery."

"Did she deny an affair?"

"Yes. So did he."

Jason snorted. "Well, she perjured herself. She's now admitted to an affair in her statement to the police in our case."

"Not necessarily," Knox said. "The sexual relationship could have started after the malpractice case."

Jason raised his eyebrows. The crusty attorney's explanation was slippery and smart. *And probably what Colleen Maples will say . . .*

"But, I'll tell you, Mr. 1-800 Get Rich, I was worried as hell that she was going to change her tune at trial. Sean put her on his witness list, and when she was called to the stand, I held my breath when he asked her if she could remember anything about the day of surgery."

"But she stuck to her guns," Jason said.

"Yes, she did," Knox said.

"So, thinking back on it, what do you think happened?"

"Off the record?"

"Yes."

"I think he was screwing her brains out and they were in a lover's quarrel during the surgery. I think their fight did cause him to be distracted, and he failed to properly delegate his responsibilities to his PA, who didn't do a timely follow-up."

"But it didn't matter, because antibiotics earlier wouldn't have made a difference," Jason said.

"So said our infectious disease doctor . . . who we paid $1,000 an hour to testify."

"You don't believe him."

"I believe his opinions were supported by the medicine, yes. But . . . there was an argument to be made on the other side, and if it had been made . . ."

"Plaintiff's verdict?"

"Maybe," Knox said.

"Damn," Jason said. "Did the family sue their lawyer for legal malpractice?"

"I don't think so, but I know that Trudy Cowan reported Braxton and the CRNA to the Board of Medical Examiners and the Board of Nursing. I had to assist him through that too."

"Did the board find anything?"

"Not against Braxton," he said. "But . . . Maples was suspended for a short time and made to pay a fine."

"How could that be?"

He took a sip of beer. "I think she chose to respond herself without legal counsel. That was a mistake."

"And a reason to be mad at Braxton."

"Right. And since Braxton didn't leave your sister, that would be another reason for her to be angry."

"True," Jason said.

"So which alternative gives you a better chance?" Knox asked. "Maples or Cowan?"

"They're both appealing for different reasons."

Knox downed the rest of his pint. "Too bad the killer's confessed that your sister paid him to do it."

Any positive vibes Jason had begun to feel dissipated with the obvious reality check.

"Sorry," Knox said. "I'm going to get another beer. You want something?"

"Let me get it," Jason said. He ordered the beer and a water for himself and brought the drinks back to the table. He had one more line of questions he wanted to go down.

"Did you meet my sister during the trial?"

"Yes indeed. Jana Waters."

"And what'd you think of her?"

"Attractive, smart, and competitive. And she seemed to be one hundred percent behind her husband."

"Seemed to be? Why do you put it that way?"

"Because she had an obvious issue with Maples, which reared its head right before trial. When Maples was on the stand, I was just as scared of Jana doing or saying something stupid as I was of what Maples might say. Your sister is a volatile woman. A few days before the trial started, I met them both at Braxton's office to go over the jury venire list and talk about our witnesses. When it got time to discuss Maples, she threw a fit and started asking Braxton where in his office he'd screwed her. She went from one piece of furniture to the next, just ranting at him, telling him that his dalliances were going to cost them everything. I finally asked her to leave."

"Great," Jason said and took a long sip of water.

"Sorry."

For a moment, they sat in silence and drank their beverages. "Let me ask you something," Knox finally said. "How'd you get bullied into taking this case?"

That was an interesting choice of words, and Jason almost smiled. "It's a long story."

"I bet," he said.

Jason stood to leave. "Mr. Rogers, I appreciate your time. When your office has those deposition and trial transcripts ready, I'll send a runner to get them and obviously pay for the copying costs and any time associated with putting that together."

"I think we have all that stored electronically. I'll send you a couple thumb drives. That work?"

"Perfect." Jason paused and gazed down at the veteran lawyer. "Can I ask you something?"

"Shoot."

"Why are you helping me? I can see in your eyes and tone that you don't think much of me as a lawyer or person."

Knox crossed his legs. "Because Braxton Waters was my client, and I liked him."

"I may be representing his killer."

Knox's eyes flickered. "Well, I can tell by your demeanor and tone that you don't believe that. Besides, that handyman killed him. You're representing the person accused of hiring the man to do the deed."

"Not much of a distinction in the criminal world. She'll be sentenced to death if found guilty."

"It'll make a difference to the jury," he said. "I worked a couple years in the Madison County District Attorney's office before branching off into civil work. I tried a lot of criminal cases as a prosecutor. We didn't have a lot of murder cases, but we had a few, and one was a murder-for-hire case involving coconspirators." He gazed up at the sky. "The defense attorneys had a field day with the deal we'd cut with the killer, and I suspect you will too." He chuckled. "Judging by your press conference yesterday, it sounds like you're already digging in. I imagine Judge Conrad gave you a tongue-lashing after that?"

"He sure did," Jason said.

"He's a good judge. We had Barber on our case, a space cadet. Conrad may be a former prosecutor, but he's fair and smart as hell."

"That's good to hear." Jason took a step backward. "Mr. Rogers . . ."

"Call me Knox."

"Knox, I can't thank you enough."

The other attorney took a sip of beer and stood. He extended his hand and Jason shook it. "You thank me by finding out what really happened to Dr. Waters. Win, lose, or draw, you hear?"

Jason nodded. "Yes, sir."

42

Trey Cowan sat on his customary stool at the Brick and stared at the television screen. The Braves were playing, and Trey typically got into the cat and mouse of a baseball game, but tonight he wasn't interested. The Dodgers had scored eight runs in the second inning, and since then, the contest had been a rout. Trey finished off his mug of Miller Lite and set the glass down on the counter.

"Another?" the bartender asked.

Trey shook his head. "No thanks. Maybe some water for the road."

"Sure thing." The woman behind the bar, Teresa, was good natured but left Trey alone. No questions about his sporting past, which was always a relief.

"Here you go," she said.

"Thanks." Trey took the Styrofoam cup of water and pushed himself off the stool. He trudged up the steps, making sure to have a firm grasp on the railing. As he did, he felt their eyes on him. The Brick had a bar area in the back of the sunken room, and then tables and booths for people and families to eat, each with its own television. At 8:00 p.m., the place was still pretty full, and he knew that there were folks talking about him as he left.

"He was such a good quarterback."

"Scholarship offers to Bama and Auburn."

"Remember when Coach Saban came and watched him play?"

"So sad."

"Sad."

"Sad."

"Sad."

Trey stepped out onto the sidewalk and gazed up Gunter Avenue. He'd been in the bar since 4:30, and he felt the buzz of at least five beers. Still, he'd paced himself, so he wasn't drunk. He hardly ever talked to anyone at the Brick, especially since Waylon Pike's arrest, but he enjoyed the background noise. It was better than the utter quiet of his apartment and more relaxing, at least to him, than being out on the lake.

Oh, he loved the water. But sometimes, when he was feeling the voices in his head telling him how sad his life had become, he wanted to jump out of whatever craft he was in and sink to the dirty bottom. Wouldn't that be an honorable way to go? *A boating accident claims the life of former five-star quarterback and major league prospect Trey Cowan.*

He didn't have those types of thoughts in the Brick. At least, not many of them. He could go in there and pretty much be left alone. He felt the stares leaving, but that was it. But he had to admit, he missed Waylon. He hadn't pestered Trey with questions about the past. Only the future.

And the future is now, he thought, remembering his last conversation with Waylon Pike the evening of July 3.

Trey limped his way down to Scott Street and crossed over. Once he was away from the downtown traffic, he picked up his pace, the limp gone. Trey walked much better than he let on, but he didn't want to make that public knowledge. *Especially now . . . ,* he thought.

Trey was quiet and had never been much of a student, but he wasn't stupid. Revenge was a powerful motive for murder. He'd also been seen with Waylon at the Brick. He'd mostly told the police the truth about their interactions.

But he had omitted one rather large detail.

Trey trotted up the stairs to his apartment. His leg felt pretty good, and there were times when he thought he might give it a go next spring. Folks in town mainly remembered him as a football star, but he'd been an All-State center fielder on the high school baseball team his last two years. He figured he could probably get a tryout with several minor league teams. He couldn't run well, but he could still hit. There might be a spot for a designated hitter or maybe a first baseman.

When he reached the door to his place, he put the key in but saw that it was already unlocked. He felt his heart flicker and stepped inside. A trail of clothes led to the bedroom.

When he saw her, his smile widened into a grin.

Colleen Maples had brown hair that she normally kept up in a ponytail when she was working. She was ten years older than Trey, which made their relationship all the hotter. She had tan skin that she kept golden brown by lying out on her boathouse dock. He hadn't been out to her place, though. When they got together, it was always here.

"Where'd you park this time?" Trey asked.

"In the Old Town Stock House lot. I had a couple drinks with friends and told them I was meeting someone. Once they'd left, I put on my cap and hoodie and walked this way."

"Stealth," Trey said, adding, "You look good in my old jersey."

She winked at him. Covering her chest, she wore his mesh crimson-and-white number 12 with *Guntersville High* embroidered across the front. She was lying on top of the covers with nothing on but the relic of Trey's past. "You like?"

Trey nodded and began to take off his shirt. "Have you figured out what we're doing here?"

Colleen crawled to the end of the bed and began unbuttoning his jeans. "You know exactly what we're doing," she whispered in his ear.

Trey closed his eyes. For a split second, he pictured Waylon Pike as he'd last seen him at the Brick. Bright eyed. Eager. Determined.

I should have stopped it, he thought.

Then, as Colleen reached inside his pants, all conscious thought melted away.

43

An hour after receiving his reprimand from the commissioners of the Alabama State Bar, Jason sat in one of the bar's many conference rooms and gazed across a mahogany table at Ashley Sullivan, the president of the Lawyer Assistance Program. Sullivan wore a forest-green suit, which contrasted nicely with her thick red hair and freckles.

"So tell me how it's going?"

Jason gave his instinctual, trademark smile. "Great. Practice is thriving. I've moved back to Guntersville to be closer to family. Can't complain."

"That's not what I meant."

He peered down at the table. "I know."

"Mr. Rich, you were supposed to reach out to my office when you returned to practice. If you'd done so, I would have assigned you a mentor to check in with regarding your recovery. Someone who's been through what you have."

He fiddled with his hands.

"Have you fallen off the wagon yet?"

"No," Jason said, looking at her.

"Thought about it?"

"Every day."

She leaned across the table. "Jason, you can't do this alone. If you try, you'll eventually fail."

"Does my mentor have to be another lawyer?"

"This is the Lawyer Assistance Program. All of our members are attorneys. Besides, who better to know what you're going through than someone who's in the same profession."

Jason stood, then walked to a window that looked out on Dexter Avenue. He could see the columns of the Alabama Supreme Court building. "Did you watch the reprimand?"

"I did," she said, her voice matter of fact.

"Then you saw . . . or felt . . . the way my peers think about me."

"That's in your head, Jason. I've watched hundreds of those reprimands. They're all the same. A lot of folks look down. Some stare off into space. And others seem to get some kind of sick enjoyment out of seeing another lawyer suffer."

"And you?"

She stood and walked over to where he was standing. "I feel empathy."

"Why?"

"Because I know, if I hadn't gone to treatment, I would have been right there too. Being disciplined like you were today."

Jason groaned. "People have your back, Ashley. You're likeable. They wouldn't enjoy your shame like they did mine today."

"I didn't enjoy it."

He glanced at her. "Well, you were the only one."

She walked to the end of the table and took a seat. "Jason, if you don't take a mentor, I'm going to have to tell Ted that you're not cooperating. As I understand it, you haven't gone to an AA meeting either, correct?"

"Correct."

"And you aren't seeing a counselor."

"None of the above," he snapped.

"And what about your counselor from the PAC?"

"We had one call. A week out of rehab."

"Well . . . that's good. What'd she say?"

"That it was unwise to take on my sister's murder case. Too stressful. Too much pressure. Too soon."

"I agree with her on all points," Ashley said.

"I figured you would, but Jana and my nieces are the only family I have, and there are extraneous circumstances."

"What are you talking about?"

He turned from the window. "I can't tell you. But Jana didn't have many other alternatives. I give her the best shot at a fair trial."

Ashley crossed her arms. "Jason, you have to know that the bar is watching you like a hawk. Ted is salivating for another chance to nail you, and I'm sure Winthrop Brooks would like nothing better than to enforce the disciplinary commission's zero-tolerance policy. If I tell them that you're not cooperating with our program . . ."

Jason sat down. "How can I prevent that?"

"At the very least, by meeting with one of our mentors."

"Ashley, I don't trust other lawyers. Especially anyone reporting directly to the bar. Seems like a recipe for failure. You saw how they were in there?"

"You didn't look all that apologetic."

"I didn't want to give Ted or Winthrop Brooks or any of the commissioners the satisfaction. I know I messed up, but they've been waiting for years to have me by the balls . . ." He looked away. "I'm sorry. I—"

"Don't worry about it."

For a moment, there was silence. "Are you familiar with the All Steak restaurant in Cullman?" Ashley asked.

Jason cocked his head. "Yes. I had a client who was in a trucking accident in Cullman. I met him for dinner once at the All Steak. Great orange rolls."

"That's the place. I want you to meet me for lunch there next week. How does Wednesday at one sound?"

216

Jason checked his phone, and the day appeared clear. "That'll work. What's this about?"

"Simple," she said. "Cullman is only thirty minutes from Guntersville."

"I still don't get it," Jason said.

Ashley folded her arms. "I'm going to be your mentor."

44

Jason decided to get a pizza at Sa Za in downtown Montgomery. He'd almost asked Ashley Sullivan if she wanted to join him but thought better of it. She'd already done him a huge favor, and he didn't want to screw anything up.

Still, he had to admit that he liked the redheaded attorney from Cullman. She seemed to care, which was a far cry from how he felt anyone else connected to the state bar felt about him. Of course, he was going to have to jump through a few hoops if he was to keep Ashley as his mentor, starting with going to at least one AA meeting between now and next Wednesday and finding a local therapist in Marshall County.

Jason gazed at the draft beer selection on his menu. What would be better right now than three or four IPAs and a pizza followed by about twelve hours of sleep at the Renaissance Hotel across the street? He remembered the sight and scent of the beer that Knox Rogers had been drinking at Yellowhammer Brewing, and his mouth watered.

Instead, he ordered unsweet tea with a calzone and a Caesar salad. He ate quickly while sending check-in texts to Nola and Niecy. He'd hoped to stop off at Birmingham-Southern on his way home and see Niecy, but she texted back that she was studying for a test and couldn't spare any time. Things were still icy between the two of them, but she had thanked him for taking in Nola at Mill Creek and had begrudgingly admitted that security for her at college was probably a good thing for now.

He'd made millions as an attorney and hadn't spent much of his fortune. He had to protect his family regardless of the cost.

As he sent back a *no problem* response to Niecy, a man sat down across from him and put both elbows on the table. Jason felt the hairs on his arms stand up. "What do you want?"

"To remind you of our deal." Tyson Cade grinned. When the waitress walked by, she asked if he'd be joining Jason, and Tyson said yes. He proceeded to order a large pepperoni and a draft beer but asked that she make his pizza to go. Once she was gone, Tyson looked at Jason. "Thanks for the treat."

"I don't need a reminder," Jason said, irritated by the intrusion and cursing himself for not bringing any security with him.

"I think you do," Tyson said. "I've seen all the people you've hired to look after your place. I assume that was because of our encounter."

"You assume right," Jason said. "But that doesn't mean I'm planning to back out on our deal. On the contrary, I'm planning to fulfill my end of the bargain."

"Jana won't testify."

"Not a chance."

"Humor me," Tyson said. "How do you plan on defending the murder charge if your sister doesn't testify?"

"I don't know," Jason answered, figuring honesty was the best policy in this instance. "But testifying that she paid money to a drug dealer as a down payment on the cocaine she'd purchased doesn't sound like a great alternative. Regardless of the murder charge, that puts her in jail for at least five years." He leaned closer to Cade and spoke in a low tone. "In other words, if she testifies, she guarantees herself a jail sentence. I may not have much criminal defense experience, but I know that would be unwise."

Tyson waited while the waitress placed his beer in front of him. Then he took a long pull from the mug. "I'm feeling better already," he said.

"Good. Then why don't you get out of here."

Tyson's grin faded. "Because there's something else I want from you."

"What's that?"

"Fifty thousand dollars."

"*What?*"

"You heard me. Fifty grand. Your sister owes me quite a bit of money for her coke habit. I've got some angry suppliers that haven't been paid."

"She paid you fifteen grand the night her husband was murdered. That's why she took out the money."

"Says who?"

Goose flesh broke out on Jason's arms. "You, I thought."

"I never said that. Is that what Jana told you?"

Jason kept his mouth shut as the waitress handed Tyson a box. He opened it and stuck a slice in his mouth.

"You're playing games with me," Jason said.

Tyson took his time as he chewed his food. When he was done, he downed the rest of his beer in one gulp. "That's not my style, Counselor." He got up and leaned close enough to where Jason could smell the alcohol on his breath. "Fifty grand cash. Meet me at the Alder Springs Grocery on Monday with it. Comprende?"

Jason found he'd lost his voice.

"Counselor? You care about those nieces?"

"Of course I do," he replied, his voice suddenly hoarse.

"Good. I'll see you on Monday."

45

An hour out of Montgomery, just south of Birmingham, Jason couldn't take it any longer. He got off at the Calera exit and stopped at a Chevron station that had a liquor store attached to it. He bought a pint of Jack Daniel's and a six-pack of Yuengling. Once back on the interstate, he opened the whiskey and held the bottle to his lips.

He'd been operating under the theory that Jana paid Tyson Cade $15,000 the night of the murder for cocaine because that's what Jana had told him.

But what if she's lying? What if she only paid Cade a few hundred bucks and bought herself some time with her body? Jason smelled the bottle but didn't drink.

What if she gave the fifteen grand to Waylon Pike?

The phone rang. He glanced at the screen on his Bluetooth radio and saw that it was Harry. He set the pint down in the cup holder and pushed the knob to answer the call.

"Yeah," he said, hearing the anxiety in his voice.

"J. R., it's me."

"You find Cowan's dad?"

"Yeah, boss. He's working a strip mall job on Highway 30A near Water Sound."

"And?"

"No insurance policy. He sends a few hundred dollars to Trey from time to time, but that's it."

"What was he like?"

"A drunk. Had a case of beer in a cooler in the back of his truck and drank three cans of Coors Light while we talked."

"Did he say anything about the mother?"

"Just that Trey's accident was the end for them. They'd put everything into his career. Every dime they had for football camps and travel ball and lessons. And they missed the big payoff. And I quote, 'All because Braxton Waters was too busy screwing his CRNA to pay attention to my son at the hospital.'"

"He said that."

"His exact words."

"Well, the Cowans all have motive," Jason said, his voice weak.

"But none of them have a pot to piss in. No way they could have cobbled together fifteen grand in cash."

"Yeah, I get it. Thanks for tracking him down."

"You all right, J. R.? You sound . . . off," Harry said.

Jason glanced at the pint of whiskey and the six-pack. "No, I'm fine."

"How'd the reprimand go?"

"It sucked," he said. "And I had another run-in with Tyson Cade."

"In Montgomery? How? Didn't you have security?"

"No."

"What?"

"I didn't think there was any way he'd follow me to Montgomery, so I asked the guards to stay at home with Nola and in Birmingham with Niecy." Jason again glanced at the whiskey. "Cade must have tailed me down here, or maybe he had someone verify where I'd be. The guy does his research."

"What did he want?"

"Money. Fifty grand. He says Jana didn't pay him the 15K on the night of the murder. He's noticed all I've spent on security and wants me to make him whole."

There was silence on the other end of the line and then a long whistle. "Jesus. What are you going to do? If you pay him now, he's not going to stop."

"What choice do I have? If I don't pay him, he may hurt my nieces."

"That's why you've spent all that dough on security. If you'd brought some for yourself today, then maybe Cade wouldn't have gotten so close to you."

Jason looked to his right and saw one of his billboards in the distance. He glared at his grinning mug as he passed. "Let's face it, Harry. I can pay for all the security in the world. But if I cross this guy, he's going to eventually kill me or hurt or kill someone I love."

Harry didn't respond, and Jason knew it was an implied concession.

"I've got to go," he said.

"You OK, boss?"

Jason hung up without answering. As he passed another billboard advising any passerby to call 1-800 GET RICH, he grabbed the pint and again pressed it to his lips.

This time, he turned it up and took a long swig, wincing as the brown liquid burned his throat. He couldn't believe he'd been so stupid.

"Jana's lying," he whispered, taking another sip of Jack Daniel's.

About the money . . . about her relationship with Pike . . .

. . . about everything.

46

He woke up with the glare of the rising sun in his face and the sound of an angry woman's voice.

"Get up, shitbird."

Jason turned toward the sound just in time to see a bucket of water being hurled at him.

Drenched, he shot to his feet, which sent a wave of nausea through his body that made him bend over and clutch his knees. "Damnit, Chase. What the hell are you doing?"

"You tell me, drunko! Spending the night in your court clothes on the dock with an empty bottle of Jack and a half-drunk carton of beer," she yelled. She wore a white tank top, shorts, and a baseball cap, appearing to have just come in from her morning kayak ride. "I ought to push you in the lake."

"Well, you've already ruined my suit."

"Are you kidding? Even with the lake on you, you reek of bourbon and beer. You smell like a damn brewery." She put her hands on her hips. "You didn't fall off the wagon. You jumped."

Jason took in a deep breath, tried to straighten up, and then bent over again. Finally, unable to control his stomach, he dropped to his knees and hung his head over the edge of the dock, puking into the water.

"Good grief, Jason," she said.

He threw up again. And then again. "Please go away."

"It's 6:15 in the morning, and Nola will be getting up soon. Don't let her see you like this. She's got enough on her plate and doesn't need to know that her uncle's a drunk."

Jason gritted his teeth. "Go away, Chase. Please."

Another round of nausea gripped him, and he vomited again. When it ended, he looked in Chase's direction, but she was gone.

"Damnit," he whispered as he beat his fists on the dock.

47

At 9:00 a.m., Jason walked through the doors of the sheriff's office. A few minutes later, he was shown into the consultation room. Jana wasn't there yet, but he was told they would bring her in shortly.

Jason waited, trying not to think about his pulsing hangover, which still hadn't gone away after three cups of coffee and several Aleve. Once Jana was shown in, Jason held his tongue until the officers exited the room. When they were alone, it was all he could do to keep his voice in check.

"I want you to tell me what you did with the $15,000 you took from the bank the day before Braxton was murdered."

She blinked. "I told you. I gave it to one of Tyson's men at the strip mall down from Fire by the Lake."

"All of it or some of it?"

"I can't remember."

"Bullshit. You're lying to me. I want to know exactly what you did with that money."

She wrung her hands, and Jason couldn't tell whether it was an act or genuine emotion being expressed. Like everything with his sister, he wasn't sure. "It was a lot of cash, J. J. I think I took out about five grand."

"Weren't you keeping up with it? You owed the bastard fifty thousand, didn't you?"

"All I could think about was doing a line of coke, OK?"

"I don't believe you."

"Well, fuck you then. I don't care."

"If that's the case, then what happened to the rest of the money?"

"It should still be in an envelope in my car."

"Well, it's not, Jana. I've looked at all the inventories. Of your house. Your car. Everything. There was no cash found in your vehicle."

"Then it was stolen, like I said before. I bet one of the sheriff's deputies took it."

"Don't be ridiculous." He took a seat across from her. "What did you do with it?"

"I told you, I left it in my car."

"Is it possible that Waylon Pike could have gotten the cash from your car? Is it possible that he thought you'd left it there for him to keep if he killed Braxton?"

She shook her head but said nothing.

"Are you sure?"

"Yes."

"Did you ever tell Waylon Pike you wanted him to kill Braxton?"

She blinked but didn't answer.

"Jana?"

"I mean, I may have kidded with him some."

"Are you serious?"

"Yes, but all wives do that. Braxton was screwing around on me. I was lonely. Waylon was at the house a lot. I might have had a couple glasses of wine and said something like 'I wish you'd kill Braxton' or something like that."

"So his statement's true?"

"No, it's not."

"The part about you asking him to kill Braxton in the past." He reached into his briefcase and pulled it out. "This part here. 'On several occasions, Ms. Rich told me that she wanted me to kill her husband.'"

"I guess so, but he knew I was joking."

"Did you ever put a number on it? Did you ever tell him you'd pay him $15,000 to kill Braxton?"

Her eyes fluttered up at the ceiling. "I may have asked him how much killing Braxton was worth, and he may have mentioned a number like that."

"Good lord. You did it, didn't you? You paid that sonofabitch to kill Braxton."

"No, I did not. I've been framed. I definitely joked with Waylon about it, but I would have never gone through with something so horrible. I got to where I hated Braxton, but I would never have taken my girls' father away from them."

"Did you tell Waylon anything on July 3 and 4 that might have made him believe you were serious about wanting him to kill Braxton?"

"Not that I can recall," she said.

"That's not good enough, Jana."

"No," she said.

"Is it possible that Waylon Pike found that money in your car and felt like you were making the payoff for him to kill Braxton?"

"No," Jana said, and Jason was relieved that she hadn't hesitated. "I think Waylon must have told someone else about my jokes, and he and that person set me up to take the fall. Someone who had as much or more reason to want Braxton dead than me."

"Who could that be? I've investigated Trey Cowan and his family, and they don't have the money."

"What about the bitch Braxton was screwing?"

"Colleen Maples," Jason said. "She could have paid Pike, but have you ever known the two of them to be around each other?"

"No."

"And hadn't Colleen and Braxton been old news for a while? What would prompt Colleen to have wanted him dead so long after their breakup?"

"Didn't you say she sent him a text a couple hours before he was killed?" Jana asked. "Wasn't that the last text he received?"

Jason had gone over the state's investigator's report with Jana, and he was impressed with her recall. "Yes and yes."

"She clearly wasn't over him."

"But Braxton was about to divorce you. He'd met with an attorney. He'd told you about his plan in front of the girls. Wouldn't that have allowed Colleen to get back in the picture?"

"Based on her text, it doesn't sound like he'd told Colleen anything about the divorce."

Jason peered down at the table. On this point, Jana was right.

"Besides, there's no way he'd have gone through with it."

Jason frowned at her. "Jana, come on. He had an attorney. He told you he was going to file, and he said so in front of Niecy and Nola. Isn't it delusional on your part to think he wasn't going to follow through with it?"

"OK, this meeting is over." She got up and walked toward the door, then hit it three times.

"Jana, are you telling me everything about what you did with the money?"

She didn't answer. "I'm tired of being treated like a liar."

"You are a liar, Jana. Were you screwing Waylon Pike? He says you were in his statement. Is that true or false?"

A deputy opened the door, and Jana held out her hands to be cuffed again.

"Jana?"

She glared at him. "Time's up."

Then, seconds later, she was gone.

48

Jason waited for Colleen Maples in the parking lot of Marshall Medical Center North. He'd picked up a bacon burger, fries, and a chocolate shake from one of his favorite high school greasy spoons, Char Burger off Highway 69, and was chowing down in the front seat of the Porsche while watching the door to the surgery center. It was 11:30 a.m., and he was hoping to catch the CRNA on her lunch break.

With his first few bites of the combo, his headache had begun to dissipate, and now, as he wolfed down the last of the bun and nibbled on the final few fries, he finally felt alive again.

And guilty as hell. *What in the world happened last night?*

It was like he shut down after Cade's demand for money, and Harry's confirmation that Cowan wasn't a viable alternative sent him over the line. He'd relapsed, which if he thought about it, wasn't all that surprising given the stress he was under.

And the failure to do what I'm supposed to be doing.

Ashley Sullivan was right. Michal was right. Izzy. Everyone. His rehabilitation hadn't ended when he'd walked out of the Perdido Addiction Center. It had only begun. If he was serious about staying sober and having some semblance of a healthy life, he was going to have to take his recovery seriously. He'd been lucky last night. He'd driven home drunk over a hundred miles. What if he'd been stopped by a cop? Gotten a DUI?

What if Nola had found him passed out on the dock? He'd been able to shower and shave before she'd gotten up, but what if he hadn't been so fortunate? His niece was beginning to trust him. Talk to him. All of that would've been pissed away with one awful mistake.

I can't make another one.

As he drank the last of his shake, he saw a woman exit the doors wearing green scrubs. She had brown hair, and her appearance matched the photographs that Harry had taken. Jason watched her approach the parking lot. She clicked a keyless entry device, and Jason heard the familiar beep of a car opening.

He hopped out of the Porsche and walked straight toward her. "Ms. Maples?"

She glanced at him but then picked up her pace. She stopped at a silver BMW 3 Series sedan. As she started to grab the handle, Jason stepped in front of her and blocked her path.

"Two minutes, Ms. Maples."

"If you don't get out of my way, I'm going to scream."

"Ms. Maples, I need to ask you a few questions about your relationship with—"

Colleen Maples let out a long screeching wail that sent a shiver down Jason's spine. Instinctively, he stepped to his left and held up his hands.

She opened the door and turned the ignition, pulling out of her parking place and burning rubber down the aisle.

"Damnit," Jason said under his breath. As he walked back to his car, he saw the BMW turning and heading right for him.

He stopped, wondering for a split second if she was going to hit him. Instead, she pulled beside him and rolled down her window. "I have nothing to say to you, Mr. Rich. I've said my piece to Sergeant Daniels, and I'm sure you have that statement. I've also spoken with your investigator, Mr. Davenport."

"Ms. Maples, my sister is innocent." He knew it sounded weak and lame, but it was all he could think to say.

"You aren't very convincing." Then she rolled up her window and sped away.

Jason looked around the parking lot, feeling ridiculous as he began to trudge back to his car. As he was about to get in, he heard a high-pitched voice behind him.

"She's a bitch."

He turned and saw a woman wearing scrubs and glasses.

"Who?" Jason asked.

"Maples," the lady said. "No one here likes her."

Jason smiled at the woman, who was pushing it to hit five feet tall and might weigh a hundred pounds soaking wet. She had whitish-gray hair cut short, and her walk was more of a waddle. If he had to guess, he figured she was in her late seventies.

"My name's Jason Rich," he said.

"Beverly Thacker," the woman said.

Miracles never cease, Jason thought, feeling a rush of excitement. It was Braxton's nurse. The one Harry said was always in surgery. "Ms. Thacker, I've been trying to reach you."

She squinted at him. "You can call me Bev. And I'm sorry to have put your investigator off. But my work takes priority, you understand?"

"Yes, ma'am."

She cocked her head. "You think all those billboards are worth it?"

Jason decided against bullshit and answered her straight up. "Bev, I wish I could buy a thousand more."

At this, she smiled. "I loved Dr. Waters. Everyone here did. He was one of the good ones. Always called me 'Dr. Bev,' because I've been a nurse so long."

"And how long is that?"

"Fifty-four years."

"Holy moly. I would have figured that was your age."

Her smile widened. "You're good."

"How long did you work for Dr. Waters?"

"I was his circulating nurse for fifteen years."

"Did you work mostly at the hospital then, in the operating room?"

"Yes. I normally circulated on Mondays and Wednesdays for Dr. Waters and Tuesdays and Thursdays for his partner, Dr. Kruza. I spent Fridays at the practice's office."

"And since his death?"

"Same schedule for Dr. Kruza, and I've been filling in at the hospital as needed."

Jason pondered her comments, choosing his next question carefully. "Can I ask you what everyone thought of Dr. Waters's wife?"

"Honest?"

"Yes, of course."

"The times I saw her, she was always dressed to the nines and very nice. A beautiful woman, mind you."

"But . . . ," Jason pressed.

"But if you listen to the gossip I've gotten here and there from other nurses and even some of the things Dr. Waters would say . . ." She trailed off.

"Go on. You're not going to offend me."

"She's batshit crazy, pardon my French." Bev shrugged. "No offense."

"None taken," Jason said. "Were you surprised that she was arrested for his murder?"

She let out a low whistle. "Honestly, kid, I was so shocked by Dr. Waters being killed that I didn't have much left in the tank to be surprised by who killed him. I mean, I heard they were having problems but not to the point of murder."

"Did you ever hear that he was having an affair with Maples?"

"Oh, yeah," she said. "That was common knowledge among the nursing staff."

"Did you ever see them . . . together?"

"Once."

Jason felt a trickle of energy. "When and where?"

"In the doctors' lounge. I went in there because I needed to ask Dr. Waters a question and walked right in on them."

"What were they doing?"

"What do you youngsters call it these days? 'The nasty.'"

Jason grinned. He hadn't called having sex "the nasty" in two decades, but he decided to be agreeable. "Yes, ma'am. So you saw them . . . having sex?"

"Does a bear poop in the woods? They were under the covers of the cot, but I could tell they were in there humping. It's been a long time for this old dog, but not that long. I still know what it looks like."

"Yes, ma'am. Bev, if I called you as a witness at trial, would you mind testifying to what you saw Maples and Dr. Waters doing?"

She looked down at the ground and back at the hospital building. "You know what? Why not? If you subpoena me, I'll have to tell the truth, right?"

"Yes, ma'am."

"I think everyone around here would probably give me a parade if I embarrassed Maples. She's bad news. A mediocre CRNA and nasty to the staff. I never understood what Dr. Waters saw in her . . . but I suspect her talents lay elsewhere . . . if you get my drift."

Jason chuckled. "I do."

"When is the trial?"

"October 22, so a little less than two months from now. I'll make sure to serve you with a subpoena a week before trial."

"It's a date then." She started to walk away.

"Bev," Jason called out, "is there anything else you can tell me about Colleen Maples? Or Dr. Waters? Or my sister? Anything at all that you think might be relevant. I hate to even ask since you've already been so helpful, but . . ."

"But you did." She kept a poker face for a second. "I don't mind your questions, kid."

"Well . . . is there anything else?"

"Yeah. They broke up on the day of Trey Cowan's surgery."

A jolt of energy surged through Jason's body. "How do you know that?"

"Because I was the circulator for the procedure. I could hear them talking back and forth. They were whispering, but I heard one part for sure."

"What was that?"

"When she told him that he had to make a choice between her or Ms. Waters."

"And what did he say?"

"He said, 'You know I can't do anything now.'"

"Did he appear distracted during the operation?"

"Yes. But he performed a good surgery." She looked down at the ground. "I think he was distracted afterward."

Jason thought back to what Knox Rogers had told him. About the failure to order antibiotics for the infection. "Did you take care of Trey in the hospital?"

"Only in the OR. Once he was out, we were on to the next patient."

"Thank you, Bev. Is there anything else?"

She took a step closer to him and spoke in a low tone, looking behind her before she did. "There was a board of nursing investigation against Maples. She was suspended for three months and put on probation for a year. Don't get me wrong. I've never liked her, and I loved Dr. Waters. But I . . . and a lot of us . . . thought that was unfair. Dr. Waters got off scot-free and Maples got hammered for her role. And I have to say this, Maples has been better since she returned. Still a bitch, but not near as bad as before. I think the investigation against her mellowed her out. I've heard her in staff meetings express deep regret for how she behaved during Cowan's surgery."

Jason also looked down at the ground. That was interesting, and the nursing investigation and discipline along with her being a jilted lover would give Maples ample motive to want to hurt Dr. Waters. But he knew a lot of this already, and there was still no connection to Waylon Pike.

"I almost hate to ask you anything else," he said.

"But you want to know if I might know one more thing, right?"

"Do you?"

"Well . . . I'm not sure I should say."

"Please, Bev, anything you think might be important could be very significant to my sister's defense."

"All right, about two years ago, I was working at the office on a Friday and I caught Dr. Waters in his office with another woman. Not Maples and not his wife."

"Were they . . . doing the nasty?" Jason asked.

"Not at that moment, but he was groping her pretty good, and her shirt was off."

"Can you identify this woman?"

She snapped her fingers. "That's just it. I remember that I recognized her, but I can't think of the name right now. I'm old and don't remember things like I used to."

So Braxton was messing around with more than one woman, Jason thought. He held out a business card, which she clasped in her hand. "If you remember, will you call me?" Jason asked.

"Sure thing. I've enjoyed talking to you, Mr. Rich. You aren't near the asshole I thought you'd be."

Jason snickered. "Well, thanks. I guess."

She started to walk away, her gait wobbly and leaning a bit to the right as if there might be something wrong with her left hip or knee.

After a few steps, she glanced back at him. "Can I tell you one more thing that I just remembered?"

"Sure."

"I worked on July 5. Maples was on the schedule, but she didn't show. That wasn't like her. She never missed a procedure. I thought that was strange before I heard about Dr. Waters's death. Now it seems more strange."

Jason tried not to look too excited, but adrenaline was flooding his system. "Yes," he agreed. "Strange."

49

He was on the phone with Harry the second he got back on Highway 69. "It's a lead," he said.

"Jason, I agree that it's more than we had before you talked to this nurse, but there's still no connection to Pike."

"We're missing something," Jason said.

Silence and then, finally, acknowledgment. "OK, yes."

"You know what I'm going to want."

"Twenty-four seven surveillance of Maples?"

"Damn right. I think she's hiding something, Harry. And I have a feeling it's something big."

"On it, J. R."

———

As he passed Fire by the Lake, Jason saw the strip mall where Jana said she'd met one of Tyson Cade's men. He turned on his right-turn blinker and pulled into the lot. There was a Laundromat, a Little Caesars, and a boutique clothing store in the small strip mall. He parked and got out of the car, snapping photographs on his iPhone from every angle. The mall was about a hundred yards from a stoplight, and Jason wondered whether there was any video surveillance from the light.

Then he checked above each of the storefronts, noticing that they all seemed to have cameras of some sort. But how long was their reach?

Shay Lankford had provided her entire file on the case to Jason, so he knew she didn't have any video surveillance from any of these stores. It was worth a shot, so he went inside the Laundromat.

Thirty minutes later, he had what he expected. Each of the stores had video surveillance, but the footage was only kept for forty-eight to seventy-two hours and then taped over. All of it had been gone by the time the police had requested it a week later.

At least I know, Jason thought, as he pulled out of the mall.

Jason took in a deep breath and exhaled. He looked at the clock on the dash. It was 3:30 p.m. He could turn right and go back to the office or left and head back to Mill Creek. Without conscious thought, he turned right onto Gunter Avenue. He was renting some space a block from the courthouse, but he passed by the building without slowing down.

He drove through town, staying on Highway 431 until he reached the brick sign marking the location of Guntersville High School. Jason turned into the parking lot and found a place near the entrance. At this time of day, most of the students had cleared out. The football team was practicing, as were the cheerleaders, but Jason didn't see any other activity. He took a deep breath and walked through the front doors of the public high school that he hadn't attended. He asked a guard where room 21 was located, and then he followed the instructions.

When he walked through the door, he saw at least fifteen people of all ages sitting in a circle in plastic chairs. Jason kept his head lowered and sat down. He wanted to bolt, but he knew he had to get this done.

Seconds later, he heard a male voice welcome everyone to the week's meeting and thank them for attending. "Who wants to go first?" he asked.

Jason didn't raise his hand and kept his eyes downward.

"OK, great. Please proceed," the man said.

When the woman started talking, Jason's eyes shot up from the floor in shock and bewilderment.

"My name is Chase," she said, looking straight at Jason. "And I'm an addict . . ."

50

When the meeting was over, Jason waited outside in the hallway for Chase. She glanced at him as she exited the room but walked past him as if he weren't there.

"Chase, wait," he said, trotting to catch up with her.

They passed a trophy case near the administrative office, and Jason caught her by the hand and stopped their momentum. Inside the glass partition was a photograph of Trey Cowan, holding a football up by his ear, grinning wide for the camera. Stenciled at the bottom of the picture frame were the words *Mr. Football, State of Alabama, 2013.*

"Were you living here then?" he asked her, pointing at the photograph.

"No," she said. "Why?"

"His family sued Braxton for malpractice. Surgery gone south. Ruined his career."

"Ah, and you think that he could perhaps have hired a hit man to kill your brother-in-law as opposed to the woman who was screwing said handyman and that was loaded with more money than she could possibly spend." She started walking again, and Jason followed.

"You don't think much of Jana, do you?"

"Never have," Chase said. "She's a troublemaker. And she's always caused you problems. Even when y'all were kids." They reached her pickup truck, and she unlocked it.

"Chase, can we talk about what happened back there? I . . . had no idea you had a drug problem."

"That's because you didn't ask, Jason. You only think about you and your problems. You've barely asked me any questions about myself since you moved back to Mill Creek."

"That's not fair. I see you almost every day and I *have* asked questions. You don't say much. Never have."

"Whatever," she said, climbing back into the truck.

"Then let me make it up to you," he pleaded. "Dinner? Tonight? My treat?"

She gripped the steering wheel and looked out her windshield but made no move to start the truck.

"Please," Jason said. "It's been a weird couple of days . . . and I could sure use some company."

"Always about you, isn't it?"

He peered down at the ground. Maybe she had a point. "OK, I'll see you." He started to walk away, but her voice carried past him.

"I need to go home and feed my dogs. Meet me on my boathouse dock in an hour. Shorts and flops. Got it?"

"Got it. What do you have in mind?"

"You'll see."

———

Fifty-five minutes later, Jason walked down the Wittschen dock wearing a T-shirt, khaki Patagonia shorts, and flip-flops. He saw Chase fire up her Sea-Doo and drive it out of the slip, then stop by the side of the pier.

"Hop on," she said.

"Where are we going?" he asked.

"One of my favorite spots," she said as he climbed onto the back of the craft.

"Chase, don't you think we should have some security?"

She patted her pocket. "I've got a nine-millimeter in my shorts pocket and a Glock in the console. And I was also in the army and can take care of my damn self. Let's live a little, J. R."

He smiled. Outside of Harry, Chase was the only person who called him by his initials, and he had to admit that he sort of liked it. He didn't often feel badass in his life, but being called "J. R." kind of gave him a rush. He'd watched the old *Dallas* reruns as a stress reliever in law school and had loved the adventures of the ultimate TV villain, J. R. Ewing. Even in recent years, Jason still found himself drawn to the scandalous adventures of one of the richest TV families from the eighties.

They went under the bridge and picked up speed as they passed a small island and made their way up the main channel toward Scottsboro. Jason remembered some of the spots. Preston Island. Mint Creek. And, of course, Goose Pond. Chase got the Sea-Doo up to sixty miles per hour, and Jason closed his eyes and enjoyed the wind hitting his face.

As the watercraft slowed, Jason realized they were coming up on the tip of Goose Pond. He saw a marina and, in front of it, a wooden-looking shack with some tables in the back. He squinted and read a sign. **THE DOCKS.**

"What's this place?" he yelled over the sound of the engine, leaning close to Chase and breathing in the smell of fruity perfume tinged with sweat. A pleasant scent.

"My favorite restaurant," she said. "No bullshit. Just great food and the best view on the lake."

———

Fifteen minutes later, they were seated at a wrought iron table on the edge of the patio. It was the table closest to the lake. After they'd roped the Sea-Doo off on the pier, Chase had walked around to the front and said something to the manager, after telling Jason to have a seat where he was now. When she'd returned, he'd asked, "What'd you tell him?"

"That I wanted my usual spot."

"Come here a lot."

"At least once a week when the weather is warm. Always by boat or Sea-Doo. Sometimes the Tonidandel gang come with me."

"I can't believe those boys all moved back home."

"Well, I can. Something about Mill Creek. Even you, the billboard lawyer himself, back on the cove."

"My circumstances are a bit different. Are the brothers still crazy as hell?"

"As shithouse rats, but they are solid gold down deep where it counts. And you better be glad the Tonidandels like me. They don't give a damn about you, but they'll do anything I ask."

"Why's that?"

"Because I'm a veteran," she said. "All three brothers were, at one time or another, in the 101st Airborne—the Screaming Eagles—and Satch was a full colonel. All honorably discharged. All a bit fucked up with PTSD, and, like me, they're like Texas toilet paper."

Jason wrinkled his face.

"They don't take shit off nobody. Anyway, when I told them I served in the army and showed a few of my scars, it was like they accepted me as one of the boys. They invite me over to watch the Bama games, and, if anyone comes nosing around my house for any reason, they've got my back."

"God, country, and Alabama football."

"Roll Tide," she said, winking at him. "Honestly, though, Jason, the Tonidandels are good folks. And damn good friends."

"Have you been . . . more than friends with any of them?"

"None of your damn business."

He raised his eyebrows.

"Shut up and order."

Jason turned to see a man coming his way. He didn't have a pen or paper and took down what Jason said by memory. Jason ordered a rib eye steak, baked potato, and salad while Chase ordered the shrimp and grits.

"House specialty," she said.

"Well, you'll have to give me a bite."

For a few moments, they drank their drinks—ice water in plastic cups—and enjoyed the ambience of the quaint restaurant. A Kenny Chesney song, "No Shoes, No Socks, No Problems," played on the outside speakers, and Jason breathed in the simple elegance of folks enjoying a meal and company with an incredible wide view of the lake. The sun was beginning to set a deep orange out over the water.

"I became an alcoholic in the army," Chase said, her voice soft. "When we were in Afghanistan, we'd have layovers here and there, and everyone would get shit faced. You know, to kill the loneliness. When I got back home, it carried over. That, and the nightmares."

"When did you get into drugs?" Jason asked.

"That wasn't until I got back. I was drinking so much that I needed an upper to get going."

"Meth?" Jason asked.

"Sand Mountain's finest." She took a sip of water. "That's another reason why I should have shot Tyson Cade the other night."

"Did you buy from him?"

"Everyone who buys meth in Marshall County gets it from Cade." She snapped the words off as if she were firing them from a gun.

Jason leaned back in his chair and stared at her. He wanted to ask more questions about the dealer, but the agitated look on Chase's face made him decide against it. "So . . . what happened?"

"I went to rehab for forty-five days. Since getting out last November, I try to make at least one AA meeting every couple of weeks."

Jason rubbed his chin, thinking through what she'd said. "You said the nightmares carried over?"

"At least one a week."

"Forgive me for asking, but did you . . . I mean, while you were in the army—"

"Did I kill anyone?" she interrupted.

"Well, yeah."

"Not directly . . . but yes."

"How?"

"I flew Apache attack helicopters. The crew in our vessel fired on targeted locations and yes, we killed enemy soldiers." She took another sip of water.

"When was the last time you flew a helicopter?"

"Last week, actually. I'm a MedFlight pilot for the hospital. It's an on-call job, and I don't get called often. I also give firearms classes twice a week at the shooting range the Tonidandels own in Grant, Alabama."

Jason looked at her. She was gazing out over the water. She wore a faded gray Rolling Stones T-shirt over mesh shorts. Her skin was olive brown, her do up in a ponytail with a couple of stray hairs dangling in her eyes that she kept batting away. She was beautiful, he thought. Just as she'd been when she was seventeen years old and they'd taken the canoe down into the back of the cove, where the water narrowed to a creek and the water was ice cold from the natural spring. Where they'd held hands and walked along the rocks, yellow wildflowers swaying in the grass. Where they'd eventually taken their clothes off and swam and splashed and kissed, and Jason placed a flower in her hair. And, eventually, after laying a couple of towels down in the small boat, they'd made love. His first time. Her first time. When they were engaged in the act, it felt like everything had stopped. His breath. His heart beating. All he could remember was the intoxicating odor of wildflowers and the incredible sensation of pleasure and fear and anxiety rolled up into long moments of bliss.

When it was over, the moment gone, a few droplets of blood on the towel and the flower dislodged from Chase's hair, Jason had felt like everyone in the world was watching them. He'd wondered whether that was how Adam had felt after eating the forbidden fruit. He was so self-conscious, and Chase's face had beamed red. They'd barely said a word to each other on the boat ride home, and she'd softly cried. Nothing had been the same after that. They'd still fished some off the dock that summer, but they'd never kissed again.

"Penny for your thoughts?" Chase asked. "You drifted away."

Jason wanted to tell her what he was thinking but, at the last second, changed course. *Too soon,* he thought. "When's the last time you had meth?" he asked.

"Haven't touched it since going to rehab," Chase said.

"And alcohol?"

She frowned and looked up at the sky. "The night after you came back, I took down a half a fifth of Wild Turkey so . . . what was that? Almost two months ago?"

"What was the trigger?" Jason asked, thinking he had a pretty good idea.

"You," she said.

He swallowed, not knowing what to say. For several seconds, they looked at each other, and then Jason broke eye contact, gazing out at the lake instead. "Well, I'm sorry," he managed.

"What triggered you last night?" she asked.

"I was overwhelmed by everything. The case. Tyson Cade. And . . . I think Jana's lying to me about what really happened."

"And that surprises you?" Chase asked, her tone incredulous. "She's so manipulative, J. R. Has been her whole life."

"I know," he said. "Sometimes I forget."

Even now, he thought. In a jail cell accused of murder, she was kicking Jason out of their meeting for accusing her of lying. She was lashing out at her girls instead of enjoying the few minutes they spent with her during visitation. Nola had told him that she'd had to leave their last session because Jana told her it was her fault that she was in jail, that she was disloyal to her own mother.

Chase's hand touched his, and he looked up just as the waiter brought their plates over. He pulled back from her, and she looked away, the moment over.

They spent the next thirty minutes eating and talking about the various stories they'd heard at the AA meeting. When the waiter brought the check, Jason snatched it before Chase could.

"Please let me get this," he said. "I owe you one for waking me up this morning."

"Whatever. Just don't let it happen again."

After he paid, they walked down the slope to the dock and reboarded the Sea-Doo. "Mind if I drive home?" he asked.

"Nope," Chase said. Once they were both on, he felt her arms close around him, and he breathed in her fruity perfume and, again, the faintest hint of sweat.

"Thank you," he said. "I . . . can't tell you how much I enjoyed that."

She leaned in and kissed his cheek. "Thank you. Now let's go. We're losing daylight."

He wrapped the key lanyard around his wrist and pushed the red button to fire up the Sea-Doo. Then he pressed down on the throttle, and the front of the Sea-Doo raised up out of the water as the craft took off.

At this time of night, the dark water was like a sheet of glass, and Jason hit fifty miles per hour in a matter of seconds. Looking ahead at the orange sun ducking down behind the clouds, he took in a gust of fresh air and was grateful for the break from his sister's case.

And the company.

———

As they neared the bridge, Jason saw an eighteen-wheeler passing from above. The rig's headlights illuminated the words that had been spray-painted on the side of the overpass. *Mill Creek.*

Jason reached a hand up and touched the graffiti just as he had done when he was a kid. After navigating through the narrow opening, he took the Sea-Doo for one victory lap around the cove and then pulled it into the slip on the side of Chase's boathouse.

"Like riding a bike," she whispered, squeezing his ribs before she climbed off the machine and onto the dock. She cranked the hoist, and the watercraft began to rise out of the water. A few minutes later, she was turning off the lights and locking up. As they walked up the dock together, Jason clasped her hand. She didn't pull away.

"Well." He looked up toward his house, where he could see Nola sitting on the island talking with one of the security guys. "I—"

Before he could say anything further, he felt her lips pressed into his. The kiss was rough. Aggressive. Wonderful.

And painfully brief. As he wrapped his arms around her, she pushed away from him.

"Let's take things slow, OK?" she said, sounding unsure of herself, a rarity. "We both have triggers, you know."

Jason felt an ache in his heart as he watched her walk away. "Chase?"

"I'm fine," she said without turning around.

"Can we do that again?"

She laughed. "If you're lucky."

Jason walked through the door to the ground level of the house and up the stairs. He knew he should be exhausted, but he was full of energy. Wired.

When he reached the top of the stairs, his sense of peace evaporated the second he saw Nola's face. She was crying and holding her phone.

"What?"

"Niecy's in the hospital. She was attacked on the way back from the library tonight."

Jason became dizzy and grabbed the island to steady himself. He looked at Nola, her lips moving, but he couldn't hear any words. He took in a breath, thinking of Niecy in her Birmingham-Southern cap. Niecy who was going to go to law school. Attacked.

No . . .

"Uncle Jason?"

His legs gave, and he collapsed down on one of the island stools. "Is . . . she . . . all right?"

"He wants to talk with you," Nola said, and the fear in her voice was palpable as she extended the phone toward him.

He took the phone. "This is Jason Rich."

"Relax, Counselor." Tyson Cade.

"What did you do?"

"Let's just say that I needed to make a statement that I could get past your security. Don't worry. Your niece is fine. I had my people hold back. But things could've been worse. You know that, right? I expect to have my money on Monday."

And then the phone clicked dead.

51

Jason called Chase as soon as he got off the phone with Cade. She came at once and helped console Nola, who appeared to be in shock. Jason grabbed his pistol and walked out the front door.

"Mr. Rich, where are you going?" one of the guards asked.

But Jason didn't answer. He heard the officer shuffling behind him and saying something over a handheld device, but he paid him no mind. His thoughts were racing, and he was on the verge of hyperventilating.

I'm a lawyer, for God's sake. I am not James freaking Bond. I don't know the first thing about negotiating with a drug dealer. I'm a personal injury lawyer. An ambulance chaser. I settle cases for money. I shouldn't be trying a capital murder case, but at least that's something a lawyer can do. But taking on Tyson Cade? I can barely even shoot a gun.

What in the literal fuck am I doing?

He stopped in the middle of the street and howled at the sky. Then he put his hands on his knees and tried to regain his breath.

"Mr. Rich?" It was the same guard's voice, but Jason again ignored him.

No, he thought, imagining Niecy lying on a hospital gurney. Then again at the bottom of Lake Guntersville with Nola right next to her. He saw Tyson Cade rolling up next to him in his Mustang and sneering.

No. No. No.

He kept walking. Across the street and into the front yard of a run-down house that he hadn't been in since he was a teenager. As he approached the door, he saw a plume of smoke rising behind the dilapidated structure. Without hesitation, he walked around back and saw a bonfire of burning junk and three men standing around the inferno.

When he was a kid, his parents hadn't had much to do with the neighbors who weren't on the "lake side," but Jason and Chase had played with all the kids in the cove. Jason couldn't say he ever liked the Tonidandels. Truth be known, he was scared to death of them. Once, when Jason and Chase were being picked on by a group of teenage boys who'd wandered into the cove on a ski boat, the Tonidandel brothers had beaten the bullies up so bad that one of them had permanent scars on his face and another was in the hospital for two weeks with internal bleeding. The sheriff had been sent out, but Grandma Tonidandel had said that all her boys were doing was defending themselves and their property. No charges were brought, and Jason had heard his father say, "Even the sheriff is scared of those crazy bastards."

"What are you doing?" Jason asked, making eye contact with each brother and gesturing toward the fire.

"You've been away from Marshall County too long, Jason," the tallest of the three said with a chuckle as he threw a sack on the blaze. "We just taking out the trash."

Jason remembered how his own father would sometimes burn their trash in the yard if there was too much.

"What's on your mind, Jason?" the big man asked.

"I'm in trouble, Satch."

Satchel Shames Tonidandel was not only the biggest but, according to Chase, the meanest of the brothers. He stood well over six feet three inches tall and weighed north of 250 pounds. He had curly brown hair with streaks of gray and a full salt-and-pepper beard. If Jason remembered right, Satch should be around forty-five years old. Massive biceps protruded from the white T-shirt he was wearing, but the physical feature that struck Jason was the man's slit-like eyes. Mean, unforgiving.

"We know. Chase filled us in." He chewed on a toothpick, and his two brothers stood behind him. In the background, the fire blazed on. "Cade."

"He roughed up my niece tonight in Birmingham. She's nineteen. Put her in the hospital. I've got to go bring her home." For a long few seconds, the only sound was that of timber crackling. "Will you boys help me?" Jason continued. "I'll pay . . . I just need someone on my side who knows how to play Cade's game."

Satch peered at his brothers, who had now stepped up to either side of him. Then he squinted at Jason with his snake eyes glowing in the light of the fire.

"We're in."

52

By the time they reached St. Vincent's Hospital in Birmingham, Niecy was being discharged. She had a purple bruise on her forehead and another below her right eye. A sling also covered her left arm.

Jason gritted his teeth when he saw her and kissed her forehead over the bruise. Though he was horrified, he was also relieved.

Things could've been worse . . .

"Honey, I'm so sorry," he said.

She said nothing and cried into his shoulder. "I really thought I could go back to school and everything would be OK." She coughed. "I thought it would be fine."

"Do you know what happened to Max?"

She shook her head. "I don't. One minute she was walking behind me, keeping watch, and the next minute I was being thrown down on the ground."

Jason wondered if anyone would ever hear from the security officer again. There were a lot of places off the grid on Sand Mountain. No telling how many bodies had been buried by Tyson Cade.

Two uniformed officers approached Jason. "Are you her uncle?"

"Yes," Jason said.

"I'm sorry, but she didn't get a good look at her assailant. It's going to be hard to catch whoever it was without more information, but we've opened a file and we're on the case."

"Thank you," Jason said, knowing full well that the investigation would likely end the second they left the hospital. The Birmingham

Police Department had bigger fish to fry than an assault on a college campus and the disappearance of a security officer. Without any leads, the case would vanish as quickly as Max had.

Jason held Niecy's hand as they walked out of the hospital. Two members of his security detail walked on either side of him.

A truck pulled to a stop at the entrance. It was a black Ford Raptor with tinted windows. The body of the vehicle was jacked a few extra inches above the oversize tires. The passenger window rolled down, and Jason saw a bearded man spying him with cold eyes from behind the wheel.

Satch Tonidandel had insisted that he drive. His brother Mickey was right behind him, driving another pickup. Chuck Tonidandel had stayed behind to guard the entrance to Mill Creek Road while the rest of Jason's security detail watched the houses and the water.

Jason opened the door, and one of the officers hopped in. Jason then opened the back and gestured for Niecy to get in. She did, and Jason climbed in after her, followed by the second officer.

Once they were all in, Satch turned and looked at Niecy, then Jason. He grunted and put the truck in gear. He glanced at Jason in the rearview mirror, his gaze stern, his voice firm.

"A man like Cade doesn't play by the rules and doesn't give a shit about who he hurts so long as he gets what he wants." He gave his head a jerk. "Only one way to deal with a man like that."

"Kill him," Niecy said, almost spitting the words.

"Yes, ma'am," Satch said.

53

"I'm going to kill him," Jana said when Jason broke the news of Cade's attack on Niecy. It was Sunday afternoon, twelve hours before he was supposed to deliver $50,000 to the meth dealer. Jana was pacing. Ranting. "I'm going to squeeze his balls until he can't breathe, and then I'm going to feed his testicles to him like he's a baby in a high chair. Nobody, and I mean no damn body, puts their hands on one of my girls."

Jason was impressed with her fight. She'd been in jail now close to two months, having lost weight and becoming gaunt. But, after she'd heard about Niecy, her eyes were fierce again.

The scene reminded him of a time when they were kids. Space Camp in Huntsville. Jana sixteen and Jason twelve. Jana had ribbed him endlessly about his bowl haircut, but when she saw one of the other campers giving him grief about it, she kicked the boy as hard as she could in the shin. When the kid complained, crying to one of the counselors, Jana had begun to sob and said the lying perv had touched her breast and that's why she'd kicked him. The kid ended up being sent home early.

That was his sister. Crazy. A liar. Could make your life a living hell. And sometimes, just sometimes, fiercely protective of family.

"Tell me what you're going to do to *really* protect my girls," she demanded. "The security crew you hired ain't getting it done."

"I've gone in with the Tonidandel brothers. They're watching the house, and Satch is now my head of security detail."

She wrinkled up her face as if she didn't believe him.

"All three of them live in their grandma's house across the street. Decorated soldiers with pretty bad PTSD. Even crazier now than when they were younger."

Jana leaned back in her chair. It was as if she were looking at him for the first time. Then her lips curled upward, and she extended her fist, which Jason tapped with his own. "You *fucking* go, baby brother."

54

On Monday morning, Jason rode shotgun in Satch Tonidandel's truck into Guntersville. Mickey and Chuck were in the back seat, and there was a security car in front of him and one in back.

Jason felt like Tony Soprano as the entourage turned left onto Lusk Street and then, a couple minutes later, hung a right onto Hustleville Road. When the Alder Springs Grocery became visible, Satch pulled off the road and stopped in front of one of the gas pumps. He hopped out of the truck and began pumping regular unleaded gasoline into the Raptor. Chuck, the middle brother, whose head was shaved clean but whose face had a long scruffy beard reminiscent of the band ZZ Top, went inside the store to get a soft drink. Mickey, the youngest, sporting a stringy mustache and a mullet haircut, got out of the passenger-side back seat and leaned against the tailgate, putting a pinch of Copenhagen under his lip. Jason took a deep breath and opened the driver's-side back door. At exactly 7:00 a.m. sharp, he took out the briefcase with the money and placed it by the back tire.

At that moment, a rusty sedan pulled into the station and parked by the pump behind the Raptor. A man got out of the truck and started putting gas in the car. He walked to the trash can between the pumps, spat a wad of gum into it, and picked up the briefcase.

"Gracias," he said and trudged back to the sedan, putting the case in the trunk. A minute later, he was gone. Jason and the Tonidandel brothers gathered around the tailgate of the truck. Jason was about to thank them when his phone rang. He didn't recognize the number, but he knew who it was.

"Yeah," he said, putting the call on speaker.

"Good for you, Counselor," Cade said.

"We're done, Cade, you hear me? No more money. No more deals. You come after my family, I'm coming after you."

"Threats are so weak coming out of your mouth," Cade said, sounding like he was eating something. "And we both know you have one very important promise to keep or all bets are off."

"And I'll keep it," Jason said. "But all bets are definitely off if you harm a hair on the head of any member of my family."

"Relax, Jason. No one's going to get hurt, and I didn't even kill your security person. You'll find Max walking down Highway 68 coming from the Fort Payne direction right about now. You'll probably want one of your folks to pick her up. I think she's pretty hungry."

"Is this all some kind of game to you?" Jason asked, glaring at Satch, who was watching the phone like it might be a poisonous snake.

"No games, Jason. I told you. That's not my style. On the contrary, this is war. If I get through your sister's trial without being touched, I win. You understand?"

"Yes."

"And if I win . . ."—he trailed off—" . . . you survive. Victory isn't going to taste very good if you, Niecy, and Nola are in coffins. Be sure to think about that if you ever ponder going back on your word and putting that crazy bitch on the stand. And tell those Tonidandel rednecks they don't scare me one bit. I crap bigger than each of them, and they'll all end up in pine boxes, too, if they cross me. Full military funerals in Guntersville. Now that would be some shit." He chewed some more of whatever he was eating. "It makes no difference to me who you have in your corner, Jason. If you screw up, they're all going—"

"Hey, Cade." Satch's voice was so low and firm as he grabbed the phone that Jason's heart fluttered.

"Who's speaking?" Cade asked.

"Colonel Satchel Shames Tonidandel. One hundred and first Airborne Division. Screaming Eagles. If you're so lucky as to knock me and my brothers off, both of whom were captains in the same division, we'll be buried in Arlington National Cemetery. Twenty-one gun salute. Horse-drawn carriages. Definitely be some shit. But if you get out of line and lay a finger on any of Jason Rich's family and we're forced to squash your skinny runt ass with one of our boots, we'll mix your ashes with some ground beef, put the meat on the grill, and have us all a nice well-done Cade burger. Then we'll shit you out the next day, and you'll end up as turd fragments at the bottom of our septic tank. Then you, son, will *quite literally* . . . be some shit."

Satch ended the call and flipped Jason the phone.

Jason looked at the device and back at Satch. He wasn't sure whether to be angry or in awe. "You think that was smart?"

"No one threatens us, boy."

As they got back in the truck, Satch grunted. "That prick has one thing right," he said, turning the key and bringing the truck to life. "This is war."

"But he's definitely lying about one thing, brother," Chuck said, taking a long sip of the twenty-ounce Mountain Dew he'd bought in the store.

Satch gave a wry grin. "Yep."

"And what's that?" Jason asked.

"He is scared of us," Mickey said, rubbing his mustache. Then, squinching up his face, he mimicked his older brother. "Then you, son, will *quite literally* . . . be some shit."

The cab of the truck rocked with the cackles of the Tonidandel brothers.

As Satch turned back onto Hustleville Road, Jason looked around the cab at each of the three bearded men, all of whom had killed before in combat and wouldn't hesitate to kill again, and a thought enveloped him like a warm blanket.

Cade would be crazy not to be scared.

55

Tyson Cade gazed at the phone for a long time after Satch Tonidandel had ended the call. He knew he ought to be pleased. His scheme to scare Jason Rich into paying off his sister's debt had worked. He'd been made whole. But he was anything but pleased.

When was the last time someone had hung up on him?

Never, Tyson thought. *No one's crazy enough to do that.*

He'd gotten what he wanted, but perhaps hurting the girl had been too much. He'd scared the lawyer, and Rich had proven to be resourceful. He might not know how to fight with Tyson, but he'd recruited some help.

The reputation of Satch, Chuck, and Mickey Tonidandel was well known throughout Marshall County.

But that didn't matter anymore. The colonel had disrespected Tyson. He'd have to be dealt with. Maybe not immediately, but one day, after the immediate crisis was over, Tyson would get payback.

He drank a sip of Sun Drop and felt his pulse slowing. He'd gotten his money back and, despite the disrespect shown, he knew that Rich wasn't stupid enough to go back on his word. *Things are working.*

Soon, Jana Waters would be convicted of the murder of her husband.

And the meth business on Sand Mountain would continue to boom.

As for handling the colonel, Tyson Cade was a patient man.

56

On Wednesday morning, Jason had his first therapy session with Celia Little, a psychologist recommended by Chase. It went pretty well, he thought, though it wasn't humanly possible to get everything he had on his chest actually off his chest. But it was good to at least check that box. He'd been to an AA meeting. He had a therapist on board. He was moving in the right direction despite falling off the wagon. Still, he hadn't been back to jail to see Jana and wasn't sure when he would. There was much work to be done, and the trial date was pressing down on him like a runaway freight train. October 22 would be here before he knew it, and it was now September 5. Two days after Labor Day. Six weeks before they started picking a jury.

Shay Lankford, to her credit, had been an open book, turning over everything the state had gathered as evidence. Obviously, their proffer agreement with Waylon Pike and his confession were the two biggest pieces of evidence, and Jason had basically memorized every word of both. He knew the state's case probably as well as or better than they did. What he didn't know was what Jana's case would be. He had Harry watching Colleen Maples twenty-four seven and was hoping to set up meetings with Braxton's and Jana's respective divorce lawyers, Braxton's financial advisor, some friends from the First United Methodist Church, and, finally, every single neighbor on Buck Island.

He still had a long way to go, but things were better now with Niecy home. He'd added five more officers in addition to the Tonidandel brothers. Chase had also given him some shooting lessons, and he'd gotten his gun permit. If Cade tried anything before trial, then he'd get what he wanted.

War.

As the Porsche hurtled down Highway 278 toward Cullman, Jason felt like he'd circled the wagons as well as he could. Thirty minutes later, when he sat down at the All Steak restaurant and put the first mouthwatering orange roll in his mouth, Ashley Sullivan smiled at him. "You look better, Jason." She paused. "Are you?"

"I don't know," he said. "Ask me in about six weeks."

"What happens then?"

He drank some tea and let out a deep breath. "My sister's trial."

PART SIX

57

On the Friday before the trial of Jana Waters, Judge Conrad called a hearing to go over pretrial motions. His Honor, who had driven in that morning from Tuscaloosa, had banned any press from being in the courtroom. Jason sat alone at the defense table. As this was a hearing only, there was no need for his sister to be present, though he planned to see her immediately afterward. The parties had agreed on most of the pretrial matters, but there was one rather significant motion left on the table.

Judge Conrad cleared his throat and spoke with a bit of a rasp. "Forgive my voice. I'm a little under the weather today."

Even sick, the man was still loud enough that Jason figured if there had been anyone in the back of the courtroom, they would've had no trouble hearing. "As I understand it, the parties have stipulated to all matters set out in their respective pretrial motions other than the defendant's motion to prohibit the introduction of evidence of any alleged extramarital affair on her behalf because it would be a violation of Rule 404 (b)'s ban on character evidence. That sound right?"

"Yes, Your Honor," Shay said, standing.

"That's correct, Your Honor," Jason said, also standing.

"All right then, my initial inclination was to grant the motion, but, as I understand the state's argument, they believe that evidence of Ms. Waters's illicit relationships goes straight to her motive for committing the crime of murder. That sound right, Ms. Lankford?"

"Exactly, Your Honor. The state's theory is that Ms. Waters was unhappy in her marriage as evidenced by her affairs with multiple men, including the killer of Dr. Waters, Waylon Pike. Evidence of Ms. Waters's unfaithfulness is relevant to motive and should come in as an exception to 404 (b). I'd also add that the state plans to introduce evidence of the victim's affair with a coworker, which also shows motive on the part of the defendant. The unfaithfulness on both sides of this relationship goes right to the heart of why Ms. Waters hired Mr. Pike to kill her husband."

Judge Conrad ran a hand through his hair and looked Jason's way. "And I'm guessing your argument is that it doesn't matter. That the state is trying to introduce evidence of these affairs to demean her character and to make the jury think that since she was cheating on her husband, she had to have murdered him."

"Yes, sir," Jason said. "That's pretty much it."

"Well, I think I'm going to split the baby. I'm obviously going to allow any evidence of a relationship between Pike and the defendant, as that is materially relevant to the state's claim that she hired Pike to kill Dr. Waters. I'm also going to allow evidence of Dr. Waters's affair as well as any nonhearsay related to the parties' separation and impending divorce. As to other affairs with additional suitors, Ms. Lankford, what's the nature of that evidence?"

Shay frowned. "We have evidence that Ms. Waters had an affair with a man from Sand Mountain named Tyson Cade."

Jason flinched at the sound of Cade's name. Was the prosecution actually planning to call him to the stand? And if so, was it fair game for him to cross-examine Cade? That wasn't a violation of his promise but would certainly seem to violate the spirit of it.

Conrad smirked. "This Cade fella is the local drug lord, right?"

Shay glanced at Detective Hatty Daniels, then back at His Honor. "He's never been convicted of any crime, but—"

"But he's the guy," Conrad said.

Shay nodded. "There's video surveillance showing Cade and Jana Waters both at the Hampton Inn on the night of the murder."

"Are they seen together?"

"Not on the video."

Conrad grunted and rubbed his chin hard. "I'm going to grant the defense's motion with respect to any evidence of an affair by Ms. Waters beyond Pike. If the state wants to make a proffer during the trial, I may change my mind." He eyeballed Jason. "And I'll certainly switch tunes if the defendant opens the door to character, so I'd be careful if I were you, Mr. Rich."

"Yes, sir."

"Very well," he said, standing and looking out at them. "I've set aside next week to be in Guntersville. We'll start picking the jury at nine a.m. sharp on Monday. Does everyone understand?"

"Yes, Your Honor," Shay and Jason said in unison.

———

Once the judge had left the courtroom, Shay Lankford approached Jason. "Mr. Rich, this is normally the time where I'd offer my best plea deal, but I can't do that in this situation or I'd be run out of town. We'll still be seeking the death penalty."

"Understood," he said, feeling a tad sick to his stomach. "With a witness with the credibility or lack thereof of Waylon Pike, I would have thought life in prison would at least be an option."

"Would Jana take that?"

He frowned. "No."

"Then it really doesn't matter, does it?"

Before he could answer, she turned and strode out of the courtroom.

———

A minute later they were all gone, and Jason was alone. He turned to the jury box and stared at the twelve built-in chairs where the citizens who would decide his sister's fate would sit. He walked over to the railing and gazed at the empty chairs.

How many times had his father, Lucas Rich, made his closing argument standing right here? What would his dad think of him now?

"See you, Monday," he whispered over the railing.

58

They gathered around his small conference room table at 5:30 p.m. on Friday evening. Izzy, Harry, and Jason. A pizza box was between them, and all but one slice had been devoured.

"Are you absolutely sure?" Jason looked at Harry and pointed a piece of pepperoni at him before popping it in his mouth.

Harry slid the photographs across the table. "You tell me."

Jason looked at them all again. Then he viewed the same shots in close-up on his laptop. "I haven't been around Cowan in person like you have, but that's definitely Maples."

"Cowan is probably still at the Brick right now. Let's go take a look."

———

Ten minutes later, the trio were at a booth near the bar of the Brick. A man in jeans and a flannel shirt sat on a stool, sipping from a pint of beer.

"Iz?" Harry asked.

She glanced at the photograph and then the man. "Definitely him."

"J. R.?"

Jason let out a deep breath. "Yep, that's him all right."

He glanced down at the photographs, which showed Colleen Maples embracing Trey Cowan on the steps outside the former football star's apartment.

"I can testify that they went upstairs and into Cowan's room."

"So let's walk through it together," Jason began. "Cowan is angry at Dr. Waters because of the botched surgery. Maples is also angry at Braxton because of the jilted romance. Maples also feels guilty for her role in Cowan's surgery and pissed that she was investigated and punished by the ABN while Dr. Waters suffered no such fate. She befriends Cowan, and they start up a romance. Cowan talks with Pike, who tells the two of them that Jana is thinking about hiring him to kill Braxton. Then Maples and Cowan decide that they'll pay Pike the fifteen grand to kill Braxton. If he ever gets caught, he's supposed to say Jana hired him."

"So Jana's withdrawal of 15K is a coincidence?" Izzy asked, the sarcasm evident in her voice.

"Not at all," Jason said. "Jana must have told Pike she was taking fifteen grand out to pay Cade, and he must have alerted Cowan and Maples that they could pay him the same sum to do the deed to make Jana appear guilty."

"I guess," Izzy said. "Still seems like a huge stretch. Do you think Conrad will let you get all of this in front of the jury?"

"Jana's entitled to defend herself and present alternative theories."

"But you're making great leaps with the evidence here," Izzy pressed. "Is there anyone who overheard Pike and Cowan talking about Braxton and Jana? For all we know they talked about ball games."

"That's not true. Teresa can testify that she saw them huddled together and talking a lot. Sometimes for at least an hour."

"That's weak," Harry said.

"I know, but it's something. All we need is one reasonable doubt. Once I take Pike apart on the stand, then an alternative will be more feasible to the jury. We just need to give them something."

"How's the Pike cross coming?"

He sighed. "Good, but his statement is vague about how Jana gave him the money. That's the most crucial part, and all he says is she gave him the money in the strip mall off Highway 69 after picking him up at the house."

"I can't believe there's not one witness to her driving down Buck Island Drive that night," Izzy said.

"I can," Harry said. "I've scoped that road out at all hours of the day. The houses are huge, most well off the road. With all the fireworks and shenanigans of the Fourth, I doubt anyone was paying attention."

"I'll just have to see what he says and react," Jason said.

"What if he says she gave him an envelope with the money? Or a package with the cash? Or stuffed the bills down his pants after sucking him off?" Izzy cackled after the last comment. "Look, I'm sorry, but you need to be ready for anything."

"I know, but I guess it doesn't matter all that much. Regardless of what he says, all I've got is his past felony and the deal he's cut with the state to cross him with. I have to discredit him with that and hope the jury doesn't believe him with respect to Jana paying him the money."

"That's right," Izzy said.

There were several seconds of silence, and then Harry cleared his throat. "J. R., you know you've done the best you can do here. Some cases simply can't be won."

"Some clients are guilty," Izzy added.

Jason stood and looked at his team, knowing they were trying to help but feeling angry nonetheless. "I'm not looking for moral victories here, guys. I have to win, do you understand?"

Harry also stood and gave him a hard stare. "Jason, if you want to win, you have to put Jana on the stand and roll the dice."

"I can't do that, Harry."

"If you show the jury that she was screwing a drug dealer as a down payment on the money she owed Tyson, then you could argue Cade as your alternative."

"I think Cade is flimsy as a suspect," Jason said. "Why would he want to kill the golden goose? You saw what he did to me. Holding the kids over my head and demanding money. He could've done the same thing to Braxton. I bet he was doing the same thing."

"Maybe so, but if Jana testifies that she gave the money to Tyson Cade's deputy for cocaine, then that sounds truthful. She's still implicating herself in a crime where she'll go to jail."

"But she's innocent of murder," Izzy said, finishing off Harry's argument. "Jason, I agree that calling a loose cannon like Jana to the stand is risky, but doesn't she have to tell the jury that she didn't pay Pike to kill her husband? Our Cowan-Maples alternative is completely circumstantial. We don't have anyone to connect the dots. Don't we need Jana's denial?"

"What do you want me to say?" Jason asked, peering down at his partner, who remained seated at the booth, and then back up at Harry. "You're both right. In a perfect world, I'd call Jana, and she'd deny everything and tell the jury what she did with the money, but this isn't a perfect world. Instead, this is a world where, if I do that, my two nieces will probably be killed, as will I. And maybe even you guys. Also, let's not forget the fact that Jana can't keep her story straight."

Izzy stood and put her hands on Jason's shoulders. "Which brings us back to Harry's original point."

"Which is?"

"You've done the best you can," Izzy said.

59

Jason stopped at Jackson Burns's home on Buck Island on the way home. When he pulled into the driveway, he was surprised to see a **FOR SALE** sign in the yard. He walked to the front door, and it was unlocked. When he stepped inside, he saw Burns sitting out on his covered deck, cold beer in hand. As he approached the car dealer, he noticed that the walls in the den were still decorated with photographs of his wife and sons. It was as if their family had never been touched by divorce. Jason hesitated at a framed photograph of Burns, Shandra, and the boys out in front of the dealership. There was a banner over a car that read *20th Anniversary Sale. Sad,* he thought, thinking about the boxes at his apartment that contained the life he'd once had with Lakin. He'd boxed his memories up, but it appeared that Jackson Burns had yet to let go.

"Hey, Burns," Jason said, taking a seat in the rocking chair next to the big man, who was sprawled out on a wicker couch. "What's with the sign in the yard?"

Burns took a sip from his bottle. "Seller's market, man. With some of the deals my neighbors have gotten, I was thinking, 'Why not?' There's nothing for me here anymore. My best friend is dead. You've taken the girls to Mill Creek, which I completely get, but I miss seeing them. I miss my wife and sons. Need a change, you know?"

"I do," Jason said. "I know very well. Where are you thinking?"

"I don't know. Maybe Honeycomb. Get a little closer to the kids but still not too far from the dealership. There are some townhomes there by Sunrise Marina."

Jason couldn't believe it. "You're gonna move from this mansion to a townhome?"

"What do I need all this space for? Hell, I hardly ever go anywhere but the kitchen, the bedroom, and the boathouse."

Jason nodded. It was time to get to it. "The state is going to call you as a witness. And based on what you told me, I bet you're probably their strongest evidence besides Waylon Pike's confession."

"I'm sorry, but it is what it is," Burns replied.

"Don't apologize. I'm grateful you're letting me talk with you. I can't get to Pike. His attorney won't let me touch him with a ten-foot pole."

"I got nothing to hide."

"So, just to go over the bad stuff. On the night of July the 3, you saw Jana sitting out on her dock having a drink. Slurring her words pretty bad. Clearly drunk."

"Right."

"You asked her how she was doing, and she said, 'Just fine for someone who's about to lose everything . . .' or something like that."

Burns nodded.

"You asked her what she meant, and she got angry and said you knew damn well what she meant. That Braxton was going to divorce her, cut her off from the bank accounts, and, because of that, she'd taken fifteen grand out of their joint account that afternoon."

"Exactamundo," Burns said, belching softly.

Jason took in a breath and finished with the closer. "Then she said she would kill the bastard before she'd let Braxton ruin her life."

Burns gave his head a jerk and finished off his bottle. "I'll never forget it."

"Here's my question, Burns."

"Shoot."

"If you'd thought Jana was being serious, you would've called the police, correct?"

"Ah, I see where you're going."

"Well, wouldn't you?"

"Yes, of course. I also would have warned Braxton." He walked to the minifridge he had on the deck and opened it, then took out another beer and cracked it.

"Exactly," Jason said. "That's all I want to accomplish in my cross of you. That you thought Jana was ranting and that she wasn't being serious."

"Well, I'll agree to all of that. Jana was always making wild threats to leave Braxton or that she was going to cuss some socialite in the Gothic Guild out. She gave everyone a lot of diarrhea, but I don't remember her ever carrying out any of her threats." He looked at Jason with dead eyes. "Until she killed Braxton."

Jason leaned back in his chair and crossed his arms. "Burns, you knew Pike as well as anyone. Did you ever see him talking with Trey Cowan?"

Burns sank down on the couch cushion. "Not that I remember."

60

"I can't believe this," Jana said, slamming her fist on the table and wincing in pain. "Damnit." It was Sunday late afternoon, their last consult before trial.

They'd gone over the conversation with Burns a million times, and the conclusion was always the same. She couldn't contradict the car dealer's testimony because everything he said was true. And even if she could rebut his testimony, she wasn't taking the stand.

"I was ranting. I mean, you know me, Jason. Burns knew me. That's what I do. Plus, I was hammered." She stared at her brother. "I mean, how stupid would I have to be to tell Burns all that and then instruct Pike to kill Braxton the next night?"

She had a point. Of course, on the flip side, a drunk person with a cocaine habit and a Xanax addiction probably wasn't exercising the best of judgment.

"There's a lot of things you can say about me," Jana said. "I'm a bitch. I'm psycho. But I ain't stupid."

"No, you're not," Jason said. He squeezed her hand. "I've gotta go, sis." He turned for the door, but before he could knock, she said something that made his knees buckle.

"Dad would be so proud of you."

Jason gathered himself and looked down at the concrete floor. "Why do you say that? He never was while he was alive." He turned. "Remember what you said after the funeral? When we were standing out in the boathouse?"

"J. J.—"

"You said *I destroyed him.* That the shame he had over my billboards and the agitation and disappointment he suffered when I turned down his offer to work for him led to his demise." Jason stared at the cinder block wall, trying hard to keep his composure. "How could you say something like that to me?"

"Because I was mad at you," Jana said, sobbing. "And devastated over Dad's death. And . . . jealous."

"*Jealous? Of me?* You were the apple of Dad's eye your whole life. You got everything. A new car. Money for college. All those beauty contests you won that he financed. You married someone he approved of. I was an embarrassment, always less than, and you were the golden child."

"You got out," Jana said, crossing her arms tight across her chest. "You weren't trapped in this town trying to please him. You had your own life."

"Which you ridiculed at every turn."

She hung her head. "I was jealous and bitter, J. J. I think Dad was too."

"*Dad? Of me?*"

"He came home to practice law with his father," Jana said. "He never had a choice. You were supposed to be the third generation, and you turned him down."

"He gave me no choice. He wouldn't make me a full partner. I was going to be his minion and make half as much money as I could make in Birmingham. And it wasn't like he was going to automatically stop treating me like a stepchild. It wasn't a fair deal. I was better off going out on my own, finding my way."

"His deal with Grandpa hadn't been fair either. I think when you said no, it made him question his own choices. Especially when you started making money. It damn sure made me question mine."

Jason was dumbfounded. "I can't believe this. Dad never said a kind word about my law practice. The man never even told me he loved me. Never! I mean, what kind of father does *that*?" Tears streamed down Jason's cheeks. A dam had been broken, and he didn't care. "And you weren't any better. You could never stand it when I got even the slightest bit of attention."

"You're right, and I'm sorry."

"No, you're not. You're just saying that because I'm your best bet at avoiding a life on death row. You ain't stupid, Jana, and you ain't ever sorry."

"I am. I was wrong. Dad was wrong."

For almost a full minute, the only sounds in the cell were their breathing and sniffles. Jason wiped his eyes and knocked on the door three times.

"Thank you, J. J."

"You don't have to—"

"I do. You came back. You've gone the distance for me, and I had no right to expect that from you. Regardless of whether you believe Dad would be proud . . . I'm proud of you."

———

Jason left the jail and walked up to Gunter Avenue. He hung a left and picked up his pace. Three blocks south of the courthouse, he stopped in front of a restaurant that advertised pulled pork sandwiches and slabs of ribs.

For five decades, a Rich had practiced law in this brick building.

It was evening, and the restaurant, which only had lunch hours, was closed. Jason sat on a wheel stop in front of the sidewalk and gazed out at the highway. One of his billboards was approximately fifty yards away. He'd wanted his father to see his advertisement every single time he walked into his office. He was that petty.

But, according to Jana, Lucas Rich had been jealous of his only son.

And would be proud of me now . . .

She could be lying, he knew, but he didn't think she was. He'd seen the pain in her eyes. He'd felt it.

As a drizzle began to fall, Jason's tears mixed with the rain.

61

"ALL RISE!"

Jason and Jana stood as Judge Powell Conrad strode to the bench. It was Monday morning at 9:00 a.m. sharp. Jason had barely slept a wink and been unable to eat more than a piece of toast with coffee. If he'd been more nervous at any point in his life, he couldn't remember it. He glanced behind their table and saw Nola and Niecy seated side by side, Nola in a maroon dress and Niecy in navy. On either side of them were Harry and Chase. Izzy was at the satellite office on Blount Avenue, keeping their other cases afloat, and would arrive by evening to brainstorm. Jason looked to the back of the gallery, where Satchel Tonidandel sat in an aisle seat wearing a sports coat and slacks. He also had security outside the courthouse, in front of his office, and, of course, at Mill Creek.

He'd be taking no chances this week.

"State of Alabama v. Jana Rich Waters," Judge Conrad bellowed. "Are we ready to roll, Ms. Lankford?"

"Ready, Your Honor."

"Mr. Rich?"

"Yes, Your Honor."

"OK. Let's bring in the panel."

———

Seven hours later, they had their jury. Nine men ranging in ages from twenty-five to seventy-eight, seven of them white and two Black. And three women, all white, ages twenty-eight, fifty-two, and sixty.

Based on the research he'd done prior to trial, Jason had hoped for more youth and diversity in the jury, as that demographic tended to be more liberal and receptive to criminal defendants, but those traits were few and far between in Marshall County.

"The women are all giving me the stink eye," Jana whispered.

They were, but Jason tried to calm her. "They're probably tired."

"Nice try."

"Ladies and gentlemen of the jury, you will be the ones who decide this case. We're going to adjourn for the day. Please report back to the jury room at 8:30 in the morning." Conrad banged his gavel, announcing the close of the day.

Jason leaned in and kissed Jana on the cheek as the guards took her away. He'd played up his relationship to his client during voir dire, saying *my sister* several times during the proceeding to gain the potential jurors' sympathies.

Based on their faces, he didn't think he was making much progress in that regard.

But they're tired, he told himself, shaking his head. *Nice try.*

62

Jason headed straight to the office. He practiced his opening statement with his partners a couple of times and then declared he'd had enough. He was dog tired, and Izzy and Harry were out of ideas. They'd have to go with what they had and let it ride. He would try to take down Pike on cross-examination and then hope the jury bought the Maples-Cowan alternative.

He wanted to go home, but he also knew that sometimes what he needed and wanted were two different things. He drove to Guntersville High School and took his place in the circle in room 21. When his turn came, he shared that the stress over the trial was triggering him to drink. He used to always have a few after a deposition or hearing. This was his first trial, and he'd just spent seven hours picking a jury for the first time in his life. He badly wanted a couple of beers or a whiskey drink to take the edge off. There were sympathetic looks and words of encouragement along with advice for getting past the trigger. Go for a walk. Talk with friends. Get to bed early.

All of it made sense, but Jason knew he was easing away from the trigger by simply being present and checking this box. He'd made one meeting a week now for two months and was nearly halfway to finishing the twelve steps. He was currently on number five, admitting his wrongs to himself and another person. He was moving slow, but everyone had their own pace.

When the meeting was over, several folks slapped him on the back as he walked to his car, his mind drifting to his neighbor. Jason hadn't seen Chase at any of the meetings since his first one. She'd told him that she needed to go to another class, so she went on Wednesdays, and he went on Mondays. They held each other accountable, but they also kept things separate. Jason knew the reason for the separation, but it still hurt him.

I'm a trigger for her, he thought as he drove home to Mill Creek.

Home. Jason wasn't sure if that was the right sentiment or not. He was on a bridge between two lives, and the outcome of Jana's trial was going to determine whether he crossed to the other side or returned to where he'd been.

He wanted to cross, but he was afraid. Fear had always been a motivator for him. Of failure. Of embarrassment. Of disappointment.

With the trial looming in his consciousness, he realized he was scared to death.

———

Jason, Nola, Niecy, and Chase had dinner together on the patio. Niecy had made spaghetti, which was delicious, while Nola peppered him with questions about the trial. Was he happy with the jury? How long would it last? Who would be the state's first witness?

Jason answered as best he could, though for most of her questions, the response was "I don't know." Since the girls were potential witnesses, they would be excluded from the courtroom up until they were called to the stand. Chase had volunteered to stay with them tomorrow, and Jason was grateful for her help and presence.

When it was time for bed, Nola gave Jason a big hug and thanked him for all he was doing. She cried a little, and then went downstairs to bed. Niecy also gave him a hug. She'd been noticeably warmer since the assault by Cade's men. As she, too, took the stairs, she looked back and asked him the question that hung in the air all the time.

"Do you think my mom killed my dad?" Simple. Direct. No bull-shit. It was a dagger, and Jason wondered how many times both girls would ask that question the rest of their lives. To themselves. Their friends. Therapists. Whether the case was won or lost this week, the question would remain.

"No," Jason said.

She looked as if she was going to say more, but she didn't. Her eyes glistened, and then she continued to walk down the stairs.

———

Jason walked Chase across the short distance to her house, and they stopped outside the door.

"Good luck tomorrow."

"Thanks." He slowly leaned in for a kiss, and she did as well. Then she turned away and closed the door. Their relationship hadn't escalated since dinner at the Docks. They talked. They took rides on the Sea-Doo and kayaks. And they kissed.

But nothing more.

Jason wasn't sure if a relationship with Chase was part of his crossing or not, but he hoped that it was.

But for now, as with his career and everything else in his life, they were on the bridge.

63

At five minutes past nine the following morning, after bringing the jury in and giving a few words of greeting, Judge Conrad announced, "The parties will now give their opening statements. Ms. Lankford, are you ready?"

"Yes, Your Honor," she said, standing and walking with purpose toward the jury railing.

"On the Fourth of July, our country celebrated its independence. In Marshall County, there were fireworks displays, barbecues, and family get-togethers. But out on Buck Island, one of the nicest areas in all of the state, a woman was plotting to commit murder. The defendant, Jana Rich Waters, conspired with a man named Waylon Pike to kill her husband, beloved local physician Dr. Braxton Waters. She hired him to kill her spouse, and when the deed was done, she gave Pike $15,000 in cash." Lankford paused. "While many of you as well as myself and most of Marshall County were enjoying our holiday, Braxton Waters was shot to death out by his boathouse on Buck Island, and his body was then dumped in the lake. And while Waylon Pike, who you will hear testify in this trial, used the instrument to kill Dr. Waters, it was the defendant, Jana Waters, who pulled the strings."

Jason watched the faces of the jury as Shay made her accusations. Several were shooting stares at Jana—the "stink eye," as his sister had called it—and Jason figured there would be a lot of that during the state's case in chief. He scribbled a note on his pad and put it in front of Jana.

Stay calm and cool.

He felt her hand on his for a moment, and he looked at her. In his life, he'd rarely if ever seen his sister scared, but he saw abject terror in her eyes now. The fear that could only come when your fate was out of your hands.

———

Shay spent the next twenty minutes going through the operative facts, starting with Waylon Pike's confession and ending with the conversation between Jana and Jackson Burns where Jana said she'd kill Braxton for divorcing her and ruining her life. The presentation was well organized and effective. When she got to the end, she was short and sweet.

"When you hear all of the evidence, I'm confident that you will reach the only verdict that justice allows. Guilty."

———

"Mr. Rich?" Judge Conrad asked, once Shay had taken her seat. "Are you ready to give your opening statement?"

"Yes, Your Honor," Jason said. He stood and buttoned his jacket. "May it please the court," he announced. "Your Honor . . ." He nodded at Judge Conrad, who returned the gesture. "Counsel . . ." He gestured at Shay. Then, as he reached the railing, he made eye contact with as many of the jurors as he could. "Members of the jury."

Jason stopped and saw the rapt attention from the twelve decision makers who would render a verdict in this case. He'd gone to see Knox Rogers last week and asked for more advice, and the sage lawyer had said that most attorneys made poor use of their first few moments with the jury. *"Don't do that, son. They'll never be more ready to hear what you have to say than in those first seconds. Make what you have to say important. Something you want them to remember."*

"As I was listening to the prosecutor's opening remarks, it struck me that it is undisputed that Waylon Pike killed Dr. Braxton Waters. So why isn't Pike sitting over at this table where my sister is?" Jason walked over to the defense table and put his hand on Jana's shoulder. "He's not. Instead, my sister, Jana, is here. She is here because Waylon Pike, after being arrested for this heinous crime, told Detective Daniels"—Jason pointed at the officer seated next to Shay—"that Jana paid him to do it." Jason paused, still pointing at Daniels. "Their entire case is based on the word of Waylon Pike, who you will learn in this trial is a convicted felon. An arsonist. A thief. And yes, a murderer." He hesitated again and let both hands drop to his side. "The only witness in this case who will testify that Jana paid Pike to kill Dr. Waters is Pike. Ladies and gentlemen, as you listen to the testimony in this case and assess the credibility of the sole mouthpiece for the state's case, ask yourself this question: Are you going to convict my sister on the word of a man like Waylon Pike?"

He stopped talking for a full three seconds, letting the seed he'd just planted sink in. Discrediting Pike was his entire case, and he'd led with it.

He again touched his sister's shoulder. *"It's important in a criminal trial to put your hands on your client if you're the defense lawyer. It shows the jury that you're not scared of your client, and they shouldn't be either."* This nugget came from Professor Pamela Adams, the dean of criminal law at Cumberland with whom Jason had set up several meetings.

"This is my sister. Jana Rich Waters. She isn't perfect by any stretch, but she's lived here in Marshall County all her life. She's served this community on numerous committees and chaired the Gothic Guild, the First United Methodist Church Women's Group, the Ladies of the Lake auxiliary board, and too many other organizations to count. She and Dr. Waters have two children, Niecy and Nola. Their relationship was strained at the time of Dr. Waters's murder. We won't be denying that. But remember something as the state trots out its evidence that Ms. Waters was unfaithful, that she was worried that Dr. Waters was going to divorce her, that she had a drug problem. None of those things speak to whether she paid Waylon Pike to kill her husband." Jason was arguing, which was prohibited in opening, but Knox had said he should push the envelope. *If the state objects, it makes them look bad. You're representing a criminal defendant on trial for her life. The judge will likely give you some leeway.*

Jason glanced at Shay Lankford, who was frowning, but she made no move to object. "Again," Jason said, as he walked back toward the jury and put his hands on the railing, "at the end of the day, when all is said and done, all they have is Waylon Pike."

Jason spent the rest of his opening discussing the virtues of the burden of proof, which was carried solely by the state. "Jana Waters doesn't have to offer any evidence in this case. The sole burden rests with the state to prove to you beyond a reasonable doubt that Jana Waters is guilty of murder. If you have one doubt . . . *just one* . . . then the court will instruct you to return a verdict of not guilty."

He closed with similar words to the prosecutor but with an obviously different expectation. "I'm confident that when you hear Waylon Pike testify and the lack of any corroborating evidence to back up his story, you'll return the only verdict that justice demands. Not guilty."

When he took his seat, Jason felt his sister's hand on his again. She gave him a squeeze, but Jason didn't look at her. He was hyped up and tried to calm himself down. He thought he'd done a good job, but as

Knox had warned: *"You never really have a clue what the jury is thinking. Don't drive yourself crazy trying to figure that out. Just do your job."*

Jason exhaled a ragged breath. *Do your job,* he told himself.

"Is the state ready to call its first witness?" Conrad asked.

"Yes, Your Honor," Shay said, standing and gesturing to the back of the courtroom for a deputy to open the doors. "The state calls Waylon Pike."

64

Waylon strode to the stand wearing a black suit, white shirt, and maroon tie. He felt ridiculous, but these were the orders of the state and his court-appointed lawyer. He'd just had a quick briefing with his attorney, Louie Taylor, who everyone seemed to call "Louie T."

"Just tell the God's honest truth," Louie T had instructed. "That's what you've proffered to do, and it's the only way you get any favor when this thing is over. With any luck, they'll give you life in prison with the chance of parole in fifteen years."

"Great," Pike had said.

"Don't screw this up," his attorney had said, his last words before the deputy had summoned him.

As he took his place at the witness stand, Waylon looked out at the courtroom. His eyes immediately latched on to Jana Waters. She wore a black dress fit for a funeral, but even though it didn't show much skin, the woman was hot. Waylon had a flashback of what she looked like under her clothes, and he peered down at the wooden bench.

Tell the truth, he told himself. He wanted to laugh as Shay Lankford approached, but he kept his expression grave. *I shouldn't be here,* he thought. *I should be on a beach in Cancún. Or the mountains. Any damn where but here.*

But alas, he'd been stupid. He'd blabbed his mouth, a problem he'd had his whole life.

"Please state your name for the record," the prosecutor said.

"Waylon Pike."

"Mr. Pike, on the night of July 4, 2018, did you kill Dr. Braxton Waters?"

As rehearsed, he didn't hesitate. "Yes, I did."

"Why?"

He looked right at Jana, again as rehearsed. "Because his wife, Jana Waters, hired me to kill him."

"Did she pay you money to kill her husband, Mr. Pike?"

"Yes, she did."

"How much?"

"Fifteen thousand dollars."

"Mr. Pike, do you see Ms. Waters in this courtroom?"

"Yes, I do." He pointed right at Jana. "She's sitting at that table there next to the guy that's always smiling on all the billboards."

Snickers erupted from the gallery, and Judge Conrad banged his gavel. "Quiet!"

"Let the record reflect that the witness has identified the defendant," Shay said. Then she looked at the jury. "Mr. Pike, where did you meet Ms. Waters?"

Pike kept his eyes on Jana. "At the bar at Fire by the Lake."

"And tell the jury about that first encounter."

He turned in his chair and focused on the jurors. "She was drinking vodka and soda. I ordered a beer. When I finished mine, she asked if I wanted another, and I said yes. We had several rounds together, and she told me that she was drowning her sorrows. That her husband was going to leave her. That he was having an affair."

"Then what happened."

"Well, one thing led to another, and we left the bar together. I asked her if she wanted to go back to my hotel room. I was only in town for a few days to do some siding work on a construction job. She said no but asked if I wanted to sit in her car and have another drink. By that time of night, the place was closing up. The streetlights were off, and there were hardly any cars in the parking lot."

"Then what happened?"

"She pushed the seats back and . . . well . . ."

"Well what?"

"We had sex."

"In the car in the parking lot of Fire by the Lake?"

"Yes, ma'am," he said, looking at Jana. If she was embarrassed by the testimony, she didn't look it.

"Then what happened?"

"She said she wanted to see me again, so we met at her house the next day. She hired me to do some patch work on the roof of their boathouse."

"And did the . . . *personal* . . . side of your relationship continue?"

"Oh yeah," Waylon said. "Pretty much every time I came out to Buck Island, we got together."

"And by that you mean you had sexual relations with the defendant?"

"That's right."

"Who was married to Dr. Braxton Waters."

"Correct."

"When did you meet Dr. Waters?"

"That first time I came out there, he showed me the spots on the boathouse that needed repairing."

"Was he friendly to you?"

"Yes, he was. He was always friendly to me."

Shay let that sink in for a few seconds. Then she changed gears. "Did Ms. Waters ever say she wanted you to kill her husband?"

"Yes."

"When was the first time she mentioned that?"

"She was always bringing that up, but the first time she said anything was at Fire by the Lake."

"How did she bring it up?"

"It was after we had . . . you know . . . when we were in the car after the act. She said she wished she could get rid of her husband so she could have more time for the kind of fun we'd just had."

"Did you think she was serious?"

Waylon cocked his head. "With Jana, it was hard to tell sometimes whether she was joking or being straight up. At that point, to be honest, I wasn't sure."

"Was there ever a time when you did become sure?"

"Yes. A week before the Fourth, she dropped by Mr. Burns's house, where I was working."

"And you're referring to Mr. Jackson Burns, the Waterses' next-door neighbor on Buck Island."

"That's right. It was the middle of the day, and I was doing some work on Burns's boat. Jana brought over a six-pack of beer and some sandwiches she'd made. We ate and then we had sex."

"Where?"

"In the boat."

"Then what happened?"

"When we were done, she asked me if I'd do something for her."

"'Anything,' I told her. She said that Dr. Waters was about to file for divorce. She said she couldn't have that, and it was time to follow through with what we'd been talking about."

"And what was that?"

"Me killing him."

Shay again studied the jury. "Since your first meeting with Ms. Waters at Fire by the Lake, how many times had she mentioned wanting her husband dead?"

"A lot. Almost every time we were together."

"When did she mention you actually killing Dr. Waters?"

"After I worked on their boathouse the first time, she came down and talked to me. Dr. Waters was on call and had to go into the hospital to see a patient. We talked a little, and she gave me a blow job."

295

There was a rustling in the jury and out in the gallery, and Judge Conrad banged his gavel again for quiet.

"Oral sex?" Shay asked.

"Yes, ma'am. I'm sorry.

"When she was through, she asked me if I'd ever killed anyone before." He hesitated. "During our first conversation, I'd told her I'd been to jail before for arson."

"I see. We'll get to that in a minute. What was your answer to the defendant's question?"

"I told her I hadn't killed anyone. Then she asked me if I would be willing to kill Dr. Waters. If the price was right."

"What did you say?"

"I think I said something crude."

"Which was?"

"Something like, 'Are you going to keep' . . . uh . . . you know . . ."

"Having sexual encounters with you?"

"I didn't put it as nice as that, but yes," Waylon said.

"Were you serious?"

"At first, I wasn't sure. But by the time she came to me in Burns's boat the week before the Fourth, I was ready."

"Why?"

"Because my work in Guntersville had dried up, and the chance to make some extra money sounded pretty good."

"Did you quibble any about the price?"

He looked down and rubbed the back of his neck. "No. I probably should have in hindsight, but I didn't."

"Why not?"

He looked at Jana. "Ms. Waters was an incredible woman. Very persuasive. I had never been with a woman like her. Sexy. Smart. I probably would have killed Dr. Waters for free. I'd have done anything she asked me."

"But you didn't do it for free, did you?"

"No, ma'am."

Shay walked to the jury railing so that Pike would have to look at the jurors when he answered the next question. Another deliberate break in the action. "Mr. Pike, please tell the jury what happened on the night of July 4."

Waylon clasped his hands together and spoke slowly and clearly. "I went fishing off Highway 69. Jana told me she'd pick me up at the Laundromat in the strip mall a half mile from Fire by the Lake. She said she was going to have a drink at the bar and then meet me at nine o'clock sharp."

"And did she?"

"Yes."

"Then what happened?"

"I got in her car, and she drove me up Buck Island Drive. She dropped me off at Burns's house, and I walked the rest of the way."

"Why'd she drive? Why didn't you drive yourself?"

"She said she didn't want my car to be seen. If her car was seen, it was no big deal. She lived there."

"Why Burns's house for the drop-off?"

"Because that was the last place I'd worked. If for some reason I was seen, I'd say I was there to pick up my toolbox."

"This was the defendant's plan?"

"Yes, it was."

"Then what happened?"

"I walked up the street to the Waterses' home and went around the back. Jana had given me a key to get inside, but then I heard music coming from the boathouse." Waylon eyed the jurors. He could tell that they were all on the edge of their seats. "I walked down to the pier and saw Dr. Waters passed out on a lawn chair. From the looks of it—there was a tequila bottle and a pint glass next to the chair—he'd been doing some drinking. He'd also been hitting golf balls off his dock."

"How could you tell that?"

"His golf bag was in the boathouse, and one of the clubs was laying on the floor."

"What happened next?"

"There were still a lot of fireworks being set on the lake." He stopped and peered at the jury. "I waited for the next big racket, and when there was . . . I shot him three times in the head."

———

The hush that came over the courtroom sent shivers up Jason's body, from his toes to his forehead. It was all he could do to keep his eyes on Waylon Pike and the jury and not steal a glance at his sister.

"Then what happened, Mr. Pike?"

"I rolled his body off the dock and into the lake. Then I walked around the side of the house and back down Buck Island Drive. Ms. Waters picked me up about a hundred yards past Burns's place."

"What happened next?"

"She drove me back to my car, which I'd parked in the back of the strip mall. Once we got there, she handed me an envelope and said my money was inside."

"Was it?"

"Yes, ma'am," Waylon said. "I counted it before I got out of the car."

"Fifteen thousand dollars?"

"Yes, ma'am."

Shay walked to her desk, looked at her pad, and strode back to her spot at the edge of the jury box.

She's good, Jason admitted. This was a symphony. A well-rehearsed play. And, judging by the looks on the jurors' faces, they were gobbling it up.

Shay looked at the jury and then back at Waylon. "Please describe your criminal background, Mr. Pike."

"I was convicted of arson in 2014. Served three years at the Limestone Correctional Facility in Athens."

"Is that a felony?"

"Yes, ma'am, it is."

"Have you been convicted of any other crimes?"

"Yes, ma'am. At least four misdemeanor thefts. Possession of cocaine. One DUI."

Shay walked again to the prosecution table and took out a two-page document. "Is this a fair and accurate depiction of the crimes you've committed?"

He looked at the document. "Yes, it is."

"Your Honor, I'd like to publish this to the jury and offer it as an exhibit."

"Any objection?" Conrad inspected Jason with a glint in his eye, knowing full well there wouldn't be. Jason again was impressed with the strategy. Shay Lankford was owning Pike's history of crime and actually making a production out of it.

And taking all the steam out of my cross . . .

"None," Jason said.

Shay handed the pages to the first person in the jury and waited for a full minute as each of them had a few seconds to pore over Waylon Pike's transgressions.

"Mr. Pike, did the defendant ever ask you about your criminal background?" She held up the exhibit as she placed it on the evidence table in the middle of the courtroom.

"Yes, she did. A lot."

"What did she say?"

"I remember her asking me how it felt to set the fire that I did and why I did it."

"Did she ever say why she'd selected you to kill her husband?"

Jason cringed as he realized what was coming. "Yes," Pike said. "Ms. Waters said she wanted someone to do it who wouldn't back out. Who would go through with killing him. Someone like me, who wasn't afraid to set a fire and walk away."

"Were those her words?"

"Yes."

Shay retrieved an additional document from the state's table. "Mr. Pike, you've entered an agreement with the state to provide truthful testimony today, is that correct?" She placed the stapled pieces of paper in front of him.

"Yes, ma'am."

"Mr. Pike, has the state made any promises to you in exchange for your testimony?"

"None."

Shay nodded at the jury and turned back to the witness stand. "Mr. Pike, a few final questions. When did Ms. Waters go over her plan with you?"

"That night at Burns's and then again the day before."

"On July 3."

"Yes."

"Where did y'all meet then?"

"She was in her boathouse. Drinking and listening to music. I had done the last of my work at Burns's and dropped by."

"Was her daughter Nola home?"

"Yes."

"Did you see her?"

"I did. I went through the house and told her that her mother wanted me to look at something that was going on with one of the Jet Skis."

"And was that a lie?"

Waylon cocked his head. "I mean, I did look at the oldest Jet Ski while I was down there, so technically, no." He stared at the jury. "But that wasn't why I had to see Jana."

"Why did you have to see her?"

"To go over the plan for killing her husband."

"And did she review the plan with you?"

"In great detail."

Shay glanced at the jury. "You said you shot Dr. Waters three times in the head. Where did you get the gun?"

"Place out at Sand Mountain. Right past the DeKalb County line."

"Remember the name?"

"No name. Just a plywood shack off Highway 75."

"How did you hear about it?"

"I can't remember. I was at the Brick, and there were some guys there talking about the place."

This was a bit fuzzy, Jason thought. Finally, a gap in the story.

"And did you purchase a gun?"

"Yes. A nine-millimeter pistol."

"And did you use that gun to shoot and kill Dr. Waters?"

"Yes."

"And what did you do with it afterward?"

"The day after the killing, I drove to South Pittsburg, Tennessee. On the way, I pulled off the road somewhere in Scottsboro that has a bridge over the lake. I threw the gun off the bridge."

"Was that also following the defendant's plan?"

"Yes, ma'am. To the letter."

Shay walked back to the state's table, taking her time. When she stopped, she didn't look back at Pike but out toward the gallery. "Mr. Pike, what was the defendant's demeanor when she was going over her plan to kill her husband with you?"

"Calm. Cold even."

"And when she picked you up after you killed Dr. Waters?"

"Same. She was a little hyped up then. Jana sometimes did some coke, and I think she may have done a line. She was a little hyper on the way back to the Laundromat."

Shay turned to Waylon. "What was the last thing the defendant said to you?"

"I was getting out of the car at the Laundromat, and she rolled down the window. And then she said, 'Good job.'"

"Good job," Shay repeated, looking at the jury for a moment. "Anything else?"

"No."

Shay turned to Judge Conrad. "No further questions."

———

Jason asked his first question on cross from his seat. "So you can't remember much about this gun, can you, Mr. Pike?"

"I've said all I can recall."

"Plywood shack out on Sand Mountain?"

"Yes, sir."

"How many plywood shacks do you think are located on Sand Mountain? A thousand?"

A smattering of laughter rose from behind him in the gallery. Jason glanced at the jury and saw a man on the front row smiling. Juror number 48. Russell Edmonson. Thirty-five years old. Owned a lawn care business. According to Jana, he'd been giving her something other than the stink eye. "That would be the 'he wants to fuck me' eye," she'd explained. "I've gotten that quite a lot in my life."

Jason hadn't argued because he knew she was right. Perhaps Edmonson was a break. He stood and looked right at the juror as he asked his next question. "So, the gun that killed Braxton Waters was purchased in Bumfuzzle, Alabama, at one of a thousand plywood shacks on Sand Mountain from a man you can't identify?"

"Bumfuzzle, what?"

"It's an expression, Mr. Pike. I'd say the correct name of this fictional town, but I suspect that Judge Conrad wouldn't approve."

"I would not," His Honor said. Jason looked up at the bench, and the sandy-haired judge had a peculiar grin on his face, like maybe he'd smelled a fart and wasn't sure who'd done it.

Jason had to admit that he kind of liked Conrad.

"Anyway, Mr. Pike, suffice it to say you've told the jury all you can *recall* about this weapon."

"Yes. That's what I said."

"And you can't recall much."

"I've said what I said."

"And you threw the gun away?"

"Yes, I did. At your sister's direction."

"You're a thief, Mr. Pike, aren't you?"

"I've been convicted of theft on occasion."

"Why didn't you just tell the jury you stole the gun? Wouldn't that have been a more believable lie than you bought it from someone you can't remember?"

"Objection, Your Honor. Mr. Rich is arguing with the witness."

"Your Honor, I'm entitled to a thorough and sifting examination of this witness."

"Yes, you are, sir," Conrad agreed. "But you aren't entitled to argue with him. Sustained. Let's move it along."

Jason walked toward the jury railing, moving his eyes around the twelve until settling on Mr. Edmonson. "You were convicted of arson, correct, Mr. Pike?"

"As I said earlier, yes."

"And theft multiple times?"

"Yes."

He approached the witness and glared at him. "And you aren't on trial today, are you?"

He cocked his head. "No."

"You killed Dr. Waters with a gun. Shot him three times in the head. And yet you aren't sitting over there where my sister is."

"She paid me to kill her husband."

"So you say, Mr. Pike. But isn't it true, sir, that the reason you aren't sitting over there beside my sister is that you cut a deal with the prosecution?"

"I wouldn't call it that. I signed a proffer agreement where I agreed to tell the truth."

"And you also gave them your signed confession in exchange for that proffer agreement, correct?"

"Yes, sir."

"Your Honor, at this time I'd like to publish to the jury the proffer agreement executed between the state and Waylon Pike, which has been marked as State's Exhibit 2."

Pausing so that each juror could have a moment with the document, Jason finally cleared his throat. "You understand that if the prosecution is happy with your testimony today, then you may get a more favorable plea offer from them, don't you?"

"All I agreed to do was tell the truth."

"That's not my question, Mr. Pike. My question is that you hope your testimony today leads to a better plea offer, right?"

Pike glanced at the prosecution table. "Yes, sir."

Jason took his time walking to the jury railing before turning back to the witness. "And you're currently being charged with capital murder, isn't that correct?"

"Yes, sir."

"And so, today, if you say the 'right' things"—Jason used his fingers to make quotation marks upon uttering the word *right*—"you could save your life, couldn't you?"

"All I'm supposed to do is tell the truth."

Jason retrieved the criminal background document from the evidence table and held it out in front of him, looking at the jury. "And it's your testimony that you've done that."

"Yes, sir, it is."

Jason smirked and looked at Pike. Then he shook his head. "No further questions."

———

There was a short recess after Waylon Pike left the stand. Jason walked out of the courtroom and into the bathroom. He went into a stall, locked the door, and took a deep breath. Then, making sure to not make a sound, he flexed like he might be Arnold Schwarzenegger. Then he beat his chest a couple of times with his fist and shadowboxed the interior of the stall. Finally, he exited the enclosure and walked to the sink. He splashed water on his face several times and looked at himself in the mirror. It was the first cross-examination he'd ever conducted in court, and he was tingling with excitement and fear.

He thought he'd done well but knew he couldn't be sure. As he came out of the restroom, he tried to calm his breathing. He saw Izzy, who'd watched from the back of the courtroom. She sidled up next to him and whispered into his ear.

"That was fantastic, Jason Rich."

He exhaled with relief as she squeezed his arm. "Thank you."

"Now what?"

Jason took in another breath of air. "We brace ourselves."

65

Knox Rogers had warned Jason that the first day of trial for a defendant, whether it was a criminal or a medical malpractice defendant, was always the worst. *"You just have to sit there and take it. And like Professor McMurtrie used to tell us at Alabama, 'Don't ever let them see you sweat.'"*

Jason had Professor Thomas McMurtrie's *Evidence* handbook on his shelf at the Birmingham office, and he'd brought it with him for this trial. He knew the great man, a legend in the state, had actually returned to the courtroom and hit a huge verdict after teaching for forty years. He'd also defended a couple high-profile murder cases in his seventies before passing of cancer.

Jason concentrated on his breathing and remembered something his father liked to say. *"A trial is a marathon, not a sprint."*

He touched his sister's hand and whispered in her ear, "Hang in there."

———

The state's second witness was county coroner Dr. Clem Carton, who testified that the cause of Braxton Waters's death was three bullet wounds to his head. He further testified that the wounds were consistent with those caused by a 9 mm pistol. Finally, he opined that the time of Waters's death was between 9:00 p.m. and 1:00 a.m.

Jason saw no reason to cross-examine Dr. Carton, so he passed the witness.

Next up was Sergeant Hatty Daniels, who was deliberate and methodical in taking the jury through her investigation and how it led to Waylon Pike and his subsequent confession. Daniels was still on the stand when Judge Conrad recessed for the day.

"Members of the jury," he said, "we've made a lot of progress today. We will adjourn until nine in the morning. Remember to not discuss this case with each other or anyone else." He then banged his gavel, and the bailiff led the jury out. As they were leaving, Russell Edmonson gazed at the defense table and smiled. Jana and Jason smiled back.

"He's our only hope," Jana said, speaking between her teeth.

Jason squeezed her hand. "All we need is one, sis."

66

The following morning, Jason began to plant the first seeds of the defense's alternative theory with Daniels.

"Sergeant, it took over a week for Waylon Pike to be apprehended, isn't that so?"

"Yes, sir. Eight days to be exact."

"And during that long time frame, you interviewed other possible suspects in the murder of Dr. Waters, correct?"

"No, that's not correct. We didn't interview anyone else we viewed as a suspect."

"OK, let's forget about technicalities. You took a statement from Trey Cowan, correct?"

"Yes."

"And you did that because Cowan's family had sued Dr. Waters for medical malpractice and lost, and you felt like Cowan might have a motive to harm Dr. Waters?"

"Well, I wouldn't say—"

"Judge, I object," Jason interrupted. "I'm entitled to a straight yes or no answer to my question."

"Your Honor, Mr. Rich has asked a compound question," Shay said in a commanding voice. "The witness should be allowed to explain."

"I'm going to sustain Mr. Rich's objection. The witness shall answer the question 'yes' or 'no.'"

"Yes," Daniels said. "We wanted to at the very least rule out Mr. Cowan as a suspect, which we did."

"He didn't have an alibi for where he was at the time of the murder, did he?"

"He said he was watching the fireworks on the Sunset Trail. We weren't able to corroborate his story. This all became irrelevant when Waylon Pike confessed to killing Dr. Waters at the direction of Ms. Waters." She snapped the words off like a machine gun, and it was all Jason could do not to take a step backward.

"You would agree that you hadn't ruled Cowan out at the time Pike came forward."

"I would."

"You also hadn't ruled out Colleen Maples, had you?"

"Actually, we had. She had a corroborated alibi for the time of the murder. She was with friends on the lake."

Jason looked at the jury. "Of course, that corroboration becomes irrelevant once Pike came forward."

She cocked her head. "I don't understand."

"Well, it doesn't matter where Maples was if she paid Pike to kill Dr. Waters, does it?"

There were several murmurs from the gallery, and Judge Conrad banged his gavel. "Quiet!" he screamed.

"Sergeant?" Jason pressed.

"Mr. Pike confessed that Jana Waters paid him to kill Dr. Waters."

"And there's no witness to that other than Pike, correct?"

"Correct."

Jason walked over to the jury railing. "Sergeant, were you aware that Trey Cowan and Waylon Pike were friends?"

She squinted at him. "No."

Jason spoke directly to the jury, though his question was for Daniels. "And were you aware that Colleen Maples and Trey Cowan were romantically involved?"

This time, Sergeant Daniels chuckled.

"Something funny, Sergeant?"

309

"This is ridiculous."

"Is it? You haven't answered the question. Were you aware that Trey Cowan and Colleen Maples, both of whom your office investigated to rule them out as suspects in the murder of Dr. Braxton Waters, were romantically involved?"

"I fail to see—"

"Yes or no, Sergeant?"

"No."

"Thank you, ma'am." Jason glanced at the jury and then back to the witness stand. "No further questions."

67

The final witness on Wednesday wasn't a surprise, but the calling of the name still sent a jolt of fear and adrenaline through Jason. He figured his reaction paled to that of his sister.

"State calls Ms. Nola Waters."

She came through the double doors and walked down the aisle. When she was in view, Jason heard the sucking of air next to him. He didn't look but placed his right foot over Jana's left. It was a signal they'd worked out anytime he was worried that she might lose it.

Nola took her seat and was sworn in. After she stated her name, Shay Lankford walked to the end of the jury box. "Ms. Waters, please tell the jury how you found your mother the morning of July 5, 2018."

"She was passed out on the floor in the den."

"Why do you say 'passed out'?"

"Because it was noon, and she still had her clothes on from the day before. And she was on the floor."

"Had you ever seen your mother in this condition before?"

"Yes."

"How many times?"

Nola sighed. "At least five."

"What happened when you arrived?"

"I shook her awake and asked her where Dad was."

"And what did she say?"

"That she didn't know."

"What happened next?"

"I heard music coming from the boathouse, and we walked down to the dock."

"What was playing?"

"Darius Rucker." Her voice was beginning to shake. "Th-th-that was D-D-Dad's favorite."

"Are you OK, Ms. Waters?"

She wiped tears from her eyes. "Fine. I want to get this over with."

Jason glanced at the jury. Each person was staring at Nola with rapt attention. She was the daughter of the victim and the defendant. Closer to the situation than even Jason. He forced himself to breathe, hoping that Nola would get through this but also hoping that her testimony wouldn't hurt Jana too bad.

"Nola, what happened next?" The move to first name was subtle, but Jason thought it was brilliant, a signal from the prosecutor to the jury that this was a teenager. A signal to Nola that a friend was asking the question, someone who only wanted the truth.

"We walked around. Saw that dad's golf clubs were down there and a club was laying on the ground. Then I saw some blood on the dock . . ." She fought back the tears and continued. " . . . and I saw his Gunter's Landing cap floating in the water."

"What did you do then?"

"Mom called 911."

"Then what happened?"

"The police came and started dragging the lake by our boathouse. An hour and a half after they started, they found the body." She put her hands over her face.

Next to him, Jason heard sniffles, and he put his hand on his sister's shoulder to console her. He was relieved to see her tears, knowing that this was a spot where genuine emotion was welcomed. What mother wouldn't cry with her daughter having to testify to such a scene?

"Do you remember talking with me in the hours after the discovery of your father's body?" Shay asked.

"Yes, I do." Nola looked at her mother.

"Do you remember what you told me?"

"Yes."

"Will you please tell the jury?"

Jason stood to object. "Your Honor, may we approach?"

Seconds later, he and Shay were standing in front of the bench, speaking in tones barely above a whisper. "Mr. Rich?" His Honor asked.

"It's our belief that the prosecution is now about to elicit opinion testimony as to who Nola Waters thought killed her father. Namely, my client. We believe this to be highly prejudicial, not to mention irrelevant. Nola Waters is not a medical examiner nor is she a law enforcement officer. Her opinions wouldn't benefit the jury and would greatly prejudice the defendant."

"Ms. Lankford, what is the witness about to say?"

"That she told me she thought her mother killed her father."

Conrad leaned back in his chair, seemed to think about it for a couple of seconds, and peered at Jason. "Objection sustained. You are not to elicit that testimony, Ms. Lankford."

"Yes, Your Honor."

Jason exhaled on his way back to the table, realizing he'd been holding his breath the entire time he'd been standing.

"Ms. Waters, please disregard the previous question. Were you aware of any trouble between your parents in the days prior to your father's death?"

"Yes, ma'am. They'd been fighting a lot. And my dad had told me and my sister that he was going to file for divorce."

Jason almost objected on hearsay grounds, but he knew he couldn't get around this undisputed fact, so he let it stand.

"When did he tell you this?"

"A few days before he was killed. Niecy came home for the weekend, and he told us all together in the kitchen."

"Thank you, Nola. No further questions."

"Cross-examination, Mr. Rich?"

Jason stood and looked at Nola and then down at his client, who was openly weeping and staring off into space. Jason had never seen his sister look so helpless, and he felt an ache in his heart for her and Nola.

"No, Your Honor. We have no questions for the witness."

68

The last witness for the state was Jackson Burns, first up on Thursday morning. Though Jason couldn't guarantee the state would rest after Burns's testimony, he thought they would. After covering the preliminaries of his name, occupation, and the fact that he had been friends with Braxton Waters for years and neighbors of the Waterses on Buck Island for over a decade, Shay got down to brass tacks.

"Mr. Burns, were you aware that the Waterses were having trouble in their marriage?"

"Yes."

"How?"

"I saw them have arguments several times in the months before Braxton's death. Course Braxton told me a lot too."

"Did you ever talk with the defendant about her marital problems?"

"Yes, I did."

"And when was that?"

"It was the night of July 3."

"And where did you see Ms. Waters?"

"She was on her dock. Sipping on a drink and listening to some tunes. I was driving by on my boat. I'd been fishing at Goose Pond."

"And what did you say to her?"

"Just hello and how she was doing. She said she'd been better, and so I asked her what was wrong."

"How'd she respond?"

"She said that her marriage was over. That Braxton was about to file for divorce and was going to cut her off their joint accounts. She also told me she'd taken fifteen grand out of one of their accounts that afternoon."

"Did she say anything else?"

"Yeah, she did." Burns glared at Jana, and Jason felt a twinge of anger at the car dealer playing up the punch line.

Shay looked at the jury and back at Burns. "What did she say, Mr. Burns?"

"That she'd kill the bastard before she let him ruin her life."

Jason could hear tapping next to him and placed his right foot over his sister's.

"No further questions," Shay said, turning to Jason. "Your witness."

———

"Braxton Waters was your best friend, isn't that correct, Mr. Burns?" Jason asked, speaking with as much enthusiasm as he could muster and hearing Knox Rogers's voice in his head. *Never let them see you sweat.*

"Yes."

"Y'all had been best friends for over thirty years, hadn't you?"

"Something like that. Since high school, for sure."

"So, Mr. Burns, surely if you had any idea that your friend Dr. Waters was in mortal danger, you would have told him, wouldn't you?"

"Yes, sir."

"If you thought someone was going to kill Braxton Waters, you would also have told the police, wouldn't you?"

"Yes."

Jason walked to the jury railing. "And isn't it true that you did neither of those things after Jana Waters threatened to 'kill the bastard,' as you quoted her."

"What's that?"

"You didn't call the police?"

"No."

"You didn't tell Braxton."

"No."

"You didn't do these things because you weren't worried in the slightest that Jana Waters was going to follow through with her threat, were you?"

"No . . . I thought she was ranting. Jana did that sometimes. She'd get mad, get to talking."

"You didn't consider what she said a true threat, did you?"

"No," Burns said.

Jason turned to Judge Conrad. "No further—"

"I wish I had," Burns added.

Jason frowned at the witness. "Your Honor, I object, and I'd ask that Mr. Burns's comment be stricken from the record and that the jury be instructed to disregard his last remark."

"Sustained," Judge Conrad said. "Members of the jury, please disregard Mr. Burns's last comment."

"I have nothing further at this time," Jason said, still staring at Burns, who was now looking down at the floor.

"Ms. Lankford?"

"No more questions, Your Honor."

"Very well, please call your next witness."

There was a half beat of silence, and Jason gazed across the courtroom at the prosecutor, who was whispering with Sergeant Daniels. Shay then turned and announced to the court, "The state rests, Your Honor."

69

After Jason's motion for judgment as a matter of law was denied, Judge Conrad adjourned the case for lunch and told everyone to be back in an hour.

As Jason started to go, Jana grabbed his arm.

"I have to testify," she whispered.

"Not only no, but hell no," Jason whispered back. "We have a game plan to follow."

"No, Jason. We can't—"

"Jana, we've been through this. There's too much risk and not enough reward."

Two guards came to take her back to the holding cell where lunch awaited her.

"Jason, please."

"We'll talk about it tonight."

She leaned in close and spoke directly into his ear. "I lied to you, J. J."

Jason wrinkled up his face. "What?"

"I lied."

"Jana."

"I'm sorry."

"Jana, we're about to start our case. You know who I'm going to call."

"I do, and that's fine. But before we finish, I have to take the stand."

Jason opened his mouth to protest, but she was led away from him, looking back one last time and mouthing, "Please."

Jesus, Mary, and Joseph, he thought but knew he shouldn't be surprised. This was Jana, after all.

As he began to walk down the aisle—he was supposed to meet Izzy and Harry at Café 336—his brain flooded with questions.

How could he call Jana given what he'd promised Tyson Cade?

And if he did call her, how could he do so without blowing up the whole case?

And finally, the big one.

What'd you lie about, Jana?

70

"Is the defendant ready to call her first witness?" Judge Conrad asked once everyone had returned from the break.

"Yes, Your Honor. Defense calls Ms. Beverly Thacker," Jason said, his voice carrying to the back of the courtroom.

Nurse Thacker waddled into the courtroom wearing green scrubs. She took her seat and nodded at the jury.

After taking his time covering her experience as a nurse and knowledge, Jason waded into the reason for her testimony. His alternative theory had three links, and Thacker provided the first.

"Nurse Thacker, did you ever see Dr. Waters acting unfaithful toward his wife, Ms. Waters?"

"Well . . . yes I did. I actually walked into the doctors' lounge to ask Dr. Waters a question, and he was in a cot with a nurse anesthetist . . . and they were going at it."

A few chuckles from the jury, and Jason was reminded of something he'd heard Professor Adams say. *"A laughing jury doesn't convict . . ."*

"Nurse Thacker, are you trying to say they were having sex?" he asked.

"Yes, sex. She was on top of him and gyrating." She looked at the jury. "It's been since the younger Bush was president, but I remember what sex looks like."

More laughter.

"Did you recognize the nurse anesthetist, Ms. Thacker?"

"Colleen Maples."

"And did you see Dr. Waters and Ms. Maples again after this encounter?"

"Oh, yes. Many times. But that was the only time I saw them knocking boots."

Juror Russell Edmonson was drinking from a cup of water and had a coughing fit.

"Did you ever hear them argue?"

"Your Honor, I object," Shay interjected. "While humorous, this all seems discomfortingly irrelevant."

Jason didn't wait for a prompt. "Judge, we're allowed to present alternative theories for the murder. Sergeant Daniels testified herself that her office investigated Colleen Maples."

"I'm going to allow it. Objection overruled."

"Ms. Thacker, did you ever see them argue?"

"Yes, I did."

"And when was that?"

"During a surgical procedure."

"What was being said?"

"They were whispering, but I heard one part of it."

"What was that?"

"Maples told Dr. Waters that he had to make a choice between her or Ms. Waters."

"And what did he say?"

"He said, 'You know I can't do anything now.'"

"Ms. Thacker, we've obtained a waiver of patient confidentiality from the patient for you to disclose his name. Can you tell the jury who it was?"

"Yes, sir." She looked at the jury. "Trey Cowan."

As murmurs and whispers filled the courtroom, Jason turned to Judge Conrad. "No further questions."

"Ms. Lankford?"

Shay stood and crossed her arms. "We will not waste the jury's time with any cross-examination."

Judge Conrad leaned back in his chair and looked at the witness. "All right then. Ms. Thacker, you're excused."

71

Jason's next witness was Colleen Maples. As described by Beverly Thacker and as he'd experienced himself during his brief confrontation with her, Maples was anything but warm and fuzzy on the stand.

Still, she admitted that she'd been investigated by the Alabama Board of Nursing in connection with Trey Cowan's knee surgery and her behavior toward Dr. Waters and the patient on the day of surgery. She kept her answers short, adding no explanation.

It wasn't until Jason got to the end of his questioning that she showed fire.

"Ms. Maples, are you currently involved in an intimate relationship with Trey Cowan?"

"Objection, Judge. This is completely irrelevant," Shay said.

"Overruled," Judge Conrad said.

"That's none of your business," Maples snapped.

"Judge, we'd ask that the witness be ordered to answer the question."

"Answer the question, Ms. Maples."

"I fail to see how my private life is any of this court's concern."

Shay Lankford joined Maples's chorus. "Judge, this is an outrage meant purely to embarrass Ms. Maples. The defense has shown no connection between Ms. Maples and Waylon Pike."

"We will, Your Honor."

"The objections by the prosecution and the witness are overruled. Ms. Maples, you will answer the question, or you will be held in contempt of court."

"I'll repeat the question," Jason offered.

"I don't need it repeated. The answer is yes. I'm involved with Trey. He's . . . forgiven me for what happened."

"I bet," Jason said.

"Objection!" Shay shot out of her chair. "The defense lawyer's comment is due to be stricken."

"Sustained," Conrad said. "Another stunt like that, Mr. Rich, I'll hold you in contempt."

"Yes, Your Honor," Jason bowed toward Conrad. "No further questions."

72

After Shay again chose not to cross the witness, Jason cleared his throat and called whom he'd originally expected to be his next-to-last witness.

"The defendant calls Mr. Trey Cowan."

The double doors opened, and in limped the former football star. Every eye in the courtroom turned toward him, and Jason knew he couldn't have asked for a better setup.

"Please state your name for the record."

"Trey Cowan."

"And what do you do for a living?"

"I work for the city."

"And were you formerly a football player for Guntersville High School?"

"Yes."

"And were you recruited by every school in the country as a quarterback?"

"Pretty much," Trey said, smiling toward the jury. There were several warm looks in return.

"You also had interest from Major League Baseball."

"I was projected as a first rounder."

"Which would have meant millions of dollars."

"Yes . . . but I would've made more money playing football."

Jason looked at the jury. "Your football and baseball dreams ended with a leg injury, is that correct?"

"Yes, sir. Broken tibia. There was an infection after surgery, and I've never regained full function of the leg."

"And you filed a medical malpractice action against Dr. Waters because of his surgery, correct?"

"I did."

"And you lost."

"Yes."

"Didn't recover a dime."

"Not a cent."

"You also reported Dr. Waters to the Alabama Board of Medical Examiners, correct?"

"Yes."

"But the board imposed no discipline on him, correct?"

"That's right."

"So you went after Dr. Waters for money and for his license, and you lost both times?"

He shrugged. "I guess that's right."

"You're dating Colleen Maples, aren't you?"

"Yes."

"And she was actually the CRNA involved in the surgery that ruined your football and baseball careers."

"True."

"And you reported her to the Alabama Board of Nursing, and the board imposed discipline, didn't it?"

"I believe they suspended her, yes."

"And now you're dating her, true?"

"Yes."

"How did that come to be?" Jason knew you shouldn't ask an open-ended question on cross, but he wasn't sure he cared so much about what the answer was here. He thought he might be able to play with whatever it was.

"She came to the Little League field where I was umping a game one day. Then she walked over when the game was over and apologized. She asked if there was anything she could do.

"I told her she could buy me a beer . . . and over time one thing led to another."

"You make a little more than minimum wage working for the city, don't you?"

"Yes."

"It would be hard for you to come up with $15,000 in cash, wouldn't it?"

"More like impossible."

"But Ms. Maples makes plenty of money as a CRNA, doesn't she?"

"I really wouldn't know her financial situation. She might have massive student loans for all I know."

"She lives out on the main channel of the lake, doesn't she?"

"Yes."

Jason walked toward the defense table. He was almost to the finish line. *One more seed to plant . . .*

"Mr. Cowan, isn't it true that you became friends with Waylon Pike when he came to Guntersville?"

Trey raised his eyebrows, and his face flushed red. It appeared the high school football star was finally getting where everything had been going. Jason couldn't tell if he was scared, angry, or both. "Yes," he said. "That's true."

Jason was relieved. He would no longer have to call Teresa. Unless he did, in fact, call Jana, he was about to end his case.

"You used to meet Pike at the Brick and talk with him for hours a few times a week."

"I'm not sure we ever planned to meet there, but we were at the Brick a lot at the same time. I wouldn't say we talked for hours, but we talked a good bit."

"Did you like him?"

"I guess I did. He didn't talk much about my high school playing days because he was new to town. Instead he wanted to know town gossip and whatnot."

"You understand that Waylon Pike killed Dr. Braxton Waters on July 4, 2018, don't you?"

"Yes, sir, I do."

"And you saw Pike pretty much every day at the Brick in the days before the murder."

"That's probably true."

Jason had planned to sit down, but he couldn't resist the urge to ask one more question. To bring it all home.

"Mr. Cowan, you and Colleen Maples conspired to kill Dr. Waters, didn't you?"

"Objection, Your Honor," Shay said, slamming her hand on her table and standing up. "This is an outrage! There's been absolutely no foundation presented for such an outlandish accusation."

Conrad gave Jason a stern look. "Overruled. The witness will answer the question."

"No, sir." His voice was firm.

"Maples gave you the money so you could take a third and final swing at Dr. Waters, isn't that true?"

"Same objection, Your Honor," Shay said, her hands on her hips. "This entire line of questioning is outrageous."

"Overruled," His Honor said.

"No," Cowan said.

"Waylon Pike had told you that he had access to Dr. Waters, and you gave him $15,000 to do the deed, didn't you?"

Shay remained standing. "Objection. Lack of foundation."

"Overruled."

"No, sir,'" Cowan said.

"Your Honor, I have nothing—"

"Waylon did tell me something about Dr. Waters," Cowan interrupted.

"—further," Jason said.

Judge Conrad cleared his throat. "Given the interruption, Mr. Rich, do you want to continue?"

"No, Your Honor. I didn't ask a question, so I'd ask that Mr. Cowan's comment be stricken."

"Response?" Conrad looked at Shay Lankford, as did Jason. The prosecutor's eyes seemed to be dancing, and Jason knew he'd just made a tremendous rookie mistake.

"We're fine with it being stricken, provided that we're able to have redirect."

Conrad smirked. "Figured you'd say that. The jury is to disregard Mr. Cowan's last statement." He bowed his head toward Shay. "Redirect?"

"Absolutely," Shay said.

Jason stood by the defense table, unable to bring himself to sit.

"What did Waylon Pike tell you about Dr. Waters?"

Trey Cowan looked directly at the jury. "He told me that Jana Waters had offered him $15,000 to kill her husband."

The answer hung in the air like smoke from a cannon.

Shay moved her eyes from the witness to the jury. "No further questions."

"Mr. Rich, any further cross?"

Jason peered down at his sister, who was looking at him with scared eyes. *Damnit...*

"Mr. Rich?"

Jason turned to the witness stand, thinking as fast as he could. "So Pike told you he was offered a deal to kill Dr. Waters?"

"Yes. By Dr. Waters's wife." He pointed toward Jana Waters. "Your client."

"Let the record reflect that the witness has identified the defendant," Shay said.

And the hits just keep on coming.

"But you didn't think he was seriously going to go through with it, did you?"

Trey shrugged. "I didn't know what he was thinking."

Jason did everything he could do to keep his voice from waning. *Never let them see you sweat.* He strode to the jury railing. "You and Maples knew what Pike had been offered, true?"

"I didn't tell Colleen about it."

"But you knew."

"Yes, I did."

"You were interviewed twice by the sheriff's office, and you never mentioned that Pike told you he was offered a deal to kill Dr. Waters."

"They never asked," Cowan said.

"That's quite an omission, don't you think?"

"Objection," Shay said. "Argumentative."

"Sustained," Judge Conrad said.

Jason knew he shouldn't sit down on a sustained objection, but he couldn't think of anything else to ask. "Nothing further."

73

Jason wanted a drink.

After Judge Conrad dismissed the jury, he told Jana he'd be by to see her in an hour. Then he walked a straight line out of the courtroom, walking past Izzy and Harry without a word. As he was about to get on the elevator, he felt a hand grab his arm. He turned and saw Beverly Thacker looking at him with a proud smile. "I remembered," she said.

Jason blinked his eyes and tried to focus. He was exhausted from the whipping he'd just received courtesy of Shay Lankford. All he wanted was a drink.

"Remembered what?" he asked.

"I told you I saw Dr. Waters with another woman, but I couldn't place who it was."

Jason snapped his fingers as he recalled their initial encounter at the hospital. "The woman you saw with him in his office."

"Right. I couldn't think of who it was, and then I saw that man at the courthouse today. You know . . . the car dealer. I got here early and was coming up the stairs when he was leaving."

"Jackson Burns?"

She slapped her hands together. "Yes, that's him. He used to do a lot of commercials with his entire family."

Jason felt a tiny tickle crawl up his arms like a spider. "His family?"

Bev nodded furiously. "That's how I recognized the woman messing around with Dr. Waters in his office. It was the car dealer's wife."

———

The closest watering hole, as luck would have it, was the Brick. Jason grabbed a booth in the back, still reeling from the disaster of his cross-examination of Trey Cowan and the revelation that Bev Thacker had just made.

Braxton was screwing around with Shandra Burns . . .

When the waitress came his way, he said, "I want the strongest IPA you have."

"How about Snake Handler made by Good People?"

"Fine."

She brought it to him, and he smelled the glass.

Then he closed his eyes, thinking again of the Cowan cross. *How could I have been so stupid? I opened the door, and he closed it in my face.*

Jason knew he couldn't leave his exchange with Cowan as the last thing the jury heard, but he was out of options.

Jason saw a man sit down at the bar, and he shook his head.

Like clockwork, he thought, watching Trey Cowan take a sip of a beer that had already been poured for him.

Without conscious thought, Jason walked away from the booth and approached Cowan. He took a seat next to him and nodded at Teresa Roe, who looked at him with wide eyes.

"So Pike told you the deal?" Jason asked, looking straight ahead.

Trey laughed. "Thought you said you had no further questions."

"I have one more."

"Too late."

Jason asked it anyway. "Was there anyone else nearby who heard what Pike said about the deal Jana offered him?"

Cowan took a long sip of beer. "I'm going to close out, Teresa." He flung a five on the bar. "Keep the change."

He started to leave, but Jason got in his way. "Please, Trey. Was there anyone with you and Pike when he told you about the deal?"

Trey looked at him with fierce disdain in his eyes. "There were several people at the bar who might've heard," he said.

"Who?" Jason asked. "Anyone in particular?"

"Only one that I remember, actually," Trey said. "Same guy that was pretty much there every time Waylon was. Waylon was doing most of his work for him."

Jason felt another tickle. "Who?"

"Jackson Burns."

74

Jason put his own five-dollar bill on his booth table and left the beer untouched. He walked back to the bar and got Teresa's attention.

"What's up?" she asked.

"Was Jackson Burns ever in here when Trey Cowan and Waylon Pike were talking?"

"Burns is in here almost every day," she replied. "He actually just left."

Jason felt gooseflesh prickling down his arms. "Thank you."

———

For the next thirty minutes, Jason walked the streets of Guntersville, thinking of all his encounters with Burns.

He's the common denominator, Jason thought.

Waylon Pike worked for Burns a lot, probably more than he worked for Braxton and Jana.

Pike's last job was for Burns.

Pike was dropped off and picked up the night of the murder at Burns's house.

Burns knew that Jana had taken out $15,000 from her and Braxton's joint account the day prior to the murder. She had told him.

And, finally, Burns knew Pike had been offered this exact same amount of money to kill Dr. Waters. He was present when Pike told Trey Cowan about the deal he'd been offered.

Yet, he didn't tell the police, and he didn't testify about it on the stand.

And he didn't tell me.

What possible reason would he have for not disclosing that . . . unless he'd used that knowledge to pay Pike the fifteen grand himself and frame Jana for it.

But why would Jackson Burns want to kill his best friend?

Because Braxton had been screwing his wife . . .

Jason's heart was pumping so fast he had to slow his stride and breathing. It was Burns who had told Jason he was sure that Jana was so guilty. The literal first person he spoke to at the crime scene. The snake in the grass. The enemy lying in plain sight.

By the time he reached the jail, he was sweating profusely. Burns's wife had divorced him. Took the kids and moved to Huntsville far away from the house on Buck Island. Why would she do that? Why wouldn't she have kept the mansion and kicked Burns out?

What if the reason for their divorce just happened to be on Buck Island?

And right next door . . .

When he entered the consultation room, he didn't bother with pleasantries. "Did you know that Braxton was screwing Shandra Burns?"

Jana blinked, hesitated for five seconds, and gave him the solid gold answer he was hoping for. "*What?* No."

75

Jason had Harry dig up the address on his way to Huntsville. He thought about calling, but he wasn't sure she'd agree to meet him. He took Highway 431 all the way into the city and then hung a right on California Street. A mile later, he turned right onto Locust Avenue. Jason remembered from his days going to Randolph that the neighborhood was called Blossomwood, one of the nicest places to live in Huntsville.

He parked in front of the house and trotted toward the steps. He knocked on the door and prayed that she'd be here.

"Who is it?" A woman's voice.

Thank God.

"Ms. Burns, this is Jason Rich," he said, having no time for pleasantries. "My sister is Jana Rich Waters. I'm defending her on the charge of murdering her husband, Braxton, in the Circuit Court of Marshall County. The trial's almost over, and I need your help."

"I'm sorry, but you're going to have to leave."

"Please, Ms. Burns. Just one question."

There was no response, so Jason blurted it out. "Braxton's nurse, Beverly Thacker, remembers seeing you messing around . . ."

The door shot open, and Shandra Burns stared wide eyed at Jason. She held a finger over her mouth. "My boys are inside this house. How *dare* you!"

"Thacker said she saw you and Braxton groping each other in his office."

"I'm going to call the police if you don't leave."

"And I'm going to start talking very loud about your affair with Dr. Waters if you don't tell me the truth."

"Momma?" a tiny voice spoke from behind the door. The boy must have been around seven years old. Behind him was an older boy, who Jason estimated to be twelve.

"What's it going to be, Ms. Burns?" Jason asked. *God forgive me,* he thought, glancing at the two kids and then back at Shandra.

She turned to her children. "Jack, take your brother upstairs and watch some TV, OK?"

"Mom, is that the guy on the billboards?" the older one asked.

"Please, Jack. Do as I say."

"Yes, ma'am." When the two boys had closed the door, she turned back to Jason with a look of utter disdain on her face.

"I'm sorry," he said. "My sister is on trial for her life, and—"

"And you think Burns killed Braxton?"

"I already have a witness to your affair with Braxton, ma'am. I don't need you to confirm it."

"What do you need?"

"All I need . . . is for you to tell me if Burns knew about it."

Tears filled her eyes as she frowned and slowly nodded. "It's why he divorced me."

76

Forty-five minutes later, Jason was back in the consultation room of the Marshall County Sheriff's Office. During his drive back, he'd called Izzy. "We got a new alternative theory," he had said. "I need you to copy the divorce file of Jackson and Shandra Burns first thing in the morning."

"Why?"

After he filled her in, she let out a whistle. "Jason motherfucking Rich . . . I think you may have a future in criminal defense."

"Thanks, but there's a long way to go, and I still have one more bridge to cross."

Now, squatting next to his sister, he was about to cross it. He spoke in a low, calm voice. "Jana, you said you lied to me about something after the state rested its case. What did you lie about?"

She spoke with no hesitation. "I didn't pay the fifteen thousand to one of Cade's goons."

"What? But Jana, you said you recognized the guy as one of Tyson's men."

"I lied. Jason, I took that money out for myself. I thought Braxton was about to cut me off. Put a hold on our bank accounts and cancel my credit cards. He'd told the kids he was going to sue for custody. I needed cash and I needed it quick."

"For what?" Jason asked, realizing that this was what she'd told him in their first meeting. Then, later, she said she'd paid Cade the fifteen grand. Now, she was back to this again. He wasn't sure what to believe.

"I had some credit card bills that were past due." She hesitated. "Some pretty big ones."

"Are you telling me the truth?"

"Now I am. I swear it."

"Jana, that's exactly what you told me in our first encounter. Why'd you change your story into paying Cade with the money?"

"I thought saying that I paid Cade would be the best out. To admit my drug problem. But then, after I told you that story, you said Cade made you promise I wouldn't testify because he was worried I'd implicate him." She wrung her hands. "I didn't want to admit that I lied to you."

"Why now?"

"Because I have to testify. I have to tell the jury that I didn't pay Pike."

"What if Shay asks you if you bought drugs from Tyson Cade? Cade isn't a man who makes idle threats. Jana, this is Nola and Niecy's lives we are talking about."

"Can't I take the Fifth Amendment to those questions? I don't have to admit I committed a crime."

Jason slapped his hands together. Now that paying Cade the fifteen grand wasn't part of the story, she *could* take the Fifth Amendment. She didn't have to incriminate herself.

Or Cade . . .

"Jana, what happened to the money?"

"I think it was in the glove compartment of my car. For all I know, Burns could have stolen it. Or maybe an officer took it."

"Jana, come on."

"Look, I don't know. I was on coke. I'm just telling you where I think I put it."

Jason gazed at her. He knew he couldn't suborn perjury, but he wasn't sure what the truth was anymore. He wondered if Jana could even tell the difference.

Jason stood and walked to the door before knocking three times.

"What are we going to do?" Jana asked.

Jason let out a ragged breath. "You're going to take the stand."

77

At 8:30 a.m. the following day, Jason met Izzy and Harry in the court-room. With thirty minutes to spare, the room was empty, but in a half hour, it would be full to capacity. Everyone expected this to be the last day of the trial.

Jason filled Izzy and Harry in on his plan.

"How do you think Cade's going to react?" Harry asked.

"Chase has the girls at Mill Creek," Jason said. "The front and back of the place are being watched by security. I have officers surrounding the courthouse, and the by God Tonidandel brothers will all be in the courthouse. Have you met them yet?"

"Just heard the stories," Izzy said.

"They're all true."

"I hope so," Harry added, "because the stories about Cade are also true."

Jason put his hands on their respective shoulders. "Jana isn't stupid. She won't implicate him."

"If you say so," Izzy said.

"Keep your eyes and ears open, partner," Jason said. "We're about to get on the roller coaster."

78

"Mr. Rich, call your next witness," Judge Conrad announced.

"The defense recalls Ms. Beverly Thacker."

The elderly nurse trudged into the courtroom and took her seat on the witness stand. After she was sworn in, Jason got right to it.

"Ms. Thacker, you told the jury yesterday about witnessing Dr. Waters having sexual contact with his CRNA, Colleen Maples."

"Yes, sir."

"Did you ever witness Dr. Waters have an affair with any other woman?"

"Yes, sir, I did."

"And who was that?"

"Well, for the longest time, I couldn't remember her name, but when I saw the car dealer yesterday, it clicked. I saw Dr. Waters making out with Mr. Burns's wife on a Friday after work. I was working late and went into his office to file something, and I saw them on his desk. Her shirt was off, and they were kissing and grinding on each other."

Murmurs filled the courtroom, and Judge Conrad banged his gavel.

"Who exactly are you talking about, Ms. Thacker?"

"Shandra Burns."

Jason looked toward the jury and saw the expressions of surprise that he'd hoped to see. "No further questions." He glanced at Shay Lankford, who stared back at him with a look of bewilderment.

"Cross-examination, Ms. Lankford?" Conrad asked.

"No, Your Honor," Shay said, still gawking at Jason.

"OK, Mr. Rich, call your next witness," Judge Conrad instructed.

Jason turned to Jana. "Ready?" he whispered.

"As I'll ever be."

Jason's heart was pounding. "Your Honor, we call the defendant, Jana Rich Waters."

His sister took the stand and was sworn in. After having Jana state her name for the record, Jason didn't waste any time.

"Ms. Waters, did you hire a man named Waylon Pike to kill your husband, Dr. Braxton Waters?"

Jana looked directly at the jury. "No, I did not."

"Ms. Waters, where were you on the night of July 4, 2018?"

"I went to Fire by the Lake, a restaurant on Highway 69."

"What did you do there?"

"I had two vodka drinks, and then I left."

"What did you do next?"

"I drove around for a little while."

"Why?"

"My marriage was ending. I was . . . upset. I'd taken out $15,000 from my and Braxton's joint account the day before, and I was worried what Braxton was going to say."

"Why'd you take out the money?"

"Because Braxton had said he was going to divorce me, and I was afraid I wouldn't have any cash."

"Did you stop at a strip mall south of Fire by the Lake?"

"I might have. I don't really remember."

"What do you remember?"

"I remember not wanting to go home. The kids were both with friends, and I didn't want to be around Braxton." She put her hands on the wooden bench in front of her chair.

Jason approached the witness stand and clasped both of his hands over his sister's. "Jana, what did you do next?"

"I got a room at the Hampton Inn. I brought a bottle of vodka with me, and I drank the whole thing in my room."

"When did you go home?"

"The next morning. I checked out of the hotel and was still pretty messed up. I drove home and must have fallen asleep on the den floor, because that's where I was when Nola found me."

Jason looked at his sister, realizing that she'd omitted Tyson Cade completely from the story. Was she lying again? Or did she not remember being with Cade?

She's making it up as she goes along, Jason thought, letting go of her hands and looking at the jury.

"Did you know Jackson Burns?"

"Of course. He's our next-door neighbor on Buck Island."

"You heard Ms. Thacker's testimony a moment ago."

"Yes, I did."

"Were you aware that your husband was having an affair with Jackson Burns's wife, Shandra?"

"No, I was not."

"No further questions."

———

Shay Lankford waded into her cross-examination of Jana with caution. "Ms. Waters, you had an affair with Waylon Pike."

"Yes."

"And you also had a relationship with a man named Tyson Cade, didn't you?"

"Your Honor, I object," Jason said. "May we approach?"

Conrad gestured to Shay and Jason to come forward. "Mr. Rich?"

"Any questions regarding an alleged affair with Tyson Cade would be a direct violation of your pretrial order."

"Your Honor, the defendant and the victim both had extramarital affairs," Shay countered. "It is our position that any relationship with Cade goes straight to the defendant's motive to kill her husband."

Judge Conrad scratched his chin and then nodded. "I'm going to allow it."

Jason took his seat while Shay strode toward the witness stand. "Ms. Waters, did you have a *sexual* relationship with Tyson Cade?"

"No, that's not true."

"Well, you'll at least admit that you were buying cocaine from Mr. Cade?"

"On the advice of counsel, I'd like to take the Fifth Amendment."

Shay put her hands on her hips. She asked several more questions about Tyson Cade, and each time Jana pleaded the Fifth. Then the district attorney changed gears.

"You admit you took $15,000 out the day before your husband was murdered?"

"Yes."

"Because you say you were afraid your husband was going to cut you off?"

"Yes."

"You knew he was going to divorce you."

"That's what he said, but I don't think he was ever going to follow through with it."

"But that's what he told you."

"Yes."

Shay slammed her notepad down on the prosecutor's table. "No further questions."

"Mr. Rich?" Conrad asked.

"Nothing further."

Jana walked back to the defense table and sat down.

"Call your next witness."

"The defense recalls Trey Cowan."

———

Jason made it short and sweet with Cowan. "You testified yesterday that you spoke with Waylon Pike quite a bit during your happy hour sessions at the Brick. Was there anyone with Pike when he would meet you at the bar?"

"Yes," Cowan said. "He was almost always with Jackson Burns."

"And the conversation you mentioned on the stand yesterday, where Pike was bragging about the deal Jana had offered him to kill her husband for $15,000, was Mr. Burns present for that conversation?"

"Yes, he was."

79

After a thirty-minute recess, Jason stood to call his last witness.

"The defense calls Mr. Jackson Burns," Jason said. As Burns took the stand, he looked rather disheveled. His shirttail was hanging out of the back of his jacket, and his hair was uncombed. During the break, Harry had called Burns and asked him to return to the courtroom. When Burns had resisted, Jason's investigator had reminded the car dealer that he was still under subpoena.

Now here he was, back on the stand.

"Mr. Burns, isn't it true that your marriage ended in divorce late last year?"

Burns wrinkled his face in confusion. "Yes, what does that have to do with anything?"

Jason walked to the defense table and picked up the file that Izzy had printed off that morning. "According to the petition, it was you who filed for divorce."

"Yes."

"But you told me that Shandra divorced you, didn't you?"

Burns frowned. "If I phrased it that way, sir, I was wrong."

"You filed the complaint, didn't you?"

"Yes, I did."

"And that was because your wife, Shandra, was having an affair with your best friend, Dr. Braxton Waters. Isn't that correct?"

"You fucking prick," Burns said. His face had flushed a deep red, almost purple. "After all I've done to help you."

Conrad banged the gavel so hard it almost broke. "If the witness has another outburst like that, then he'll spend the rest of the day in jail for contempt. Understand, Mr. Burns?"

"Yes, Your Honor," he said, staring a hole through Jason.

"Do you remember the question?"

"I do."

"Well, are you going to answer it, or are we going to have to bring Shandra here?"

"Your Honor, I obj—"

"I'll answer it," Burns interrupted the prosecutor's objection. "Yes. They were having an affair."

"And you divorced her because of it?"

"Yes."

Jason walked over to the jury railing and leaned his hands on it. "Mr. Burns, why didn't you tell the police that Waylon Pike had bragged to you and Trey Cowan about being offered fifteen grand to kill Dr. Braxton Waters?"

"Because I never heard him say that."

"So you're calling Trey Cowan a liar?"

"No."

"Well, that's what Trey said on this witness stand. That you were there and heard every word."

"If he said that . . . then yes. He's lying."

Jason walked back to the table. "Mr. Burns, you didn't tell anyone about what Pike said because you decided to pay him fifteen grand to murder Dr. Waters. Isn't that correct?"

"That's the most ridiculous thing I've ever heard."

"You've previously testified that, on the night of July 3, 2018, Jana told you herself that she'd taken out fifteen grand earlier that day from one of her and Braxton's joint accounts. Correct?"

"Yes."

"You knew she'd withdrawn the money, and you knew Pike had been offered that same amount to kill Dr. Waters."

"I knew she'd made the withdrawal, but I didn't know anything about any deal offered Pike. If Trey says that happened, then he's lost his mind."

Jason watched the jury, who all seemed engaged. He could see the questions in their eyes, and that gave him hope. "Mr. Burns, you decided to get revenge on your best friend, didn't you?"

"That's preposterous." Burns had started to sweat and wiped his brow with one of his meaty palms.

"You paid Waylon Pike yourself to kill Braxton Waters and framed Jana to take the fall. Isn't that true?"

"No."

Jason kept his eyes on the jury. He'd done all he could do, and now it would be up to them. "No further questions."

When Shay Lankford said she had no questions, Jason peered at Judge Conrad and spoke in a firm voice. "Your Honor, the defense rests."

80

Jason splashed water on his face and looked at himself in the mirror as he stood in the men's restroom of the courthouse. Judge Conrad had given the jury a fifteen-minute recess before closing arguments. Jason took in a deep breath. He was exhausted, but he'd almost reached the finish line.

As he ran more water in the sink, he found himself becoming emotional. *We could win,* he thought. *We could really win. I've made mistakes. I bungled the Cowan cross. But we still have a chance.*

He gaped at his reflection and did a full flex in front of the mirror and slapped himself in the face a couple times. "I can do this," he said. "I can do it."

The door swung open, and Harry stepped in. "Showtime, J. R."

"I'm coming," Jason said. As Harry left, Jason leaned over and grabbed his knees, taking in a deep breath. Then he straightened and exhaled slowly. "Showtime," he whispered.

81

Jason entered the courtroom and sat down next to his sister. "You OK?" she asked.

"I'm about to throw up," he admitted.

Jana squeezed his hand. "Quit being a pansy. You'll do great," she said.

"Aren't you scared?" Jason asked.

"Yes. But I believe in you. You're a fantastic attorney, and I'm proud that you're my brother."

Jason stared at her. It was perhaps the nicest thing she had ever said to him. "Bullshit," he finally said, and she snickered.

"OK, maybe I overshot," she said. "But, by damn, you've gotten us this far."

"You trust me?" Jason asked.

She didn't hesitate. "Yes."

"Good . . . because my closing is going to test that."

"You say what you have to say, baby brother. You aren't going to hurt my feelings. But do something for me, OK? Leave it on the field."

Jason smiled. It was one of their father's sayings. Something he'd always said, in fact, before Jason would participate in a golf tournament or when Jana ran for student government in high school. "I plan to," he said.

———

Shay Lankford was methodical in her closing argument. She went through the facts and each of their witnesses, focusing mostly on Waylon Pike's testimony that Jana had paid him to kill Dr. Waters. "Mr. Pike's testimony is uncontradicted. He confessed that Ms. Waters paid him $15,000 to kill the victim. It is undisputed that Ms. Waters removed $15,000 from the couple's bank account within twenty-four hours of the murder, and no plausible explanation has been offered why. It is undisputed that Dr. Waters was going to divorce the defendant. Ms. Waters told Mr. Pike and Jackson Burns that she wanted her husband dead. She had the motive. She had the exact means to pay Mr. Pike to kill Dr. Waters—$15,000. And she had the opportunity. She was constantly in contact with Mr. Pike, and Mr. Pike has testified to her driving him to her home the night of the murder and whisking him away after he killed Dr. Waters."

After going over the jury instructions, she closed with her final request. "Members of the jury, the state has proven beyond any reasonable doubt that Jana Waters paid Waylon Pike to kill her husband. I'm confident that you will render the only verdict that justice allows. Guilty."

———

"Mr. Rich?" Judge Conrad asked. "Are you ready to give your closing argument?"

"Yes, Your Honor," Jason said. He stood and walked around the defense table, taking a seat on its edge. He looked at Jana and the twelve jurors who would decide her fate.

"I'll be the first to admit that the prosecution has proved a lot of things that don't paint a pretty picture of my client or her family." He let out a ragged breath. "My family."

Jason pushed off the table and gestured with his arm toward Jana. "My sister was *not* a great wife," he said. "I think that's undisputed. She cheated on her husband with Waylon Pike. And the victim, Dr. Braxton Waters, wasn't all that great a spouse. He had affairs with Colleen Maples and Shandra Burns. And you know what the state has also proved? My sister wasn't a great mother either. It is undisputed that she spent the Fourth of July in a hotel room, and was found by her sixteen-year-old daughter passed out drunk at noon on the fifth of July."

Jason peered at Jana, who was looking down at the table, unable to meet his gaze. Her posture was perfect.

"My sister isn't going to win Mother of the Year or Wife of the Year." Jason scratched the back of his neck. "But . . . ladies and gentlemen, what the state hasn't proven is that she's a murderer."

Jason walked to the edge of the jury railing. "You heard how desperate Jackson Burns was on the stand. He even had the gall to call Trey Cowan a liar. Burns knew that Jana had withdrawn $15,000 from the bank on July 3. He'd also been present with Trey Cowan at the Brick when Pike revealed that he'd been offered that same amount of money, $15,000, to kill Dr. Waters; Burns knew Pike well, and Pike was, in fact, working at Burns's house on the day of the murder. And, perhaps most importantly, Braxton Waters had ruined Burns's marriage." Jason licked his chapped lips. "Jackson Burns paid Waylon Pike $15,000 to kill Dr. Waters and then framed Jana Waters for it."

Jason walked back to the defense table. "Can I prove that Burns paid Pike to kill Dr. Waters beyond a reasonable doubt?" Jason shook his head. "That's not my job. The defendant doesn't have any burden of proof in this trial. That task rests with the state, and they haven't met it." Jason looked at his sister and then beyond her to his law partner, Izzy, and investigator, Harry, in the front row. He felt emotion welling within. "This is my sister," he said, hearing a slight crack in his voice. "Warts and all. She took the stand and said she didn't hire Waylon Pike to kill her husband. The only question you should have is whether you have any doubts in the evidence the state has presented." He walked around the table, standing behind Jana's chair. "When you deliberate, think about the state's two *star* witnesses. Waylon Pike, a known felon, an arsonist, and a thief, who was given a deal by the state to testify. Do you have any doubts in Pike's story?" Jason moved his eyes down the line of jurors. "*How could you not?* And then there's the state's other star, Jackson Burns, who we've shown had the motive, means, and opportunity to kill Dr. Waters. I am confident that when you consider the weaknesses in the state's evidence, you will, as Ms. Lankford so eloquently put it, reach the only verdict that justice allows." He put his hands on his sister's shoulders and nodded at the jury. "Not guilty."

82

The jury deliberated for seven full days before coming back with its verdict at 4:30 p.m. the following Friday, November 2, 2018.

After bringing them in, Judge Conrad asked the foreman to read the decision. When Russell Edmonson stood up with a piece of paper in his hand, a warm sensation ran through Jason's body.

"We, the jury, find that the defendant, Jana Rich Waters, is . . . not guilty."

———

The next few moments were a blur of hugs, shakes, and kisses. Jana had latched on to Jason and wouldn't let go. Then Izzy and Harry came in for a group hug. Jason shook Shay Lankford's hand as well as Sergeant Daniels's and Sheriff Griffith's.

The sheriff gripped Jason's hand and spoke in a low tone. "We're going to see about charging Burns. He hasn't been in to work since he testified, and his family hasn't seen him. Once we locate him, we hope for your client's cooperation."

"I'd hope for that too," Jason said, before pushing past the sheriff and making his way to the back of the courtroom, where Satchel Tonidandel was standing by the door. "We good with Cade?" Jason asked.

"I think so," Satch said. "He wants to talk, but he said there'd be no trouble from him."

Jason exhaled with relief.

He turned when he felt his hand being squeezed. "I want to see my girls," Jana said.

Jason nodded. "Let's go home."

83

As they exited the courtroom, the sun had almost completely set over downtown Guntersville. It was 5:10 p.m. Jason had parked in front of the Brick, and he was tempted to go in and thank Trey Cowan but decided against it. He wanted to see his nieces. He and Jana walked side by side down the walkway with Harry leading the way and Satch Tonidandel behind them.

Maybe it was the shadows. Maybe it was the exhilaration of the moment. Maybe it was just plain carelessness.

But Jason didn't see the man standing under the awning of the Brick. He clicked the keyless entry to his Porsche and started to walk across the street. That was when he saw the man step out from under the covering.

Jackson Burns pointed a pistol at Jason's chest. "You damn fucking prick. You ruined my life."

Jason put his hands up instinctively. As a cacophony of gunfire exploded, he was engulfed in a hug by his sister, and he fell backward onto the pavement as more shots and blasts peppered the air.

Seconds later, he rolled out from under Jana and looked at her. Blood covered the front of her dress.

"No!" Jason screamed. He jerked his head around and saw Burns sprawled on the sidewalk, riddled with bullets. Dead.

Jason turned to see Harry kneeling with his pistol pointed at Burns's dead body. Smoke swirled out the end of the barrel of the investigator's weapon. He looked at Jason and mouthed, *"You all right?"* Behind and to the right of Harry, Jason noticed Chuck and Mickey Tonidandel holding shotguns pointed at Burns and Satch cradling the handle of a Glock. The brothers had also fired on the car dealer.

Jason tried to blink away his shock and gazed down at his sister. "Jana," he whimpered, wiping at the blood on her dress and looking at his hand. "Jana, we have to get you to the hospital." He yelled at Harry and the Tonidandels. "We need an ambulance!" But he already heard sirens closing in the distance.

He felt a hand grab his own and looked into his sister's eyes. "Jana." He was sobbing. This wasn't how it was supposed to end. "We won," he said. He leaned close to her face. *"You won."*

She touched his face. "I love you, baby brother." She coughed, and Jason again darted his eyes. Harry and Satch Tonidandel were now standing above him. "Help me," he whined, but neither man said anything.

"J. J. . . ." Jason could barely hear her voice over the sirens.

"You're gonna make it, Jana. You'll be at the hospital real soon."

"Come here," she managed.

Jason leaned down and placed his ear next to her mouth.

"Will you take care of Niecy and Nola?"

"Yes, but you're gonna do that yourself."

"J. J. . . . thank you."

"Jana, don't leave me."

"I . . . love . . . you."

"I love you too, sis."

And then her eyes went blank. Her hand dropped from his face, and Jason felt his grip on reality . . . and his heart . . . breaking. "Jana?"

When she didn't answer, he screamed. "Jana?!"

Jason stood and stumbled backward. Someone kept him from falling, but he didn't look to see who was holding him up. "Jana!" he wailed again.

"She's dead," Jason said, turning and looking into the eyes of Satch. "My sister . . . is dead."

84

The funerals for Dr. Braxton Waters and Jana Rich Waters were officiated together at the First United Methodist Church. At least five hundred people attended.

The front page of the *Advertiser-Gleam* lauded Jana as a hero who'd saved her brother, Jason, from certain death by taking the bullets meant for him. The article, written by Kisha Roe, also labeled Jason a hero.

"Not only did Mr. Rich obtain a defense verdict for his sister, he solved the mystery," Kisha wrote in her story, concluding, "Though Jackson Burns will never be tried for the murder of Dr. Waters, his actions in the aftermath clearly demonstrate his guilt."

Later, after most of the visitors had left the cemetery, Jason, Niecy, Nola, and a few others stayed behind and watched a crew lower the caskets into the ground. The two daughters cried as they threw dirt on the graves. For days, Niecy had been chatty and hyper and had to be put on a sedative to sleep, while Nola had barely uttered a word since learning of her mother's death.

Both of their parents were dead. Both murdered. It was too much for any child to bear. Jason honestly didn't know how anyone could withstand such a burden. He was taking it day by day, but he was worried for their futures.

Eventually, Chase escorted the girls to her car.

"I'll be behind you," Jason said.

"OK," Chase said, kissing his cheek.

Once the funeral workers and burial laborers had all left and Jason was alone by his sister's grave, he cleared his throat. "Jana, there's so much . . . I wish we could have discussed. So much I would like to have said." Jason wiped his eyes and peered back at Chase's car. "I'll do my best to make sure the girls will be OK. They're struggling now . . . we all are . . ." He hoped he sounded thoughtful and not crazed or desperate. "Jana, I meant what I said when you were . . . dying." He kissed his hand and placed it on the dirt that covered his sister's final resting place. "I love you very much."

He wiped his eyes. "I always will."

———

Jason drove back to Mill Creek, his mind a jumbled, exhausted mess. He knew that his nieces were going to need him more now than ever. And once the shock was over, the real hurt would set in. Their father was dead. Their mother was dead. And they were living with an uncle they barely knew, who battled alcoholism. And there was also the matter of a certain Sand Mountain meth czar who, according to Satch Tonidandel, still wanted a word with Jason.

"He said he'd let me know when he wants to meet," Satch had said.

As he stepped out of his car, he saw Chase waiting on the steps.

"Where are the girls?" Jason asked.

"Satch took them down to the waterfront store. They're going to buy some bait and go fishing in his boat."

Jason plopped down next to her. "That's a good idea."

"You OK?" she asked.

"No," Jason said.

"I have a thought, if you can spare a little bit of energy."

"I'm up for anything that will take my mind off . . . everything."

"I think this may do the trick."

Jason followed her around the house and down to the boathouse.

361

A canoe had been tied to the pier.

"Chase?" Jason started, but she took his hand and dragged him toward the waiting boat. They climbed inside and took seats opposite each other.

Chase reached into her pullover and pulled out a yellow wildflower. She smelled it and then held it out to Jason. "Will you . . ."

Jason felt his heart rate speed up as he took the flower in his hands and tucked it into the folds of her hair. "You're beautiful," he whispered.

"Been a while since we've been down to the creek." Then she leaned in for a kiss, and as his lips brushed hers, he breathed in the intoxicating scent of berries, sweat, and wildflowers.

In Jason Rich's mind, he envisioned himself taking the final steps across a long and rickety bridge. "Yes, it has."

EPILOGUE

A week after the funerals, Satch Tonidandel knocked on Jason's door at 8:30 a.m. Nola was in school, and Niecy had decided to study at JaMoka's coffee shop downtown.

"Tyson Cade wants you to meet him at the Alder Springs Grocery at ten a.m. sharp," Satch said.

"Today?" Jason asked.

"Yes. He's promised no trouble but says you gotta come alone."

Jason sighed. "Do you think that's wise, Satch?"

"No, I don't. That's why my brothers will be camped out across the street in a clearing I'm familiar with. I got a friend who owes me one."

"Thanks. Really appreciate that."

"You know what Cade wants?"

"I have no idea."

———

Tyson Cade was standing by the side of the cinder block building when Jason arrived. The dealer was eating a Twinkie and drinking a Sun Drop.

He walked over to Jason and hopped in the front passenger-side seat of the Porsche. "Here," he said, reaching into his pocket for another Twinkie. "A little nourishment for you."

"What's this about?"

Cade pulled up something on his iPhone and then gave the device to Jason.

Jason studied the screen. It was a video of the Laundromat in the strip mall on Highway 69. The words at the bottom of the screen read, *July 4, 2018. 9:00 pm.*

Jason's stomach clenched when he recognized Jana's Mercedes SUV and a woman in the driver's seat. It was Jana, no doubt about it. A few seconds later, a man climbed into the passenger seat of the SUV.

"Oh, no," Jason whispered.

It was Waylon Pike.

Jason's hand began to shake, and he peered at Cade, who was grinning at him.

He handed the phone back to Cade and gazed over the steering wheel out at Hustleville Road. "How'd you get that?"

"Let's just say I have a close, personal relationship with the folks who run that Laundromat. They gave me the tape before the sheriff could ask for it."

"Why'd you hold on to it?"

"Because I wanted my money. Jana owed me $50,000."

"And I paid that. Why didn't you have the tape magically turn up after I paid you?"

Cade glanced up at the sky. "It's not in my nature to help the police."

"Then why are you showing me now?"

"Because you broke your promise. You called Jana to the stand."

"And she did you no harm. I looked out for you."

Cade chuckled and hopped out of the convertible without opening the door. "And that's why you're not dead." He leaned his hands on the side of the car. "But there had to be some repercussions. Besides, you should feel even better about yourself now. You helped a guilty client go free. I know who I'm calling if I ever get in trouble."

Jason fought the urge to tell him to go to hell.

Tyson started to walk away and stopped. He took a long sip of Sun Drop and then crushed the plastic bottle in his hand. "You know something, Counselor? You want to know the real reason I didn't do anything with that tape?"

Jason said nothing.

"I liked her." Cade threw the bottle in the trash and gave his head a jerk. "I really liked her."

Then he began to walk down Hustleville Road.

ACKNOWLEDGMENTS

My wife, Dixie, is my first editor, and this story hatched during our many long walks together. I love walking through life with her.

Our children—Jimmy, Bobby, and Allie—are my inspiration, motivation, and joy.

My mother, Beth Bailey, as always, was, is, and will always be my biggest fan and greatest supporter.

My agent, Liza Fleissig, kept me focused and on task during a difficult year. I am so lucky to have an agent who is also my friend.

My developmental editor, Clarence Haynes, provided much help in the characterization of Jason Rich and the plot of the story. Excelsior, Clarence!

To Megha Parekh, Grace Doyle, Sarah Shaw, and my entire editing and marketing team at Thomas & Mercer, thank you for your support and encouragement.

My friend and law school classmate Judge Will Powell, as he has done for all my legal thrillers, gave insights and advice on criminal law matters and was one of my first readers.

Thank you once again to my friends Bill Fowler, Rick Onkey, Mark Wittschen, and Steve Shames for being early readers and encouraging me along the way.

My brother, Bo Bailey, has supported my writing dream from day one, and I am grateful for his help and steady presence in my life.

My father-in-law, Dr. Jim Davis, continues to be a source of positive energy and, as always, gave me an insightful read of the story.

My friend Jonathan Lusk was a valuable source of information for all things Guntersville and Marshall County.

My friends and lake neighbors Jason and Christy Reinhardt introduced my family to the Mill Creek area of Lake Guntersville.

My friend and classmate Roman Shaul, the general counsel for the Alabama State Bar, provided insight into the workings of the bar's disciplinary process.

My friends Joe and Foncie Bullard from Point Clear, Alabama, have provided tremendous support during my writing quest, and I'm so grateful for their friendship.

ABOUT THE AUTHOR

Photo © 2019 Erin Cobb

Robert Bailey is the *Wall Street Journal* bestselling author of the Bocephus Haynes series, which includes *The Wrong Side* and *Legacy of Lies*, as well as the award-winning McMurtrie and Drake Legal Thrillers series, which includes *The Final Reckoning*, *The Last Trial*, *Between Black and White*, and *The Professor*. He is also the author of the inspirational novel *The Golfer's Carol*. *Rich Blood* is his eighth novel. For the past twenty-three years, Bailey has been an attorney in Huntsville, Alabama, where he lives with his wife and three children. For more information, please visit www.robertbaileybooks.com.

Printed in Great Britain
by Amazon